THE KORB KONSPIRACY

VIVIAN UÍBH EACHACH

Copyright © 2013 Vivian Uíbh Eachach
All rights reserved.
ISBN: 1481922416
ISBN 13: 9781481922418
CreateSpace Independent Publishing Platform
North Charleston, South Carolina

To Maureen and Kevin

Téicht doróimh
Mór saido becc torbái
Inrí chondaigi hifoss
Manimbera latt ní fogbái

[Going to Rome
A lot of trouble, little profit.
The king you seek there
unless you bring him with you,
you will not find]

(Irish verse, circa 1250 AD
Codex Boernerianus
Msc. Dresd. A 145b)

1 ARRIVAL

WHAT WOULD YOU THINK if you woke up in a prison in space 37 years from home? What would be your first thoughts, your first reactions every morning? Even after so many years, would you experience a miniscule millisecond during which your consciousness remained at default setting – at home with family and friends, relaxing in the bosom of your family, enjoying the company of those you love? Even then, the realisation must rapidly set in, like a dark cloud suddenly forming over a bright green meadow. Almost immediately, the blue sky of contentment – the legitimate expectation of happiness in the day ahead – would be cruelly painted over and replaced by a threatening claustrophobic blur. Cruelly, you would then find yourself wide-awake, already despairing and chillingly aware of the hopeless reality surrounding you.

Thus it was for Kevin Kane, Prisoner 313 in Korb Kolony One, an energy-producing prison, 37 years distance from Earth. And thus had each and every dreary morning, since his arrival more than three years before, begun. Sometimes Kane would attempt to postpone the onset of reality by hanging on stubbornly to a fragment of a dream or even a memory that he had raked up somewhere in his subconscious. But the real world would always be there, waiting like a hunter for its prey, and inevitably the prisoner's only option would be to reluctantly drag himself out of his bunk and join the hundreds of others who had just awakened to the same cold reality and must now face another prison day.

Going to sleep at night wasn't much of a release either. Frequently, the prisoner would lie on his bunk, thinking about his plight. How had it happened? Could it have been avoided or was it all predestined? How would it end? Would he manage to escape or would he die, as others had done, far far away from where it had all begun? If he was lucky, the prisoner would have something new with which to exercise his brain – an incident in the work chamber that day, a new theory of some kind put forward by one of the inmates, an upcoming sports event amongst the prisoners – but, no matter what occupied his thoughts, the dark fact of his banishment from everything he loved was never far below the surface in his mind. The night's sleep ahead would always be an unsettled one, the demons of the present and the friends of the past doing battle in the tormented prisoner's head. Then would come the awakening, when Kane would have to reluctantly let the memories go and accept his painful reality for yet another day.

Kane wondered, as he had done for so long now, where it had all gone wrong. He had gone over the entire episode a myriad of times but had always failed to identify that moment when disaster had struck. Every time, he would strain his mind to the limit in an attempt to squeeze out the last drop of memory of those final days, striving tirelessly to identify every second that could have mattered. But the prisoner's efforts were always fruitless. Time after time, his meditation produced the same painful result. Time after time, his efforts left the prisoner in the same tortured state as before.

Sometimes, Kane would just lie there, his hands behind his head, and think about what he called the 'critical line'. This was the point in time when a decisive action was taken, whether consciously or unconsciously, the results of which might not be felt immediately or indeed for some time, but whose effect, sooner or later, on the life of the individual involved would be considerable. Prisoner Kane would spend night after night, day after day, time after time, analysing the events of his life in recent years. Every word, action or deed by him, to him or about him that he could recollect would be dissected in the laboratory of his mind to identify that critical line. As time passed slowly on the kolony, the importance of that moment to the prisoner grew and grew until identifying when *he* had crossed the line and started the train of events that had led him to his present unhappy state became an obsession.

Kane would wrestle at length with the idea of the line. He had long concluded that it was almost always a fine one and crossing it usually an unnoticeable experience. The invisible, intangible, shifting nature of the line, however, created a fatal trap into which the unwitting would always fall, from bliss to misery, from love to hate, from freedom to captivity.

It was the beguiling ease with which the fatal line between happiness and despair could be crossed that angered the prisoner. How unfair, he would brood, that this unseen, uncharted demarcation could be traversed with beguiling ease while any attempt to cross back to normality was a seemingly impossible task. How unreasonable, Kane felt, that a seemingly innocuous incident could ultimately turn out to be a momentous event in life. Those unlucky enough to make that sad journey would have passed a milestone in their lives without being aware of the magnitude of that moment. Sometimes even, Kane concluded, although crossing the line could involve a major event or a decision consciously taken, the ultimate consequences of the occasion might still not be apparent at the time. That, the prisoner believed, was the fashion in which life had changed for him, how the happiness of a young man's carefree existence had been cruelly transformed into the drudgery of a life without liberty, without pleasure, without hope.

Kane remembered his life just before his arrest and transportation as a time of happiness and untroubled youth. Despite having a positive outlook on life, the young servant of the administration was never really an idealist, a pragmatic engagement with the establishment being his preferred approach. Then he met Sheena Strauss, a young woman who exuded confidence and seemed to be driven by an unusual inner certainty. Kane soon discovered that his new companion had a more questioning view of the establishment than he had, but he had no idea that his meeting with Strauss was about to set in train a series of events that would eventually lead to the apolitical young man arriving on Korb Kolony One as a convicted 'information terrorist'. Somewhere in that chronology of events lay the critical line and the prisoner was determined to identify that demarcation of the damned and those who had played a part in pushing him across it.

Regardless of the how, why and who of his undoing, one thing was certain nonetheless – Kane's three years of labour on the kolony had had their inevitable effect, the young man changing dramatically in those brief intervening years. The once indifferent employee of the state had now been transformed into an implacable enemy of the regime, whose mind rarely strayed far from a burning determination to turn his situation around and retrieve control of his life once more. In Kane's mind, there could only be one goal in life for someone unjustly deprived of their liberty forever – escape. A sentence of incarceration for a definite period, be it long or short, carried with it the expectation that liberty would be regained at some specified time in the future. A sentence of banishment to a korb kolony years and years away from home *for life* was a punishment which it was intended would have only one conclusion – *death, sooner or later*, in the same cell that had welcomed the reluctant victim on his or her first day of enforced exile. Escape would be the only way to thwart such an ending. Then, and only then. could the waking nightmare that began on the prisoner's arrival be brought to an end.

It was ironic, Kane believed, that one of the few things he could remember of his arrival on Korb Kolony One was the assertion by the Master of the kolony that escape was physically impossible and any attempt to leave therefore a waste of time and energy. As was the case for his fellow inmates, the prisoner had been oblivious to most of the events surrounding his Arrival Ceremony, as the Master would euphemistically describe it. His first memory of his arrival was waking to find himself facing a 'welcoming party'. Kane wouldn't have seen the earlier stages of the 'ceremony', including the magisterial march to the Arrivals Dock by the Master, accompanied by the tyrons and the reluctant 'prisoner witness'. Neither would he have seen the almost flamboyant wave of hand with which the Master had signalled to his tyron soldiers to release the lock on the prisoner tray compartments in the newly arrived craft. He wouldn't have heard the sudden loud sound of the lock being opened, a noise which momentarily startled the prisoner observer in the Master's entourage.

Kane remembered gaining consciousness, though, the air almost scorching his lungs as he attempted to catch his breath and come to terms with his new surroundings. In front of him and his colleagues, the Master waited patiently, a look of pleasure on his face. A mixture of fear, surprise and confusion showed in the eyes of the gasping arrivals, their light-blue body vests emphasising their vulnerability. Disorientated and attempting to cope with their sudden return to consciousness, the prisoners found themselves in a totally defenceless position, confronted by armed guards. The faces of some of the captives expressed a surprise verging on panic, some assuming they had been awakened to face the firing squad. The confusion of the new arrivals was compounded by the fact that the leader of this clearly unsympathetic reception party immediately proceeded to deliver a 'welcoming' speech.

Speaking with an air of arrogant detachment, the orator treated his captive audience to a brief address, one that seemed to involve the regular use of the words "work", "happiness" and "cooperation". Still struggling with the intake of air, the new arrivals were not in a position to pay much attention to the welcoming speech. Almost all they would remember afterwards would be the concluding phrase, repeated for emphasis – "no point in trying to escape – no point at all!"

It appeared to Kane that the Master was enjoying delivering his oration. He smiled occasionally and nodded his head slowly and slightly when emphasising a point, but presented a serious countenance when explaining the futility of escape to his captive audience. Although the prisoners were obviously unable to pose a threat of any kind, the tyrons nevertheless stood guard as the sermon was given, their weapons at the ready and their attention totally focused on the 'convicted criminals', as they had been trained to view them. The prisoner witness stood motionless, her expression barely concealing her distaste at the show taking place before her eyes.

On the wall behind the Master, the large Northern Confederation emblem left none of the prisoners in any doubt as to the jurisdiction into which they had arrived. The emblem consisted of a large eagle chasing a comet above the planet Earth, with a banner in its beak displaying the letters NC. The message was a positive one, brimming with energy and promise – the Earth was blue and yellow, the comet black, the background crimson and the eagle a dark blue. A black outer circle completed the design.

Kane spotted the same emblem on the top left of the orator's tunic, his purple uniform and cape a contrast to the military appearance of the tyrons, in their plain red uniforms. Here was a man used to the trappings of power. Unnoticed by the prisoner, however, the orator's eyes scanned the features of his new 'guests' as he spoke, searching in particular for any signs of a rebellious spirit. This was a good opportunity, the Master believed, to note any reactions that might complement or contradict the *prisoner attitude files* he would receive on each new arrival. On this occasion, his experienced eye focused on Kane but, having given his subject a moment's consideration, he decided that none of that day's batch displayed any emotion stronger than the 'normal' trauma associated with awakening from a 37 year-long sleep.

Afterwards, Kane's recollection of his journey through the Reception Area would be of a forced march punctuated by a number of physical impositions by a variety of functionaries in what he later learned were euphemistically called 'Registration Tunnels'. An assortment of implements was directed at the captives, readings taken and recordings made. Occasionally along the trek, some prisoners would peer at their fellows, attempting to guess the kind of company with which they would probably be spending the rest of their lives.

Passing through the large chamber, some of the new prisoners were driven by curiosity to look up and see a large glass dome in the centre of an expansive grey ceiling, beyond which appeared to be a purple nebulous sky. Seemingly composed of a dense mixture of smoke and cloud, the sky appeared to change its form and shape almost continuously but one feature of its appearance was unchanging – its unwelcoming and hostile countenance. Kane sensed a threat of violence in its dark purple heart as it observed, brooding and menacing, the sad procession passing below.

On reaching a long corridor that seemed to continue almost out of sight, its low glass outer wall carrying a black handrail, the newcomers marvelled at the scale of the scene that greeted them below. A host of prisoners in yellow uniforms sat at large tables, busily dining and conversing. The dense hum of their conversation carried up through the vast chamber, past the bemused arrivals, and floated innocently towards the sky that glared through another glass dome – the same murky mixture of threatening gases and cloud that had greeted the visitors only minutes before.

Eventually, the blank wall on the left-hand side of the corridor gave way to one containing a long line of cells. Most of them had their grey doors closed, but there were no bars or beam-locks to be seen. Afterwards, Kane remembered that the air had seemed reasonably fresh, a relief after his lengthy sojourn in a confinement tray. No noticeable odour greeted the nostrils of the newly arrived and, here and there, ventilation grills broke the monotonous appearance of the walls. Making their way around the corridor, the group stopped, when instructed, at the doors of various empty cells. Then the name of a prisoner and his or her new number was called and an instruction given to stand out. Having moved forward, the prisoner was told to enter the cell, don the yellow uniform on the cell bunk and await further instructions. Relieved at the relatively pleasant appearance of their new abode and weary after their long spell in confinement state, the prisoners, Kane included, followed their simple instructions and walked meekly into their new home.

Being the last one directed into a cell, Kane turned to see the Master and his troupe march away down the corridor, leaving Prisoner 313 to prepare for his first night of regret and recrimination on Korb Kolony One.

2 THE KORB PROJECT

SITTING IN HIS CELL three years later it was the intense heat following his emergence from confinement that Kane remembered more than anything else about his arrival on Korb-1. Three years later and three years further away from Earth and the life he would never see again, his memory of the Master's speech was limited to the cold cruel warning that the new prisoners had better like the atmosphere on Korb as they would never breathe the air on Earth again.

Many's the night those brutal words echoed in Kane's mind as he remembered the life he had left behind. He would think of the friends, the places and the experiences that had made him the man he was, the man who had endangered and ultimately lost the comfortable lifestyle he once enjoyed – by challenging the *status quo*. With his background and education, Kane could have done well within the Administration. He was clever enough to play the middle ground and sensible enough to know when to close an eye. His parents were totally conservative, thoroughly believing in the system and entirely lacking in the doubting genes that lead one to question official information. How often since had he asked himself in the uncertainty of a sleepless night why he had crossed that thin unseen line and left his comfort zone behind, if it would have been easier to look the other way and enjoy the company of his fun loving friends in the 6741 District of NCR (Northern Confederation Region) 435.

Kane didn't take the safe road, however, and when he and Sheena Strauss were caught copying information disks on Development Sector Finances for network dissemination, retribution was swift. The following day, a Northern Confederation Court, sitting *in camera*, found the two guilty of Information Terrorism and sentenced them to hard labour for life in the Korb Kolonies – Kane to Korb-1, Strauss to the distant Korb-3. In a matter of days, the prudent servant of the Administration had been transformed forever into an exiled convict.

THE KORB KOLONIES WERE established at the turn of the 22nd century in order to boost the stocks of korb fuel available on Earth. Although korb supplies were substantial then, the project – and the huge cost involved in setting up the kolonies – was justified by the Northern Confederation Administration as an investment in the future and an important insurance policy against the withholding of korb supplies by the Saladdan States as a lever against the Northern and European Confederations. As korb was by that time the premier energy source for industry, defence, services and domestic consumption, ensuring continued supplies into the future was a sensible and popular move, particularly as security sources indicated a Saladdan move on korb was imminent. Establishing kolonies in extra-planetary locations where sources maintained the korb supply was plentiful was also viewed as stealing a march on the other super-states and getting a hold on valuable resources for the future before anyone else did. The project was a major success and, by the third decade, four kolonies had been established to process the fuel.

The establishment of the Korb Kolonies was a major project for the Northern Confederation. Massive amounts of capital were allocated and NC citizens were encouraged to contribute financially to its success. *Invest in the Future!* was the slogan used to motivate public opinion behind the venture and many supported the fund. The campaign was slick and handled by one of the NC's top PR firms. The marketing gimmick of spelling with a 'k' everything that began with a hard 'c' created a recognisable and vigorous brand image for the new project. When some questions were asked about the necessity for such a scheme, the Administration officials simply asked the public whether they wanted their children and their children's children left at the mercy of the Saladdans or whether they wanted to take a bold step into the stars to ensure a permanent supply of energy into the future. The response was massive – and vigorous. The support for the project was such that the initial planned target of two kolonies was doubled.

The work on the kolonies was originally supposed to be done by robots, androids and machines, and the general population marvelled at the impressive plans produced by the Administration and networked around the Confederation. Soon after the inception of the scheme, however, the Administration announced that the success of the project was under threat and that it had received information that a number of Saladdan agents had been sent to carry out a sabotage campaign. In order to protect the project from the Saladdans, it was decided that the Korb Kolonies Project would have to be coded red – defined as top secret. The public was asked to assist in foiling any Saladdan attempts to gain information about the venture by not alone accepting the strict coding of the project as top secret, but also by avoiding any reference to it at all. The future of the Northern Confederation and its civilisation depended on the success of the Korb Kolonies Project and no reasonable patriotic citizen would want to jeopardise that. There was general public acceptance, therefore, of the request for secrecy and soon the KKP, as Administration people affectionately referred to the project in the inner circle, became one of the great unspoken achievements of the NC. The way was now clear for the Administration to put the second stage of its plan into operation.

Since the beginning of the Saladdan scare, the Northern Confederation had become a highly security-conscious regime. When the Saladdans' alleged armament campaign was first revealed, it was considered a natural reaction to the growth of the African Alliance. The Northern Confederation clearly understood the need for self-defence. But the African Alliance was by no means strong enough to form a threat to the Saladdans or anyone else for that matter – so what were the Saladdans really up to? The NC became alarmed. What were the Saladdans arming for? The Mao Republic, the Caucasian Republics, the Russian Federation and the Indian States were all locked into a long-running cold war, and there was no real threat to the Saladdans from any of their neighbours. Why then the need to arm to the teeth? It wasn't long before that question was answered. The Confederation's Intelligence and Policy Institute produced a 'confidential' report, which was almost immediately leaked, which stated that the Saladdans' real objective was the break-up of the Northern Confederation. This was to be done by bringing the Confederation and its economy to its knees by depriving it of energy supplies. Then, by threatening war on the weakened superpower, the Saladdans hoped to encourage regional disaffection with the NC Administration within the Confederation itself. This would be done by 'encouraging' NC regions to sign 'friendship' agreements based on the supply of energy. The destabilisation campaign could be summed up in one word – korb.

Most of the world's stocks of korb, a rock discovered deep under the surface of the Earth and producing, after processing, an intensely powerful fuel, was in Saladdan territory. Since its discovery late in the middle of the 21st century, korb had rapidly become by far the cheapest and most efficient source of energy throughout the globe. A century later, however, korb stocks in many parts of the world, particularly in the Northern and European Confederations, were reported by the security information services to be depleting at an alarming rate. It was predicted that the Saladdan States would soon have an extremely lucrative product to sell – or an extremely strong bargaining chip with which to influence the course of events on a global basis. The Intelligence and Policy Institute now reported that the Saladdans intended to use that chip.

On disclosure of the Saladdans' plans, NC attitudes towards the secretive empire immediately hardened and it was soon announced that diplomatic relations were to be sundered. The Confederation initiated an armaments campaign and a clampdown on the discussion of sensitive information was begun. The Saladdan States 'premier status' as a diplomatically was changed to 'potentially hostile' and then to 'hostile'. Saladdans in NC territory were deported and NC citizens in Saladdan jurisdiction brought home. After a brief stand-off period, the Intelligence and Policy Institute then announced that it had become aware that the Saladdans had a large contingent of sleeper agents in NC territory and that their campaign of sabotage was about to begin.

On hearing this report, the NC population became alarmed. The enemy was now within the walls and getting ready to strike and extreme vigilance was essential. The Administration acted swiftly. The Information Laws were temporarily tightened. Anybody apprehended in possession of unauthorised information would be deemed to be a participant in destabilisation. Destabilisation was declared to be a 'Category A' offence.

It wasn't long before a wave of arrests swept the entire Northern Confederation. Anyone who had been 'reported' by more than three citizens as being suspected of involvement with the Saladdans was categorised as a 'prime suspect', arrested and detained. Interrogations were carried out by special Enquiry Teams who exhibited a high degree of success in uncovering enemy agents. Soon the atmosphere in the Northern Confederation was heavy with conspiracy and accusation.

Not all the citizens of the Confederation were enthusiastic supporters of the anti-Saladdan campaign. A group called *Question?* was established, which claimed that anti-Saladdan hysteria was being deliberately whipped up by the Administration in order to achieve its real aim – total control of the dissemination of information. The group's leader, Clayton Towning, circulated a statement on the networks that the Saladdan States were in fact friendly to the NC and had no hostile intentions at all. He promised to visit the Saladdans soon to extend the hand of friendship. Young radicals swelled the ranks of Towning's group and rallies were held in some of the biggest NCR population centres, although the threatening atmosphere created by the large security presence at these demonstrations kept the attendance down. Towning swore to defy the latest NC law banning contact with the Saladdan regime and to carry out a bridge-building mission of peace to the Saladdan capital.

Three weeks later, however, the *Question?* campaign suffered a major blow. A video broadcast from the city of Deeltus, the Saladdan capital, was shown on all NC networks. It showed the new Solemn Leader of the Saladdans addressing the 29th Grand Saladdan Assembly. The Leader declared that the Saladdan States were the cradle of human civilization and that the process of civilization had not yet matured in other parts of the world. He claimed that previous Saladdan administrations, including the recently overthrown one, had "shamed their ancestors" by associating with barbaric regimes abroad. He reported that both the Northern

Confederation and the European Confederation were conspiring to destroy the Saladdans and their culture and had saturated the States with *agents provocateurs*. He claimed that the leader of this "foul plot" had been arrested and was now being interrogated, declaring that, in order to save himself, this "spineless excuse for a human being" had given the names of thousands of conspirators all over the States who were being arrested even as he spoke. Two days later, the broken body of Clayton Towning was hung from the Grand Tower of Truth in Deeltus.

In the light of these traumatic events, apart from the actions of a number of hardliners, the *Question?* campaign soon fizzled out. Now, more than ever, the necessity for vigilance against the Saladdans was clear and unchallenged.

The anti-Saladdan campaign was a huge success for the Administration. All opposition had been stifled – and the Administration's hold on information was now almost total. But the massive wave of arrests and convictions had left them with a considerably large number of prisoners. What was to be done with them? The ever-reliable Intelligence and Policy Institute soon came up with an answer – korb! Instead of the expense of producing and maintaining a force of robots and work androids, the Administration could transport its troublesome subversives to the Korb Kolonies, killing two birds with the one stone.

The Administration regarded the Intelligence and Policy Institute's proposal as very attractive. Not alone would the costly exercise of manufacturing the work force be overcome but the problem of what to do with a large prison population, many highly radicalised and holding a gripe of some shape or form against the Administration could also be addressed.

The implementation of the scheme still contained many difficult challenges for the Administration, however. How would the prison population be transferred to the Korb Kolonies? Who would guard and control them when they arrived? How would the issue of the passage of time between transportation, korb production and product shipment be managed? How would the policy of banishing people to another galaxy, many years travel away, be viewed by the general population – if they found out? What would the relatives and friends of the transported be told? The Intelligence and Policy Institute was asked to draft a plan for the final implementation of the Korb Kolonies Project. The result was ingenious .....

Thus fell into place the series of events that led Kevin Kane, servant of the Administration, to a convict labourer's cell on Korb Kolony One.

3 NO ESCAPE

MANY YEARS AFTER THE Towning Affair, the Intelligence and Policy Institute's Progress Report on the Korb Kolony Project gave details on the status of the project, describing the unprecedented progress made in establishing the four kolonies in the Taurus constellation, a location only accessible after a voyage of many years. Korb-1 involved a journey of 37 years, Korb-2 33, Korb-3 47, and Korb-4 21. These journeys were based on travel capabilities at the time and the Institute maintained that a steady supply of korb would begin to arrive just at the time that global deposits of korb were expected to be finally exhausted.

Obviously, as a return journey to Korb-1 would involve a round trip of 74 years, anyone sent there could never expect to see the Earth they knew again – unless, of course, the NC's space travel capabilities improved dramatically. The Institute's intervention had solved the problem of providing labour for these distant kolonies and, true to form, they had also come up with a solution to the problem of providing managerial personnel to administer them. The Institute proposed that only those whose loyalty to the Confederation was beyond question, who had no relatives or family, and who had a unique appreciation of the need to protect information could qualify for the job. Power and status would be assured on the kolonies to those willing to take on the task and security would be handled by a battalion of tyrons, whose loyalty and dedication to service knew no bounds.

Getting the prisoners there would be the easiest part. When overpowered and sedated, new prisoners for the Korb Kolonies – called *novos* – were placed in confinement state. This involved removing all oxygen from the body and replacing it with suan gas. The subject was then placed on a 'confinement tray' in a container and stored at -10 Celsius. When the long journey to the kolonies was completed, the docking system on the host port interfaced with the visitor craft's system and the process was reversed. Then, following their lengthy confinement, the novos could breathe again, the sudden rush of oxygen into their bodies tearing them from their dreamlike state to introduce them to the nightmarish reality of their new abode.

Kane's recollection of those first few moments, his first on Korb-1, were patchy. Confusion tinged with fear was his first reaction as the oxygen tore its way in through his lungs, but this soon gave way to a mixture of anger and resentment as he realised where he now was, that the Administration had actually carried out their sentence, without hesitation or the slightest compassion. As he and the other novos who accompanied him on that journey three years earlier marched meekly after the Master and his tyrons, their minds were all, to a man and woman, concentrated on the Master's 'welcoming' speech and his cold advice that they should make Korb their home as, thenceforth, they would have no other.

This dreadful message lodged deeply in Kane's mind and in the minds of his fellow prisoners during their first few minutes in their new home and was repeated at regular intervals in the ensuing years, for fear anybody doubted its veracity. For Korb Kolonists, the past was indeed another country, the Earth a place never to be seen again. At the regular Kolony Report Sessions presented by the Master, the message was briefly but effectively conveyed: even if one succeeded in leaving Korb-1 – the Master didn't like the word 'escape' – the kolony's distance from Earth and its isolation in the Taurus constellation almost certainly meant a slow and lonely odyssey to oblivion. The alternative wasn't that unpleasant really, the Master would suggest – play one's part in the success of the KKP, a project judged by the regularity with which korb was dispatched to Earth, and enjoy a simple, if somewhat contemplative, life amongst the stars.

Three years on and Kane still hadn't come up with an alternative to the Master's work ethic. Frustrated, he would lie on his bed after his day's labour and attempt to find a hole in the Master's cold reasoning but so far only failure and a reluctant admission that his previous life – all that he had ever had – was gone for good were the fruits of his intellectual exertion.

There were now 1,314 prisoners on Korb-1. Most of these were as 'guilty' as Kane, some less, some more so. Some had been duped into appearing to commit an offence by those in a position to benefit from their absence. Awakening in Korb-1 37 years after such an incredibly gross injustice, they had only one option – forget about it and make a new existence in the kolony. Some members of the Korb-1 Kolony's prisoner community were neither 'information terrorists', as the unfortunate Kane was officially termed, nor the pathetic victims of personal vendettas. On Korb-1, as on the other Korb Kolonies, there was a substantial body of common criminals. These included serious criminals – those guilty of murder, grievous assault or theft 1. Prisoners generally mixed with those of their own ilk – even on Korb-1, birds of a feather flocked together.

There were exceptions, though, and those imprisoned for crimes not regarded as heinous by the political prisoners were generally free to associate with whomever they wished.

Kane spent most of his leisure time in the company of a small band of prisoners who worked with him on his first Korb Chamber shift, plus one or two others he had got to know well since his arrival. In the evenings, he would play squash, bowling, target-ball, ice hockey or hurling-ball with this small coterie of fellow deportees. They were a tightly knit group who had grown to know one another well and, crucially, to trust one another. Andrea Thorsen, Andrew Dayton, Sandra Nielsen, Tadhg O'Hara, Sarah Gilmore, Lauren Reilly and Clarence Gibney were all of a kind – strong-willed and imbued with a common trait – the will to survive. All having arrived around the same time, they had gone through the various phases together – the initial shock, the deepest despair that followed, the acceptance of their lot and the rekindling of an innate sense of hope were the shared experience of this kindred band.

Kane trusted them all and felt able to discuss openly with any of them his views on their common plight. Dayton, a year younger than Kane at thirty-one, was a bright and superbly fit former athlete. From NCR 56, the seat of government, his successful running career and success on the track for the Confederation seemed about to ensure a lucrative insider Administration career when his partner and childhood sweetheart, Anna Serentino, was suddenly arrested and accused of replicating Development Contract Files. Dayton insisted that the whole episode was a mistake, that he had known the woman all his life and was familiar with her every thought but then – just before her trial was to begin – the District Controller announced that the prisoner had taken her own life in her cell – "an action which was obviously provoked by the realisation of the gravity of her offence and a sense of shame at her betrayal of the Confederation's trust in her as a citizen".

Dayton was horrified and, knowing Serentino would never commit suicide, denounced the Controller's announcement as a lie. The young man felt betrayed by the Administration's treatment of Serentino and distributed files on the information networks calling for an enquiry and full disclosure of the facts surrounding his partner's death. Within hours, Dayton himself was arrested and, on the basis of his own admission that he was familiar with the dead woman's every thought, was summarily convicted of Information Terrorism and sentenced to hard labour for life on Korb-1. Nearly three years on the kolony now, Dayton seemed to have come to terms with the cruel series of events that had deprived him of his love, his career and his happiness in one fell swoop. He now occupied himself with an active sports regime and displayed a friendly demeanour which successfully disguised the hurt he felt inside.

Kane regarded Dayton as a man who, having come through the mill himself, would stand by his comrades when the situation demanded. He believed that Dayton was of a kind that would make a difference in any situation. But, of all Kane's associates, Thorsen was his real soul mate. She had arrived almost a year after him, but almost immediately they had felt a bonding between them that overcame even the depressing realities of Korb-1. Initially, Kane was reluctant to become involved with another woman. Strauss, although 37 years in the past, was still part and parcel of Kane's dream world – a world he regularly visited when the warm sticky nights of Korb-1 forced him into a balmy semi-conscious state. She was still there, deep in his mind. But Thorsen lived in Kane's physical world. Thorsen was the now, and Thorsen seemed to see in Kane what he saw in her – someone who understood, someone who could 'handle' it.

Thorsen had as much reason to retreat into a numbed cocoon of bitterness and despair as anybody else. She had been an insider – part of the Administration itself. Working in Taxes and Excise, she had risen through the ranks to a middle management position. Never having reason to question the system, Thorsen was a happy and fulfilled employee – an effective functioning cog in the wheel. Then she met David Player, another rapidly rising star in the Administration sky. He was above her own immediate boss and still rising. They met at an official presentation and, after some meaningless and forgettable banter on the night, she found herself the object of intense interest by the focused Regional Director. Thorsen demurred initially but eventually yielded to Player's persistent efforts to woo her. After a brief and unfulfilling affair, however, Thorsen decided to end what she felt was a smothering relationship. Player had other ideas, however, and threatened to terminate Thorsen's rapid rise through the system and indeed send her hurtling as speedily in the opposite direction. Thorsen dismissed Player's threats but, less than a week later, she awoke to find her flat being ransacked by Administration agents. In the early hours, still trying to come to terms with her predicament, she found herself facing an NC Court, accused of offering sensitive Administration documents for sale to a foreign power. In a traumatised state, Thorsen refused to confess to a lesser – and equally fabricated – charge of Carelessness in the Management of Sensitive Information, and was immediately found guilty, on the written evidence of two Administration Regional Directors, of wilfully endangering the Confederation by breaching the Information Laws. In a matter of hours, Thorsen was on her way to Korb-1.

Thorsen hadn't handled the first few days of her 'new life' in the kolony too well, violently refusing to accept the new reality and ending up in *The Void*, an SDU (sensory deprivation unit) on the kolony, for a week and a half. Eventually, though, the realisation set in the young woman's mind that Korb-1 was forever and that thoughts of revenge on the hopefully since-dead and decayed Regional Director were useless tools in her new environment. Kane helped the spunky newcomer over the first – and highest – hurdles and now they were able to face their new challenge together as one.

Usually, the two would lie together in one of their cells and talk. Often they would agree not to make any reference at all to the past. Their thoughts and minds would be directed at the present – and if possible, the future. Sometimes they would play each other at *War-Raok!* – a game in which speed of thought and tactical skills were tested in a battle between opposing forces on various levels to enter the inner sanctum of the enemy and overpower him. Thorsen was a tough opponent, but Kane had gained the upper hand more times than not so far. Other times, they would make love.

When alone, Kane would often just lie on his cell bunk, thinking and his mind would go over the events that had resulted in his ultimate banishment to another time, another world. He would attempt to identify anything he had overlooked that could possibly have been the cause of his catastrophe. Time and time again, he would examine what he had said and done in an effort to discover what went wrong. He felt a need to rationalise the entire series of events. The prisoner felt it would be easier to control his anger, his disappointment, his despair if he could discover what exactly had gone awry, what one element in what had taken place had precipitated the disaster. If he could do that, then the reason for his plight would be easier to bear – it would be simply a question of something having gone wrong. His overall judgement would be vindicated and he could apportion blame to that one decisive factor. Kane would wrestle with his torment for many hours but the key element in the calamity had yet to become clear and he would usually be left in a mire of self-doubt that would only be broken by a visit from Thorsen or one of his other friends. He would sometimes drift into an uneasy sleep in which the spectres from his past would haunt him mercilessly once more. Other times, he would pit his skills against the system computer in advanced games of *War-Raok!* Kane rarely won, but often gave the system a run for its money.

Whatever Kane did, the day usually ended in an unsettled sleep and confrontation with the ghosts of the past. On occasion, the night's slumber would be broken by a sudden awakening, provoked by reveries about friends or times past. Kane's mind would travel over time and space and visit people and places he would never see for real again. A kaleidoscope of colours alien to his present world welcomed him on these regular journeys. He would spend time talking to his friends or merely enjoying their presence and sense how they had fared since he left. But no matter how vivid the dream, no matter how lucid the recollection, the sultry surrounds of his cell in a night dimly lit with stringer bulbs would always be Kane's final destination.

4 KORB CHAMBER 10

THE CHAMBER WAS QUIET. The six large grey tunnel machines silent. Then the turbo motors began to turn. Slowly, steadily, the noise increased until the screech of the turbines went beyond the decibel level and could be heard no more. Inside the tunnels, the korb liquid was received from one of the Generation Chambers, rapidly moved along and deposited in the huge protective transporter containers. The progress of the liquid could be seen on the colour scanner screen upon which the sensors inside the tunnel relayed an image of the advance of the substance through the system. As the liquid filled the tunnel, the screen gradually turned red. With the korb stream leaving the tunnel, the screen became yellow. When the contents of the tunnel had been consigned to their container, the operator at the control panel instigated the decontamination process. Following this, a dark blue colour returned to the screen. If, as rarely happened, the process was incomplete and the blue-red-yellow-blue sequence was not reflected on the screen, the operator released the valves on the funnel machine and opened the tunnels. The operator then had to clean out the tunnel using a high-powered hose. This was a highly dangerous procedure and if an unskilled hand directed the hose, it could result in backsplash and korb contamination for everyone in the Chamber. If the hose did its job, however, and the screen showed blue, the tunnel was closed and the whole process begun again.

The decontamination stage was important because korb, when in a liquid state, had to be kept running. If allowed to rest, it would quickly solidify. Once in the transporter containers, the korb would return to a solid state but, if a residue of korb remained in the tunnels, for whatever reason, it would soon congeal and inhibit the movement of the flows into the containers. Therefore, after every 'gush' – the term used for the movement of a consignment into the containers – the tunnels had to be made korb-free.

Kane wiped the sweat from his brow as he finished hosing the tunnel, closed the doors and sealed the funnel valves again. He had presented himself for work today at Korb Chamber 10 just as he had done every morning since first being placed on korb loading duties over two years previously. Loading liquid korb into giant metal cylinders, although a dangerous occupation, was certainly not as unpleasant as participating in the generation process, during which korb stones were ground by querns driven at the speed of light, and liquidised while in an energy-rich state. Constant exposure to the intense heat generated during this process was debilitating and almost all Kane's free time while on that duty was spent recovering from the previous shift. Invariably, novos were given generation duties initially, with the intention of wearing them down and dissipating any energy they might have intended expending on subversion or even on an escape plan, however futile. After a year toiling in the heat of the Generation Chamber, any other duty seemed pleasant and would be carried out with something resembling enthusiasm.

Work on any part of the korb process was teamwork and any carelessness on the part of a member of the team could endanger the life and limb of their fellow members. This interdependence and reliance on the KC team resulted in an atmosphere of cooperation and a culture of common purpose. It surprised Kane that the obvious camaraderie that grew up within teams did not seem to unduly trouble the Kolony Administration. Surely it would be in their interest to break teams up regularly and frustrate the growth of solidarity amongst prisoners on the kolony, but this development was apparently not regarded with alarm by the authorities.

During their shift, Kane and his fellow toilers, dressed in their grey work suits, mechanically did what had to be done and attempted to break the boredom of the daily routine with the jokes and pleasantries associated with any 'ordinary' day's work. The fact that this jolly little troop was engaged in their labour a journey of 37 years away from home sank into the subconscious as the friendly banter of the day filled the spaces between gushes. Dayton was the main entertainer on the shift, although Nielsen was a close second. Quizzes of all varieties were his speciality. Dayton's quizzes usually kept spirits high and almost everybody found them testing and stimulating, though towards the end of the day they generally petered out following a bogus challenge to the quizmaster's official answer. When this happened, spirits would rise even higher because everyone knew the loading shift was coming to an end.

Generally, the camaraderie in KC teams was such that if a member of the group wasn't on top form, the others would generally carry him or her on that shift, in the knowledge that when their turn came they could expect the same level of support. On the other hand, if one member of the team was disliked by the others, the Administration would be approached and requested to move him or her on. The authorities generally complied with these requests on the basis of the Master's conviction that a happy workforce was a productive one.

This team spirit extended beyond the production line and team members generally hung out together in the kolony. Prisoners were identified as working on a particular team, and when sports competitions were organised, they were almost always based on the KC unit. Prisoners themselves identified one another by their KC chamber and shift number – Clarke: KC16-1 or Griffith: KC19-2 or Nguma: KC5-3. There was sometimes rivalry, and even dislike, between KC teams. In the first year of the kolony's existence, a mini-riot took place after a squash tournament ended in a tightly contested game between KC3-1 and KC3-3. Surprisingly, there were no repercussions for the prisoners after the disturbance was put down by the authorities and, apart from the injuries inflicted by the tyrons in quelling the disturbance, no other punishments were imposed. Many of the prisoners regarded this leniency as a wonderfully magnanimous gesture by the Administration and a display of understanding. This led to a series of repeats of the incident over the years, which elicited the same response. Others, Kane and his associates included, regarded it as an indication of the extent that violence by prisoners would be tolerated as long as it was directed against other prisoners and not against the Administration. Some regarded this view as unduly suspicious.

The KC10-1 crew were amongst the more politically aware shifts on the kolony, acting more as a unit than many of the other shifts. There was generally a 'KC10-1' view of any new development rather than a variety of individual ones and, if any prisoner wanted a good 'political' analysis of any issue that had arisen, he or she would approach a member of the KC10-1 team.

An hour after a KC shift team had finished its work, another shift team would begin in the same Korb Chamber. Thus each Chamber had three shift teams, each carrying the number of the Korb Chamber plus the number of the shift - 1, 2 or 3. Each shift lasted seven working hours plus a changeover hour, and thus the Chambers were active for 21 hours out of every 24. Although there was nothing but continuous night on Korb-1, the earth clock of twenty-four hours was used to count time. The Master had decided that this was a "good way to maintain an Earth atmosphere on the kolony". It certainly created an impression in the minds of the prisoners that, despite the continuous use of artificial lights and stringer bulbs, and the unremitting presence of the murky purple sky overhead, day did, in some eternally logical way, follow night. In reality though, the 24 hour clock was actually divided into three, allowing the day to be divided between shifts. It worked like this: K1-3 would be three hours into the first korb shift – 3a.m., K2-4 would be four hours into the second korb shift – 8 + 4 = 12 hours or 12 midday, K3-5 five hours into the third shift – 8 + 8 + 5 = 21 hours or 9p.m., and so on.

Today went as did most workdays on Korb-1. The target of 200 kerons of korb was easily met, without a hitch, and there were no quality warnings. Leaving the KC to the next team, KC10-1 headed for their respective cells to clean up for mealtime. As Kane and Dayton walked together towards their cells, they saw the Master heading down to the Reception Chamber with three tyrons. He marched ahead, they followed behind on each side, their polished red helmets a warning to those who valued their existence to stay well away. The Master's purple cape, his sign of office, showed the way for the tyrons through the area ahead.

"Another package holiday", Dayton joked. "Do you think they'll be happy with the weather?" he asked Kane. Kane smiled a dry smile as he watched the Master and his tyrons head for the Reception Chamber to re-enact the drama that was every prisoner's first experience of Korb-1.

At the meal later on, the Dining Hall was filled with an assembly of people chatting after a day's work. All dressed in the yellow suits provided by the Administration for non-work occasions, they provided a welcome break for the eye from the grey and blue of the Hall. Their conversation generally concerned Korb-1 or the 'latest' news from Earth which arrived with every shipment of novos. Direct links with Earth were not possible as there was reportedly a bacanite concentration in the constellation that broke up radio signals. News from Earth was networked around the kolony by the Administration and read avidly by most of the prisoners. Some couldn't motivate themselves to read it as it was already 37 years out of date but most of the prisoners couldn't resist the temptation, and the latest news from the Old World would be a major conversation piece in the Dining Hall. KC10-1 types were always quick, though, to advise their fellows to remember that this was 'official' news, and not necessarily the whole story. Novos, of course, were the source for most of the interesting news, those stories held back by the Administration as 'irrelevant information'. Novos who went beyond the realms of truth to fulfil the demand for news and actually invented information were generally ostracised when their fabrication was discovered, following comparison with other novos' accounts, and regarded as untrustworthy.

As the teams dined on their never ending supply of food – some Korb-1 grown, some shipped in with the latest batch of novos – recent arrivals were informing their associates that the Saladdan scare was being beefed up again just as they left. NC President Lindon had been networked appealing for extreme vigilance as reliable information indicated that the Saladdans had just established three colonies in Taurus, one of them a mere twenty years distance from Korb-1. Attacks on NC bases were considered a real possibility and it had been discovered that a number of Saladdan agents had been despatched to the Northern Confederation to gather information. Citizens were asked to be on the watch for these agents and to report suspicious activities.

"Oh, no," Kane moaned, "not again!"

"'Fraid so, friends, the show goes on!" replied a fair-haired novo from NC Region 822.

"Must be time to build a new kolony – and labour is required!" another quipped.

"Hey, maybe we can apply for a transfer to a new kolony," Dayton ventured. "It would only take a few decades to get there. If we were really clever, we could keep transferring from kolony to kolony. In that way, with all our confinements, we could live for centuries!"

A hail of uneaten crusts was the reaction from his fellow Korbs.

AFTER THE MEAL, KANE and Dayton made for the squash courts in the Leisure and Sports Area (L+S). On the court, the monotony of the day's labour and the healthy rivalry between the two players produced an excellent game. Following a tough encounter, Dayton notched up a last minute winning hit and contended that his opponent was showing an energy deficiency, requiring an immediate injection of korb!

"Maybe I'll send you into the tunnel to get it for me!" Kane threatened jokingly, stretched on the ground, covered in perspiration.

Returning to their cell quarters, the two men saw the latest contingent of novos being marched to their cells. Observing the sorry band of travellers plodding along confused and helpless, 37 years away from the only world they knew, Kane couldn't help but feel a sense of sorrow at their loss, an eternal empathy. They seemed dazed by their New World surroundings and unable to react coherently, just as Kane and his fellow time travellers had felt on their first day on Korb-1. As the novos passed by, however, one of them – a bearded man with piercing eyes – stared at Kane as if he knew him. Kane, following a puzzled glance, continued on with his companion.

5 DEATH IN A DISTANT PAST

KANE LIKED THORSEN'S CELL. There was something about the way she kept it that he pleased him, something he couldn't really put his finger on. He liked all the mini-holograms she had constructed and positioned in different places around the cell. In particular, he liked the one of the Taurus constellation. Often when visiting her cell, he would look deep into that conglomeration of stars, and wonder would he ever see them at close quarters. Starting with Korb-1, he would map out a path through the constellation, a path through time and space which would lead to the only destination he still craved to visit – the planet Earth. He had studied his route so often now that he knew exactly the way he would go – not in a straight line to Earth, but initially in the opposite direction, then take a curved turn towards the EC Skomal Colony, followed by a sharp about-turn and a journey to the edge of the constellation, from where he would set course for Earth. His reasoning here was that a direct journey from Korb-1 to Earth would be the first thing NC Space Control would be watching out for. By heading in the direction of the Skomal Colony, it might be concluded that sanctuary in the European Confederation's jurisdiction was his intention. If the Korb-1 Administration was to be believed and there actually was a bacanite concentration in the galaxy that broke up radio signals, then it might just be possible that his about-turn would go undetected and he would arrive at the periphery of the constellation, unnoticed by the NC detector system. The last step in the voyage was the most perilous – how could he complete his return journey to Earth without the knowledge of the Confederation, particular with such a long flight path? He knew that, like most challenges, there must be a way – but how? He just hadn't worked that bit out yet.

"Let's guess what you're thinking about!" teased Thorsen as they lay together. "Could it be a one-way ticket to Earth?"

Kane smiled a pensive smile. Thorsen might tease but he was deadly serious. He wanted a mass escape. "If there *is* a way out, we should take everybody. One thing is certain, after an escape, successful or not, it will be ten times harder to do it again."

"Surely the less people who know, the less chance there is of an informer spilling the beans", Thorsen warned.

"If several hundred people are sailing away, on the law of averages, some are bound to make it", Kane replied, with untested logic.

"Make it to where?" Thorsen wondered. "Back to Earth? Even if it was possible to do so, we'd be going back to a world that we probably wouldn't even recognise?"

"The Taurus constellation is a big place. In the Tayvok sector, there are planets that are habitable by humans, and …", Kane added hesitantly, "apparently there's a colony close by".

"What – you want to visit the Saladdans! You're losing it, Kane!" Thorsen exploded.

"O.k., o.k., but the European Confederation has the Nebula and Skomal colonies, and they're not too far away."

"The European Confederation has a cooperation policy with the NC. You'd have wasted a long journey by going there."

"We can argue about that later. The urgent thing is to find a way."

Thorsen said no more, as they both lay looking into the constellation hologram, and wondering .....

LATER ON, IN HIS own cell, the green screen of Kane's computer reflected in his eyes as he pitted his wits against the mechanical skills of the system in a game of *War-Raok!* Occasionally, however, his concentration drifted from the screen to the line of newly arrived prisoners lining up in his mind and the man whose glance of apparent recognition had triggered something in Kane's mind. Kane wondered who he was? Where had he seen him before? What was *his offence?* Every time he got close to answering these troubling questions, his electronic adversary would make a clever move, leaving him struggling with the strands of a memory fragmented by time and distance. Inevitably the computer flashed the word *War-Raok!* across the screen in crimson letters. Kane, defeated again, was tired.

The prisoner lay on his bunk, trying to rack his brain to uncover the identity of the bearded novo. Trawling through various times and occasions in his previous existence, he made a determined effort to recognize the man. The newcomer obviously knew him, but how? Kane was frustrated. Every time he got close to identifying the novo, his mind would go blank, as if there was something there blocking his view. *Why couldn't he remember?*, he asked himself in frustration. Kane developed an ache deep in his head as he tried to see the stranger in his mind, numbing him to such an extent that he gradually just drifted off to sleep.

KANE AND THORSEN MOVED down the corridor slowly, warily. Although there was no sound, they expected to meet a party of tyrons at any minute. Armed with zennors, they could put up a fight against the well-trained seasoned soldiers but, with no cover, they could hardly expect to survive an assault by a tyron unit. Still, they continued. Moving cautiously, watching behind as well as in front, they carefully made their way towards the Master's Quarters. Negotiating the bends and curves of the corridors, the regime's centre of operations eventually came into sight. Kane looked at Thorsen, and she returned his satisfied glance. Slowly, step by step, they approached the door.

Suddenly, two tyrons walked out the door and straight into the two prisoners. As the tyrons overcame their surprise and went for their weapons, the prisoners didn't delay. A zennor flash from both sent the tyrons to the ground. Excited by the engagement, the prisoners rushed in the door, ready for more action, and were met by three tyrons, zennors rising. Thorsen took one out, Kane the other, but the third wasted no time and sent Thorsen flying with a sharp burst. Torn between concern for Thorsen and the knowledge that he was next, Kane hesitated slightly and saw the eye of the tyron's zennor focussing on him. He fired a blast and the tyron hit the workstation behind him as he fell.

Immediately, Kane turned to see how badly his companion was wounded. Thorsen lay slightly on her right side, blood streaming from a burn on her shoulder. Kane bent down on his knees and held Thorsen. "Go ahead on your own", she uttered, short of breath. "No!" Kane said firmly, "we're going together." As the two spoke together on the ground, Kane noticed Thorsen's eyes suddenly look up in terror at something behind his back. Turning around, Kane felt the cold muzzle of a zennor against his cheek.

"Guess who?" was the question Kane heard, mockingly posed. While Kane attempted to figure out what his response should be, the standing figure added coldly: "Time up!" With that, the zennor gave Kane a searing kiss that burned his cheek and passed through the very fabric of his skull. He himself smelt the burning of flesh as he collapsed, almost in slow motion, to the ground.

As his senses began to rapidly desert him, Kane looked up to see it was the bearded novo who had blown him away – and the stranger was now lining up his zennor to deliver the *coup de gras* to Thorsen. Gathering up all his dwindling strength, he roared at him not to pull the trigger – "Noooooooooo!"

Kane woke up in a cold sweat, his tunic drenched with the perspiration of cold fear. His head burned with an ache so intense that he thought it was going to burst. Sitting up suddenly in the bed, he could see no sign of Thorsen, the bearded novo or fallen tyrons. There was no sound except the echo of his nightmarish scream as he awoke. Sluggishly, in a gradually emerging consciousness, Kane got up and prepared to go down to the Dining Hall for breakfast.

THE DINING HALL WAS almost full with the prisoners, in their yellow tunics, having breakfast before their shift was due to begin. Most of them were now used to the Korb-1 mornings, though the idea of a morning with none of the natural sounds and appearances associated with an Earth morning always took a long time to get used to. In reality, there was nothing whatsoever to distinguish between the three work shifts on Korb-1, as the only difference between them was the personnel involved. Be it 8, 16 or 24 hours of the clock, the atmosphere was almost always the same. The outgoing and incoming shifts would sit together, and their repast would depend on whether they were going on to their shift or had just finished it, and even then that was a matter of taste.

Kane sat beside Dayton, Thorsen, Nielsen and other team members. As they sat down, Kane cast a wondering glance at Thorsen. She noticed and asked what it was – "Oh-oh! Have Have I been seared again?"

Kane was embarrassed – "'Fraid so, only this time I saw his face."

"Really?" Thorsen wondered, "Maybe I should get to know him – then I can get him first."

"It was him", Kane replied, nodding in the direction of the bearded novo.

Thorsen looked around, trying to carry out a physiognomic read on the newcomer. "He looks like a killer to me", was her instant judgement, a fake look of terror on her face.

"Do you recognise him?" Kane enquired, more seriously.

"Do you think I could forget him after last night? was Thorsen's ambiguous reply.

Kane laughed – "Bitch!" he added. "He was right to sear you!"

THERE WAS NOTHING UNUSUAL in the shift in KC10 as the team went about their chores and the korb gushes resumed. Dayton was his usual pleasant self and managed to raise any flanking spirits with a constant flow of repartee with his fellow toilers and humorous descriptions of various individuals in the kolony. He was particularly good at imitating the Master's supercilious gestures, particularly his facial mannerisms. Dayton would purse his mouth and hang his eyebrows, looking down his nose at the rest and inform them that they were all one happy family and should "just have fun". This performance usually resulted in a rain of dirty rags or whatever lay at hand and Dayton would seek shelter behind his tunnel. Nielsen would then take up the act.

Today, Gilmore told the team that one of the novos had informed her the night before that there was talk of an attempted coup having taken place in the Confederation just before they left. Apparently the coup failed and, as a result, there had been a widespread sweep of arrests of information activists and other 'subversives'. Rumour had it that the coup organisers were from the liberal wing of the government party and would have relaxed the information laws, if successful. After the failure of the plot, the Confederation Administration had released statements maintaining that continuous vigilance was required if the Saladdans were to be prevented from subverting the Confederation.

The novo had other depressing news for the prisoners. Apparently, the Administration had been regularly reporting that bomb attacks had been carried out by "enemy agents". These attacks generally involved casualties but the names of the victims were usually not released – "for security reasons". However, when he had told one of the guards that his friends would be looking for him, the response was: "Don't hold your breath – you were blown to bits in a terrorist bomb attack this morning!"

A stunned silence fell over the Chamber when the prisoners heard this news. Although they had always known that they must come to terms with the knowledge that they would never see their friends and relations again, the injustice of this situation was compounded by the discovery that, on top of the loss of their family and friends, a cruel deception had been perpetrated on the ones they loved and cared for.

"The bastards!" O'Hara spat, "The bastards!"

The rest remained silent, having fallen into a sad recollection of their former lives. In quiet, sometimes bitter, reflection, they scanned their memories, as a flood of faces, most of them smiling, came into view. For the prisoners, it all only seemed like yesterday. For them, 37 or 337 years was all the same – the past, no matter how far away, had been stolen and they would never get it back.

"I think it was the best thing to have happened", Kane said. The rest looked at him in surprise, awaiting an explanation. "For us, this has been a torture ..... because we know the truth. For our families and friends, it has been a simple bereavement – death in a bombing – sad, but acceptable, and life moves on. I think it was the best thing."

Nobody responded, but most nodded their heads ever so slightly in agreement. For the rest of the shift, the team mostly remained silent – pondering, wondering, remembering.

6 IN A CAVERN LONG AGO

IN THE TWENTY-FIRST CENTURY, the question of global energy supply was a major issue. Initially only the environmentally conscious were concerned, and industry and business continued burning their merry way through the fossil fuel stocks of the planet. Talk of damage to the ozone layer and climate change was dismissed as a scare tactic of extreme environmentalists who wanted to return the world to a primitive fundamentalist lifestyle. Big business was of the view that environmental issues were the concern of scientists and that the duty of business was to trade and make money.

Most people seemed to share that view as well, and few even of those who thought that there was perhaps something to the theory that the ecosystem was being damaged believed that anything practical could be done to redress the situation.

This negative attitude began to erode, however, towards the middle part of that century when it became obvious that real climate change was actually taking place. The decades from 2000 to 2050 were years of one natural disaster after another. As humans continued to puff smoke into the face of nature, nature struck back. Tidal waves, floods, droughts, disease and pestilence became almost everyday occurrences on the planet. Seasonal confusion reigned, with traditionally mild climates suffering heavy rain, and even floods, in the summer and sunny spells in the winter.

Everybody but the greediest and most short-sighted eventually agreed that the days of burning carbon fuel were numbered, but nobody could come up with an alternative. Nuclear power was a discredited and deprecated form of energy, particularly after a series of disasters in the former Soviet Union, the United States, Europe and Japan and the poisoning of many of the seas around nuclear plants with radioactive discharge. Anyway, uranium stocks were almost used up. Only the Chinese insisted on continuing to use that form of energy after 2050 when the Treaty of Sarajevo declared nuclear energy a "redundant option in the search for alternatives to carbon fuels". Wind and solar power were the preferred choice of the environmentalists but decades of experimentation had shown wind to be inadequate, producing energy only 25% of the time it was actually required. Solar energy carried a similar drawback in that dense cloud could greatly degrade energy production and only cloudless climes could fully rely on it. Also, the climate changes brought about by the burning of carbon fuels had, ironically, made the climate so unstable that it could not be depended upon for the main alternative green options.

The initiation of the Greeyan Project, a joint US-AE-Russian venture in 2047 was a breakthrough. This involved positioning a number of satellites in space carrying optimum capacity batteries that captured the sun's energy, compacted it and beamed it back to energy stations in America, Europe and Asia. But the project was extremely costly and came to be regarded as dangerous after an out of control satellite sent a shaft of energy over Canada, blowing the entire Canadian grid asunder.

Other projects were equally disappointing. The use of hydrogen to produce energy was unsuccessful as the reserves of pure hydrogen were extremely limited and the manufacture of pure hydrogen was energy-intensive in itself.

In the year 2071, when the only realistic solutions to the global energy crisis were identified as being the most costly ones, something remarkable and totally unexpected occurred. An anthropologist called Heinrich Rudemeyer read a paper to the National Geographic Society in New York on a five-year study he had carried out on the Klishtah people in southern Sudan. During the course of his dissertation, Dr. Rudermeyer mentioned the fact that this nomadic people carried with them an unusual substance, called korb. This was a dust originally discovered by an ancestor of theirs and called after him. Korb dust was used in small amounts in open fires. Its main property was that, once shaken onto the fire, it lit and remained aglow for days on end, emitting intense heat.

When Rudermeyer enquired as to where the famous tribal warrior, Korb, had originally discovered the dust, he was told of a deep cave in the Nuba Mountains into which Korb and other warriors of the tribe had descended almost two centuries before. The cave was regarded by the Klishtah as sacred, referred to as 'the opening to the womb of the Earth'. Carrying lighting torches, Korb's group explored the fissure, continuing deep into the bowels of the cave. Amazed at the distance they had succeeded in travelling, the party manoeuvred its way through a narrow passage that opened out into a large chamber. Passing through the opening, one of the party stumbled and let his torch fall. Almost immediately the cave floor in front of him lit up, as if by magic. The party of warriors fell back in astonishment at the sight of the ground on fire but, after a while, when it became clear the fire was not going to subside and they could see the extent of the huge cavern, they were eager to establish the cause of the wondrous event. They eventually concluded that the substance responsible for the continuous heat was a heavy dust that littered the floor of the cavern, lying in heavy concentrations here and there. Korb ordered his explorers to gather as much of the magical dust as they could and bring it up to the surface.

On returning to their camp, the delighted scouting party called a tribal assembly and produced their new discovery. The tribe were mesmerised by the action of the dust in producing light and heat and concluded it was a gift from the Earth Mother. The tribal elders decided that the new substance should be called after the warrior leader who had discovered it and thus *korb* was born. The elders also judged that such a gift from the Earth Mother was an honour worthy of celebration every year by the performance of the Earth Mother Fire Dance. The elders made one other pronouncement: the existence of the new substance was to kept as a secret of the tribe lest its existence might cause other tribes or nations to become jealous and invade their lands in an attempt to gain possession of the substance. From that day to the year of Rudermeyer's lecture, the Klishtah were extremely protective of their wonderful discovery, and had only given the details of the story to the scientist after he had become an honorary member of the tribe. Unfortunately for the Klishtah, however, Rudermeyer's incidental mention of the existence of korb was to bear serious and long term results.

Rudermeyer's paper was well received by the Society that evening and, although the revelation of the existence of korb dust was regarded as 'interesting' by most of those who attended, it did not provoke any major discussion. Rudermeyer, on reflecting on the repercussions for the Klishtah if multi-national energy companies were to become interested in the substance, decided to remove any reference to the story from the published version of the talk. In the attendance that evening, however, was a member of the Society, a scientist who had connections in the Administration of the newly formed Northern Confederation (an amalgamation of the United States of America, Canada and Greenland). The following morning, the official contacted an associate of his in the Confederation's Intelligence and Policy Institute and arranged to meet him for lunch. A number of events ensued.

The extremist regime in Sudan had been for many decades persecuting the peoples in the central and southern areas of the country. With no international interest being expressed in their plight, only the courage of these peoples stood between them and total extermination. Then, to the surprise of many, the Northern Confederation announced that the "genocide of the southern Sudanese people was an affront to civilisation and could no longer be tolerated". This statement was followed by a number of verbal attacks on the Khartoum regime. These attacks increased in virulence over time. The southern Sudanese were delighted to discover that the world was now concerned about their plight and could finally see a ray of hope through the cloud of oppression that had hung over them for so long. They were further encouraged by an announcement by the European Confederation that it would have no choice but to put serious measures against the unlawful Khartoum regime in place "if its war against the peaceful people of southern Sudan and its attacks on EC aid workers" did not cease immediately. Less than a month later, a unified NC/EC strike force invaded Sudan. Within another month, Sudan had been divided into two states, separated by a demilitarised no-fly zone. The people of the new northern state of Sudan were told that the international community would only cooperate with them if the dictators in Khartoum were overthrown. The new interim government of Nuba, the southern state, concluded a treaty with the NC and EC, involving a massive aid package and rebuilding programme, in return for which the Nubans allowed the two superpowers to explore for natural resources in their territory, a small price to pay for freedom, particularly considering the apparent lack of natural resources in the new state. Over the next few years, both Nuba and the Sudan settled down to become stable democracies and peace reigned in the land. Eventually, both states became active participants in the establishment of the African Alliance and a new era of cooperation in the region began.

The rest of the story is now history. At the same time as the new political dispensation in northern Africa began to take root, the NC and the EC announced that they had jointly managed to develop a new natural fuel which they hoped would eventually prove to be the alternative sought after for so long by the governments of the world. The two superstates offered to share their discovery with all other interested states, particularly with a view to 'opening up and maximising access" to the natural resource required. The substance in question was identified as a non-carbonate substance with enormous energy potential. It was called korb. Scientists explained that korb was an igneous rock from the inner mantle of the Earth produced during the later formation period. It was extremely hard but when liquefied by a process using querns driven at the speed of light in a vacuum, it could be containerised and used in that form to produce large amounts of energy over extremely long periods. No mention was made of the dust found in the Sudan or how the substance came to be found in a powdery state.

The reaction of the general public to the announcement of the discovery of a new fuel was muted, mostly due to the failure of previous ventures that had been heralded with much ado. The reaction of the corporate sector was different, however. The news caused an unprecedented level of excitement there, resulting in a frenzied scramble by many of the established energy corporations to get on board. The NC and EC administrations announced public-private ventures to locate, access, exploit and produce the new fuel and soon a new, vibrant and lucrative industry was born. Most of the new corporations were reincarnations of the old energy companies though one or two individuals close to the governing parties in both Confederations were to the fore in establishing consortiums, bringing together new investors in the sector. One of these – The Korb Konsortium, was particularly effective in locating korb veins. Although established in the Northern Confederation, its successful activities were not confined to that political area. Within a few short years, the Konsortium had hit it lucky in a number of other parts of the world, particularly in ULAS (The Union of Latin American States), Africa and the South Pole. A related group, based in the European Confederation, was equally impressive in hitting the korb spot, with major strikes in Africa and the Caucasian Republics.

Soon, the korb industry became literally the shining light of the new political super-structures that had now come to rule the world. Its aim of solving the global energy crisis and providing the ordinary citizen with a reliable and relatively cheap fuel was a noble one and a service to society. The new industry provided energy, employment and a sense of security for the future. To be associated with this progressive sector, particularly with the Korb Konsortium, was a badge of honour. The development of the new energy source was the beginning of a new era in keeping with the emergence of the new super-states. All the power-driven comforts and conveniences of modern living were provided by korb. To avail of them was to live in the future. The only ones to complain in all of this were those who objected to the Earth's core being disturbed once again. But few paid any heed to them. The world's energy spectre had been slain and the magic lance was called korb.

7 ENERGISING THE PAST

AS THE GUSHES CAME and went in Korb Chamber 10, they took with them minutes, hours and days of a prisoner's life. A prisoner could spend the greater part of his or her days standing by the operating screen, shift in, shift out. Sometimes that very thought occurred to Kane as he stood by his tunnel, ushering vast amounts of korb into containers to energize a planet he would never see again. Sometimes he wondered would the sons and daughters of his former friends and relations benefit from the energy provided by their long 'dead' and probably forgotten benefactor. Other times, the korb containers only served to remind the deportee of the distance between him and his real home. That thought never failed to depress Kane and at those times even Dayton's fun and frolics couldn't lift his flagging spirits.

Despite these sad reminders, every day the crew would put in their shift, loading korb into massive containers and storing them for transport to Earth. It was a task now carried out with routine efficiency. Every fifteen minutes, an operator filled a container. This was then hermetically sealed and moved by a conveyor to a Kollector Bay to be taken to the Despatch Port. There it would be loaded onto a transporter ship to be delivered to a new generation in an old world.

Initially the idea of sending fuel to keep a world functioning that one had left 37 years before – fuel that wouldn't arrive for another 37 years – caused a strange sensation. How could you be sure the fuel would get to its destination? How could you be sure there would be a planet there to accept the delivery, particularly as each and every one of the global states had the capability to blow the world to smithereens a thousand times over? What if a fuel was developed which was easier and cheaper to produce? Would anybody bother telling Korb-1 and the other kolonies? Would they just store the continuously arriving korb away somewhere for a 'rainy day'? Or would they just dump it when it arrived? Either way, it would take 37 years to inform the kolony and put the workforce there to another useful purpose!

Whatever the answer to these confusing questions might be, the korb supplies which left KC10 were earthbound. Kane found it ironic that this inanimate fuel was guaranteed something that had been stolen from him – a journey to Earth and a meaningful role on the planet. He felt troubled by this thought and even jealous of the substance that would visit a world that his eyes would never see again. Eventually, though, Kane realised that his hatred for korb was simplistic and illogical. He remembered the old American proverb "Don't get angry, get even!" and concluded that his anger and frustration could be more usefully directed at those who had deprived him of a life in his world.

Over time, Kane began to regard korb as a symbol of his own predicament, a substance that was rescued from it's primordial imprisoned state and released into a form of extremely powerful energy. In this potent condition, it was sent to Earth. This, in Kane's view, was something to aspire too. Perhaps there was a lesson there for him – a prisoner in a strange rocky planet. Perhaps *he* could be liberated to a new state – the state of freedom. Perhaps *he* could discover a way to develop himself in his prison environment and eventually free himself from his plight, escaping to a new world – or even back to his old one.

Sometimes these thoughts filled Kane's mind, even inspired him, as he filled the transport tanks with korb for despatch to the old world. Eventually every korb tank that left the kolony became a symbol for Kane of his own liberation. He smiled in his mind as the tanks lined up in the Kollector Bay for removal and shipment. Although he himself had never seen the actual departure of the tanks – prisoners were not allowed access to the Despatch Port for obvious reasons – he experienced an inner sense of satisfaction when a complete batch – 5,000 containers – was ready to go. One day, he felt, korb – the cause of his incarceration and deportation from Earth – would be the vehicle for his deliverance. This was not, in *his* mind, just a hope, it was a certainty. The only remaining task was to work out *how* – that was now Kane's sole challenge on Korb-1.

As Kane developed his new challenge in his mind, he originally decided to keep his own counsel on his intentions, but as the idea grew in his head, he had taken Dayton, O'Hara, Gibney, and, of course, Thorsen into his confidence. Their reactions were very similar – sympathetic but sceptical. O'Hara even emitted a sad, helpless laugh. Gibney was the only one who wanted to hear more. In fact, Gibney had returned to the subject with regularity ever since. Only the other evening on the squash court, he punctuated his shots with probing questions like "Who would try it with you?", "What exactly would you do?" and "How would you get through the tyron guards at the various levels?" Kane, encouraged by his fellow prisoner's enthusiasm, told him he had a plan (which he hadn't yet), to keep cool and wait for "the word".

If the shift was dull and tedious in the Korb Chamber, the Generation Chamber was a different proposition. The first thing to strike a novo on his or her first day on generation duties was the intense heat that turned the entire area into a furnace. On passing through the door, a wall of hot dry air hit the prisoner in the face, and it was this, an essential part of korb generation, that was the enduring feature of work in the chamber – but certainly not the only one.

A Generation Chamber consisted of seven large tanks, each controlled by an operator and an operator's assistant. Each of the seven tanks was fed a supply of korb rocks by conveyor belt channels, from a central pit, into which rocks were being continuously loaded from the korb mine, operated by machine robots, directly underneath the kolony. When the operator judged that the tank was full and ready for the liquidation process, the belt feeding into the tank was stopped and a signal given to the assistant to close the door. If, when the feed belt was stopped, a rock was blocking the door of the tank, it was the assistant's job to direct the team of six to move it and allow the door to be closed. The smooth efficiency of this system depended on the ability of the operator to judge the capacity remaining in the tank and the flow of the belt so that, when the tank was almost full, the belt could be stopped without any rocks being left blocking the door.

The heat in a Generation Chamber wasn't the only uncomfortable feature a generation worker had to bear. Although the noise of the rocks being deposited in the korb pit from the mine was cloaked by a noise suppressor, the continuous rumbling and banging in the feed channels left a dull thudding noise almost permanently sounding in the generation worker's ears. The seven hours continuous toil was broken halfway through by a twenty-minute rest period and punctuated by occasional ten-minute breaks as the korb rocks were broken down and liquidised, but then it was back to business.

In Generation Chamber 9, the production of korb was continuing apace and the team involved had just been joined by a new member. Novo 1319 was getting his first taste of the working day and night on Korb-1 – and didn't like it. The intense heat and hard graft in the chamber wasn't easy to take after a confinement of 37 years, and 1319 was feeling the pressure. His plight was by no means lessened by the presence on the shift team of Wilson Leonard, a criminal banished to Korb-1 for a series of violent assaults. The ferocity of the violence involved in these attacks was not a reflection of any imposing physique – rather an indication of the disregard shown by Leonard for the life and welfare of others.

It was more or less an open secret that Leonard was a spy for the Kolony Administration and, for that reason, most of the other prisoners treated him with nothing but contempt. Only a small band of fellow lowlifes, mostly on the same generation shift as himself, associated with Leonard, and even they, out of earshot of their fellow creature, called him by the name everybody else, both Administration and prisoner, did: 'The Ferret'. Thoroughly disliked by the prisoners in general, Leonard survived by a combination of toadying to the Administration, attempting to ingratiate himself with some of his fellow workers, and abusing some of the more disorientated new arrivals in the kolony. Having been kicked out of three KC shifts at the demand of the other members, he had been finally deposited in a Generation Chamber with other misfits and whatever unfortunate novos happened to be assigned there. As a reward for his information gathering activities for the Administration, the Ferret had been given the job of Chief Operator, leaving him in a position to avoid the more strenuous aspects of generation duties and also to torment whoever had the misfortune to end up on his team. A recently departed member of the team, Jack Kerne, who had just graduated to Korb Chamber duties, had reacted to this situation by toadying to Leonard and massaging his ego, and this had made life slightly more bearable for him while in the Ferret's clutches.

Kerne's replacement was Novo 1319 and, as soon as the new prisoner arrived, Leonard had judged him to be a genteel type, not suited to physical toil and strain – an assessment based solely on the novo's restrained attitude rather than on his physical appearance – and had therefore decided he was a man to be pushed to the edge. Time after time, during the novo's first shift, he had imposed the most difficult and strenuous of tasks on the new prisoner.

1319 obliged every time and, although on the brink of collapse, never waned in his execution of whatever had to be done. Sweat poured down his cramping muscles as he manoeuvred rugged korb rocks, up to 3 korb stone in weight, into the generation tank or moved them out of the way in order to close the tank door. When the tank was loaded with rocks, the heavy metal door was closed and double-locked. Once the door was locked and the Ferret had nodded to the Assistant Operator at the control panel, 1319 could rest for ten minutes as the nuclear driver inside the tunnel shot a multitude of quern cells at seventeen times the speed of light through the korb rocks, disintegrating them into mush and eventually liquidising the mixture. As this liquidising process took place, a red light flashed on the side of the tunnel, reflecting on the sweated-covered faces of the team. When the process was complete, the red throbbing light gave way to a green one. At this, the Assistant Operator pressed a button to release the highly reactive substance into the main funnel, to be passed on to a Korb Chamber team further down for loading. When the substance had passed out of the tunnel, another button began a decontamination process, and the light turned to blue. The decontamination complete, a yellow light indicated it was time for Novo 1319 and his fellow toilers to load again.

The intense heat in the Generation Chamber and the continuous cycle of coloured lights – red, green, blue, yellow, red – on top of the labour involved in shifting 7 tons of korb rocks in a seven hour shift left the loading team members disorientated and in a state of almost total exhaustion. This cut no ice with Leonard, however, who continually pretended to be frustrated by the length of time involved in the liquidation process, and shouted and roared continuously at Novo 1319 to "get stuck in". When the yellow light indicated that it was time to load again, the little Ferret's eyes lit up and it was never going to be long before he called on the team to clear a boulder from the opening, his beady eyes and rasping voice concentrating primarily on the novo. Watching 1319 struggling with a large boulder, he would roar that he was far too slow and that his attitude was all wrong. "You'll learn how to work around here!" he would shout, as the novo was attempting to load a particularly heavy rock into the tunnel, "this is the place for you!"

The novo appeared to be oblivious to the Ferret's constant barrage of abuse, silently loading the rocks and taking advantage of the liquidising rest period. Leonard was surprised at his inability to bring the novo to his knees, a goal easily achieved in previous cases. When the siren sounded the end of the shift, Leonard approached the novo as he left the Chamber and warned: "You'd better shape up or we'll feed you to the korb!" Sneering, he waited for a reaction. The bearded novo said nothing and just walked away. Leonard squinted after him. He was convinced he had a meek type in his clutches and he would push him all the way.

WALKING SLOWLY ALONG THE corridor, Novo 1319 felt every muscle in his body ache. His spine felt as if it had been bent in every direction and his head spun. He found the bright lights of the corridor almost blinding after the gloom and flashing lights of the Generation Chamber. Trudging slowly back to his cell, he wondered how much more of this treatment he could take. The foulmouthed Ferret was a minor irritation compared to the wearisome toil involved in the generation process itself and it was all he could do after every shift to recover in time for the next one. But 1319 decided he would have to ride the storm and see this through. At the end of the day, he had no other choice – for the moment.

Passing a group of tyrons, the novo grew slightly tense, not knowing what to expect. The soldiers glared at him momentarily, their zennor shoulder guns an intimidating sight, and their stunner batons looped on to their uniform legs ready to be grasped and put to use. They also carried handheld zennors, an indication to a seasoned prisoner that trouble was brewing somewhere. Novo 1319 wasn't on Korb-1 long enough to read those signs, however, and, rubbing his black beard with his hand, passed by, though, he couldn't but note that, armed to the teeth in their red uniforms and helmets, the tyrons were an imposing and menacing spectacle, and it was common knowledge that their willingness to use their deadly weapons was beyond question. 1319 had already heard from the other prisoners of the tyrons' cold efficiency in putting down any attempts at insurrection on the kolony, and their legendary 'Code One' missions against the Saladdans were popular subjects for the entertainment media. Nevertheless, he displayed no fear as he walked by and, having sized up the threatening guards with a passing glance, went upon his way.

As Novo 1319 passed by Cell 313, the occupant was awaking from an uneasy sleep, his mind preoccupied with a matter that had lately become almost an obsession – the journey home.

8   NOVOS

THE DAY AFTER THE arrival of new kolonists was always an exciting one on Korb-1. Where were the new prisoners from? What had they done to be sent there? What had happened in the years after the present inmates had been transported? What state was the Old World in when they left? Had the Saladdans eventually proven the Administration correct and attacked or had they moved on the African Alliance, as they had been really threatening to do? Had the Caucasian Republics faced down the territorial demands of the Mao Republic?

And there were other questions too – more important ones. "Have you ever been to District 2251 in NCR 112?" "Did you ever hear of the artist, Breena Remo? I once knew her." "What's happening in the Area Ball League? Who are the champions?" And other, sadder, despairing questions that no one would answer, particularly if they knew the truth.

Such was the life of the prisoner on Korb Kolony One, time spent in a world which ignored the seasons that normally tracked the path of the earthling through his or her brief sojourn on the blue planet. So many questions could be answered by novos and so many gaps filled into a fading picture that the weeks following an Arrival were usually filled with a buzz that covered the entire kolony. This excitement would continue for quite a while and only begin to fade when the novos had little else to offer in the line of interesting news. Prisoners would then patiently wait for another Arrival and the excitement would reach fever pitch again. This was the situation for most of the prisoners – but not all. Some had long lost interest in their old existence and found the best way to survive in the New World was to forget all about the old one. The arrival of novos was a dark period for them, a time when long suppressed feelings were aroused once more and old spectres returned to haunt their sleeping and waking hours. The Master's message that there could be no escape from Korb-1 was the mantra they would repeatedly whisper to their souls as they tried to sleep in the quiet Korb night.

THIS EVENING ALMOST EVERYBODY congregated in the Dining Hall to interrogate the latest arrivals properly. Some of the novos were still too depressed or traumatised to participate but most told their stories. One told of his action in support of his striking colleagues in a manufacturing plant. The strike committee were arrested *en masse* and never seen again. Then, in a cruel deception, the staff were invited by radio message to a meeting in a secret location to re-establish the strike committee. When 15 turned up, they were immediately arrested and despatched, after an efficient and speedy trial, to the Korb Kolonies.

Another told of a brief career of petty larceny which culminated in the theft of computer disks from the back of a *ptv* (personal transport vehicle) left unlocked outside one of the most exclusive pleasure venues in one of NCR 771's biggest municipalities. Within twenty minutes, a homing device had lead the Special Information Police to the small time thief who found himself accused of stealing Administration Budget Files and convicted of "financial espionage for a foreign power". A one-way ticket to Korb-1 brought the miscreant's career in crime to a conclusion.

A woman, still in a state of shock, told of how her partner, an employee of the Administration and in his early thirties, had died suddenly. As she left the obsequies with her friends and family, a work-associate of her deceased partner approached her, acting suspiciously and asked her had she any knowledge of a set of green disks that were in her partner's possession when he died. She said she hadn't and the man left. When she arrived back at her apartment, however, she found a team of men in Administration security garb there, systematically searching the premises. Having been surprised by the woman, the agents announced that a security issue had arisen and that they expected her total cooperation. Regarding the team's presence in her home as an unwanted and untimely intrusion, the woman refused to cooperate and demanded that the intruders leave. She was immediately arrested and questioned about the set of green disks. Having spent three days attempting to convince her interrogators of her innocence, the woman then found herself heading for a confinement tray, having been found guilty of Information Terrorism. When she had finished her sad tale, Thorsen's consoling hand on her shoulder introduced her to her first friend on Korb-1.

All of those who spoke had a sad story of some kind to tell, either a life of petty crime or an interest in freedom of information. Amongst those who chose not to tell their tale was the novo who had seemed to recognise Kane. When asked by the more inquisitive what bad luck had brought him to Korb-1, the bearded newcomer announced that he had "wanted a change of scenery", leaving his inquisitors speechless.

Thorsen looked at the bearded newcomer suspiciously as he left, then continued to talk to another novo who claimed to have worked in the Administration Information H.Q. and had intimate knowledge of the Information Control structure. This novo said he had worked on a variety of very sensitive projects and that, when one of them leaked, the finger was pointed at him, probably by the real culprit. The rest of the story followed the same script as everybody else's and finished at the table in the Korb-1 Dining Hall.

Thorsen seemed to have a particular interest in this novo's story and asked him a number of questions about areas of his former career. The novo appeared to be surprised at Thorsen's knowledge of projects and individuals in Information Control, and wondered how she knew so much. Thorsen replied that she had had contacts in the IC area before her capture. The novo seemed delighted to meet someone who had knowledge of his area of interest and offered to meet Thorsen again to talk some more. Thorsen agreed and left, arranging to meet later on. Leaving the table, she noticed the bearded novo observing her from the other side of the Hall.

Playing *War-Raok!* later on, Kane still wondered who the bearded novo was, but was coming to the conclusion that perhaps he hadn't seen him before at all and was just imagining a spark of recognition in the stranger's eyes. Tonight, having left the Dining Hall early, he gave the system a good game, concentrating the bulk of his forces on the left flank third level, and retaining two smaller bands of cavalry on the right and in the centre at first and second levels. Suddenly, the mechanical mind moved a force of infantry through the centre of his right flank with speed and took his citadel with a clinical strike. Once again, the crimson letters

War-Raok! flashed on the screen. Defeated again and tired, Kane failed to notice another message flashing on his screen. He lay down on his bed to spend another night travelling far away from Korb-1.

Kane's mind bought him back to his days at Development Sector Bureau 375 in NCR 435 with Sheena Strauss. He remembered the way they had both agreed that the wall of information suppression had to be breached and that they were the ones in a position to do it. He relived their preparation and the planning of the operation. They had been extremely meticulous in the preparatory stage, but yet they had been arrested almost immediately. What had gone wrong? he wondered. What had they overlooked? How had the information leak been so rapidly traced to them?

Strauss had decided that the easiest part of the operation for systems experts like her and Kane was accessing the information. In order to do this, they first had to locate the relevant information cells in the system. When doing this, they had to be careful not to access the numerous sleeper cells placed in the system to trap sweepers – those sweeping the system for information. Once a sleeper cell was activated, it immediately notified the Control Centre that an unauthorised sweep was taking place, homed in on the sweeper's search path and locked in on the sweeper's machine, freezing it immediately. Strauss was an expert in sweeping the system, however, having helped construct it, and knew how to bend her search path around the waiting sleepers.

The most difficult part, though, would be copying the files. All files had an anti-copy device that would immediately incapacitate an unauthorised copier's machine and inform the CC that an unofficial copy was being attempted. As only the CC was authorised to copy files, Strauss's plan to get around that was to hack into one of the CC's own accounts and do the copying from there. The chance was that one of the seven staff there would not have changed their password in the last two months despite being required to do so, thus giving Strauss time to crack it. Strauss was right and not alone did she manage to get one password but got a second one just in case.

The next factor Strauss had to control was the timing of the operation. The system worked on two shifts – an early morning to noon shift and an early afternoon to midnight one. The period from midnight to 6 a.m. was used for backups and maintenance. Strauss realised that if the sleeper system was triggered during the working shifts, the sweepers would be caught red-handed by office colleagues. The only other option would be to strike at night. Kane agreed, but how to do so safely was another question. Surely, he pointed out, if the system was down at night, any activity at all would trigger an immediate response.

"Correct!" replied Strauss, with a glint in her eye. "During the night, the system is not used and backup is carried out on all files. Therefore the only usual activity at that time, apart from a maintenance task, is in the backup area. We will search only backup files. Thus, no usual activity will be noted in the general area. We will do so from a CC member's identity file and hopefully avoid sleepers."

Kane wasn't totally convinced. "We know we can't hack into the Document Control System from outside. So how do we get back in to the building in the middle of the night?"

Strauss smiled again – "We don't!"

Kane was puzzled but before he could pose the obvious question, Strauss obliged.

"The security system is very careful about letting people in. All access is based on thumb print profile and iris identification – as you are aware. Approach areas are covered by camera. Gaining unauthorised access wouldn't be easy. Leaving the building, however, is another matter altogether. Despite its great efforts to control entrance, the system doesn't seem to be that worried about letting people out. So we won't go! We'll remain in the building after our shift, and then strike. We'll then have to conceal ourselves until the end of the first shift and leave with everyone else, returning shortly afterwards as normal for our own shift. The best place to hide is on top of the systems cabinets. As long as we don't nod off and fall off, we'll be o.k."

It all seemed too simple to Kane. Strauss, sensing his doubt, placed a finger on his lips, saying "Don't worry. If we're cool, everything else will fall into place."

Kane kissed Strauss's calming finger and they both lay back on her bed and vanished into the twilight.

As if looking down from far above, Kane saw himself and Strauss lying together. When their movement together slowly came to a climax, Kane sensed the image of a face in the corner of the room – a shadowy scary kind of figure which hovered in a misty cloud. The figure appeared to smile and move closer to Kane. Suddenly, an abrupt move by the shadowy form startled Kane. Leaping up from beside Strauss, he awoke to find himself alone in his cell, the oppressive heat of the night a reminder that Prisoner 313 was still in his cell.

9 PURPLE NIGHT

Most Korb-1 'mornings' were the same to Kevin Kane. Having awoken in the early hours, the prisoner would lie on his bunk and wrestle hopelessly with all his fears and regrets. He always felt the silence in his cell at that time to be almost unbearable and, although he realised it was a victory for those who had taken everything he had away from him and left him to live, work and ultimately to die in another world, he always looked forward to the beginning of another working day and to the company it would bring.

Reluctantly, he would find himself looking forward to the sound of the wake-up gong for his shift, beamed into his cell, almost as a liberating sound. In Kane's mind, the sound of the gong was sweet, almost like that of a lark or a blackbird, creatures he had heard in his youth when visiting his grandmother in NCR 427. It signalled a new day for him and his fellow first-shifters – and an end to another purple black night, with its ghosts and spectres. The rest was predictable. After the reveille gong for the shift, the shift teams had a half an hour to get to the Dining Hall for breakfast. After a half an hour in the Dining Hall, they had fifteen minutes to get to their respective korb chambers.

The Dining Hall was enormous and was overlooked by the large dome high up in the centre of the ceiling that Kane had observed on his first day there three years earlier. Through the dome could be seen the dull purple atmosphere of Korb-1. The depressing starless sky was a permanent feature. Because of its position in the constellation, light reaching the planet from the nearest star was negligible. Whatever natural light managed to get as far as the forlorn rock, however, had no chance of permeating the dense atmosphere, composed as it was of thick heavy gases, none of which would be welcome in a pair of human lungs.

The dome, rather than being a window on the outer world, was a depressing reminder that Korb-1 was a place that didn't encourage departures. Anyone adventurous enough to venture outside the kolony without an *iwv* (inter-world vehicle) of some kind would end up travelling to a place from which there would be no return. Unlike the blue sky above the Earth, the murky purple sky above Korb-1 was the end of a journey, not the beginning.

For a novo on Korb-1, the purple sky was an appropriate backdrop to a first morning on the kolony. New arrivals were usually too pre-occupied trying to come to terms with the significance of their experience to pay it much heed, however. Awaking in a prison labour camp 37 years from home, surrounded by strangers in a unknown environment, with no prospect of escape, was enough to keep any mind, no matter how strong, in a depressed state. Understanding the plight of the newcomers only too well, the established prisoners, with the exception of those who had reacted to their new existence by withdrawing from social contact as much as possible, sought at all times to make the novos welcome, especially those of the opposite sex.

Originally, all the prisoners on Korb-1 were 'political'. The Confederation decided that to mix criminals with those who were motivated by antipathy to the Regime, an antipathy perpetuated by a life sentence on a korb kolony, would be to facilitate the development of a very dangerous alliance. Such an alliance could prove to be an extremely effective one and could never be countenanced. On the basis that criminals would not organise themselves in any effective coherent manner, they were sent exclusively to Korb-2 and Korb-3. Korb-1 and Korb-4 were reserved for those who had had the temerity to challenge the authority of the Confederation. Nonetheless, after a short period, the Confederation concluded that the introduction of common criminals to the political kolonies could in fact be useful, particularly in terms of securing information. Prisoner 477 (Ferret Leonard) was one of the first OCs (ordinary criminals) to be introduced.

IN THE NORTHERN CONFEDERATION of 2070, due to the huge costs involved in the production of paper, the use of that material to record information was banned. According to the law, information could now only be stored electronically. With the initial crisis brought about by the amalgamation of the Middle Eastern territories into the Saladdan States, and the declaration by the Northern and European Confederations of a state of DMP (defensive military preparedness), an order requiring the registration of all information networks was issued. This effectively made the operation of an unregistered information network an illegal act and an attack on the security of the Confederation. When the crisis with the Saladdans intensified in the following years, the Confederation tightened its control of the information systems and declared that, in the face of a grave threat to Confederation security, the operation of all information systems must be placed in the hands of the Administration.

As was the way of the Old World, when the threat posed by the Saladdans became less immediate, those who had tightened up the law could find no good reason to loosen it, rather the idea of further controlling the flow of information became irresistible, and in the interests of the 'financial security' of the Confederation, the movement of information, by whatever means, without the prior express permission of Confederation Information Control, became a serious offence.

Within a few short years, the Confederation Court had ruled that an offence against the Information Laws in the context of the continued threat against the Confederation by 'alien forces' and the Clayton Towning affair, could only be for the purposes of propaganda, was therefore an act of terrorism and must be dealt with as such. The offence of 'Information Terrorism' was born. Eventually, even a reference to the existence of the Information Laws was interpreted by the Courts as a breach of those very same laws. The structure was in place.

ON THE NOVOS' FIRST evening in their new home, they were generally welcomed by Nevin, the kolony prisoners' leader. Nevin was the patient type, never one to panic. He had natural leadership qualities and was the obvious choice for any prisoner who needed direction or advice. As he showed the novos around the prison area, he would put a positive gloss on everything, almost like a *holiday city* agent showing his clients around the latest location. Most novos benefited from his positive approach, however, in coming to terms with the finality of their predicament. After all, if he was so happy after his years on the kolony maybe it mightn't be that bad at all.

Nevin was the longest-serving resident on the kolony, having been amongst the first six to arrive fourteen years earlier. The other five died when their Korb Chamber – the first – exploded. Nevin survived, but minus the fingers on his left hand. This deformity, a badge of honour in the eyes of the prisoners, coupled with his intimate knowledge of the kolony, made him an instinctive choice as leader of the prisoners of Korb-1, most referring to him amicably as 'old steel fingers' because of the false fingers on his damaged hand.

The Kolony Administration acknowledged Nevin's special role and even welcomed it. He was not called upon to perform any labour. The Administration's view was that the existence of a prisoner leader was a calming influence on the kolony and that at the end of the day it was easier to deal with a reasonable man like Nevin than to have to deal with the unpredictable demands of an entire kolony. Nevin had formed a union with Karen Kenning, another ideologically strong prisoner, and they now shared a cell. Unions were approved by the Administration when the participants had spent at least three years in the kolony. What the prisoners didn't know, however, was that their unions could never produce offspring, as all male deportees were vasectomised before movement to the kolony, just one of the many cruel deceptions of which prisoners were, perhaps fortunately, unaware.

THE DINING HALL WAS a sea of yellow as the first shift prisoners had breakfast. The atmosphere was good and the prisoners were discussing the news brought by the latest batch of novos. Together they built up a picture of the world that had developed since they had left the Earth – politics, sport, economics, the arts – and, of course, the dispute with the Saladdans.

At one of the tables in the Dining Hall, Thorsen was deep in conversation with the former IC novo when Kane arrived. Noticing that Thorsen was engrossed in discussion with the new arrival, and might possibly be receiving some interesting information from the Old World, Kane decided to join Dayton, Nielsen and Gibney at another table instead.

Dayton welcomed his friend and, after a few minutes, asked him had he heard the news that some of the novos had brought about a daring tyron rescue mission to the Mongolian States, at that time engaged in negotiations with the Mao Republic for admission to that giant entity. Apparently a visiting group of NC scientists on a research visit to the Gobi Desert had been arrested and accused of espionage by the Mongolian authorities. Such was the paranoia of the MS regime that the scientists were charged with economic espionage – an offence against the security of the Mongolian States and punishable by death. The Northern Confederation deplored the draconian treatment meted out to mere scientists and demanded the return of the captives. The Mongolians refused. As attempts were being made to negotiate, a force of tyrons was despatched to Ulan-Bator, the Mongolian capital, and all the captives were brought home safely, with the tyrons receiving minimal casualties. The Mongolians States declared the NC intervention an act of war, and said that they would punish the Confederation. The Mao Republic announced it was breaking off diplomatic relations with the Northern Confederation due to "this grossly irresponsible action". Unofficially, the word was that the Confederation was very eager to ascertain the korb capacity of the Mongolians prior to their assimilation into the MR and had been attempting to quantify the extent of the korb resources remaining untapped in the Gobi Desert. The NC regime made no reference to this claim in its official world briefing on the incident, concentrating instead on the bravery of the captives and their liberators.

"You've got to give it to them, Kane", Gibney announced, as Dayton finished his story. "They're a hard bunch of guys."

Kane didn't respond. Gibney continued: "Whatever about our situation here, those guys in Mongolia were ours, and the tyrons did a good job."

Kane remained unimpressed with Gibney's generous admiration for their jailors and ignored his remark. Dayton and Nielsen remained silent too, though they were considering the significance of the story in the context of Korb-1. How could anyone overcome a fighting force of that calibre?, they wondered.

Kane was deep in thought. He was trying to figure out why the Confederation was so interested in korb resources on Earth, if it had such a supply from the kolonies. Perhaps they were trying to monopolise production outside the Saladdan States, or prevent Mongolian korb getting into the hands of the MR. He wondered.

When the gong sounded in the Dining Hall, it was time for the prisoners to return to their cells and prepare for KC duty. Finishing their meal, Kane, Dayton, Nielsen and Gibney left the Dining Hall. As they did, Kane winked at Thorsen, who was still talking to the novo.

Later, on his way to the Korb Chamber, Kane met Thorsen. In ebullient form, she told him that the new novo she had been talking to was very interested in helping his fellow prisoners in any way he could, and hoped that any information he possessed about the IC system might someday be useful. Thorsen felt this could be the case, as the novo – Nathan Winslow – held a reasonably senior position in the Administration and could have vital information.

"After thirty seven years?" Kane responded cynically, and almost immediately felt guilty for responding negatively to Thorsen's enthusiasm. His partner's features betraying annoyance, Kane spoke again, smiling this time: "No, you're right. Keep at it!" Then, touching her on the tip of the nose with his finger, he smiled and strolled off to Korb Chamber 10.

In Kane's Korb Chamber, the gushes flowed, and the prisoners talked in between. Not unusually, today's conversation centred on events that had happened 37 years previously. The 'latest' news was always tempered with the thought that the events in question were probably irrelevant now, even to the participants themselves, but could in some strange way impact on the lives of the kolonists on Korb-1. Every bit of information brought to the kolony was examined in that context and the possible consequences of any event, no matter how remote, was always analysed. Kane was thinking of Thorsen's new contact. He found it hard to be enthusiastic about 'new' information when it was 37 years old, but maybe Thorsen was right, maybe something useful could be gleaned from the newcomer. Lying against a feeder pipe, Kane saw 'screen yellow' indicate it was time to load another gush.

Kane hadn't spoken to Thorsen after work that day and when 'night' fell, he decided to just relax in his cell. The prisoner's mind was sharper and more focused than usual and he gave the system a good game. With three troops of cavalry on assault on all three dimensions, he had his foe under pressure. At the last minute, however, having feigned retreat at its fortress perimeter on dimension two, the system suddenly swept forward in strength on dimension three, snatching victory from Kane's eager hands. As the screen flashed *War-Raok!* at Kane's disappointed eyes, the player was amazed to see another message momentarily flash before him – "Hard luck - you came close!" No sooner had Kane read the message then it vanished before his eyes. Kane hit the reshow button but nothing re-appeared except the victorious message from his mechanical adversary. Kane was puzzled, but soon forgot the event, lay back on his bed and eventually fell asleep.

Kane dreamed that night of the sun, as he often did. Sometimes it was huge and orange. Sometimes it was small and yellow, tucked comfortably in the corner of a blue sky. Sometimes it was red, weeping from the bottom of a sad dark backdrop. Tonight, he saw himself with Sheena Strauss lying on a lakeshore in a spot the two had discovered and used to visit regularly, the sun warming their browned skin as they lay together on the bank. The water lapping against the shore called out to them and only now he understood what it said. It was a warning, a warning to the enthusiastic youngsters with a zest for life of what was to come. As the waves washed rhythmically on the pebbles, their sound rose gradually to become drum-like, beating out a pulse that almost deafened the prisoner. While Kane attempted to understand the beat, it became a crescendo — then suddenly stopped. Kane awoke in the heat of the Korb-1 night, his heart pounding in his ears.

10   DEADLY NEWS

"**H**EY, I'VE DISCOVERED SOMETHING!"

Kane was lying on his bunk, attempting to focus on another Korb day when Thorsen's head appeared at the door, unannounced. Startled, he focused his eyes on her welcome form, but couldn't form a verbal response.

"Do you hear me? I've discovered something!" Thorsen said, excitedly, as Kane rose up on an elbow and stared at his surprise visitor. Thorsen was already in her work suit and seemed excited at her discovery.

"Yeah, what is it?" asked Kane eagerly.

"There's a NC agent among us", Thorsen exclaimed baldly.

Kane was surprised. It had never occurred to him that the Confederation would need an agent on the kolony. After all, if nobody was going anywhere, what was the point of keeping close tabs on them? He would have thought that a few scumbag informers would have been sufficient for that role. Kane asked who it was.

"An old friend of yours", Thorsen replied.

"An old friend of mine! Who?" asked Kane, his mind already trawling through a lifetime of faces, images and personalities, all of them at least 37 years away.

Thorsen noticed two tyrons observing her in the corridor, became anxious and, as suddenly as she had arrived, departed, saying she would talk later.

Kane fell back in his bunk. His head was fuzzy after what was a poor night's sleep, and Thorsen's surprise arrival and puzzling announcement did nothing to help him clear his mind. Lying on the bunk trying to identify Thorsen's alleged spy, his mind became even more clouded as he remembered the message he had received the night before on his pc. "Yes!" he said to himself, almost aloud – "who – what – was that?" He jumped out of his bunk and sat at the pc, switching on the monitor. Calling up his received mail, he could see no record of any message resembling the one he was trying to recall. Had he received the message at all or was he just imagining it? Perhaps he was just tired and dreamt the whole thing – after all, it had been a fairly uncomfortable night. His recollection of the wording of the message wasn't too good either, and perhaps that was an indication that he had imagined or dreamed the whole thing. But had he? It had all seemed so real, but then most broken dreams and nightmares do for a time. Kane found the whole incident, coupled with Thorsen's intervention, confusing, and his head began to ache as he attempted to sort it out in his brain. He got into the shower and tried to clear his mind.

The reviving water running down his face, Kane wondered about Thorsen's announcement. Could she be right? Was there an agent operating on Korb-1? It certainly wouldn't be that difficult for the regime to plant one amongst the prisoners. Kane was as aware as anybody else of the probability that the Administration had a number of spies and informers on the kolony. He assumed that most of them would be OCs – human nature being what it was – especially in a space kolony, though he wouldn't rule out the involvement of one or two 'politicals'. But an agent? A trained and commissioned agent? The puzzling question was what would the Administration want with an agent on Korb-1? Everybody had been told there was no escape – there seemed to be a wide consensus on that. For that reason, a relatively lenient atmosphere existed, and a *modus operandi* had been established, by which the Kolony Administration had no difficulty achieving its targets on korb production. The *quid pro quo* was that the prisoners led a fairly relaxed lifestyle, consisting of a day's work and a leisurely existence after that. Indeed, many of the prisoners regarded the work shift as an excellent way to keep themselves in shape and wondered how they would get sufficient physical exercise if it wasn't for their korb duties! Why an agent, then? Kane asked himself. What had the regime to fear?

Having changed the shower to dry mode, Kane stood under the warm air blowing on him from all sides and wondered what he was missing. Perhaps, he concluded, it was merely the nature of the beast. Perhaps, the idea of having an agent amongst the prisoners was something the control freaks of the kolony just couldn't resist. Perhaps they had a whole load of them? As he put on his tunic for the Dining Hall, Kane entertained himself by going through all the likely candidates for the role of Administration agent that he could think of.

IN THE DINING HALL, most of the KC10-1 Team were seated and having breakfast. Collecting his tray, Kane looked around for Thorsen, eager to have the name of the Administration's agent revealed, but there was no sign of her. Sitting down with Dayton, Nielsen, Gibney and O'Hara,

Kane asked had they seen Thorsen. Dayton said she had been talking to novo Winslow earlier on and that they had left together. Kane wondered was Winslow Thorsen's informant. Perhaps he had recognised somebody on the kolony and was about to blow their cover to Thorsen. Kane began to eat, excited at the prospect of the impending unveiling. He decided to say nothing to his colleagues of Thorsen's announcement, for the time being. Quieter than usual, he finished his meal and returned to his cell to prepare for work.

In KC10, Kane and his colleagues indulged in their usual light-hearted banter as the working day passed by slowly. The prisoner's mind was full of unanswered questions – "who was the agent Thorsen had identified?", "why was there an agent among the prisoners?", "had he really received a message on his communication player the night before and, if so, who had sent it?" Questions, questions, questions. Kane decided it was time to bring the others in on what was going on. During a break, he told his colleagues that Thorsen had received information that suggested there was an agent in their midst.

"Hey", O'Hara responded immediately, "are we important again? Yippee!"

"Maybe they think we know something that they've forgotten on Earth since we left!" Dayton exclaimed. Everybody laughed and it occurred to Kane that his comrades weren't taking the idea of an agent in their camp as seriously as he felt they should. Tongue in cheek, the team wondered why the Administration would need an agent in the first place, suggested that Kane and Thorsen were "getting too much rest" and came up with some more smart comments on what the agent was looking for and who it might be.

Kane, surprised at his workmates' flippant reaction to what he thought was an important development, shrugged his shoulders in a gesture of frustration and returned to work. Dayton was shouting above the noise to the effect that the story was probably only an Administration plot to make the prisoners suspicious of one another and Kane was concentrating on another gush when Gibney, working on a machine beside Kane, suddenly roared with pain. Having touched off a loader tube – a silly mistake for a seasoned pro – his left hand was scorched. "Gotta go to the TU", he groaned as he left the Chamber, grimacing in pain.

As the day passed in KC10, the conversation inevitably returned to Thorsen's discovery. "An agent in our midst – but why?" was the recurring question. The team discussed possible candidates, and everybody had a suggestion to make, invariably based on an individual they didn't like. However, the general consensus seemed to be that the agent must be a relatively recent arrival who had been sent in amongst the novos from Korb-1 Administration personnel, as there would seem to be little point in sending an agent on a 37 years' long trip to a kolony from which there would be no return. Alternatively, the agent could be just a lowlife informer like the Ferret, who would sell any of his fellow prisoners in order to impress the Administration. Any common criminal who was willing to gather information for the regime could be styled an agent, but Kane get the impression that Thorsen was referring to the real thing.

When the lay-off gong sounded the end of the shift, Kane swore his comrades to secrecy on the question of the agent and told them he would keep them informed, adding that Thorsen herself would probably reveal the agent's identity later on that evening.

Leaving the Korb Chamber, Dayton, Kane and O'Hara passed through the Atrium. "Let's wait for Andrea here", Kane suggested. "Maybe we can get more information now." The three stood in the middle of the large passageway as the shift workers returned to their cell areas following the day's toil. Most of them walked in groups, moving slowly. Almost all of them were involved in a conversation of some kind or other. One animated group were playing keepball with a colleague's cap.

Kane and his friends watched as almost all the grey-clad workforce walked by. Although some of her Korb Chamber shift-mates had passed by, there was no sign of Thorsen. The three waited eagerly to see their accomplice but she wasn't appearing. As the workforce traffic thinned out, two of Thorsen's KC31-1 labour mates passed by.

"Where's Andrea?" Kane asked impatiently.

"Oh, didn't you hear?" a redheaded woman replied sympathetically, "She opened the tunnel too early. The korb filter burst all over her. She's in the TU right now."

"Wh... when?" Kane asked, stunned.

"Early this morning."

Kane hesitated for a moment, wondering was it all true. Then he awoke, as if moving from a bad dream to a nightmarish reality. Shocked, he pushed his way past Thorsen's KC mates and headed for the Treatment Unit, followed by the other two.

The trio rushed up the corridor and up three flights of stairs without saying a word, all equally shocked – and concerned. When they arrived at the Unit, there was no sign of Thorsen. One patient receiving blood cleansing treatment for korb poisoning sat silently in the detox machine, hoping the treatment would succeed in giving him back a year or two. There were no other patients there. The staff seemed surprised when the three men burst in.

"Where is she?" Kane demanded.

"Where is who?" the doctor in charge asked blankly.

Kane grabbed her by the throat, and repeated accusingly: "Where is she?"

"Upstairs in the Special Unit," she replied coldly.

Kane pushed her to one side and all three headed upstairs. As they rushed out the door, the doctor added: "She won't survive!"

THE SPECIAL UNIT WAS a collection of ten dimly-lit wards surrounding a central control area, where the monitoring equipment for the wards was operated. From this area, the progress or otherwise of the occupants of each of the wards could be observed. All organ activity was monitored here, including vital life functions.

At present there were two medical operators at the monitoring centre. Behind the panel, the Master and two of his kontrollers, Windsor and Overly, were discussing the situation.

"Don't act the fool. Finish it!" Windsor said, impatiently, the red light above the Special Unit door reflecting on his balding head.

"It might be better to let things take their course", the Master replied. "If we can be seen to be doing our best, it will reduce the level of suspicion. If we handle it badly, we could have a difficult situation on our hands."

Overly, happy that the Master was taking his side in the argument, seized the initiative. "Precisely, let the drama play itself out and we can all act our parts. If things aren't going well, we can finish it then."

"Agreed", the Master announced, just as Windsor was about to rejoin the discussion. "We'll let it ride, monitor closely and make sure there are no mistakes."

Fixing his gaze firmly into Windsor's agitated eyes, he warned: "*Make sure* there are no mistakes!"

Kane, Dayton and O'Hara burst in past the monitoring centre and straight into the first ward on their left. They stopped in their tracks when they saw their friend's condition. Thorsen was lying on a bunk, bandaged almost from head to toe.

"Andrea!" Kane announced in a soft tone, "It's me – Kevin."

The body on the bunk shook in agitation. Kane got down on one knee beside the bed and asked what he could do. A gurgling sound emitted from Thorsen's throat. "Kevin", she whispered. Kane feared that his name would be the last word Thorsen would ever speak. But the dying woman continued: "The secret....... the secret ...." As Thorsen hesitated – the words catching in her throat – Kane wondered what she meant. Struggling to speak, she continued: "isn't there.... it's not ... there!"

Kane was trying to make sense out of Thorsen's hesitant words when Windsor suddenly burst into the room accompanied by four tyrons.

"Out!" he roared. "Out!" The tyrons moved to carry out his order.

Kane rose to react and lunged himself towards Windsor, while Dayton and O'Hara braced themselves for a struggle with the tyrons. As chaos reigned, Thorsen's Vital Signs Monitor began to emit an alarm. In the middle of the turmoil, the alarm bottomed out to zero and Thorsen lay dead. Kane, struggling with Windsor, stopped on hearing the VSM emit its final message. Immediately, Windsor sought to seize the advantage and subdue Kane. As realisation of what was taking place set in, Kane went berserk and rushed past the others out into the passageway, not knowing where he was going to go. Dayton and O'Hara attempted to follow but were easily overpowered by the tyrons and brought to the ground.

Making his way blindly down the corridor, followed by tyrons, Kane knocked over trolleys and anything that got in his way. Surprising two tyrons as he swung around the corner to enter the Administration Area, he was partially halted by a stun shot which hit him in the shoulder. Stumbling and almost falling, the fleeing prisoner avoided another two shots that shattered the panel on the door beside him. Kane pushed on as far as the next door and, as he was about to collapse at the mercy of the following tyrons, it opened before him. Falling into the room, he saw a woman in a green Administration uniform. Landing at her feet, he noticed her push the door closed behind him. Kane saw the title "Assistant ….." on the door as it closed. After that – nothing.

11 DEPARTURE CEREMONY

KANE AND THORSEN WERE talking. It was dark and Kane could just about make out Thorsen's facial features in the weak light. The two were having their usual conversation on how best to execute their escape from Korb-1. Kane told Thorsen he had finally decided he was going – that the time was right to organise a mass revolt, take over the kolony, destroy it, and head off into space to seek a new home. If luck smiled on them, they might even someday make their way back to Earth and pay their tormentors – or their descendants! – a courtesy call.

Thorsen smiled that smile of patient understanding that usually greeted Kane's more outlandish flights of fancy. Despite her lack of enthusiasm for his big plan, the prisoner continued to explain what he had in mind. He would organise the politically aware inmates under the leadership of Nevin. Together they would prepare an escape strategy that would be implemented with military precision. Central to that strategy would be the instigation of a revolt amongst the other prisoners on an issue carefully chosen to provoke an emotional reaction among them. When that explosion was taking place, the rebels would make their move – disabling the security system and effecting their escape.

Thorsen continued to smile her slightly dismissive smile and Kane plodded on. In order to ensure success, it would be necessary to capture some of the systems and navigational staff on the kolony to supplement the skills of the escaping prisoners. Beforehand, these people would have to be identified and targeted. Most of them would probably cooperate, once the prisoners were out of range of NC craft and assault capabilities. The prisoners would then make their home in a safe location and plot their revenge.

Kane was sweating in the heat of the Korb-1 night as he lay beside Thorsen on her bunk. Totally enthused by his desire to escape and his belief that this was now a real possibility, he held forth on the kind of society the escaped prisoners would create as an example to the entire universe, old and new.

Thorsen's lack of response disappointed Kane and he looked around at his partner, challenging her to find fault with his plan.

"Well," he said, confronting his soul mate, "what have you got to say? You know we can do it, don't you?"

Thorsen's reply was barely audible: "Yes, but you know *I* won't be there!"

Kane stopped in his tracks, realising there was something wrong. He stared at Thorsen. Despite the heat in her cell, there was no sign of warmth on her face, no bead of sweat to trickle down her brow. She just lay there statue-like, coldly beautiful.

"Andrea!" Kane called, recoiling in horror at the sight of the lifeless body beside him. "Andrea! Don't leave me! Andrea!"

The room spun around Kane as he realised what was happening before his eyes. He tried to reach out to Thorsen but found himself unable to move his hands. It was as if they were tied down. Struggling to release them, he became totally agitated, falling back on the bunk and shouting his lover's name – "Andrea! Andrea!"

Continuing to struggle and shout, Kane gradually realised he was alone, in a hospital bunk, strapped down and totally helpless. Regaining his faculties, he saw the dim lights of the stringer bulbs on the ceiling and the watching eyes of the tiny multi-cameras positioned around the room. Gradually, he could make out a human shape standing over him. It was the Master.

"Well, Kane", the Master enquired in his usual arrogant tone, "have we recovered from our little attack?"

"You bastard, I'll kill you!" Kane threatened.

"Now, now, Kane", the Master rejoined, chuckling in a condescending tone, "You're hardly in a position to do anything like that."

Almost as if to prove the Master's point, Kane sought to burst open his straps but to no avail.

"You swine", Kane roared, "You killed her!"

"Come on, Kane. Be reasonable. It was an accident. Thorsen made an error and paid the penalty. I understand your grief and even your anger but there really is no point in blaming anybody else. Believe me, we all regret such incidents in the kolony. It hurts and saddens us all. I'm sure that when you have time to reflect on that you'll see the sense in what I'm saying."

The Master's comments and the cold reasoning they revealed confused Kane. Was the bastard telling the truth or was he engaging in his usual clever evasion? Kane was too confused to figure it all out and could only manage to fire questions at his foe.

"Why was Thorsen in the Special Unit?"

"She suffered dreadful injuries. We did our best for her."

"Why were tyrons posted?"

"A dreadful accident like that is classified as a security lapse. It's a question of procedure."

"Why were we attacked – and where are Dayton and O'Hara?"

"You were in a crazed state and endangering the life of the patient by agitating her. You saw what happened yourself. O.k., the tyrons may have over-reacted. In fact, to be honest, only for one of our own Administration Personnel, they would probably have finished you off."

The Master turned to go and, as he left, added: "Oh, yes, your friends are already back in their living quarters. Have some more sleep, Kane!"

Lying there, helpless and distraught, Kane mused over the Master's coldly logical response to all his questions. Could it be the truth? Could it? The prisoner couldn't think straight. Was Thorsen really dead – or was this some kind of cruel nightmare from which he would awake in the Korb-1 night? As he attempted to reason it all out in his head, the lights in the room seemed to get into the deepest recesses in his mind and turn it inside out. They became ever stronger as Kane blinked in an effort to keep them out of his head. Gradually they merged to become one great light. The light shone brighter and brighter until Kane had to look away. As he did so, he saw Thorsen walking away from him towards the small lake he had once visited with Sheena Strauss. As she reached the lake, she looked back and smiled at Kane, then continued to walk away. Kane called out to her to come back, but to no avail. Suddenly, the reflection of the sun on the lake began to blind Kane and he shouted Thorsen's name in desperation: "Andrea! Andrea!" Desperately focussing on the light, Kane struggled to find Thorsen again only to realise he was staring once more at the stringer bulbs on the ceiling and calling Thorsen's name. Two orderlies, accompanied by a tyron, entered and an injection in the shoulder sent Kane far, far away.

DEPARTURE CEREMONY

When Kane awoke, the Master was beside his bed again.

"Felling better now, Kane?" he enquired.

Kane didn't respond.

"Come, come, Kane, cat got your tongue?"

Kane still didn't respond. Silently, he studied his visitor. A tall, well-built man, the Master had the bearing of one used to having things his way. He always appeared to be relaxed, never displaying any sign of the tension and stress that one would expect to show, even occasionally, on one with ultimate responsibility for the administration of a korb kolony 37 years journey from Earth.

The instant – and abiding – impression the Master made on Kane was that of a man at peace with himself, one who had found his mission in life and was totally at ease in the execution of his duties. What motivated him, nobody seemed to know. Most of the prisoners dismissed him as a control freak who wallowed in the knowledge that his prisoners were in a no-escape situation – the ultimate control. The Master seemed to relish telling his latest arrivals this terrifying fact and enjoyed repeating it as often as possible when he thought they were about to forget it.

Strapped to the hospital bunk, Kane now understood better than most what those words, 'no escape', really meant. In a way, Thorsen was the one who had found a way out of Korb-1. But it was an exit of finality. And it was the finality of Thorsen's departure that tore deep into Kane's soul as he lay, helpless, staring at the Master.

The Master spoke again. "You're obviously still upset, Kane. We all understand that, but it's time to move on. Thorsen would want you to do that. Her departure ceremony takes place tomorrow evening. Surely, you should be there. Get some sleep and you can get back to your living quarters then. We'll talk again tomorrow."

The Master left and Kane wondered what to do next. He knew that whatever he had to do couldn't be done strapped to a bed. Whatever course of action he was going to take could only be followed if he was back amongst his fellow prisoners. Kane knew he had to talk to Dayton, O'Hara and the others as soon as possible.

IN THE ASSEMBLY AREA, the lights were dimmed and the purple sky of Korb-1 observed the proceedings dispassionately as Thorsen's departure ceremony began. The Master read the Ceremonial Introduction in a solemn voice, dwelling on some of the words in a theatrical fashion. The Master's performance added a certain gravitas to the ceremony that, despite their deep dislike and distrust of him, made an impression on many of the prisoners. He referred to Thorsen's many qualities and regretted the "terrible accident" that had deprived the kolony of her valuable contribution. Despite his grief and seething anger, Kane listened carefully to the Master's words. If he hadn't known better, he himself would have been impressed. But even though his mind was still in a state of confusion at the sudden and final turn in events, he still knew that whatever had happened, the Master and his cronies were up to their necks in it. Suppressing his anger, Kane realised even now that if he was ever to avenge Thorsen's death and achieve what they had both talked of for so long – escape to freedom – he must be calm and ensure that whatever course of action he took would be effective and as final for the Master and his regime as was this departure ceremony for Andrea Thorsen.

When the Master had finished his Introduction and an appropriate silence had followed, Nevin began to read Thorsen's Departure Declaration. The prisoners' leader referred to Thorsen's intellectual abilities and her steadfast belief in information freedom. The prisoners would be much the poorer for her loss, whatever the cause of her death. Nevin stressed the last few words whilst casting an eye in the direction of the Master. The purple-clad Administrator didn't blink an eye as those present watched for a reaction and the tyrons in the background tensed visibly. When their leader had finished his moving speech, the assembled prisoners applauded loudly what they interpreted as being an ultimatum to the Administration to come clean with the facts. When the applause died down, the Master moved forward to commend Thorsen's spirit to the Ultimate Power, lowering his head in respect, as the body tray slowly moved away.

The ceremony over, Kane stood in silence at the head of the prisoners as the casket moved into a haze of starlight holograms and out of sight. With Thorsen's remains consigned to the laser incinerator, the Master declared the ceremony at an end and, turning to leave, nodded respectfully in Kane's direction. At that, a multitude of Kane's fellow prisoners gathered around the shaken prisoner to express their sympathy. Later, when the long line of sympathisers had passed, Dayton, Nielsen, O'Hara and Gibney remained with Kane. Noticing a tear in his comrade's eye, Dayton placed his hand firmly and supportively on Kane's shoulder and the two turned away.

"Come on, Kevin, we've got to talk, he said, ushering his friend out of the darkening Hall.

BACK IN DAYTON'S CELL, Kane's friend gestured to him to be quiet as he turned on the music system. Stellar music drifted around as hologrammed images wafted their way choreographically throughout the cell. Kane sat down on the bunk, Dayton moving around as he spoke.

"What are you going to do?" he asked Kane, seriously.

"I really don't know." Kane replied despondently.

"What's going on?" Dayton asked.

"I'm not too clear on that either", Kane announced almost despairingly. "All I know is that Andrea is dead and there's a NC agent in our midst."

"Who is it?" Dayton wondered.

"I don't know. But that's not the only question. Who killed Andrea and why? Why have they placed an agent amongst us? How do we locate the agent before they can do any damage? How do we avenge Andrea's death?" Kane thought for a minute before answering his final question himself: "Escaping from the kolony and destroying it in the process would be a good start!"

"But, Kevin, look at it this way", Dayton responded, "If we get out of the kolony, where do we go? Earth – the Earth we knew – is another planet in more ways than one. Everything we were a part of is gone and by the time we got back there – taking it for granted we could elude NC forces and get there in the first place – we would stick out like Rip Van Winkle. It's not a realistic option."

"We could go elsewhere. The European Confederation's Skomal Colony is accessible. We might even be welcome there!"

"True, but that would involve a journey through Saladdan controlled space. You wouldn't get many takers for that."

"What do we do then? Roll over and die?" asked Kane.

"No," Dayton replied, his eyes lighting up "– there is another option."

"What's that?" Kane enquired.

"We stay here!"

12   PUERTO LIBRE

IN HIS CELL THE next morning, Kane couldn't relax. Still in a state of shock after Thorsen's sudden death, he thought about Dayton's plan, wondering was it really an option. Daring it certainly was. Carefully organise a revolt in the kolony. Take control, and then ... stay! Make Korb-1 a new republic, a society of free people, a port of call in a lonely universe for those seeking liberation – *Puerto Libre* – and transmit the good news of emancipation throughout the galaxies. It was certainly a thought that hadn't occurred to Kane. There was no doubt that it would solve the problem of finding a way out and establishing a new world elsewhere and all the hazards associated with that – but was it a realistic option? Surely there was no way the Northern Confederation would allow such an alternative world to exist, particularly on one of its own korb kolonies. Even if the public on Earth were ever to discover that the mutiny had taken place, they would be led to believe that it was the work of criminals sent there, and would be supportive of a strong security response. If truth be told, many of the relatives of those housed on the Kolony, believing their loved ones to be long dead and buried, would probably support a crackdown against criminals who took over a korb kolony anyway. Despite all this, Kane still felt Dayton's idea had a daring edge that deserved further consideration.

To help clear his head, Kane decided to challenge the system player on his communication player again. He played a mean game ending up in a siege scenario and threatening to storm his enemy's citadel. The system hesitated and finally played an advance thrust on the left flank of the third level. Kane had to withdraw immediately to defend his own fortress. The only options left now were all ties. "Option Tie" flashed on the screen. Kane was pleased. Suddenly however another message flashed on the screen – its bold orange letters lighting up Kane's face. "Well done. Good game. But watch out .... "

And then, as quickly as it had arrived, the message vanished from the screen. Kane was fazed. Another message, so he wasn't imagining the last one! But who was sending them? Was it a friend? It seemed to be. But could he be sure in the present climate who was friend and who was foe? He scoured the electronic mail records for his pc. There was no trace of the messages he had received. "How?" he wondered, "and who?" Who could leave messages that could not be traced? Only someone in the Kolony Administration could do that, he suspected, and if that was the case, why were they doing it? Perhaps it was the Master trying to play with his mind again. Obviously the fiend was aware that Kane was considering something and wanted to know exactly what it was. He wouldn't put it past him to cleverly manipulate his mind by introducing the red herring of a phantom correspondent. But how could he be sure?

Sitting at his media station, the prisoner concluded that the only way to find out was to play along. Only then – perhaps – would it all become clear. Despite the Master's advice that he "take a few day's rest", Kane decided the best thing to do was return to work. He went to shower and get ready to go.

IT WAS THE SAME toil as before for Novo 1319 as he cleared the rocks from the mouth of the Korb Generator. Covered in sweat in the sticky heat of Generation Chamber 9, he laboured silently under the jibes and harassment of the Ferret as he went about his daily grind. His colleagues observed, inactive, as the Ferret shouted and roared at the quiet novo. With Leonard directing a continuous stream of abuse at the novo, they wondered how long all this would last? When would the novo break? Only once during the entire day did the venomous creature give another member of the team a comparably vicious berating. As a stocky muscular prisoner with long black hair in a ponytail was trying to push a heavy rock into the generator, it slipped through his arms and crashed to the floor. Leonard leapt in the direction of the commotion, shouting and roaring a series of expletives. The prisoner stopped and looked coldly at Leonard, saying nothing. Reading the menace in the prisoner's eyes, the Ferret backed away, leaving the prisoner to pick up the purple-black rock and toss it into the dark opening.

Leonard appeared to be taken aback by the longhaired prisoner's reaction, and seemed to realise he had allowed himself to be carried away by his treatment of Novo 1319. No one else would take that kind of harassment from Leonard and deep inside he considered himself lucky to have escaped retribution by the longhaired man. The novo was the only one who was willing to suffer the level of abuse that Leonard was heaping on him, and *he* would therefore continue to get more. As if to confirm this to himself, he called back Novo 1319 as the gong sounded and the team left the Chamber to harass him once more.

The other prisoners ignored the two as they left, happy to see the end of another hard day in the Generation Chamber. If Novo 1319 wouldn't stand up for himself against the little Ferret, why should *they* defend him? Making their way, tired but relieved, out of the Chamber and down the corridor, having left the door slightly open behind them, none of them noticed the red light throbbing inside Generation Chamber 9.

In KC10, as the team waited for a gush, the talk was of death, intrigue and revenge, following the tragic death of Andrea Thorsen. Dayton was for sitting tight and planning carefully, suspecting the whole affair could be the handiwork of the Master – any knee-jerk reaction could be disastrous, he believed. Nielsen agreed. O'Hara wanted blood. He claimed that Thorsen's death was only the beginning and that a campaign of assassination was probably being planned by the Kolony Administration – an open revolt was the only choice. Gibney wanted the agent located. He said a novo had already replaced Thorsen in KC31-1. He could be the one. He should be taken out and then the Administration would get a clear message to back off. Reilly, a feisty little redheaded woman, was of the view that nothing should be done until Kane returned.

"We must see Nevin", Dayton insisted. "We need to talk this through." The others agreed.

The korb gushed into its container tanks and the procedure started again.

Walking slowly down the corridor towards KC10, Kane felt the time for decisive action was approaching. If escape was desirable, it was possible – that was the logic he now chose to employ – it was only a question of how. Thorsen's death had shocked everyone but if her death was not to be in vain, the Master and his kolony must pay the price – that price must be the liberation of the inmates and the fall of the Administration. But how? How?

It occurred to Kane that an essential part of any plan was a map of the kolony. Apart from their own areas of activity, the prisoners had very little knowledge of the other areas of Korb-1. Unless that information was obtained, no attempt at liberation could possibly succeed.

He thought of his phantom correspondent. Perhaps it really was an Administration insider. If so, what was their angle? Could they be genuinely interested in helping him? Perhaps they knew him. Maybe it was an old flame. But he really doubted that. To volunteer to work on Korb-1 was to choose to live a hopeless future on a godforsaken cinder in outer space. Only those who wanted to escape from a particularly unpleasant present would go for an option like that.

Maybe it was someone who had seen the light, someone who had discovered there *was* a way out and had decided to take it? Maybe *they* needed assistance to get away? Whatever happened, he must meet them soon. The time for action had arrived.

Kane was still wrestling with these puzzling thoughts when he arrived at KC10. Entering the Chamber, his surprise arrival prompted a warm welcome from his friends and colleagues. As they worked, his colleagues asked Kane what he thought would be the consequence of Thorsen's death, but the prisoner, still puzzled and shocked by events, had to reply despondently that he really didn't know. Most were agreed on one thing, though – the prisoners on the kolony needed to be organised in case the Administration was planning repression – and Nevin was the man to do that. As for revolt and possible escape, Kane sensed that his friends didn't really believe in that course of action enough to have formed any serious opinions.

NEVIN AND KENNING'S CELL was larger than Kane's, it being the comfortable love nest of the kolony's prisoner leader and his permanent companion. The two had struck it off almost immediately after the tough blonde had arrived in the kolony, and Kenning had apparently been mesmerised by the charisma of the former rights and information campaigner. Most of the prisoners were surprised at the match that was taking place before their eyes. Although a man with natural leadership qualities, Nevin had always been a loner, appearing to be always at peace with his own thoughts. The arrival of an attractive young woman into his life surprised many, but most of the prisoners were happy for their elder statesman and wished him well in his new union with the strong-willed woman.

Many felt that his relationship with Kenning had changed Nevin, making him more relaxed, though some would say complacent. He certainly had become more of a domesticated type, spending most of his time with his partner and appearing to be less interested in the affairs of the kolony and his fellow prisoners. Of late, he and Kenning had taken to the construction of a large hologram model of the Korb-1 Kolony as viewed from space. Where they were getting their geographical details, nobody knew. Most assumed the work was based on creative imagination. The two were spending a lot of their time working on this project and Nevin seemed particularly impressed at the fruits of his artistic efforts.

In Nevin and Kenning's cell, when Kane and Dayton arrived, the two occupants were busy at their keyboard working on their masterpiece, Nevin's false fingers making an echoing sound. Covered in a light purple cloud, the kolony looked almost noble as it stood strong and firm on the surface of an unwelcoming rocky planet. The light and glow of human activity on the kolony seemed to be in obvious contrast to the dark brooding nature of the planet, whose rocky surface seemed to begrudgingly reflect some unseen light on its surface. The kolony appeared to stand proud as if aware of the wonderful achievement its construction had been. It shone out like a beacon in the dark space around it, piercing the purple cloud and sending a message deep into the darkness that humankind had reached a level of civilisation that touched the very heart of the universe and tapped into its infinite potential.

Knocking on the side of the door, Kane stepped inside. Dayton followed.

"Nice", Kane observed.

"Thank you", replied Nevin quietly.

"A work of art!" Kane emphasised, nodding his head slightly. Dayton said nothing. Nevin and his companion continued to work.

"Where did you get the view?"

"Imagination, Kane. That's all we've got to work on here."

"It would be nice to be able to go and see for ourselves, wouldn't it?" Kane responded, watching for the reaction of the others.

Both Nevin and Kenning took their eyes away from the keyboard and focused on their visitor. These were words that no one spoke on Korb-1, redundant ideas that had been gradually whittled away by the regime and replaced with an air of impossibility, an air of acceptance.

"Dream on!" said Kenning, dismissively.

"Some people dream dreams", Kane quipped.

"That's what got us here in the first place, Kane", was the sour response.

"Our dreams were the only possessions we brought from the Old World. Why should we abandon them now?" Kane enquired.

"Maybe our dreams abandoned us – here – forever!" Nevin intervened.

"Is that what you really think, Nevin?" Kane asked provocatively. Dayton watched Nevin closely for a reaction. Nevin became quiet, as if hurt by Kane's words.

"That's what we *all* think", Kenning leapt in.

"Really?" Kane enquired sarcastically, "Have you been doing a survey?"

Dayton sensed that things were taking a negative turn. "Excellent piece of work", he declared, reluctantly dragging the conversation back to the hologram. "I remember when hologram technology was first produced, my father just couldn't believe it. He bought me a package and told me he wanted me to be become an expert."

Kane was surprised at this little anecdote and enquired with genuine curiosity: "And did you?"

"Become an expert – not as good as that!" Dayton replied, nodding in the direction of his hosts' creation.

"You're too kind, Dayton!" Nevin remarked, relaxing. Kenning continued to work.

Nevin turned towards Kane. "What happened to Linda was awful. She was a good person", he said softly. "How are you holding up?"

Kane merely nodded in recognition of the sentiment, and silence ensued.

Then Kane changed the tempo: "It's a while since you played squash, Nevin! Maybe a tough game would do us all some good. We could meet you in the L+S in, say, two hours?"

Nevin seemed surprised, and threw a glance at Kenning. She didn't respond.

Kane and his companion left. As they did, Kane looked back: "Good luck with the hologram!" he said softly.

13 POSSIBLE OR EASY?

There was an atmosphere of 'normality' on Korb-1 since Thorsen's death that disturbed Kane. Normality, following the events of the past week, was certainly not what one would have expected. But the concept of 'normality' on a korb kolony was a bizarre one anyway. What could be normal about any of this?, the prisoner wondered, as he saw young men and women do their best to retain their sanity in a large glass jar in outer space when everything they ever wished for was aeons away, unattainable and literally unreachable? To deal with this 'normality', those who were on work shift worked and those who were off-shift attempted to fill the void in their souls with the simplest of social and leisure pursuits. When Kane entered the L+S, he found Dayton and Gibney enjoying a game of doubles with two other prisoners, Fox and Marsden.

"Think he'll turn up?", Dayton shouted to Kane.

"Maybe", was Kane's noncommittal answer. In his mind, Kane knew that whether Nevin turned up or not, he was going to proceed with his plans. With the experienced Nevin on side, he felt success would be that bit closer, and mistakes that Kane himself might make due to lack of experience could be avoided. But, Nevin in or out, Kane was certain in his mind that he would be leaving Korb-1 behind sooner rather than later.

Dayton nodded in the direction of the stairway, where Nevin, his left arm across his chest and his right arm massaging his chin, stood watching the two.

"Maybe we'll be doing business after all!" was Kane's upbeat response.

When Nevin approached, Dayton nodded a welcome.

"Ready for a game?" Kane asked.

"Bit late to back out now, Kane!" Nevin replied, with a smile.

ON THE COURT, KANE and Dayton played Nevin and Marsden in a double, while Fox stood out. If anyone thought Nevin was going to be a pushover, they were mistaken. Gradually he worked up into a frenzy of assault play, seizing on plays that everyone thought were beyond redemption. Eventually, he and Marsden won by two points.

"I'm impressed", said Kane, genuinely surprised.

"So am I", replied Nevin, "After the explosion, I thought I'd lost my appetite."

"Shall we go again?" Kane asked.

"O.k., but let's down it a gear or two", was Nevin's response.

"I think we're all agreed on that", Dayton remarked, wiping the sweat off his brow.

A new game began, at a more leisurely pace, but Nevin still tried to kill the last ball.

"You like to win!" remarked Kane, as Nevin threw everything at a final ball.

"Only if it's possible", said Nevin.

"Do you mean *possible* – or *easy?*" Kane riddled.

"I think you know what I mean".

"How do you know what's possible?"

"Look around you, Kane", asked Nevin, "What do you see?"

"A prison", replied Kane, simply.

"Do you see any doors or windows?"

"Prisons don't usually have them. But I know we all came in and that we can therefore all go out again."

"I don't know if the formula is that easy", responded Nevin.

"See what I mean!" Kane responded instantly, "You're talking *easy* again." Irritated, Nevin whacked a final ball off the angle of the right and back walls.

"That's the spirit", Kane goaded.

Nevin seemed annoyed, but Kane continued. "Are you in?" he asked.

Nevin responded with another hardball.

"Will you organise us?" Kane asked. "Can you devise a plan?"

Kane missed a play. With that, Dayton popped in with a sly backhand to the bottom left corner and the game was won.

"Whatever we do will have to be done right", was Nevin's only response. "We'll talk again", he promised as he sauntered away, wiping the sweat from his neck with a small towel.

Kane was content as he watched the prisoners' leader leave the L+S. He now believed that Nevin was in, and that was a big positive. The active support of a man like Nevin was an absolute necessity for the success of any kind of effort at revolt. His knowledge and experience of organisation and the regard in which he was held by the prisoners could make all the difference between success and failure. Kane sensed the balance was shifting in favour of a successful insurrection and, if Dayton's theory was to be the decided option, Nevin would certainly be the one to mould the liberated prisoners into an organised community of free men and women. But, whatever the final option was to be, if the revolt was to have a reasonable chance of success, Kane was convinced that Nevin was the one to make the difference.

"How about some more?" Kane asked his colleagues.

"Count me out!" declared an exhausted Marsden.

"I'll chance it", offered Dayton.

"I'm finished!" added Fox.

"Is old steel fingers in?" asked Dayton, as soon as Marsden and Fox had left.

"Looks like it", responded Kane.

"Excellent!" concluded Dayton.

As the two played, Kane noticed the bearded novo in the court beside them playing on his own. Kane glanced at him occasionally, puzzled. Once, the novo momentarily returned Kane's glance but looked away almost immediately. Kane wondered. Shortly after, Kane noticed the novo was gone.

LYING ON HIS BUNK after a shower, Kane was pleased with the day's events. With Nevin on board, he was becoming confident. For the first time since his arrival on Korb-1, he felt as if escape was a realistic option. It saddened him that the price of this realisation was Thorsen's death. He knew she herself would have willingly paid the price, but she was a stronger person than him, patience and steely determination her main attributes. How much poorer life would now be without her. It was only now that she was gone that he realised how important she had been in his life. Of course, he had valued her friendship, her support and her many qualities, but only now was he realising the many different ways in which she had enriched his life. It was at times like this that her coolheaded advice would have tempered his hot-headed response to a challenging situation. An invisible tear rolled silently across his mind as he remembered all they had been together.

He thought of the anger that he really wanted to unleash, but realised that Thorsen would have advised calm in a situation like this. She would have totally controlled the raw emotion that was dragging Kane towards what would have to be, one way or another, the final act. He tried to think rationally, attempting to plot the course of events. Only a successful uprising would justify Thorsen's death – and only the death of her murderers would avenge it. When the opportunity presented itself, he would be the avenging angel. Then the Master and his puppets would pay a high price. But if his dream of revenge was to succeed, he must be calm and think clearly. That would have been Thorsen's way and it would be his way too.

In the L+S, Nevin stood in the middle of a small group.

"How soon could the Korb Chamber Teams be organised?" he asked.

"It wouldn't take long. A week", a tall young man from KC14-1 replied.

"You're beginning to sound like Kane", Kenning remarked.

The young man looked to Nevin for assurance.

"Good", Nevin responded, nodding his head slightly.

"What about the Generation Chambers?"

"Same", replied a broad low-sized man, whose features betrayed the years of hard labour to which his body and mind had been subjected.

"The prison areas would be o.k.", a man with a particularly wrinkled face replied, "but how would we access and subdue the operational areas in the kolony?"

"A fair question", Nevin commented, looking around and inviting suggestions.

"The Master is the key", Angela Clarke from KC16-2 replied, her dark afro hair glistening under the light bulbs. "Grab him and all doors will be opened onto you!" she proclaimed, biblically.

"O.k!" Nevin seemed commanding as he outlined the structure he required. "There will be ten sector commanders, all of them responsible to me. All ten will decide over the next three days who is to be trusted, who has a talent for what – and who the Administration agent is!"

"What about Kane?", one the conspirators wanted to know. "It's too dangerous to rely on him. He's out of his head since Thorsen died."

"Kane's a good man", Nevin defended. "He's totally motivated."

"He's *too* motivated", Kenning added, coldly. "He's not seeing straight. If we're to succeed, we'll need clear heads. I think Kane should be held on a lead."

The others looked at Nevin, and seemed to agree. The veteran listened. "O.k!", was his only response.

THE TURBOS BEGAN TO turn in Generation Chamber 9 as the team set out on another shift. As usual, the sweltering atmosphere in the Chamber was filled with toil and sweat, but there was one unpleasant aspect of work in GC9 that wasn't present today – the Ferret Leonard.

The obnoxious little overseer hadn't turned up for duty today and the relief in the Chamber was palpable. In his absence, Assistant Operator Garcia took over, appointing Nadia Kovacs as Assistant for the day. The generation process progressed efficiently, without acrimony or rancour – a new experience for the members of the GC9 shift. Novo 1319, the object of the absent Ferret's daily spleen, worked away silently without any obvious sign of pleasure that his tormentor hadn't turned up today.

Everybody wondered where the Ferret was. Was he sick? Had he been called in by the Administration? Had he just slept it out? Everybody wondered but nobody seemed to know the answer.

In the absence of the odious Ferret, the environment in GC9 was transformed and a new atmosphere obtained. The team spoke to one another between chores and everybody appeared to be relaxed. For the first time since he arrived, Novo 1319 was made to feel welcome by his teammates, conversations began and friendships took root. Normal banter was so unusual in GC9 that initially many members of the team seemed to be uncomfortable with the idea. Eventually, however, barriers broke down and normality – of the Korb-1 variety – descended on the Chamber.

By the end of the shift, GC Team 9-3 had bonded into an effective cooperative unit and when the gong sounded the end of the day's labour, the team went on their way, some of them conversing, others merely appreciating how different the day had been and dreading what it would be like when the Ferret returned.

ON HIS BUNK, KANE was wondering what kind of plan Nevin would devise to organise the prisoners when he sensed someone standing at his cell door. Leaning out over the side of the bed, he peered out into the corridor. As he did, he thought he saw the bearded novo passing by. Kane wondered. There was something really suspicious about him. Kane was convinced he had seen him before but just couldn't figure out where.

Kane felt he seemed to be always hanging around. What was his game? Perhaps he was the agent Thorsen had uncovered. Perhaps *he* was the one who had caused her death. Kane swore that if the novo was the guilty one he would pay the price. In the meantime, Kane would watch him like a hawk.

Inevitably, Kane began to think of Thorsen's death and how it had all happened. He seemed to remember her speaking before the tyrons burst in, causing her death. But what did she say? Kane wracked his brain to recall Thorsen's last words. What exactly did she say? If only he could remember. He recalled being puzzled by her words, as if they didn't make sense but what did she say? Kane struggled to recall.

Slowly, Kane began to remember. It was about something that didn't exist. But what? What didn't exist? Who didn't exist? Could it be that she was mistaken over the existence of the agent? That was unlikely, otherwise there would have been no reason to kill her. Maybe she wasn't killed? Maybe her death *was* an accident? Maybe the Master *was* telling the truth after all?

Kane became confused. What was the truth? Would he ever know? After a while, however, another explanation occurred to Kane. Perhaps there was no agent but the story of the existence of one had been concocted for some other reason – and Thorsen had just figured that out. But what reason could there be for that? Why all the subterfuge? Kane knew there was at least one person in the kolony who knew the answers to all these questions, and that person was the Master. Only when he had the Master in his grasp could he expect to find the answer to all the questions in his mind. Revolt or no revolt, he must seize the Master. Then all would be revealed.

INVIGORATED BY THE CHALLENGE he knew he would have to face, Kane played a cool game tonight. Staring with a foray on level two, he tore into the system's defences. The system responded with an incisive cut along the right flank on level one, leaving a tight battle for control of the middle terrain between Kane's defence forces and the system's invaders. When the system tried a pincers movement from both flanks, Kane responded with an unexpected attack on the system's citadel on level two. As a possible final blow loomed, the system pulled a counter offence out of the hat. "Game Tied" flashed across the screen. Disappointed with his opponent's late rally, Kane awaited a message from his correspondent. He wasn't disappointed. "Maybe you're not good enough!" splashed across the screen. Kane immediately typed a reply. "How good are you?" A moment elapsed before the response – "You'll see!"

"Give me another game!" Kane demanded.

Again a moment elapsed before the reply: "O.k. If you feel lucky!"

The game began with some tame jousting in mid-board. Some infantry were lost as the protagonists sized one another up. Then things heated up. Kane's peripheral defences came crashing down. But Kane struck back with an attack on his opponent's cavalry on level two, capturing many and scattering the rest. A flurry of activity followed, which ended with Kane making a mistake in venturing his citadel guard into battle, rather than digging in under attack. After a carefully manufactured moment of tension that his opponent obviously savoured, the *coup de gras* was delivered with the arrival of another enemy force that entered Kane's citadel unopposed. Kane was annoyed, but felt he had been beaten by a skilful opponent.

"Hard Luck!" was the victor's message. "Perhaps we should play again?"

"Perhaps we should meet?" Kane suggested.

A long hiatus followed, then the reply: "We"ll see!"

"When?" Kane enquired. But there was no response.

14   A SILHOUETTE

In the Korb Chamber the following morning, Kane was quiet as Dayton entertained the team with his jokes and antics. His friend's spirits were even higher than usual today and the crew was treated to a string of jokes, mostly at the expense of the tyrons.

"What do call a tyron with eight legs?" Dayton enquired. The crew thought for a minute and awaited the answer.

"A spider with a helmet", was Dayton's punch line, as his fellows winced with feigned pain.

Inexplicably encouraged, Dayton continued: "Why do tyrons wear posterior protection?" Silence.

"To protect their thought process device."

"You're getting worse, Dayton. Give us a break!" pleaded O'Hara.

"Don't worry, Éamonn, it gets even better!" Dayton promised.

"What do you call a tyron with a brain?" Dayton enquired. The crew demurred.

"A prisoner!" was Dayton's response.

The team wasn't sure how to take that one – the idea that a prisoner was as formidable a force as a tyron, with the added advantage of intelligence, appealed to most of them, though the idea of comparison with their dull-witted jailors left most of them uncomfortable.

"Take a break!" Gilmore, a tall blond woman, advised.

As the banter continued, Kane retreated into his own thoughts. A further futile attempt to work out in his mind the identity of his mysterious correspondent was inevitable. Kane churned it all over again in his head. Who was it? Where were they? How had they access to the system? Why were they contacting him? What were they after? Why him? The questions were easy, the answers a little more difficult. Was it a friend who had somehow breached the communication system? Highly unlikely, especially 37 years from Earth. Maybe it was someone in the Administration who had an agenda of their own and wanted to use Kane to achieve it. Maybe it was the Master, playing another cruel trick and laughing in the knowledge that Kane was racking his brain trying to figure the whole thing out. A ruse like that would be a major source of enjoyment to him – controlling people's lives was his preferred form of entertainment and playing with their minds would be a bonus. Either way, Kane felt it highly unlikely that it was a friend. It certainly was an unexpected and, Kane believed, an extremely welcome development. Even if it did turn out to be a ruse, there was still the possibility that it could be turned to advantage. The important thing was to get to meet the phantom – only then would he have enough information to make a judgement on his midnight caller.

Happy in the knowledge that he had somehow clarified his immediate objective, Kane's mind returned to his immediate environment – and Dayton's suspect jokes.

"Why do tyrons wear helmets?" the young man quizzed. No response.

"Easy", he replied, feigning disappointment at his colleagues' failure to work it out, "without them, their vacuous crania would float up into the atmosphere and implode!"

The team laughed, more at the idea of the tyrons floating skyward than anything else, and Dayton was happy.

At their mid-shift break, the team talked about Thorsen. Most of them had anecdotes about her – positive, reassuring ones – stories that showed some of the qualities that Kane had come to know – and love. Nielsen told of Thorsen's intervention in a disagreement she had had with a criminal novo who had decided to help herself to Nielsen's supper one evening. Nielsen found the newly arrived woman intimidating. Thorsen had merely approached the novo with a friendly introduction and a welcome to Korb-1. As soon as she was close enough, however, she got the bully in a nerve grip on the neck and explained to her in no uncertain terms how she was expected to behave in her new environment. Only when the novo signalled that she understood *and accepted* the rules did Thorsen loosen her grip. The novo, after taking a few moments to recover, left, having learned an early and a valuable lesson, was well behaved after that.

Kane smiled slightly, remembering the strength and perseverance that Thorsen's light frame disguised. He smiled again as O'Hara told of Thorsen's jousts with a muscle-bound prisoner in one of the Generation Chambers. The lard-head had challenged all comers to a hand-wrestle in the Dining Hall. Having defeated four of the strongest men in the kolony and six others besides, Thorsen challenged the strongman. Smiling an ugly toothless smile, the strongman thought that if a woman wanted to be made a fool of herself, he would be more than happy to oblige. Grasping Thorsen's hand, the witless one decided to make a game of the challenge, dragging it out and feigning imminent defeat. Suddenly the bonehead frowned, glared at Thorsen as if some realisation had hit him and tried to remove his hand. Thorsen held on for dear life and with her opponent more interested in extricating his hand than winning the contest, she went for the kill, slamming the big man's hand to the table to the loudest of cheers from the assembled prisoners. Shocked, the fossil-head looked at his hand, expecting to see major burns. Seeing no marks whatever, he looked unbelievingly at Thorsen. Smiling, she graciously accepted the adulation of the crowd, having ground up and tossed away the silver paper that had been next to her palm and the industrial cleaning pepper she had carried on it, used in the kolony kitchen to scour badly burnt cooking vessels. Leaving no marks, the pepper was about the nastiest little skin-biter in the galaxy. Even the deposed dinosaur brain realised he'd been had, but still couldn't figure out how.

"She was good, was Thorsen!" O'Hara said quietly, placing his hand softly on Kane's shoulder, as the group returned to work – "She was good". Kane nodded in reflective response.

LEAVING THE CHAMBER AFTER their shift, the KC10-1 team were in relatively high spirits. Kane and Dayton left together, heading towards their cells in order to prepare for the evening meal. In the distance, they saw Nevin, Kenning and a number of others huddled together in conversation. As the two approached, the huddle broke up and the group scattered in different directions. Kane and Dayton walked past Nevin and Kenning.

"Well, Nevin, ready for another game of squash?" Kane asked.

"No thanks, Kane. I'm still paying for the last one", Nevin replied, rubbing the muscles on his right arm. Kenning ignored the two, waiting patiently for Nevin to move on.

"Have we made progress", Kane enquired discreetly, his face taking on a more serious look.

"Take it easy, Kane", Nevin counselled, "These things take time if they going to be done right."

Kane was a little disappointed, but saw the point. "O.k.", he replied, "Just keep us informed". The three men nodded and parted again.

"What do you think, Andy? Has he got what it takes?" Kane asked, as he and Dayton made their way along the corridor overlooking the Dining Hall.

"It's o.k., we can trust him", was Dayton's simple but reassuring reply.

RAIN. LOTS OF RAIN. A torrent. Kane sheltered under a small group of trees with Strauss as they returned from a visit to her folks. It had been a good day. Meeting her parents for the first time was always going to be a chore, but in the end it hadn't been so bad. Her father was a serious type – a pillar of the establishment. His conversation at the dinner table was more like a speech in which he extolled the virtues of the Northern Confederation and forcefully contended that the NC was a natural development in the civilised progression of humankind through the ages. When Kane suggested that the Administration had too much power and too much control of information, Sheena's father exploded. Only the perfectly timed intervention of her mother defused a potentially violent situation. The angry host calmed down after a few drinks and then the compulsory viewing of the family disks – showing births, weddings, the kids' NC citizenship days, birthday parties and other records of milestones in the lives of Sheena's folks – followed, and a more relaxed conversation ensued.

On the way back to NCC 48 the following morning, the two passed a lake beside a small wood. Oasis-like, it stood alone on the green plain. Kane and Strauss thought it strange that such a wonderful spot was free of the usual conglomeration of *ptv*s (personal transport vehicles), *dippers* (large glass torpedo-like amphibious craft which were very popular in lake, river and sea leisure pursuits) and *cocoons* (plastic bubbles which were inflated over *ptv*s to provide a tent-like environment for the holidaymaker). It appeared to be a natural lake, not one of the many artificial ones created by developers to enhance their projects. Untouched, unmarred by human hands, it seemed to be an aberration in a totally controlled environment. The small wood, less than a hundred yards from the lake, added to the appearance of perfection.

As soon as she had noticed the lake, Sheena had instinctively slowed down and glanced at Kane. They looked at the scene in wonder, then looked at one another again. Almost immediately, Sheena spun her *ptv* past the sign 'Chestnut Farm' and down the narrow track leading to the lake. Coming to a halt between the wood and the lakeside, the doors of the *ptv* opened and the two stepped out. After a cursory look around, they ran to the lake, tossing off their clothes as they ran. Two splashes – and two people swam in unison, like graceful dolphins in a pool of dreams. Then the rain fell.

The falling rain seemed to have a magical effect on the lake. Large ripples appeared all round the swimmers and the air cooled as they glided around on the surface. The rain was getting heavier. It was as if the Earth was just one great torrent of water and the two were merely drops in its natural flow. Swimming together, they embraced, kissed and became one with the lake.

With the rain continuing to fall, the young ones left the lake and ran, hand in hand, towards the trees. On the edge of the wood, they lay down together on some velvet grass and sensed the world all around them. Lying there as one, they saw the rain cease and the sun begin to shine until the heat became overpowering, and eventually oppressive. It seemed to lie heavily on the two, almost pressing the breath out their lungs. Alarmed, Kane noticed that Strauss seemed to have passed out. He himself gasped in an attempt to breathe.

Then Kane suddenly awoke. It was dark and the heat of the Korb-1 night surrounded him, smothering his mind. In a galaxy far from home, a lonely man tried to come to terms with overpowering solitude.

Suddenly Kane heard a beep on his communication player – a message. He leapt from his bunk and dashed to see the screen. On the dark background, the orange scroll flashed: "Fancy a game?"

Kane shook his head in disbelief. Then replied: "Don't you sleep?"

"A woman's work is never done!" was the response.

Kane typed in his message with enthusiasm: "Let's go!" noting at the same time the important piece of information that his correspondent was – or was pretending to be – a woman.

The game took over an hour and the pace was furious but, after Kane slipped up on an outflanking exercise, leaving his leader's personal cavalry exposed to a massive attack on level 3, his challenger seized the initiative and suddenly it was all over.

"Kicked your ass!" was the triumphant message flashing at Kane.

Kane sat silent for a few moments, then typed a message across the screen – "Can we meet?"

After a brief delay, the response came – "first junction, Purple Area – ten minutes!"

Kane couldn't believe his eyes. Had his fellow jouster actually agreed to meet – and almost immediately? He was excited, but couldn't help wondering – was it safe? Deciding he had no choice if he wanted to move this relationship further, the prisoner sent a brief reply: "I'll be there."

KANE LEFT HIS CELL, full with a sense of expectation. In his three years on Korb-1, he had never had an experience like this before. Who was the phantom correspondent? What was her role on the kolony? If she could communicate on the system untraced, she must have supervisor access. If she could confidently predict that the security system would not detect him entering the Purple Area, she had control over that too – not bad. A prisoner could never gain access to communication or security controls. That would be disastrous for the Administration. All of which meant that she had to be 'one of them'. If she was, what was going on? What was she trying to do? What was her game? Was it all a cruel deception or even a trap? Perhaps a team of tyrons was waiting for him in the Purple Area with zennors at the ready, laughing at how easily he had been duped? Nevertheless, Kane gathered his composure, focused his mind and walked out of his cell into the corridor.

Moving silently, the prisoner's heart beat quickly in his breast. He could hear its rhythm in his ears as he moved slowly, warily into the Purple Area. Oddly, Kane felt himself become keenly aware of the smell of the kolony, that neutral bland odour that was the same no matter where the prisoner went. It was as if there was nothing at all on the kolony with the courage to produce an individual scent, as if all the matter there had decided to relinquish its right to be different, to be distinct. Approaching the first monitor, he wondered would it immediately sound an alarm and call the tyrons to the spot in a matter of seconds. He hesitated momentarily before pushing his toe across the line. Nothing happened. So far, so good. When he reached the second monitor, again there was no reaction.

Everything seemed totally calm as Kane approached the first junction. Maybe things were too calm, he thought. He waited for what seemed a lifetime. Then, the prisoner's heart jumped as a panel in the wall to his right suddenly opened. Ready to defend himself or to run if numbers deemed that to be the best policy, Kane waited for someone to emerge. The panel opened slowly. As it did, it revealed a dimly lit corridor about three feet wide. Peering inside, the prisoner could see the silhouette of a female. Nervously, he entered, and the door closed gently behind him.

15 ENCOUNTER

BEHIND THE PANEL, KANE found himself in a narrow corridor with a curved ceiling. There were no markings or fittings of any description on the walls and, with the exception of weak red stringer bulbs that seemed to stretch as far as the eye could see until the corridor turned gradually to the right, it seemed to contain nothing at all. Nothing, that is, except the form of an attractive female who stood motionless as Kane's eyes accustomed themselves to the dim light.

The light was soft as it reflected on the vision in front of Kane. Still fazed by the idea of this unexpected encounter, the prisoner tried to focus on the figure that stood before him, whose powerful eyes, set in a face of clear marble-like skin, were fixed upon the nervous visitor. His eyes focusing on his host, Kane realised she was wearing a Kolony Administration uniform – and filling it beautifully.

Unsure as to what to do next, and worried by his continued suspicion that he was being lured into a possibly fatal trap, Kane stood cautiously in front of the woman. "You play a hard game!" the stranger said in a friendly voice, looking Kane plainly in the eye. "Not as well as you!" Kane replied, his game-companion's soft tone of voice calming him somewhat.

A silence followed during which Kane tried to assess the situation. The woman's bearing and approach certainly signalled that this was a friendly contact, but that in itself raised a myriad of questions that he was finding it hard to answer. Kane decided not to ask too many questions though, lest he scare his new friend away.

"Why don't we sit down?" the lady suggested and the two sat on the floor of the corridor, their backs propped against opposite walls. The woman took a small case, the size of her palm, out of her uniform belt, opened it and placed it beside her on the floor. It consisted of a small black screen. She touched a button at the left corner at the base of the screen and it lit up. When she touched her finger on a button at the right corner, two red spots showed on the screen, and a green network of lines continually moved around them.

"We don't want to be interrupted, do we?" she announced, looking at Kane. Impressed by the sophisticated gadget, Kane nodded weakly in reply.

"I suppose you're wondering what this is all about" the lady asked calmly.

"Kind of", was Kane's weak reply.

After a second or two, the woman spoke again: "I'm sorry about Thorsen".

Kane nodded again, then added seriously: "What do you know about that?"

"I'm the one who took you out of the line of fire when the tyrons were trying to sear you."

"Aha!" Kane remembered, taken aback. "Thanks", he said, "looks like I owe you a big one." A brief silence ensued. Then Kane asked what he realised almost immediately was a silly question: "Do you work for them?" he asked.

The lady looked at Kane, glanced at her uniform and then back at Kane. "What do you think?" she asked calmly. Kane shrugged his shoulders and smiled.

"Thorsen and you were close, weren't you?" she asked. This time it was Kane who gave an amused glance in reply.

"They killed her", she continued "– but you know that already."

"Can you prove it?" Kane asked. Taken aback at the speed with which the stranger had approached such a serious issue, the prisoner was both surprised and encouraged.

"To whom? For what? You know the truth, that's all that counts, isn't it?" the Administration officer replied cynically.

Kane became depressed. "What's this about then?" he asked his host, as if he felt it was time to come clean.

Just then, a low burring sound came from a device on the officer's wrist. Looking at it, the woman's face took on a serious expression.

"I've got to go", she exclaimed. "The local system has been down for nearly twenty minutes now. If I don't re-activate it immediately, it will do it itself. We'll talk again", she said, and Kane, becoming anxious, stood up.

"Don't worry!" she reassured him, "I'll be in touch again. Be careful!" Then, moving her palm across a part of the wall to the right of the door, she opened it and ushered the mystified visitor back out into the corridor.

His head full of strange and unexpected thoughts, Kane hurried back to his cell. Once there, the prisoner lay on his bunk and tried to work it all out.

THE EARTH WAS QUIET. Kane and Strauss sat in the dark sipping rosé wine in the window of her apartment on the 39th floor. NCC 48 was lit up in front of them, lights of every description dotting the view. Brightly-lit sky-buses cruised the air, carrying their passengers gracefully through the night sky, their hologrammatic advertisements trailing behind them. Occasionally, an *r-rav*, a security rapid response air vehicle, would pass by, its dark sinister colour a contrast to the colourful sky-buses, and a spotlight would cut through the air threateningly.

"There's something magical about the city at night", Kane remarked.

"The city hides many secrets", Strauss replied, "by day and by night."

"There are some things we are better off not knowing", Kane contributed.

"Perhaps", Strauss replied, "but who decides?"

"The Administration. Isn't that why we pay them?"

"Do you trust them?" Strauss asked, pointedly.

Kane noticed the seriousness in Strauss's voice. He thought for a moment and then, looking into her eyes, asked "Why? Don't you? What do you know?"

"Can you handle it?" Strauss asked.

"I can if you can", Kane replied, slightly offended.

Strauss smiled, sipped from her glass and peered into the distance.

"Tell me!" Kane insisted, Strauss's knowing smile annoying him.

In the ensuing years, Kane had regularly wished, in the darkness of a Korb night, that he had never insisted on hearing what his companion had to say that fateful night. Before morn, the young man had discovered that there were entire information tracts in the central administration system involving foreign policy that were in conceal mode, that these files gave a totally different appraisal of the 'Saladdan menace' to the one released for public consumption, that only herself and two other operators had access to them, that contravention of the conceal mode was a Grade 1 offence under the Information Laws and that it would take a committed activist to risk the wrath of the administration by divulging any of this information.

Kane's initial response was 'why divulge any of it? Maybe what was going on was wrong, but why bother?' But it soon dawned on the young functionary that his companion had already made up her mind. There was a strange look in her eyes, a look of determination.

"What exactly is in the files?" he enquired timidly.

"You see," Strauss replied, finishing her glass of wine, "people always want to know!"

KANE FOUND THE MEETING with his contact slightly surreal. There he was in the middle of the Korb-1 night, in a secret tunnel, talking to a woman he had never met before, a woman who, although clad in Administration uniform, seemed to be offering to help him. Reflecting on the brief encounter, Kane tried to make sense of it all. Was she friend or foe? She seemed to be a friend but one couldn't believe anything anymore. Anyway, maybe the important question for now was could she be used either way to help the prisoner effect his escape? An accomplice in the nerve centre of the Kolony Administration, no matter what their agenda was, could only be an *invaluable* asset in any attempt to escape from the Master's dungeon.

But what could the woman's agenda be? The Master had driven his mantra of *no escape* deep into the psyche of the prisoners. To hold out the merest suggestion of escape to any of these unfortunates would be totally contrary to his cruel but simple strategy. Maybe there was a bigger game going on here – perhaps there was opposition to the Master in the administration – maybe *they* wanted to encourage revolt? That was a reasonable theory. Kane would be an obvious candidate for such a scheme – and probably confused enough after the death of Thorsen to fall for it. Mmm, Kane realised he could be merely a pawn in a power struggle – being used against one Master by those who would wish to be another. A depressing prospect, Kane thought, but one that he might somehow be able to exploit for his own ends. If he was wrong and his contact was genuine, better still, but in the meantime he would play along – and caution would be the foundation of his approach.

At breakfast the following morning, Kane kept quiet about his strange night time encounter. No matter what happened now, he knew he must play it cool. Normality – or what passed for that on the prison rock – must be the order of the day. Any divergence from that, any suggestion that things might be not be what they seem, would only titillate the Master's antennae and any chance of escape would be immediately suppressed. Kane kept his thoughts to himself then, as Dayton and Gibney discussed the case of a speed-runner called Maria Tarantini who broke every record in the NC's official sports-book and then disappeared from the face of the Earth. Gibney claimed to have heard that she was pulse pumping – shooting performance-enhancing drugs – and that she had died after a bad pump. Dayton suspected that the unlucky athlete had somehow incurred the wrath of the Administration and was now pumping korb on one of the other kolonies.

"What do you think, Kane?" the others asked, as the loner tried to focus his mind on his companion's words. "What do you think?" they repeated.

"About Tarantini?" Kane checked. "I think Andy's right – she's probably another victim – just like us".

"Ah, come on", Gibney urged. "You can't blame the Administration for everything".

As they spoke, a loud crash was heard from another table at the far side of the Dining Hall. Looking over, the KC10-1 team saw two of the KC27-2 team rolling over a table as they wrestled like bears. Both muscular brawny types, the two fought hell for leather, damaging the seats fitted to the ground as they grappled with one another. As one of them appeared to be gaining the upper hand, a tyron security horn sounded and a team of tyrons descended on the two. The encounter was brief. Both of them relaxing their mutual animosity at last, they realised what was happening and attempted to direct their attention at their common enemy. Immediately stunned by zennors, the pair were soon overpowered. The other prisoners watched, unsure what to do, as their fellows were carted away unceremoniously by the tyrons.

Kane and his colleagues looked at one another, wondering what lessons could be drawn from the incident. O'Hara was the first to speak.

"Why is it always so easy for them? Does it have to be that way?"

The others tried to reason an answer to their comrade's question that wasn't as depressing as a simple 'yes', but it wasn't easy.

"What gives them their advantage?" Kane asked.

"Their arms, their training, their strength – and our lack of all those things", was Dayton's honest reply.

"O.k. then", Kane replied, "but what advantages have we got that they haven't got?"

Silence seemed to be the universal reply from the assembled team.

"That's what we have to work on", Kane concluded, leaving his friends to consider the meaning of his words.

Relaxing after his Chamber shift, Kane still had only one thought on his mind – his mysterious new contact. Walking up and down in his cell, he couldn't wait to hear from her again. He wondered what he would do if he *didn't* hear anything. What could he do? He would just have to walk away. But it was a bit early to assume that events would take that course. For now, Kane felt confident that the lady would contact him again and the obvious way would be through his terminal. Sitting down at the pc, he started to play a game of *War-Raok!*

This evening, Kane wasn't playing too well. He seemed to have too much on his mind – too much thinking to do. His head was full of Sheena Strauss, Andrea Thorsen and the lady in the tunnel. He wondered what her name was? If they met again, that would be the first thing he would ask the mysterious woman. Sitting in front of his pc, he wondered would his encounter with the stranger end up as tragic as his relationships with the other two. Maybe he should warn her away, tell her to have more sense. Then again, maybe she already had and was playing a cruel game with him, like a cat plays with a mouse. Maybe she and the Master were laughing out loud at his gullibility already. Maybe this was to be the final indignity – to be set up as a victim of a phoney escape plan. One thing the stranger had mentioned that Kane couldn't but respond to was her contention that Thorsen had been murdered. If Kane could push her on that, perhaps the encounter could be worthwhile, no matter what hidden agenda she was following. Kane stared blankly at the screen. Suddenly, a message flashed before his eyes. The prisoner immediately became alert.

"Nice meeting you – you're not as ugly as I thought you'd be!"

"Thanks", Kane replied with speed, "you're not too bad yourself!"

The screen remained clear for a while. Kane became impatient – and worried. "Are you still there?" he messaged anxiously.

"Yes", was the simple reply.

"What's happening then?" Kane enquired.

"Patience is a virtue, you know!" came the admonishment.

Kane took exception. "After three years here, I suppose I wouldn't know that", was his sarky reply.

"Sorry", the lady responded, "I should have thought."

"Apologies!" Kane returned, "I should really lighten up. .... Can we meet again?"

"Later on – I'll be in touch", came the reassuring reply and then the screen went blank once more.

Kane sat back in his chair, took a deep breath and threw back his head. He would be meeting the mysterious woman again.

16 DO YOU BELIEVE THE MASTER?

KANE WAS ONLY TWO months in his new job in the NCR Development Sector Bureau 375 when he met Strauss. He liked her almost immediately, though she was in what appeared to be a rock-solid relationship and didn't seem to notice him the way he would have liked. Occasionally, they would meet at lunch in the canteen or at various staff events, the majority of which were organised by management. Because of her red hair, he could always pick her out in the crowd, and when he approached she would be unfailingly friendly. It wasn't until her partner left suddenly to work in another sector that Strauss seemed to pay more attention to the young programmer and a warm fulfilling two years in Kane's life began.

Kane recalled observing Strauss at a staff seminar once. Attendance at the seminar was compulsory and the theme was the importance of information protection – the Administration's euphemism for censorship. As the staff listened attentively to the Chief Executive extol the virtues of Northern Confederation society, Strauss looked over at Kane and displayed a cynical smile. The value of NC information to those who had carried out the most repulsive acts of torture against their own people could not be underestimated, the Chief explained, in solemn tones. Any act of negligence by those entrusted by the Administration with the care of sensitive information could be used by these violent regimes to damage the free world. Because of this, a reluctant Administration had 'reluctantly' decided to classify more and more information as secret and it was up to the servants of the state to ensure the success of this policy and deprive the enemies of the people of a crucial weapon. Having shown examples of the uses to which these foreign terrorists had put information which had fallen into their dangerous hands in the past, the Chief finished his presentation to a round of sustained applause. Kane looked towards Strauss and, having noticed her joining weakly in the ovation, did likewise himself.

It wasn't long after the seminar that Strauss approached Kane at a club not far from the Administration building and begun a relationship that was to become a strange mixture of friendship, sexual attraction and intrigue. The club was called *The Colony*, an ironic name Kane thought now – though spelt in the conventional manner rather than in the Master's PR version with the K – and the prevalent theme was one of time travel, with a variety of dance rooms and lounges dedicated to different periods in the history of the Northern Confederation and its territory. The treatment wasn't entirely reverential and the Presidential Room had corners dedicated to Marilyn Monroe, Monica Lewinsky, Kate Bernard and Jeff Torman – four individuals whose relationships with Presidents had impacted on society at the time.

Strauss asked Kane did he want to dance and suggested the Presidential Room – as they were both "servants of the Administration". Kane agreed and spent the next four hours of his life jousting with the intellectually agile systems expert. At the end of the evening, they parted, promising to meet there again the following night. Kane agreed with Strauss's suggestion that they wouldn't reveal their new relation in the workplace, though at the time he wasn't really sure why. The following day, they both stuck to that arrangement, and after what seemed to be an unusually long eight hours, Kane met Strauss in *The Colony* once more. After that, there was no going back – the two became friends and lovers at night but remained polite workmates during the day.

Though they never met anybody from their workplace on their many outings together, Kane seemed to feel deep in his mind that somehow they had always been under observation. Something in his head sensed that somewhere along the line there had been another face in the background, another pair of eyes. It was a strange, almost irrational, feeling but Kane couldn't recall those days now without his memory being invaded by a third party in the darkest recesses of his mind – listening, watching, waiting.

KANE WAS UNEASY. SOMETIMES lying on his bunk, other times sitting on the side, his head in his hands. Then again he would sit at his media station, staring at the screen, afraid he would miss an important message from his new friend. Most of the time, however, the prisoner would pace up and down in his cell, trying to clear his head and identify the issues he should be addressing in his contact with the stranger. Who was she, really? That was something he would have to find out – but if she was an impostor or an Administration agent, she wasn't going to tell him the truth anyway. What was her role on the kolony? Again he would have no way of proving anything she would tell him about that either. What could he find out then – and how could any of it be verified? Bouncing to his feet and walking up and down in his cell, Prisoner 313 explored every area of his brain in an attempt to discover some way of testing his contact. Eventually, he found one.

WHEN KANE FIRST BECAME aware of the existence of the Korb Kolonies, he didn't really appreciate what it all meant. He had heard that there were space stations that were being prepared to receive colonies of people from Earth – mostly scientific researchers and space espionage experts – but he had no idea there were bases being set up to which citizens could be banished, never to return. The idea of a one-way ticket to a remote rock in space was a frightening concept for Kane and when the guards told him of his sentence, he freaked out. Coming out of sedation two days later to be informed that Strauss was already gone, Kane was overcome by a sense of powerlessness, a sense of immense failure. His immediate response was to withdraw into himself and refuse to communicate with his jailors.

The thing was, Kane realised later, that apart from basic instructions, delivered by gruff guards, the Administration didn't seem too interested in communicating with him anyway. He had been convicted – end of story. Obviously, they knew he wasn't involved in a major information conspiracy, because they never even bothered to question him about that. The system worked efficiently. That was all that mattered.

Kane didn't get much of an opportunity to come to terms with his sentence. After three days, a guard came into his cell and informed him that he was 'lucky' – a Korb Transporter was leaving in two days time. When that day arrived, Kane was dragged unceremoniously out of his cell and given a jabber. He awoke 37 years later on another planet, with a major headache.

Three years there now, he wondered could it all have been avoided, if Strauss had decided to turn a blind eye or if he had tried to talk her out of it. He had missed his former companion a lot during his first few weeks in the kolony. Their lives had been inextricably bound together and now they had been brutally torn apart. They had been soul companions, sharing their live experiences. Then suddenly it was all over – and 37 years in the past. In a strange way, the fact that so much time had elapsed helped Kane to handle his loss to an extent, but the idea that those 37 years had passed in what appeared to be only a single night's sleep added to his sense of confusion. If Strauss was still alive, it would take a lifetime to reach her and even if he did manage to escape and transport himself to wherever she was, unless she had been in suspended animation too, she would be an old woman to whom Kane would be a traumatic reminder of a really bad dream a long long time ago. That idea always filled Kane with a rage that he could only defuse by turning to his communication player to play a game of *War-Raok!* and vent his sense of angry frustration on his opponent there.

For the last year, since the beginning of his relationship with Thorsen, Kane had been a calmer person. Thorsen, herself the survivor of a tough passage, had held Kane's hand when the pressure of the emptiness on the kolony rock had threatened to crush his mind to nothing. It was Thorsen who had kept Kane together and helped him recognise that as long as he kept his sanity and his will to survive, the Master's numbing message would never permeate his inner shell. This lifted Kane and helped him to reach a clearer view of his new reality. It eased the pain.

With Thorsen's death, however, Kane realised he was on his own again. This sense of being alone was a heavy burden to carry in the silent purple darkness of Kane's Korb-1 night. Where he had once had the knowledge that no matter how dark the night the morning would bring a chance to talk to Thorsen and sooth his injured soul, now even that chink of light in the wall of solid korb rock that obstructed his view of the sane world had been cruelly blocked.

Kane's anger and frustration were leading him more and more to feelings of revenge. Revenge for Strauss, revenge for Thorsen, revenge for himself and the life that had been stolen from him. This thirst for revenge was a burning fire in his soul that couldn't be quenched. Only total victory against the Administration could redeem him now – from now on, escape and the destruction of the kolony were the objectives that would inspire him. Survival and re-union with Strauss would be his ultimate dream, however fanciful, but his immediate objectives were now very clear – how to achieve them much less so, unfortunately.

Kane's communication player emitted a beep and suddenly the prisoner was back in the silent reality of Korb-1, Strauss and Thorsen merely images from the past. Taking a second to adjust his thoughts, Kane rushed to the player to see if a message had been received. He wasn't disappointed.

The prisoner's eager eyes read the words on the screen: "Two minutes – same place – confirm". Kane confirmed and left.

"NICE PLACE YOU'VE GOT here", Kane remarked as he sat down beside the lady in the tunnel.

"I've better places", she replied, confidently, as she placed the same small black case beside her on the floor and activated it.

The two strangers sat quietly for a moment. "What's going on here?" Kane asked, softly, "am I dreaming?"

"No, you're not dreaming. The dream – or the nightmare – is out there", was her reassuring reply, pointing towards the panel through which Kane had just come.

"Can I awake from that nightmare? I'm told it's impossible."

"Everything's possible in space – don't you know that?"

"Only the darker things, as far as I can see."

"Maybe you're not looking in the right direction."

Kane stopped and considered what his contact might be telling him. Then he continued: "Where should I look?"

"I had a friend once", the lady responded, "who thought for a long time that a beautiful spot in the country she came across once was off limits because there was a gate on the way in. No sign – just a gate, an unlocked gate. Sometimes we see barriers that aren't really there."

"Are you telling me we're not locked in here at all?"

"Oh, it's not *that* easy, Kane!" the woman exclaimed, laughing.

Kane thought for a moment, wondering where this was all going. Then he asked: "What are we saying here? Is escape really possible?"

"The Master says it isn't. Do you believe him? Do you believe the Master?"

Kane hesitated. After all, the lady was asking a fair question.

"You've loads of questions, but I don't hear too many answers", Kane remarked testily.

"Now, now, Kane! Don't be like that! Maybe you'll have to come up with *some* of the answers."

"Riddles, more riddles!" Kane exclaimed, exasperated.

"Don't worry, Kane. Relax – all will be revealed!" the woman reassured.

Kane didn't know whether it was the impression that he wasn't going to get anything out of this woman that she didn't want to divulge or her disarming smile, but whatever it was, he decided to relax and just listen to what she wanted to say. "O.k.!" he said, shrugging his shoulders.

Content that the prisoner understood the ground rules, the woman appeared to believe she could now move on.

"You're here over three years now, aren't you?" she asked sympathetically. Kane nodded.

"It's not easy to .... forget, is it?"

Kane looked at her intently.

"What are you going to do about it?" she asked.

Kane was surprised at what he thought was a stupid question. What *could* he do about it? She knew as much as he did how limited his options were.

"What *can* I do?" he asked, deciding to play along.

"What do you want to do?" she asked provocatively.

"Don't play games with my mind", Kane warned, looking the woman in the eyes.

"I'm not playing games. I'm trying to open your eyes."

Kane thought again. Was this for real? Was this woman telling him the door was really open? Or was it all a cruel game. He decided to play along. He looked at his new partner in the smart green uniform of the Administration, hesitated and then replied, with a laugh: "I want to go home!"

"That's what I wanted to hear", the lady said, "– and I want to go with you!"

As Kane struggled to understand this latest twist in his bizarre contact with the mysterious woman, a device on his friend's wrist beeped. She immediately looked at the device beside her on the floor and announced hurriedly: "Sorry, I must go back. We'll talk again."

Kane was disappointed. Getting to his feet together with the woman, he held his index finger in the air as if to stop her going any further and asked her what her name was.

"It's too dangerous to tell you that yet. But don't worry – I will soon", she promised.

As she waited for him to leave through the panel, Kane asked something else of his anonymous lady. "There's something I'd like to have. Can you do it?"

The Administration officer seemed slightly alarmed, then nervously asked what it was.

"A plan of the kolony", Kane announced; then repeated calmly: "Can you do it?"

The woman hesitated, obviously going over the risk in her mind. A decision made, she responded: "I'll do my best", adding: "Tell no one of our contact – or we'll both be departing in lead caskets! I'll be in touch."

With that, Kane found himself back in the corridor, hurrying back to his cell.

17   A STRANGE QUESTION

VROOM, VROOM, VROOM, VROOM, *vroom!* The noise in the massive Korb Distribution Chamber was piercing as the korb boulders were hurtled around like pebbles and sent hurtling up the giant suction-feeder tunnels. They would eventually land in any of the thirty Generation Chambers. The small team in the Chamber, all of them with a noise-cloaking device in each ear, ignored the conspirators huddled in the corner and sat in their respective positions, watching their screens and occasionally throwing an eye around the huge rock-strewn area below them. The arrival of korb boulders from the bowels of the planet was represented on their screens as a thick red line. If the red line got thinner, this meant that the supply was slowing down and the operator would speed it up, if the red line got thicker, he or she would slow it down. Equally, the ten green lines on each screen displayed the korb supply to the feeder tunnels and the same supply fluctuation procedures applied to them. Watching for fluctuations on the screens, noise cloakers tucked in their ears, was enough to keep the operators occupied in their own little worlds as Nevin, Kenning by his side, gathered with his lieutenants to discuss their plans.

It wasn't easy to converse in the Distribution Chamber. The swirling sound of the vortex tunnel as the boulders were sucked up into the chamber got deep into the brain and created a numbness that made it hard to concentrate. This was compounded by the pounding of the rocks as they emerged on the chamber flow and were carried away on conveyer channels to their respective Generation Chamber suction-tunnels. To attempt to talk in this environment, not to mention attempt to hatch a conspiracy, was almost an impossibility, but Nevin persisted. It was important that the Administration didn't get wind of the prisoners' intentions before it was time to act and Kenning had suggested the Distribution Chamber as a suitable venue for a strategic discussion.

Beneath the din, the conspirators talked. "It's time to start gathering information", Nevin explained. "Until we have reliable knowledge of what we're up against, we can't move."

"How do we obtain information here?" Mirambeau, a thin dark-haired prisoner with penetrating eyes, wondered. "We're in a totally controlled environment. They watch our every move." His comments made the rest of the group feel uneasy. Some of them looked around nervously.

"What kind of information do you want?" Clarke, a KC15-3 member, wanted to know.

"Everything – what kind of numbers have they got; where are their weakest points; when do they relax, if ever; where should we direct our forces; what should our initial target be? To get the answers to all these questions, we need to gather every bit of information we have and don't even realise we have. People have seen things over the years. You'd be amazed at what we already know! Let's get it all together and take it from there", Nevin explained. "We know it's not going to be easy. How could it be? the leader asked rhetorically, attempting to reassure. "But we've got to start somewhere."

A STRANGE QUESTION

The group's response was a nervous silence.

"We'll have regular information debriefings. Karen will coordinate all information received. When we have enough, we'll move", Nevin explained. "Any observations?"

"What about Kane?" Pirri, a low-sized prisoner with a dark moustache, asked. "Is he under control?"

"Don't worry about Kane", Nevin reassured "He's outside the loop".

After a few moments, Nevin nodded, pointing to his ears and scowling, to indicate the meeting was over. The participants then left the chamber in pairs.

WITH THE CONSPIRATORS RETURNING to their cells, leisure areas or korb chambers, the Master turned away from the monitor and looked at his kontrollers.

"Well, it would appear we've got a little rebellion brewing. This could be exciting! he remarked, with feigned enthusiasm.

The kontrollers, standing in their dark blue suits and white capes against the backdrop of the NC emblem on the wall, nodded with approval. The penalty for conspiring or attempting to escape was death and, with the evidence provided by the visual monitors in the Distribution Chamber, there were more than a dozen gooses cooked already. But the Master was a practical man. Escape from Korb-1 was impossible. The penalty of death for attempting the impossible was slightly harsh, in his view. His main concern was for the efficient and productive administration of the kolony. If the prisoners wanted to indulge in harmless fantasies, that was of little concern to him – in fact, it could be quite entertaining. If the prisoner population allowed these fantasies to become a threat to order in the kolony however, action would be required – and action would be taken. In the meantime, why should he deprive the kolony of a force of efficient workers? The activities of the conspirators would be monitored and a close eye kept on the movements of the participants.

"You all know what you have to do. Watch out for developments – but don't precipitate anything!"

The kontrollers held their gleaming helmets in their hands as they listened to the Master's instructions. Most of them respected the Master and valued his judgement. Kontroller Windsor, however, had a different view. He had long come to the conclusion that the Master, having no military experience, was unsuitable for the leadership position in which he had been placed by his political cronies and would inevitably lead the kolony to disaster. Windsor believed that the Master had been around too long already and had no idea what real discipline was. In Windsor's view, firm action was required in the kolony now. A conspiracy was taking place before the authorities' very eyes, yet "the fool" whose duty it was to stamp out rebellion thought it a mere sideshow, an entertainment! Windsor was clear on what the penalty for rebellion should be. All of those involved in the conspiracy should be rounded up without delay and given a "deadly kiss", slang for a fatal inhaler dose of gas. Such decisive action would end the plot immediately and leave none of the remaining prisoners in any doubt about the price of conspiracy. According to Windsor, the Master was a "total idiot" and seemed to be unaware of the slippery slope towards which his policy of inaction was leading the entire kolony. If this strategy was allowed to continue, the result would be a growth in rebellious activity and descent into mayhem.

Leaving the Master's Kolony Kontrol Area, the Kontrollers were obviously stimulated by the prospect of a war of wits – and perhaps the opportunity to try out some of their 'kontrol' hardware on the prisoners. They talked little, and seemed to be attempting to control their excitement at the prospect of action. Windsor looked at them coldly, disgusted at their childish exhilaration at the prospect of playing games with the prisoners. A serious man, with an advanced receding hairline and a scar above his right eye, Windsor was one who had transferred from military rank to become a kontroller when others would have considered retirement. A severe man, he regarded his fellows as incompetent fools, unworthy of their commissions. Storming down the corridor alone, on his way to his quarters, he felt that his chance might yet come to expose his fellow kontrollers' ineptitude and the Masters' loss of touch with reality. When that moment arrived, he would not be slow to react.

RETURNING FROM THE DISTRIBUTION Chamber, Nevin and Kenning met Kane.

"How goes it?" Kane asked, his raised eyebrow suggesting it was not the construction of the hologram that interested him.

"As I told you already, Kane, it's too early to say anything. We need information first. If you have any information or observations on Administration security arrangements or on the overall layout of the kolony, please let me know."

"Have you given any thought to our overall objectives?" Kane wanted to know.

"It's too early for all that."

"But what do we do if the project is successful?" Kane asked, as Kenning pretended to be looking elsewhere.

"It's a bit premature for that, Kane", Nevin replied, impatiently.

"It's not, you know. There might be a number of options", Kane replied.

"To have a choice would be a victory in itself", was Nevin's judgement as, nodding to Kane, he moved on with his silent partner.

In the Master's office, Kontroller Overly was explaining the situation to his superior. Wilson Leonard was missing. Since he finished his shift in GC9-3 twelve hours previously, he hadn't been seen by anyone.

"Where is he, then?" the Master enquired.

"Nowhere", replied Overly.

"Nowhere?" the Master repeated cynically. "And where's that exactly?"

"He just can't be found", the minion replied.

"Korb-1 isn't that big, Overly, and it's not that easy to slip away, is it?" the Master retorted.

"No, sir."

"Then where is he?" the Master enquired again, firmly.

"We've searched all the chambers, leisure and assembly areas, and we're about to begin a search of the cells, but there's no sign of him anywhere."

"What about the prisoners on his team – what do they say?"

"They claim they left him in the Generation Chamber, as they usually do."

"Are they lying?"

"We don't know – probably!"

"What do the surveillance cameras in the GC show?"

"They show nothing unusual."

"None of them?" the Master asked incredulously.

"Two of them show nothing unusual."

"And the third?"

"The third was out of action."

"Out of action!" the Master exploded, "Out of action! You idiot, what do think those cameras are there for – home movies?" The Master fumed.

"Make sure all surveillance cameras in the kolony are working within one hour. You have another two hours to find Leonard. Now get out!"

As the chastised kontroller left his office, the Master looked at the hologrammed plan of the kolony on the wall. It had taken many years of hard work and clever manipulation to build Korb-1. Like the others, it was a monument to the ingenuity of the Confederation. It was functioning excellently – production of korb was meeting all targets – and it had been a major success in removing from circulation most of the Confederation's undesirable elements. The Master was proud of the achievements of the Korb Project, most of which he put down to his own masterful leadership. Nearly fifteen years established now and not a blip on the screen. Although proud of what he felt any reasonable person would consider an excellent record, the Master realised that what a team of geniuses had developed, a single fool could destroy. He could not allow that to happen. Overly was lazy, but he wasn't big enough a fool to destroy the kolony. Windsor, though, was a different kettle of fish. He had delusions of grandeur and felt his role was to lead rather than to follow. Lunatics like him would bring down the roof on anything if they felt it was their 'destiny' to do so. The Master decided, as he looked at the hologram of the kolony, that Windsor must never get the chance to destroy what the genius of others had built. Windsor would have to go – and that would be arranged soon.

As for the prisoners, the Master believed that they were nearly all suffering from traumatic detachment from their previous realities but, equally, he felt that all most of them wanted to do now was live out their lives in comfort on Korb-1. In the Master's mind, Nevin's conspiracy was not to be taken too seriously. As soon as he thought the time was right, it would be sorted out, with little bother. The Master's preferred option was to allow the conspirators to talk and plan away and then, when things were at an advanced stage, impose a crackdown. Nevin would be sensible enough to realise the game was up then and return to his hologram hobby.

The rest would park their escape notions for another day and concentrate on keeping out of trouble. The only individual the Master viewed with concern was Kane. He was relieved that the conspirators were reluctant to rely on him. Since Thorsen's "accident", Kane was now a man with a cause. The Master believed that, apart perhaps from the prisoner's immediate circle of friends, Kane was the one most likely to attempt to inflict damage on the kolony. A dangerous element had been added to his antipathy towards the Administration – the desire for revenge. He believed that Kane was the only one with any real determination to actually carry out his threat. As long as the troublesome prisoner remained isolated by the leaders of the conspiracy, it would be easier to handle him but, if he crossed the line, he would be dealt with firmly and effectively.

The Master was confident. His stewardship of the kolony had been effective from day one. He had shown himself to be a firm but understanding Master, one who knew when to be harsh and when to be kind. His judgement in these matters was second to none and he felt the vast majority of the prisoners understood this and appreciated it. In the event of a revolt by a bunch of hotheads, he was convinced that the bulk of the prisoners would even side with him. They knew where their bread was buttered.

Wallowing in a mire of self-admiration, the Master was a happy man. After all, it was his ability and skills that had made the kolony the success it was. Lesser men or women would have handled things differently – with disastrous results. The Master had followed a wise path. He prided himself on his unique ability to read the criminal and subversive mind. The criminal would push it as far as he could, and then accept whatever he got. The subversive would resist as a matter of principle, but if he felt that he was not being kicked around, he would put his weapon back in his holster. After all, most people just wanted a reasonable existence, even on a korb kolony – particularly on a korb kolony!

18 CONFRONTATION

Kane sat in Nevin's cell, waiting for the elder statesman to return. Patiently, he watched Nevin's companion put the finishing touches to her hologram, every keystroke carefully considered. Kane remarked on the progress she was making on the structure. Kenning didn't respond. An embarrassing silence ensued.

As she input some final data, Kenning spoke to Kane without raising her head. "I see you've talked him into becoming involved. Some people never learn."

Kane didn't like the condescending tone of Kenning's voice. "I don't write the script for Nevin", he replied calmly, "He knows what he's doing."

"Sometimes he follows his heart too easily – and listens to fools. It's people like you that got him sent here in the first place", Kenning replied acidly.

"Lucky for you!" Kane replied.

"Fucker!" was Kenning's emphatic response.

As Kane considered leaving, Nevin returned.

"Time to talk", Kane quipped. Nevin nodded. "Won't be long, Karen", he said as he left the cell, Kenning's eyes following Kane angrily.

The two men meandered around the Atrium Balcony and then down towards the L+S.

"It's time to decide when", Kane declared.

"Fools rush in", Nevin replied.

"It's time", Kane reiterated. "I can feel it."

Nevin didn't reply.

"Have you had the chance to think about what we do if we succeed?" Kane asked of the older man.

"By the time the Confederation realises what has happened, it will be too late to intervene. It would take 37 years to send an intervention force and by then anything could have happened. They probably wouldn't even bother."

"They could send a screech missile, that would only take about ten years", Kane rejoined.

"Even if they did, we'd have ten years to take evasive measures."

"You're presuming we'd have detection equipment functioning."

"You worry too much, Kane", Nevin replied, irritated. "At the moment we've got nothing."

Kane decided not to pursue the issue. Nevin was an important man to have on board. He presumed his lack of interest in what happened later was merely restraint based on bitter experience. Maybe Nevin was right, but Kane preferred to plan ahead. If things started to happen, they would happen fast. There might not be time to think straight at that stage. There was no point in effecting an escape from the kolony if a shipload of escapees were to die of hunger drifting in space. Eventually, Nevin would have to address that issue. Kane decided to give him more time.

CONFRONTATION

As Nevin returned to his cell, Kane noticed the bearded novo watching them again. This time the novo didn't run away. He looked Kane calmly in the eye, then walked on. Watching him move away, Kane got a strange feeling that it wouldn't be long now before he established the identity of the NC agent who had destroyed Thorsen's life.

IN THE L+S, KANE and Dayton played a tough game. Ball after ball bashed off the end wall as the two tested one another's endurance to the limit. A speedy return from Dayton found his friend slow to react.

"Gettin' old, Kevin, are we?" the youngster asked, feigning surprise. Kane didn't reply, deciding to let his next shot answer that particular question. Swinging savagely at Dayton's serve, Kane hit a rocket towards the back wall. Dayton, expecting a reaction, was ready and returned an equally fierce missile. Kane just about managed a return and a ferocious encounter ensued. For almost a quarter of an hour, the two prisoners gave as good as they got, neither willing to allow a ball to go unmet. Twice, Dayton nearly broke his opponent, and once Kane almost gained the upper hand, then a seemingly harmless return from Dayton hit the angle of the walls and spun straight at Kane. Desperately trying to adjust his body to meet the shot, the elder of the two succeeded in volleying the ball off the wall, but only at the expense of a heavy fall, leaving him helplessly spread-eagled on the floor. Dayton, not expecting a return, was caught wrong footed and joined his comrade on the ground, totally exhausted.

"Good thing I went easy on you there, Kev. I thought you were going to bust a gut!" he uttered, gasping for air.

"Yeah, I owe you one", Kane replied sarcastically, equally drained.

"No problem", Dayton added, a wicked smile on his lips, "that's what friends are for!"

As the two lay on the ground, Dayton spoke earnestly to Kane.

"Kevin, if you're thinking of going it alone, I want to go with you. I'm not sure Nevin has the right stuff anymore."

"Nevin's o.k. It's Kenning we have to watch."

"But Nevin's strongly influenced by her. He's not his own man anymore."

"Nevin can organise the Chambers. We need that kind of support."

"The more people on board, the more the ship lists in the water."

"Ah, those ancient proverbs can mean anything, Andy. You know that."

"Kevin, you know what I'm saying is true. That's why a lot us are here in the first place."

Kane sat up on the floor, his arm on his right knee. "Maybe you're right", he uttered, looking the young man in the eye, "but if a mass escape is on, why not involve everybody. Not to do so would be to abandon them to their fate – they're our comrades after all."

"Sooner or later, you've got to be realistic", Dayton returned. "If you involve a hundred people, ten of them will be spies. You can't risk that kind of exposure.

"At that rate, if you involve ten people, one of them will be a spy – and one spy is one spy too many! Anyway, if your plan for taking over the kolony is the way to go, we'll need everybody!"

Dayton drew a heavy breath and, holding out an arm to his companion, helped him to his feet. "Time to go", he announced, and the prisoners moved away.

Leaving the L+S, Kane and Dayton didn't notice they were being observed. At a discreet distance, the bearded novo from GC9-3 was watching. When they got to the Lower Atrium, Dayton parted with Kane, telling him he wanted to talk to Gibney and O'Hara in the swimming pool. Tapping his friend on the shoulder with his towel, Kane jokingly advised him to get an early night after his exertion, and then walked on towards his cell.

Walking along the corridor towards his cell, his mind full of the thoughts that he hoped would result in freedom in the weeks ahead, Kane suddenly got the feeling he was being watched. The prisoner pretended not to notice and turned the corner. Certain that no one was around, Kane stood against the wall, waiting for his observer to follow. As he turned the corner, the pursuer hesitated to see where his target had gone. With that, Kane pounced – it was the bearded novo. Punching the novo in the stomach, he then kneed him in the face and, as the surprised stalker attempted to regain his composure, Kane pushed him up against the wall.

"What's your problem, spy?" Kane asked, contemptuously, his forearm across the novo's throat, as he emphasised the last dirty word.

"I'm no spy", the novo gasped.

"Oh, yeah, so why are you following me then?" countered Kane.

"I want to talk to you", the novo protested.

"Really, about what? About how the NC planted you here as an agent?" Kane asked.

"Don't be so damned stupid", the novo responded, staring his adversary in the face. Suddenly, however, the novo shifted his gaze towards something behind Kane's back. Kane turned to glance around his shoulder and, with one deft manoeuvre, the novo upended him onto the floor. Before Kane realised what was happening, he was on the flat of his back, with the novo sitting on his chest.

"Listen, for god's sake," the novo growled impatiently, "I am not an agent. I'm a victim just like you. But unlike you, I'm going to do something about it. Now I've been told I should talk to you. Am I wasting my time?"

The novo hesitated, waiting on an answer. "How about it?"

Kane was hardly in a position to argue. Lying on his back, he wondered what his other options were. As he considered his response, the unmistakeable sound of the steps of a team of tyrons could be heard approaching around the corner. Hearing the approach of the tyrons, both men looked at one another. Almost immediately, the novo allowed Kane to get up and pretended to be conversing with him. Both men started to walk.

Turning the corner, the tyrons glared at the two as they passed by, their zennors at the ready and a cold robotic stare in their eyes. The novo put his hand on Kane's shoulder as the tyrons watched. "Seriously," he said, "I really think you were unlucky to lose that game. Your last shot was a beauty." The tyrons continued on and the two stopped again.

Kane pushed the novo's hand off his shoulder. "Don't push your luck", he spat.

"When can we talk?" the novo asked calmly.

Kane walked away in anger.

THE TYRONS WHO HAD passed by Kane and his friend in the corridor continued on their way down through the Green Level and into the Tyron Kontrol Centre. Marching in an apparently synchronized manner, the soldiers seemed to be able to look forwards at all times, while still being aware of what was going on around them. This ability of the tyrons to remain focused while being ready to react immediately was clearly illustrated to the prisoners when a recently arrived novo, seated in the Dining Hall having enjoyed one of his first Korb-1 meals, decided to have some fun at the tyrons' expense. As a group of four tyrons marched past in perfect formation, their backs to the novo, the young man gathered a nice lumpy portion of Korb Stew on a spoon and, having steadied himself to achieve an effective aim, let fly at the helmet of one of the tyrons. Prisoners looked on in amazement as the projectile flew through the air and squelched on the shining red helmet. Most of the prisoners waited for a reaction, while the most experienced in their midst looked on in disbelief at the novo's daring, knowing full well what the result was going to be.

In an instant, the tyrons turned, as a unit, to face the guilty party and, almost in the blink of an eye, propelled themselves towards him. In one continuous movement, the hapless novo was hit with a stunner baton, rendered unconscious and dragged away. While one tyron dragged the offender away, the other three casually protected their flanks from a hostile reaction amongst the prisoners. The incident had occurred so suddenly that few of the prisoners would have had time to react, even if they had been brave enough to do so.

In similar arrogant fashion, the four tyrons that had passed Kane marched into their Kontrol Centre. On arrival inside, the men stopped at a duty desk, entered their identification prints by placing their thumbs on a sensor, clicked their heels and separated, removing their helmets as they walked away. One of them, a dark-haired man, walked past the entrance to a large hall in which a group of ten tyrons were undergoing training in close combat. Observing them were Kontroller Windsor and one of his Security Officers, Steevens.

"I want you to study all prisoner files, Steevens. Make sure you can identify the ones whose motivation is ideological. If matters escalate, they're the ones who must be taken out first. Without them, the rest of the rabble will be unable to function as a unified force, and we can pick them off."

Steevens seemed unsure, but was obviously of the view that disagreement with his Kontroller would not be a good idea. He nodded his head slowly in agreement and uttered an almost inaudible "mm".

"Make sure you look at their faces too, Steevens. Some of them have the mark of the rebel stamped across their stubborn features. Get to know those faces, Steevens. Become familiar with them – their eyes particularly. Their eyes betray them. No matter how hard they attempt to disguise their purpose, their eyes display their true intent. It will be important, in the heat of the moment, to be able to identify those faces, read those eyes, know what their rebel minds intend to do. When you know their minds, you know what their reaction will be. Then you can direct your men to strike – decisively and effectively!"

Steevens nodded his head slowly again. "I understand", he responded respectfully. "I will follow your command."

"Good!" Windsor responded. "If only the rest of them were as aware as you, we would have a team that would make the rebels shake in their prison-issue boots." He stopped, looking into the distance, then continued, as if awakening from a trance, "but they'll see the light, Steevens. They'll come to heel. Yes, they'll come to heel."

Saluting one another, the two men parted.

19 TIME TO GET CLOSE

Kane wasn't able to concentrate on his game. There was too much happening – Thorsen dead, Nevin on board, a Confederation agent at large, and a contact in the heart of the Korb-1 Administration. There seemed to be *too* much happening. Thorsen's death was enough to blow the prisoner's mind but that seemed to be followed by everything under the Korb sky. *What next?* Kane wondered to himself – a meteorite scoring a direct hit on the whole damn lot? Who could predict? The important thing now was to remain sane, keep a clear head. He was convinced that another momentous event was only a question of time. As he grappled with *War-Raok!* a message flashed across the screen: "Would you like to play?"

"What are the stakes?" Kane enquired.

"The future against the past – are you willing to risk it?" was the reply.

"It seems to me that I lost both a long time ago", Kane ventured.

"I don't think you're a loser at all, Kane. You haven't forgotten how to win – that's the important thing."

Kane liked what he was hearing. Maybe it was just his ego, but he felt the void left behind by Thorsen being filled somehow by this outsider who had chosen to become his friend.

"Let's play!" he messaged.

The game was tough and rapid. Three times Kane had his opponent's fortress under siege. Three times she repelled his attacks and succeeded in seriously damaging his outer defences in return. This woman knew how to play and wasn't afraid to take risks if she sensed the possibilities were there. She read the game with a speed that was uncanny and Kane was pressed to the full to defend his territory and personnel from his competitor's penetrating raids. Sweat poured down Kane's brow as his opponent's attacks became more frequent and ferocious. Successfully fighting off a raid on his left flank, he watched in horror as a long-range clinical strike took out his command centre. Forced to abandon his HQ and without the technical support required to organise and direct his forces, Kane would now be easy prey for his skilful rival.

"Had enough – or will I humiliate you?" was the blunt message flashing on the screen.

"Bitch!" was Kane's defiant reply.

"In one moment of madness, Kane directed his forces at the centre of his opponent's defences. As the defenders backed away, Kane sensed he could grasp the initiative. Pushing through, he could see the fortress defence centre in view. Victory was near.

Suddenly in successive moves, the enemy flanks closed in behind Kane's weary probing assault force. Kane gave his all but was rapidly surrounded and overcome. Mentally drained, he dropped his head on the keyboard.

"You're pushing me too hard. I'm supposed to win easily", the victor flashed.

"No kidding?" was Kane's tame response.

"I'll contact you soon – it's time we got to know one another a little better", the woman messaged and signed off.

More than anything else, the last sentence in his contact's message was music to the prisoner's ears. The better he got to know this woman, the sooner he could hope to see where his new 'relationship' was going. Then he would know if his new friendship was going to really change his life or not.

Kane sat back in his bucket chair and felt, with some excitement, that the time of atonement was at hand, that a chain of events was in train that would put an end, once and for all, to the Master's regime. In Nevin, the prisoners had an experienced leader who could make the difference in organising the kolony in revolt; with Dayton, O'Hara and himself, they had young people who could make bold choices for the future of the prisoners, and with his new contact within the system, they had someone whose inside knowledge could provide the vital edge that any revolt would need to succeed.

Before any uprising could begin, however, Kane knew that he would have to eventually inform Nevin of his contact within the Administration, and probably even organise a meeting between the two. With Nevin's organisational expertise and the woman's inside knowledge, an effective plan could be developed which could catch the Master unawares, and maybe even enable the prisoners to take control of the kolony with a clinical strike.

Kane respected Nevin and was sure that his involvement in the revolt would strongly enhance its chances of success. His leadership qualities were well known and respected and his advocacy of the enterprise would ensure widespread support amongst the prisoners. The only worry Kane had in regard to Nevin was his relationship with Kenning. Kane didn't like Nevin's companion. He had never liked her – from day one. He always felt she was a conservative, almost a draining, influence on her companion. That wasn't surprising, really. Since her arrival two years previously, she had settled into her new life on the kolony without any difficulty at all. It was almost as if she was at home on the purple planet.

Now that he thought of it, Kenning had never really explained what her origins were and why she had been banished to Korb-1. Surely she must have told Nevin. Perhaps it was time to find out. Kane remembered noticing the new arrival at the time; her blonde hair and attractive figure made her immediately conspicuous to her new neighbours. But he never felt the urge to get close to the lady – she seemed to exude a coldness that Kane found entirely unattractive. Not everybody felt the same alienation from Kenning – a stampede of eager males beat a track to the nubile novo's cell in those early weeks, but none received more than a curt dismissal. Then, only a matter of months after Kenning's arrival, it was something of a surprise for many to discover that the blonde was ensconced in Nevin's cell, having received a special early cohabitation exemption because of Nevin's status as leader of the prisoners. She was soon the inseparable partner of the veteran information campaigner.

Although many were surprised, and not a few jealous, at the same time most recognised that Nevin had a certain charisma and that his leadership qualities were beyond question, and as everybody knew, the air of authority was an aphrodisiac. The kolony soon got used to the new item and Nevin settled down to an urbane existence with his partner. Shortly after his relationship with Kenning began, Nevin arranged clearance for his cellmate from KC labour, and the grateful lady took to domestic life with the kolony's elder statesman like a fish to water. They were now the kolony's first family.

Kane had never been too close to Nevin, although he respected his obvious abilities, but having succeeded in enticing the leader to lend his support and skills to the revolt, he wondered now if the older man's relationship with Kenning might jeopardize the whole affair. That could not be allowed to happen and Kane felt that it was up to him to ensure that it didn't.

Lying down for the night, thinking thoughts of rebellion and intrigue, Kane gradually fell into an uneasy sleep. When he did, all his ghosts came to haunt him and all his disappointments gathered to torment him. His hopes seemed impassive as he wrestled with whatever his fate would be. In his struggle, he sensed Sheena Strauss lying beside him. They were on the ground beside the lake, just after the rain fell. Sheena sat up and looked into Kane's eyes.

"What do you think it would be like?" she asked.

"What", Kane replied.

"The world, if we were the only people in it."

Kane thought for a minute. In his mind's eye, he imagined a world of pristine beauty, high green trees proudly displaying their foliage to the blue cloudless sky, a river flowing healthily out of the woods and down the slopes of a verdant glen, in the sky a single eagle hovering and watching over his ancient dominion.

"Well?" Sheena intervened.

As Kane prepared to reply, the noise of an approaching machine disturbed him. It was the sound of an *r-rav*, approaching from behind the wood. Instinctively Strauss and Kane jumped up, threw on their clothes and made for their *ptv*. Swinging out towards the main road, they saw the large stalking form of the security vehicle appearing from behind the wood. Slowly, it emerged and cast a long dark shadow over the lake and the meadow where Kane and Strauss had just been.

Speeding towards the main route-way, Strauss turned to her companion and said "You never answered my question – and it's too late now!" Kane stared at her, trying to make sense of what she was saying. Then suddenly he noticed the huge shadow of the security vehicle covering the *ptv*. A probe light shone in on top of the pair. Kane started to shout with excitement as the light shone into his eyes, almost blinding him. He covered his eyes with his hands. Suddenly he felt a strong grip on his arms as he was pulled up towards the *r-rav*. Opening his eyes, Kane focused to see two tyrons standing above him pulling him out of his bunk, the strobe light beaming on the far wall behind them. Struggling, the prisoner was eventually overcome and dragged out of his cell into the corridor.

THE MASTER WAS STANDING by his desk watching something on his screen when Kane was brought in. At first, he didn't look up, pretending to be occupied with something important and to be almost unaware that his visitor had arrived. As Kane steadied himself between two tyrons, he threw his eye around the Master's office, rapidly taking in the layout of the room. The predominant colour, if one could call it that, was grey – shades of grey. Everything was a grey of some hue and no other colour penetrated the boring unimaginative greyness that surrounded the occupants of the suite. There were no decorations of any kind and Kane could see nothing that could be regarded as a concession to aesthetics anywhere. There didn't seem to be any files or working disks or any kind either and Kane quickly concluded that the Master did most of his dirty work in his head.

Suddenly, the Master looked up at Kane, feigning surprise at his presence.

"Ah, my dear Kane," he croaked, "how nice to see you!"

Kane didn't reply.

"Kane – always the shy one!" was the Master's patronising comment.

Kane pretended to be bored.

"I'm really surprised, Kane", the Master continued, "I thought we'd have a nice little chat. I'm quite disappointed."

"What do you want?" Kane finally asked, impatiently.

"Oh, I think you know what I want", the Master replied coldly.

"Do I?" Kane replied, now his turn to feign surprise.

The Master nodded to the tyrons and they left the room, leaving Kane all alone with the Master. Kane took no heed of this, knowing that the guards could return in a matter of seconds.

"Come now, Kane", the Master said, with a forgiving intonation, "I'm sure we can sort all this out. But you've got to help me."

Kane didn't reply.

"I know what you're up to you", the Master announced, almost like a schoolmaster speaking to his errant pupil.

"Do you?" Kane responded, pretending to be puzzled and deliberately jousting with the Master.

"Yes, yes", the Master quipped, pretending not to be feeling a sense of exasperation at his prisoner's obduracy, "Yes, I do."

Kane nodded, as if impressed by the Master's brilliant powers of deduction.

The Master looked at the screen, and the suddenly glared at Kane. "Where is Wilson Leonard?" he asked coldly.

"The Ferret?" Kane enquired.

"You know who I mean", the Master responded sternly.

"What would I know about him?"

"That's what I'm asking you. Don't play games."

"I've no idea where that stinking little swine is. Why should I?"

"Leonard has made a significant contribution to the success of the kolony. His leadership skills have been invaluable in motivating new arrivals in the Generation Chamber and the results have been impressive. Granted," the Master continued with his genteel tone, "he is inclined to be somewhat abrasive, but his intentions are good and he has the welfare of the kolony at heart."

"Maybe that's why he decided to leave," Kane replied cheekily, grinning at the thought.

"Kane, I've been doing my best for you but you are testing even *my* resilient patience to the full. If Leonard is not found, the culprit will pay a heavy price. I hope it's not you, Kane. I hope it's not you."

Kane didn't respond, and the Master, clearly disappointed that his charm was not enticing the prisoner to respond, shook his head sadly, and added a gentle word of admonishment: "Ah, Kane, sometimes I wonder about you. You seem to have closed your mind to me!"

Kane's raised his eyebrows to emphasise his expression of boredom.

The Master, realising that progress would not be made on this occasion, held his open palm towards the door and invited Kane to leave, adding a slightly sarcastic "Thank you, Kane!" as the prisoner turned around and was met at the door by his tyron guard.

RETURNING TO HIS CELL to prepare for the coming day, Kane wondered what the Master's little session had been all about. The Ferret was an obnoxious creature that preyed on weary disorientated novos and was obviously an agent of the regime. That he was gone missing *now* was a surprise only to the extent that nobody had ever bothered to deal with him up to now. The real question, in Kane's view, was how it was done. Nothing ever happened on the kolony without the knowledge of the Administration and if prisoners were responsible for Leonard's disappearance, Kane was puzzled as to how they managed to do it. Perhaps it was time to talk to Nevin again.

Beep! When Kane entered his cell, he heard the 'message received' signal on his pc. Rushing over to open and read the communication, Kane wondered could it be the woman. He wasn't disappointed.

"Welcome back! Hope that wasn't too gruelling!" the message read.

"Tough going!" Kane replied mockingly.

"Relax – we'll talk soon – tomorrow. Take care!"

"You too", replied Kane, sensing that tomorrow could be an interesting day.

20 FINISHING THE JIGSAW

SEEING HIS MYSTERIOUS LADY'S shape forming a silhouette as he entered the tunnel relaxed Kane. He had left his cell immediately on receiving the invitation to meet and was relieved once again to see his ally waiting for him rather than a gang of tyrons. Such was the prisoner's uncertainty that he felt anything was possible at any time and a double cross at a crucial moment as much a likelihood as anything else. Illogically, the attractive femininity of his contact added to the prisoner's sense of security, it had to be admitted, and Kane even managed a smile as his eyes met hers. Kane's pulse raced somewhat, though, when he thought of what was at stake here. Standing before him was either the possible key to his liberation or a device to ensure his permanent incarceration. "Hi!" the lady said, tilting her head slightly to the side, "fancy meeting you here!"

"You take me to all the nice places", was Kane's response, smiling. Holding her hand out in an exaggerated gesture of courtesy, the lady invited Kane to sit down.

Being seated beside an attractive woman in the uniform of the Kolony Administration was still a strange sensation for the prisoner. Uniforms and symbols of officialdom and authority had never impressed Kane and, since his imprisonment, had become symbols of his own personal oppression. Nevertheless, he sensed a soothing element in his contact's personality. There really was something about this woman that reassured and calmed Kevin Kane. He sat back.

"Well, what's the story?" he asked boldly. "When does the revolution begin?"

The lady smiled. "Well, in many ways", she replied, "That's up to you."

"How's that?" Kane asked, intrigued. "I'm only the prisoner here."

"You may be the prisoner but you might hold the key to your own prison."

Kane was intrigued, but decided to play it cool. "More riddles?" he asked, raising an eyebrow to signal a note of cynicism.

"Riddles are for those with the intellect to work them out. Can't you see what I'm saying?"

"Three years on this rock have dulled my senses, I'm afraid. How could I have the key to my own prison – the Master says there is no escape from here at all?"

"The Master says a lot of things but, if you want to believe him, it's you – not him – that's blocking the portal. We've been through this before. Don't you want to escape?" The lady waited for a reply.

"Of course I do", Kane replied, irritated that he had to make what he thought was a statement of the obvious, "but wishes, despite what our grandmothers used to say, don't light up the galaxy at night."

"Ah, Kane!" the lady replied with exasperation, "my dear Kane! Don't be too hard on your grandmothers! They knew a lot that is lost now."

"O.k. – look – what are you saying here?" Kane demanded, frustrated with his contact's riddles and half statements.

"Listen", the woman replied, bearing a slightly more serious expression. "You say you want to be free. Let's start there. Let's see where we can go from there".

Kane listened carefully as the woman continued.

"You want to be free – so do many others. What have you got that they haven't got?"

Kane thought for a minute then replied – "YOU!"

"Got it in one – who said your intellect had been dulled?" the lady said, her ruby-red lips framing a smile of satisfaction.

"But that begs a whole load of questions", Kane interjected. The woman waited for Kane to identify those questions himself. "What can you do to help me, would it be enough to get me out, and why would you want to get involved anyway?"

"You're full of questions – Kane – I told you that before!"

"Maybe", Kane admitted, "but I don't seem to be too good at getting answers!"

The young woman waited a while as if in the process of making a decision. Hesitantly, she began to speak: "Look, Kane, don't take this the wrong way, but there are ..... some things ..... some things .... I know I can't tell you ....because .... because .... they'd just blow your mind!" Kane looked at the woman with an air of scepticism. "Believe me, I know!" she beseeched, attempting to reassure her unconvinced listener.

A tense silenced followed, Kane offended by his contact's reluctance to be open with him, the woman uneasy with having to tell the prisoner straight out that she wasn't going to give him the whole story immediately. "Look, Kane, you have to trust me. I know what I'm doing".

"Look, if you're worried I'm going to tell all the lads at breakfast about you, you really must think I'm mad! Nobody knows about my contact with you – nobody! You asked me if I wanted to be free – the question itself is an offence. Of course, I want to be free. Of course, I want to go home. I know you're just trying to psyche me up – I understand that – but if it's possible to get off this stinking rock, I want to be the first to do it. Don't have any misapprehensions about that! If the Master says we can't escape and you say we can – I believe *you*! O.k.? Is that *that* cleared up?"

Kane looked at his companion expectantly, awaiting a confirmative response after his animated outburst. The woman looked at Kane patiently but didn't commit. Kane continued: "As for whether you can trust me or not – that's a decision *you* have to make. It was *you* who contacted *me*." Kane hesitated again, waiting for that simple fact to sink in, then went on: "In a korb kolony riddled with spies, agents and informers, it would be suicide to confide in anybody. If you're my key to freedom, I'm certainly not going to e-mail the kolony to spread the good news. If you want to help me, I'm not going to endanger either of us in any way."

Brushing back her short black hair, the woman seemed impressed by Kane's assurances. She had always known that at some stage they would have to trust one another. She just hoped that one day he would understand why she couldn't bring herself to tell him the *whole* story.

KONTROLLER WINDSOR WAS EAGER as he sat down with Security Officer Simpson and the Critical Information Technician. The Technician, as he was known by everybody, was a dark figure, always on the edge. His brief was "critical information" but what exactly did that mean? How did his domain of activity differ from that of the Security Officer and anybody else involved in gathering information relating to security? What was 'critical' about what he compiled? The answer to these questions was never discussed in any depth or even referred to in any clear sense by anyone, but most understood the Technician's task as being the discovery and use of information of a nature that would almost certainly result in success when applied to any particular human subject or any given situation involving human subjects. It was never felt necessary to verbalise the Technician's role beyond that.

"O.k.", the Technician asked, "what do we want to know?"

Simpson activated her screen. "We need information on Leonard's disappearance. How did he disappear and who was involved?"

The Technician input a note onto the screen in front of him, and Simpson continued: "We also want information on the escape conspiracy. Who's involved? Are all those involved reporting to Nevin? Are there many involved? Are there different groups?" The Technician noted the Security Officer's requirements and listened intently as Simpson outlined other issues the Administration wanted to know more about. "What kind of a timescale are the rebels working to? When do they intend to strike? Also what do the conspirators know of the layout of the kolony? And — an important issue indeed — where do they intend to concentrate their efforts in order to effect their escape?"

"Good!" Windsor announced, "Good!" Turning to the Technician, he added "You know what you have to do. Have you got some background material on this one?"

The Technician was slow to respond, irritating Windsor slightly. "I think we're ready", came the cold reply.

"Good!" Windsor exclaimed again, with a forced smile, "Hopefully you'll succeed where that other fool failed. We can proceed."

"SO TELL ME, THEN", Kane asked, half joking, "are we really going to get out of here?"

"I think we can", was the earnest reply.

"When can we start?" Kane asked, looking his companion in the eye.

"No time like the present!" was the reassuring reply.

"I'm Kane, Kevin Kane", the prisoner announced, holding his hand out in a challenging gesture.

The lady hesitated, as if unsure that divulging her identity was a good idea. Recognising his accomplice's reticence, Kane raised a disapproving eyebrow and awaited a response. The woman replied resignedly: "Zeena. Zeena McKenzie – nice to meet you!", and, taking the prisoner's hand, shook it cordially.

"Zeena – mmm, nice name. And what do you do around here?"

"Keeping dangerous people like you under control is my job."

"Mmm, interesting occupation. Is it rewarding?"

"Only when I fail", was the lady's rapid response, followed by a wicked smile.

"Fascinating", Kane opined, finding every word uttered by his friend an encouragement.

"And when do you think you'll fail again?"

"That – as I've said already – depends on you!"

Kane thought for a moment, as the realisation set in that this was becoming real. It really *did* seem to depend on him.

"What do I have to do?"

McKenzie took a deep breath, as if about to embark on a journey from which there was no turning back. Then, opening an arm pocket in her tunic, she produced a slimline disk reader and presented it to guest. Kane's eyes opened wide.

"I think you asked for this. This reader contains a plan of the kolony. The file has a life of 72 hours. When you open it, you will have three days to memorise its contents. When I think you've had enough time, I'll contact you again." McKenzie stopped to see if Kane realised the gravity of her action. He nodded slowly, as if to reassure. She continued: "If you're caught with this, you're on your own. But I hope you'll make sure that doesn't happen. I may be able to warn you if there's going to be a search. But don't bank on that."

Kane looked at the palm-size reader in his hand and attempted to fathom the reality of it all. A plan of the kolony! Unbelievable! Could he really be holding the key to his liberation in his hand? He looked at McKenzie and, taking hold of her arm, thanked her profusely.

"How can I ever repay you for all this?"

"Make sure you don't fail!" was her simple reply.

EMERGING FROM THE PANEL in the corridor, Kane was gripped by the excitement of it all. In his tunic, he held either the key to his escape from the kolony or sufficient evidence to convict him of conspiracy to escape. The former could be the beginning of freedom and a new life for the prisoner, the latter a death sentence. With all the appearance of a Korb prisoner who had long ago accepted his fate, Kane walked slowly along the corridor towards his cell, head down, shoulders hunched. Inside, he was spreading his wings like an eagle about to fly.

EXCITING, FRIGHTENING, THOUGHTS MADE their way through the caverns of McKenzie's mind as she walked back to her office. She realised that there was no going back at this stage. Kane now had enough on her to make *her* an inmate of the prison, if circumstances forced him to do so. Somehow, however, she felt that that wasn't going to happen. She trusted Kane – why, she didn't know. It was an instinctive thing. Sometimes in life, one had to make calls that were not couched in the safety of everyday certitude. The only thing to do then was to balance the risk of failure against the goal that could possibly be achieved. In this case, McKenzie had no problem with the decision she had made. She knew she needed someone who was properly motivated if she was going to succeed in achieving *her* aims. She was certain that Kane was the one.

APPROACHING HIS CELL, KANE felt his heart beat faster and faster. Purposely, he slowed his stride over the final few metres of his journey. It was important at this stage, he was sure, not to attract attention by displaying any exceptional mood changes that could be picked up by a monitoring sensor. Making his way along the corridor overlooking the Dining Hall, he consciously avoided making eye contact with anybody – fellow prisoners and tyrons alike.

The Kolony Plan! Kane's heart started to beat faster as he realised the momentousness of what had just transpired. The Kolony Plan! In *his* possession! Ready to read! What would the Master think if he knew this? What unctuous blather would he utter if he found all this out. Turning in through the door of his cell, Kane was almost overcome with the excitement of being about to put the Master's claim of invulnerability to the test. Throwing himself on his bunk, he lay down for a few minutes to catch his breath. Then, instinctively, he jumped up, and in almost one movement, turned off the light and slipped the reader behind the light fitting on the wall. Deciding not to create suspicion by turning the light back on again, Kane lay down on his bunk in the darkness.

All kinds of emotions went through Kane's mind. Was he about to discover the answer to the questions he had so often puzzled over with Thorsen? He remembered those pleasant hours with his companion – his source of strength when times were bad. She had been murdered by the Master and his crew – Kane was convinced of that now. Perhaps he was getting closer to finding out why. Thorsen had been Kane's greatest support in his desire to be free again. Now she was his greatest inspiration as he attempted to make that desire a reality.

Kane was sure that Thorsen had discovered something the Administration couldn't allow her to reveal. Her death 'by accident' shortly after she had informed Kane she had discovered something couldn't have been a coincidence. What exactly had she discovered and how had she discovered it? It must be still possible, Kane believed, to find out what Thorsen's deadly secret was. That secret would be another vital piece in the jigsaw that would put together the full picture for Kevin Kane.

Memories of his time with Thorsen came flooding back to Kane – her calmness under pressure, her fortitude in the face of adversity, her healthy cynicism counterbalancing his own exuberant enthusiasm. All those qualities combined to produce what was essentially an oasis of strength in a desert devoid of hope. Thorsen's legacy to Kane was the ability to control his anger and frustration and concentrate his efforts in the right direction. He was certain that her advice in this situation would be to keep his head and act wisely. That he would do.

21 HARDBALL

BASHING A BALL AGAINST the wall with a racket was always a good way to grind aggression out of the bones and allow the mind to see more clearly – that was Kane's approach, anyway. The harder you hit the ball the quicker it would bounce back, and the quicker it bounced back, the faster you had to react – a simple formula. Eventually, both brain and brawn realised that rapid coordination was required. This demanded concentration – and there was no room for anger and other irrelevancies. When this realisation set in, both body and mind were ready – and the machine was finely tuned.

Kane considered, as he slammed the ball with vigour against the glass wall, what the weeks and months ahead would hold in store. Would he become the first prisoner to escape from Korb-1? Would he lead a mass revolt? Would McKenzie be his salvation? Would he avenge the cruel fate that befell Strauss and Thorsen? Or would he become a thoroughly defeated man, a prisoner in the complete sense – one with *no hope* of escape?

Kane wondered about Nevin. He certainly had the pedigree and held the respect of the prisoners – but was he going a bit soft? His approach certainly seemed to be cautious, to say the least. Had he really got the ability to organise the entire kolony in revolt? Whether he had or not, Kane knew in his heart that a more important player than Nevin in all of this would be McKenzie. If she was for real, she could make all the difference in effecting an escape. If she was acting as a decoy for the Master, she could not only scupper the escape bid, but in so doing ensure that it would be a long time before the prisoners had the imagination and courage to even consider trying again. Kane was impatient for another meeting with his apparent guardian angel. Eventually he would have to make a judgement on her, a judgement that could decide the fate of every prisoner on Korb-1.

His favourite hologram of Korb-1 glowing in his face, the Master sat at the top of the table listening to his kontrollers giving update reports on the latest security situation. A kontroller with a red face and a thin moustache was talking: "They're beginning to organise – there's no doubt about it. The prisoners in my area are up to something. It's clear."

"It's the same in my zone", said another kontroller with short red hair. "There is an air of conspiracy everywhere. It's as if the word has gone out."

"My zone is the same. There's something going on – without question", reported another.

Kontroller Windsor listened intently, as the other kontrollers reported on the position in their respective areas. With every confirmation of subversive activity, Windsor's heart soared. There could be no question now — a revolt was being organised and must be nipped in the bud. When the Master turned to him for a report on Zone 12, Windsor was too intense to notice the sarcasm in the Master's voice.

"Well, Windsor, have *you* anything to report?"

"Yes", Windsor replied in serious tones. "There is obviously a conspiracy in train. A concerted effort is being made to organise the Chambers. There can be no other purpose for such organisation but *REVOLT!*"

The kontroller stressed the final word with a ferocity that surprised his peers, but the Master merely said "very good" and moved on to the next kontroller. Windsor was taken aback, and was about to interject but hesitated. When the three remaining kontrollers had reported and all confirmed the evidence of their fellows, the Master concluded:

"Gentlemen, I have asked you all for an appraisal of the situation. What I have received is your impression that a revolt is being planned. Were we not here only a matter of days ago to hear with our own ears that a revolt *is* being planned? And now, all you can collectively tell me — in dramatic fashion", the Master hesitated momentarily to cast a derisive glance at Windsor, "is that a revolt is being planned! Am I to be impressed with that? Is that the level of intelligence that is to be presented to me?" The Master stopped for theatrical effect, enjoying the sight of his underlings squirming in their seats, Windsor in particular finding it difficult to conceal his fury. The Master concluded his broadside clinically: "We *know* there is a revolt being planned. What we want to know is at what stage the plan is now and who is involved? We shall meet again tomorrow and maybe then you will be capable of shedding *some* light on the situation in the kolony. Good day, Gentlemen."

Windsor was appalled at the relaxed manner in which the Master had dismissed his warning of a serious revolt. Unable to restrain himself anymore, he burst out in a horrified voice:

"But the kolony could be overthrown in a matter of days, if we don't act now. Don't you realise the consequences of your inaction? If the leaders are not detained immediately and an example made of them, the results will be disastrous!"

There was stunned silence amongst the other Kontrollers as they waited for the Master's reaction. The Master remained unperturbed, however. Fixing a cold glance on Windsor, he warned his arrogant underling:

"That is the last time you will ever speak to me like that. I am Master of this kolony and *I* shall decide in *my* wisdom what any given situation demands. You will have noticed, gentlemen, that Kontroller Overly is not with us today. Despite an extensive search, he has failed in the simple task of locating agent Leonard and has been relieved of his kommand. Kontroller Windsor, *you* now have that onerous duty to fulfil. If Leonard is not found within one week, you will join Kontroller Overly in the recycle bin."

Before he stood up to terminate the meeting, the Master glared at Windsor. "Understood?" he asked pointedly.

"Yes!" Windsor replied, barely repressing his anger.

Windsor ignored his fellow kontrollers as he left the meeting. He was irate that the Master had dismissed his warning that a major revolt was about to explode in the kolony, but content that the record would show that he had attempted to warn the old fool of the consequences of his poor judgement. He was also happy that the Master had given him the task of finding Leonard. He had already been active in gathering information on that case with the assistance of his accomplice, Chief Security Officer Simpson and the Critical Information Technician. He was now fully authorised to continue that operation openly and he fully intended to capitalise on the opportunity now given to find out exactly what was going on – and act accordingly. A slight smile broke out on Windsor's pained face as he walked to his office. He now believed 'the stupid old fool' had unwittingly handed him an opportunity to show his worth to the other Kontrollers and stake his claim to the leadership of the entire kolony. Then, the stern servant of the Administration believed, the Master would regret his arrogance.

On returning to his office, Windsor summoned Simpson. "We have two days to find Leonard or discover what happened to him. Get me a list of all suspected agitators in all chamber areas. Have the first six on the list interviewed by the Technician. Interview all informers, at high and low level, yourself. Have all cells searched immediately and all information obtained collated for consideration by tomorrow morning. If you fail, the Master will demote you. If you succeed, I will reward you", he informed his loyal assistant. Simpson smiled, then left to about her task.

WHEN HE GOT BACK to his cell, jaded after his punishing session with the wall, Kane was just about to shower when he heard activity outside. Rushing to the door, he saw a large body of tyrons entering cells in groups of two. As Kane observed, wondering what was going on, two tyrons approached his cell and, pushing him aside, entered and proceeded to carry out a search. A nervous Kane received no reply to his query regarding the objective of the intrusion. After what the prisoner considered a fairly peremptory search, however, the tyrons left in silence and entered the neighbouring cell. Relieved, Kane cast a glance at the light fitting behind which his key to freedom was concealed.

Kerner, Kane's neighbour, wasn't too happy.

"Who do these automatons think there are?" she asked angrily. "Can we not have some privacy even in our cells?"

"I wonder what they're looking for?" Kane thought out loud.

"Trouble, that's what they're looking for – trouble!" bawled Kerner at the two as they left her cell to enter the one next door. The tyrons ignored the irate prisoner, not even batting an eye as they passed her by.

Eventually, having searched all the cells, the tyrons left to search another level and the prisoners, relieved that nothing more serious had occurred, returned to normality.

KANE WAS LYING DOWN for the night. He thought about the search carried out by the tyrons and wondered what they were after. Perhaps they had got word of Nevin's efforts to organise the prisoners and were looking for information? Perhaps they just wanted to show who was boss? More seriously, however, maybe they were looking for the Kolony Plan that McKenzie had given him? But the probability was that they were really looking for the Ferret, whose disappearance was now the talk – and celebration – of the kolony. Kane wondered where the disgusting creature had gone, but was sure somehow that wherever he was he wouldn't be coming back. Either way, the Kolony Plan was safe so far, and Kane would be feasting his eyes and his memory on that fairly soon.

Kane's thoughts inevitably returned to McKenzie. The jury was still out on whether he could trust her or not, but certainly the weight of the evidence was in her favour at present. But even if his newfound friend's *bona fides* were proven, the next question would have to be had she the ability to pull it all off? The answer to *that* question could decide Kane's ultimate fate. But then all the original doubts began to return. The woman certainly *seemed* genuine, but actors were ten a penny and it would be typical of the Master to play a cruel trick like that. If it was a trick, where would that leave the prisoner? Bogged further down in the mire of deceit, control and captivity, he thought. Somehow, though,

Kane felt his new ally *was* genuine. Though, no matter how hard he might try, he couldn't rationalise this impression, this gut feeling. Deep down, although he wouldn't like to admit it, he knew it was the look of determination in McKenzie's eyes that had convinced him, that look that he had seen before a lifetime away, the look that had changed – and ultimately destroyed – his life. Perhaps that same element of determination would be the factor to change his life once again? Perhaps it would undo the damage that had been done? Perhaps he could return to the life that had been stolen from him long ago? Maybe, somehow, the raw determination in that glance that had got him into Korb-1 in the first place might be the catalyst that would gain him his freedom once more. But for Prisoner 313 that could only be a dream for now. Kane closed his eyes and went to sleep.

WINDSOR READ THE LATEST security update on the screen in front of him, then sat back in his chair. The kontroller smiled to himself as he considered what he now realised was a golden opportunity to take control of the kolony. If he handled the situation well, he could end up as Master, with the stupid old bugger in his fancy cloak consigned to korb generation duties. Carefully considering the future, it occurred to him that perhaps the best approach would be to allow a revolt to actually take place and then, when the Master had lost control of the situation, take decisive action to bring matters under control. If he played his cards right, he could be the big winner in the game and his destiny as Master of Korb-1 fulfilled. But first he must find Wilson Leonard.

After a short Korb night, Kane allowed the water in the shower to splash on his face and prepare him for the Korb day ahead, his mind still firmly concentrated on McKenzie. She hadn't made contact since. Why? Maybe she was biding her time. Maybe she had a different picture of what she intended to do and Kane was merely an insignificant pawn in her greater game plan. Maybe he would have to be patient and wait. On the other hand, maybe she had been uncovered and was now under arrest. Maybe that was why there had been no word. Maybe that was why the tyrons had searched the cells. If that was the case though, why hadn't Kane been arrested? Obviously the woman hadn't given his name to her inquisitors. But surely it wouldn't take them long to find out? Maybe, maybe, maybe .... Steadying himself, Kane dismissed his negative defeatist thoughts as mere weeds on dry rocks, planted in his mind by the Master.

The prisoner wondered how long he could keep the story of his contact a secret. If Nevin eventually got his act together and organised a meaningful effort to effect an escape, he would obviously have to be brought into the loop. And what about Dayton? He would have to be told too. And what would McKenzie herself think of her identity being passed on to other prisoners in the kolony, particularly as she had already asked Kane not to compromise her in any way? Kane knew she wouldn't approve. Anyway, he would keep the news of his contact to himself for the time being. If the woman was for real, he would only be endangering her by bringing more people into the equation. If she was an agent, he would be imperilling his friends by bringing *them* into contact with *her*. He would say nothing yet.

Kane used his air-razor to give himself a perfect shave. Cupped in the palm of his hand, he moved it slowly over his cheek, his chin, his throat, slightly touching the skin. Looking in the concave mirror that almost surrounded him and lit by the blue light emitted from behind the glass, Kane had a sense that perhaps a new age in his destiny was about to begin, that his state of disorientation and confusion was about to end, that he could see more clearly now the path that lay before him. He felt himself invigorated by the thought that his deliverance would soon be at hand, that he would soon be 'the Master' of his own destiny. He sensed a new inner strength brewing up inside him, the strength of a man confident in his ability to change the course of his life for once and for all.

Having put on his yellow tunic to go down for breakfast, Kane left his cell. In the corridor outside the door, however, four tyrons were waiting. One of them looked at Kane and nodded to him to come with them. Despite the prisoner's surprise, no words were spoken. None were necessary. All five marched away together.

22 PRISONER AT LARGE

UNDER TYRON ESCORT ALONG the corridors of Korb-1, Prisoner Kane wondered what lay in store for him now. He had thought things had settled down somewhat since Thorsen's death and that the kolony seemed to be drifting back into its former docility. Why then was he now the object of attention for the Administration once more? Had they become aware of his contact with McKenzie? If so, he could be facing a difficult situation. As the party moved through the cell quarters, past the massive korb feeder pipes and down past the Reception Area, he understood he had to decide what he was going to do if confronted with his association with the woman. Denying everything seemed to be the only reasonable option. At least in that case, he would not be implicating her – if she hadn't already implicated him! – and it would be up to the Administration to prove a connection. But what if evidence of his contact with the mysterious lady was produced by the authorities? What would he do then? What if the woman was genuine and her life depended on him clearing her in some way? Thoughts of what lay before him, particularly if he was given a jab of *feer*, the so-called truth drug, troubled the prisoner's mind as he passed the office of the Master.

OUTSIDE THE CELL OF Novo 1319, four tyrons awaited the inmate as he walked out his cell door. The prisoner, surprised to see a 'welcoming' party outside, was startled and stood momentarily staring at the arresting party. The tyrons gave the prisoner a few seconds to compose himself, then one of them nodded for him to accompany them. Suddenly, to the surprise of the tyrons, the novo threw himself on two of them with such force that they flew backwards across the corridor with the novo on top of them. The other tyrons reacted immediately and darted towards the novo in an attempt to overpower him. As the tyrons were about to grab him by the arms, the novo made a bounding leap that threw him clear of the tyrons and saw the two space warriors land on top of their fallen comrades. As the tyrons got to their feet, Novo 1319 fled down the corridor and around the corner. Running after the fugitive, one of the tyrons fired a stun round at the novo which hit the side of the wall as the prisoner turned the corner. The fleeing prisoner showed such speed that a clear gap opened up between himself and his pursuers. Showing a clean pair of heels, he was heading for the Atrium when all four tyrons let fly with a volley of stun shots. Luckily for the bearded novo, none of them hit the target and he continued to create space between him and the angry and frustrated tyrons.

As the novo arrived in the L+S, a group of about thirty prisoners were preparing for a game of hurling-ball. When Novo 1319 burst through the group, some of the players were knocked to the ground. Surprised and angered, they were attempting to regain their feet when the four tyrons burst through, throwing them to the ground once more. This time, however, the players were ready and, using their hurling sticks, brought the soldiers to the ground. Soon the floor in the hall was a mass of bodies and sticks, with the prisoners taking every opportunity they could to paste the tyrons with their sticks and bare fists. Novo 1319 looked back, the sight of his pursuers wrestling on the floor with the prisoners a welcome sight, and quickly left the area.

The scene Prisoner 1319 left behind in the L+S was one of mayhem and chaos as the prisoners attempted to prevent the tyrons from using their weapons and injuring any of the group. Old scores and indeed anticipated ones were settled as the tyrons were pinned to the ground and treated to hospitality L+S style. Three of the tyrons passed out with the whipping they received and the third wasn't far off joining them when, managing to free his right arm from those holding him, he hit his alarm button on his left wrist. As a blow from a stick sent the tyron into a peaceful state and left the prisoners in a position to admire their handiwork, a team of ten tyrons burst in through the L+S door and, firing stun rounds, soon levelled the group of prisoners to the ground. The tyrons then walked through the fallen group, standing on some of the prisoners as they went. One unfortunate who hadn't been totally immobilised by the stun rounds received a kick in the face with a tyron space boot and immediately joined his colleagues in the land of the unconsciousness. When the dust had settled, there was no sign of Novo 1319.

KANE SAT IN A swing chair in a room he had never seen before. The chair consisted of a seat, into which the occupant was locked, hung by two wires from the ceiling. Kane was worried. The idea of the swing chair was to enable those in control to adjust the balance of the chair, either suddenly or subtly, depending on the effect required by the Technician, in order to convey to the prisoner a feeling of total helplessness, a sense that the inquisitor was in control. The swing chair could be moved rhythmically from side to side to give the occupant a sensation akin to sea sickness or lifted up and down slowly and continuously to produce space sickness. The very fact of being left sitting in the chair was enough in itself to worry any prisoner, conscious as he or she must be that something unpleasant was in store. Sitting in the seat, Kane awaited whatever might come, steeling himself as he did. The prisoner squinted as he attempted to get control of his nerve, concentrating his entire consciousness on resisting whatever interrogation technique was to be applied. Fear, he was convinced, was the main enemy. If he could persuade himself to suppress his fear, he would be able to survive whatever ordeal his inquisitor had in store for him. Kane sensed that the impending battle would not be between him and his jailors but between the prisoner and fear itself. Sitting in the swing chair, waiting for his Technician to arrive, Kane decided to face fear down, to look it in the eye and not to blink. Suddenly, he heard the door open and close behind him. The hair stood up on Kane's neck. The battle was about to begin.

Novo 1319 realised he couldn't escape. Resting up against a korb pump outside KC35, he considered his position and where he was going to go from here. In a space prison, surrounded by a poisonous atmosphere, he knew his choices were few. One option was to go down fighting, taking as many of the tyrons with him as he could. Another was to do as much damage as possible to the kolony administrative and security apparatus before he was recaptured, as he inevitably would be. He considered the option of giving himself up and attempting to convince the authorities that the whole episode was a mistake, an unfortunate misunderstanding mishandled by the tyrons. That would be hard to get away with. The tyrons would be fairly angry by now at the ease with which Novo 1319 had escaped their clutches and humiliated them in the process. They would be eager for payback. Presuming the microchip under his skin would be used to pinpoint his exact location, Novo 1319 was well aware his options were becoming more limited by the minute.

KANE BRACED HIMSELF AS the Technician approached from behind. The prisoner knew he was there — even imagining he could feel his breath on the back of his neck — but the inquisitor said nothing, preferring to stand still and silent behind his prey. Kane waited nervously as silence prevailed in the interrogation room. The prisoner decided not to allow his interrogator to dictate the pace.

"Nice evening, isn't it?" Kane quipped boldly. "I can see Lake Huron from here."

Silence. Kane waited again. Kane froze as a fingertip touched the side of his neck slightly, chillingly. Then, slowly, a spaghetti band was placed around the prisoner's head. Although his natural inclination was to resist, Kane decided not to. He knew resistance in this situation would be a futile act and hoped that a display of indifference might unsettle the Technician and make it more difficult for him to focus on his target. Kane *was* worried, though. 'Spaghetti band' was slang for *cerebral wave distorter*. This was a device that identified the wave pattern of the subject's brain and immediately discharged electric signals to distort the natural pattern. Depending on the strength of the signals emitted by the band, the effect on the subject could be anything ranging from disorientation to nausea, from occasional spasms to an uncontrollable fit. Prolonged use could have long-term consequences. Kane was aware of this, although he tried to put his worries on that score out of his mind. Walking around slowly to face his captive, the Technician looked Kane in the eye and smiled the smile of one in control. He knew what Kane was thinking at that moment and it pleased him to know that his subject's main concern now was what his Technician's next move was going to be.

The Technician was a grey man, a short-cropped head of grey hair capping a colourless face with no significant characteristics. His could easily be the features of any of those silent anonymous beings whose tired forms populated the trams and airbuses upon which Kane would have made his nightly journeys home once upon a time in a long-lost life.

"Well, Kane! Comfortable, I hope", the Technician suddenly sneered in a condescending voice. Kane didn't respond. "Ah, don't worry, Kane", the Technician continued, "it generally isn't as bad as you expect", then added with a sick smile, after a theatrical silence: "– or maybe it is ...!"

Kane still didn't respond, looking his captor in the eye as if observing a mildly interesting case of behavioural abnormality.

"Time to begin", the Technician announced. Kane stiffened in the swing chair, as it began to rise.

Novo 1319 was becoming desperate. If he was to have any chance of survival, he would have to get to a large group of prisoners before he was inevitably caught. Only then would there be a chance that he would be taken alive. He was convinced that the murder of a prisoner by the tyrons in front of his fellows would spark a riot situation that would bring the kolony to the verge of disaster. He hoped that even the tyrons would realise that. Still, if they caught up with him before he got to his fellow prisoners, he wouldn't be expecting cakes and biscuits.

1319 decided Generation Chamber 9 was the nearest location in which he would stand a chance of getting enough support to prevent the tyrons taking the law into their own hands. It was only a matter of time before they pinpointed his location and called him to account. Novo 1319 moved fast, running rapidly along two corridors and down the short stairs to the GC9. Nearing the door of the chamber, he heard a commotion, the sound of the tyrons grip-boots bringing a cold sweat to his brow. Slamming the door closed behind him, he heard the first kling shots bounce off the outside of the door. These were single bullets, designed to kill immediately by bursting one second after impact and releasing the instantly fatal *morav* chemical inside the body. The tyrons meant business. Rushing into the chamber, he shouted, "Help! Stop them – they're trying to kill me!" The workers in the chamber – the novo's own workmates who had just begun their shift without him – looked in amazement as he launched himself under one of the large conveyor belt channels which moved giant pieces of korb towards the generations tanks. Then the tyrons burst in, firing indiscriminately as the workers dived for cover.

ON THE OTHER SIDE of the viewing wall, Kontroller Windsor looked coldly at the prisoner in the chair. Windsor's icy eyes focused on Kane, not as one human would view another but as a predatory animal would view its prey. His eyes fixing on the form in the swing chair, he saw before him an object that, if crushed and controlled, could open the door for him to fulfil his destiny. Windsor almost looked the prisoner in the eye as he stared in his direction, but in reality all the kontroller could see was an opportunity that would not be wasted.

In his hand, Windsor held a screen-viewer on which he could consult the prisoner's general file.

ID: Prisoner 313

Name: Kevin Kane.

Korb Assignment: KC10-1.

Origin: District 6741 NCR435.

Born: 12.12.2119.

History: Worked in NCR Development Sector Bureau 375 in NCR 435.

Offence: Information Terrorism.

Convicted: 03.02.2148.

Accomplice: Sheena Strauss - Prisoner 275, Korb-3.

Recent Events: Relationship with Prisoner 393, Andrea Thorsen, KC31-1, terminated following 393's accidental death. Sedating and calming procedures followed.

Psychological Status: Mood swings between demoralisation and defiance.

Present Security Profile: Intermediate.

Windsor thought about the Thorsen incident. It was just another example, in his view, of the Master's mishandling of a perfectly simple situation. It was the Master's prevarication that had allowed that matter to get out of control. Pussyfooting and play-acting, that was all the old fool was good for, while the situation deteriorated around him. Windsor wasn't like that. He wasn't going to be fooled by "intermediate profiles". Kane was a dangerous motivated criminal who would take any and every opportunity to escape and destroy the kolony. Windsor's responsibility was to prevent him doing that – using whatever means at his disposal.

As the Technician sat back in his comfortable chair, he placed a narrow metal ring on the index finger of his right hand. The room darkened and a halo of light focused on the suspended prisoner. Slowly, the Technician moved his right hand over a small sensor area at the end of the arm of his chair. In response, the prisoner's perch began to sway. Then it began to move up and down. Finally, the chair began to tilt slightly from side to side, with the result that the prisoner had an immediate sense of being about to topple to the ground, instinctively attempting to retain his balance lest he fall. The Technician exercised full control. If he moved his ringed finger upwards and to the right, the chair followed the movement exactly and the occupant attempted to rebalance his body to respond to the unpredictable motion of the chair.

His subject in position, the Technician relaxed, sat back and passed his palm over the control panel on the arm of his chair. A laser light shot out from the panel and focused on the prisoner's forehead and, immediately, the prisoner's coded serial number and all the information recorded on his file appeared on a hologram screen in front of the Technician. Kane's ordeal had begun.

23 INTERROGATION

MOVING THE HELPLESS PRISONER at will in any and every direction, the Technician applied himself with silent pleasure to his duties. A slight smile curled up the right side of his lip as he relaxed and got into his routine. Kane attempted to keep his mind clear while struggling desperately to keep control of his physical faculties. Slowly, gradually, the Technician moved the prisoner in the air while Kane reacted to every move in an eventually vain attempt to keep his equilibrium. The Technician always enjoyed this part of the interrogation procedure. The movement of the prisoner reminded him of his first ever shuttle ride to the Lunar Colony in the early days of his career. The atmospheric adjustments when landing were so turbulent at times that passengers were shaken around like rag dolls for a number of minutes until the shuttle regained an even keel. Things were so bad that civilian travellers had to sign disclaimers stating that they would not hold the shuttle company responsible for any injuries received on the journey. The Technician smiled wistfully as he thought of the good old days. But now there was work to be done. Returning to his subject, the Technician moved him back and forth and up and down like a medieval marionette on strings.

Outside the viewing wall, Windsor breathed a deep breath of satisfaction as the interrogation began. He was convinced that in Kane he had a big fish, one who could do great damage to the morale of the kolony, if allowed. He had a suspicion Kane was the culprit in the Leonard case and had every intention of extracting a full confession from him on this and many other issues. Windsor was convinced that the Leonard disappearance was a direct and deliberate challenge to the authority of the regime by the prisoners. If he could break the Leonard case, he would have the initiative on both the Master and the subversives in the kolony. He would then be a force to be reckoned with and the shilly-shallying approach of the Master would be shown up for all to see as being criminally negligent. The prisoner in the Interrogation Room was the key to the success of Windsor's plan and the kontroller would pay particular attention to him. As Windsor waited impatiently for the business to begin, however, he received a message on his communicator. He immediately became excited. Another prisoner, Novo 1319, had escaped from the custody of his tyron escort and was now gone missing. *What?* Windsor thought, *is the uprising about to begin?* He contacted his security staff immediately. "What's going on? I want a full report on my screen in one minute!" he ordered. Windsor rubbed his chin with his left hand and wondered. Could this be the beginning of the revolt he had warned the idiot Master about? Or was it a spontaneous act of bravado by a fool? It didn't really matter, though, Windsor thought – any incident of this kind was grist to his mill and he would use it to the full. Anyway, maybe this fugitive had good reason to flee – maybe *he* knew something about Leonard.

Windsor's communicator screen flashed and a report on the missing novo appeared. The kontroller read it eagerly:

ID: Prisoner 1319

Name: Thomas Pedersen.

Korb Assignment: GC9-3.

Origin: NCC 12 of NCR 41.

Born: 01.07.2120.

History: Activist for Informed Decision Party – 2142.

Offence: Information Terrorism.

Convicted: 05.04.2151.

Accomplices: Martin Fleering – Prisoner 1271, Korb-2; Orla Klune – Prisoner 1299, Korb-3.

Recent events: Escaped – At Large!

Psychological Status: Highly Motivated.

Present security profile: Emergency.

The words 'At Large!' flashed in red on the screen. Windsor concentrated. This seemed interesting. Novo 1319 looked like the kind of hardened terrorist likely to be to the fore in any planned resistance in the kolony. A seasoned campaigner like that would know exactly what he wanted and how to go about achieving it. As well as that, GC9-3 was Leonard's Generation Chamber Team! In fact, GC9 was the last place the ferret had been seen. The missing novo had actually been on Leonard's Team .... mmmm ..... perhaps there was now, at long last, a break in the case, an opportunity for Windsor to show his metal. The balding kontroller squinted as he considered how lucky a development this could actually turn out to be. Touching his communicator, he contacted Security Officer Simpson.

KANE HUNG ON LIKE an oversized parrot on his perch as the wire moved in every conceivable direction. The movement was such that it was difficult for the prisoner to concentrate even for a moment. Just as he felt he had regained his equilibrium, he was forced to struggle to gain his balance once more.

"Comfortable, Kane?" the Technician enquired with a seemingly sympathetic voice. "I hope this isn't too much of an inconvenience ... but maybe we won't be too long ... then again maybe we will ... it's really up to you!"

Kane heard the Technician's voice waft around the room, expanding and spreading until it seemed to fill the very air itself. "I often wonder about you, Kane," the inquisitor announced, as his sickeningly sweet tones entered the prisoner's ears once more. "I can never understand how someone like you – intelligent, sensible, able – ends up in a place like this. How did it happen? It seems so strange. What went wrong?"

Despite his earlier resolution not to heed anything the Technician might say, Kane, hanging in mid-air, found himself listening intently to every word his interrogator uttered. Somewhere in his mind, the very questions now being posed by his persecutor lay unanswered, deserted in a dark recess. The Technician's seemingly simple question discovered that spot with surprising ease and a shaft of blinding light burst in – demanding recognition, demanding satisfaction, demanding answers.

All Kane's ghosts suddenly emerged to haunt him again. Faces and scenes from his Old World flooded past into the ether surrounding the pendant prisoner. Family, friends and distant acquaintances lined up to ask Kane the same painful question: "Where had it all gone wrong?"

Kane was now on a spit. Tortured physically and mentally, body and soul, within and without, skewered on the end of a piercing lance – the lance of doubt. No matter how he struggled in the air to regain physical and mental control, he could not break free. Almost sensing, with predatory animal instinct, that his first salvo of arrows had struck true, the Technician remained silent, watching, observing his prey struggle on the wire above. Kane attempted to fight back, to recover, all the while being shunted, jolted and shaken in the air. He was particularly shaken with the speed with which his interrogator had hit the spot and identified his weakest point. The prisoner tried hard to concentrate, to direct his mind on what he wanted to think about rather than follow the pathway being laid out for him by the Technician. Kane fought hard to regain control of his thoughts, gradually succeeding in directing them towards someone he had always relied upon for strength and support – Andrea Thorsen.

Thorsen was a mine of inner strength. Anything she set her mind on doing, she did. Anything she decided to resist, she resisted. Determination was her middle name and her sheer doggedness in the face of adversity had always been a source of inspiration to Kane. When she died, Kane had felt a void where that resource of strength and support had been. Now, he thought, perhaps that mine hadn't entirely collapsed in on itself. Maybe it was still there and would always be there – maybe that was Thorsen's eternal gift to him. Inspired by that thought, Kane tried to model himself on his lost comrade, trying to imitate what he felt her reaction to all of this might have been. Suddenly, as the Technician rejoined the fray, he was now facing a new and more formidable foe, a man newly-motivated by old memories.

The Technician resumed his attack. "Really, Kane", he asked, "what a shame you left behind all those you loved – and who loved you. What a shame you threw it all away!" Kane, still struggling on the wire, concentrated on rebutting his interrogator's efforts. 'Rubbish', he thought to himself, 'it was the Administration that took all that from me and left me to spend my years on a rock in space.' The Technician continued: "Can you still see the faces of those you left behind? Can you imagine how they felt when they realised you had abandoned them for a silly cause? Will you ever understand how hurt and betrayed they must have felt?" Kane ignored the goading of the interrogator and instantly dismissed in his mind his malicious suggestions. 'It was the Administration that betrayed those people and everyone else besides', he thought. 'It was the Administration that must ultimately pay the price for that mass betrayal – and I will play *my* part in bringing that day of atonement about.'

As the Technician worked on sewing the seeds of doubt deep in the troubled soil of Kane's mind, the prisoner began to dig deep into his resolve. Whatever the Technician had to say, he would redefine as further proof that it was the Administration that had had been the cause, not only of his own misery and pain, but of that of the thousands of prisoners and millions of innocent and trusting citizens all over the Confederation who had believed them.

OUTSIDE THE VIEWING WALL, Windsor had become impatient. His mind had now moved from the subject of the inquisition inside to the whereabouts of Novo 1319. He was convinced that the runaway novo knew something of the ferret's disappearance. He must be located immediately and interrogated in order to solve that case once and for all – and to show the idiotic Master how things should be done. Animated, the kontroller told Simpson to get every available tyron on Novo 1319's trail.

KANE'S INTERROGATOR WAS ENJOYING his work. The wave band graph on the screen extending from the arm of his chair showed the prisoner to have an agitated emotional state. Gliding his hand over the control panel, he moved Kane back and forth, up and down at will.

"Kane", he asked, pausing, as always, in order to create a sense of expectation in the subject, "Do you remember your mother?" The

Technician knew well the reaction that was going on in his victim's mind. He knew that the effect of his question would be to plunge his subject back through the years, through all that had happened, to a time when life was simpler, happier, safer. He waited awhile for Kane to make that journey, sitting back comfortably as the prisoner opened his eyes in a time so much a part of the prisoner's psyche that it could never be far under the surface of the present.

Kane opened his eyes in another world. His mother was in the kitchen, making him his favourite pie – apple and almond. The sun was shining through the window, pouring through her blond hair and filling the room with a blinding radiance. The young boy was dazzled by the light – overawed by the brilliance and intensity of the illumination. It seemed now as if he stood there for hours watching his mother, bathing in the glow. It was probably just a few moments, but it was a memory that he had held with him ever since. Radiance, brightness, illumination – that was his indelible memory of his mother.

The Technician watched the graph with interest. Kane's memory was obviously positive. The Technician watched and then asked: "Your mother, Kane, didn't she" – he hesitated again – "didn't she" – another pause – "have a ..... relationship ..... with another man? A man called Brant?"

Kane heard the interrogator's words and tried to make sense of them. He had never heard of a man called Brant. His parents had had a very close and happy relationship. He wondered. Was there something unsavoury in his parents' relationship that he had never known? Had his mother really been involved with another man? Could it be true? As Kane tried to reason it all out, the interrogator gave the wire a series of jerked movements. Kane struggled to keep his composure while all the time searching his distant past for anything that might suggest that the Technician spoke the truth. Searching and searching, Kane uncovered views and recollections of his parents that he had thought he had long forgotten – little arguments, minor disputes, trivial disagreements. Worried, Kane tried to patch these scenes together to create a pattern, a pattern that would explain the interrogator's question.

The Technician sat back silently as his prisoner struggled on the wire. Experience told him it was time to be patient. Kane remembered his father hitting the table once as he and Kane's mother talked. Could they have been arguing, could they have quarrelling about ..... Brant? The Technician moved in: "Don't worry about it, Kane", he advised sympathetically, "these things happen – it's usually no-one's fault." Kane wondered. Perhaps the Technician was right, perhaps these things do happen, perhaps it is nobody's fault, perhaps life is like that and perhaps his parents were no different to anyone else's. As Kane was drifting into an acceptance of the Technician's allegation, suddenly his vision of his mother returned – radiant, bright, aglow. 'The bastard', he suddenly thought, 'he's a liar, a scummy liar. He's making it all up. The bastard!'

The Technician noticed a sudden change in his subject's brain patterns. Now the patterns indicated anger, strength, resistance. The Technician had to make a quick decision. Should he continue with this line of questioning and attempt to convince Kane of the truth of his fabrication? Should he try to portray himself as understanding and sympathetic or should he move on, exploring another cavern deep in his subject's mind? The Technician had to make his judgement call now.

24 THE MEMORY ZONE

THE WORKERS IN GENERATION Chamber 9 watched in amazement as their workplace was suddenly swarmed by tyrons. The object of the invaders' interest wasted no time in placing himself as far under the conveyor belt channel as possible, the tyrons pouring into the chamber behind him. The pursuers sprayed the lower part of the channels with kling shot in a vain attempt to stop the fugitive, but the gap between the channel and the floor was too narrow for a standing tyron to hit his target. After a torrent of fire which lasted the best part of a minute, the tyrons ceased fire and moved to cover both sides of the belt channel. Having done that, one tyron then lay on the ground in an effort to get a view of his target. The fugitive novo lay sweating and exhausted under the belt channel, not even blinking when the tyron made eye contact with him. Seeing his target, the tyron set about aiming his weapon at the defenceless novo. The prisoners, appalled at what was about to take place, began to hurl abuse at the tyrons, shouting "Stop!", "Don't shoot!", "Murderers, murderers!"

A prisoner standing at the back of the group beside the manual controls looked around to see if he was being observed and then, having assured himself that he was safe to act, hit a switch on the panel, unnoticed by the tyrons. Immediately, the conveyor belt's caterpillar wheels, used to transport the large piece of equipment from chamber to chamber, were released and, coming down on both sides, soon made any view of the undercarriage entirely impossible. In anger, the tyron let his shot go anyway but it merely bounced off the caterpillar wheels and ricocheted back into the chamber, creating an unmerciful din and a blinding flash.

In a moment, the noise and uproar that had reigned in the chamber faded away as the tyrons tried to work out their next move. Like cats after a mouse, they gathered around the carrier, poking and clawing at the bulk of metal that had lowered down and was now tantalizingly shielding from them the prey they so eagerly wished to devour. The chamber crew watched nervously as the tyrons swarmed around the channel, growing more and more frustrated as the realisation set in that their quarry was now beyond their reach. Suddenly one of the tyrons, kicking the carrier in anger, swung around and fired a shot above the heads of the prisoners, shouting: "Get back, you bastards! Get back!"

The prisoners moved back to the wall behind them, raising their hands in the air in an attempt to pacify the furious tyrons. The atmosphere in the chamber was explosive and most of the prisoners were aware that the tyrons knew they could act with impunity in situations like this. A tense stand-off took place as the tyrons glared at the prisoners, visibly angry, and the prisoners stood nervously awaiting their fate.

"Lift the wheels!" one of the tyrons roared.

With a decision to make that would probably prove fatal for somebody in the Chamber, tension mounted. Suddenly, however, the chamber door burst open and a tyron kommander rushed in, accompanied by four more tyrons. "Cease fire!" he barked at the tyrons, "Hold it!" The frustrated tyrons reluctantly lowered their weapons and backed off, accepting that control of the situation had now passed out of their hands. Satisfied that calm had been restored, the kommander pointed his zennor baton at the prisoner immediately beside the control panel. "Lift it – now!" he roared. The prisoner, satisfied that the fugitive's life was no longer in immediate danger, pressed the button. The caterpillar tracks began to lift. Soon, the huge belt channel was left to stand once more on its outer legs. Immediately, the tyrons threw themselves on the floor, all of them focussing their weapons on the trapped prisoner underneath. "Come out!" the kommander ordered. "Now!" Slowly, the fugitive emerged, four tyrons pouncing on him as soon as he was out. Novo 1319's dash for freedom was over.

"Kane", the Technician called, "do you remember your friends, the ones you shared your youth with, the ones you grew up with, the ones you left behind?"

'The bastard!' Kane thought. 'He's trying again, but he won't succeed. I'll fight him.'

The interrogator watched and waited, noting the waves of resistance emanating from his subject's brain. Then he placed his middle finger on a red ball in the centre of his control console and moved it slightly to the right. With that, Kane felt a throbbing pain begin deep in his brain and pulsate out till it filled his head. Still struggling to maintain his balance on the wire, the prisoner felt totally oppressed by his exterior environment and the pressure waves inside his head. The Technician moved in.

"Do you remember Sheena Strauss, Kane? Do you remember her?" He waited. "Now there was a strong lady...... Do you remember the time you met?"

Despite the pain, Kane's mind travelled to that time so long ago when his and Strauss's paths first crossed. It was a memory tinged with sadness and framed with anger – sadness at the thought of what had been lost and anger at the realisation that somehow it could have all been avoided.

The Technician sensed Kane's feelings and decided to probe. "Whose fault was it that you were caught, Kane? Was it yours? Were you the one who made the mistake, the fatal error for which two young people paid with their futures? Were you the one who threw away your own life and that of a talented young woman too? Surely you should admit it, Kane. Surely it would be better for your own peace of mind? Surely it's time you realised that, for you, the enemy is within? Instead of spending your life blaming everybody else for your misfortune, isn't it time to lay the blame where it should really lie – with yourself! The Administration had no option but to punish you for your crimes. What else would you expect it to do? You left it no other option."

Kane shuddered at the cold logic employed by his tormentor. It was certainly undeniable that if he had never become involved with the resistance, never played along with Strauss, his future would have been very different, his happiness intact, his peace of mind undisturbed.

"You know I'm right, Kane. Your very soul calls out to you in the quietness of the night to tell you so. You were the one who destroyed everybody else's lives and, indeed, your own. You were the one who left nothing but tragedy in your wake, nothing but unfulfilled promises and empty barren futures."

Kane listened in silence to his interrogator. Despite his best efforts, he could not entirely convince himself that the Technician was wrong. Struggling to maintain control of his own mind, he found it impossible to dispel the doubts that dwelt there, the raw painful wounds that he had hoped had healed but that had been so expertly probed by his tormentor.

He could see the faces of those he had left behind – his parents, his relatives, his friends – floating in his mind. Taking turns to look deep into his eyes and remind him of the ones he left behind, they moved silently about, some now to the forefront, others in the background, then more faces appeared to reactivate other painful memories. Every face that Kane saw was a stinging cut, every smile a reminder of things left behind. "Tell me about Strauss", the Technician interrupted, "you and her were very close, weren't you?"

Kane immediately thought of the last time he had seen his former companion. Even then, struggling in the arms of the information security police, as they both realised that their plot had been uncovered and that dire consequences would ensue, Strauss's rejection of the Administration's authority was complete. Kane, looking to her for a reaction to their plight, was surprised and, in a manner, uplifted by her defiance. Her face, framed by her short red hair, told it all. While her body resisted the guards as they attempted to place the necklock around her, her eyes, lit up like fire, revealed the total rebelliousness of her nature. Here was one who would never submit, one whose mind would resist as long as there was breath in her body. Inspired by his companion's spirit, Kane had decided that he also would defy his captors. As the two were dragged away, Strauss advised her fellow conspirator to "tell them you know nothing!" Kane thought afterwards that that was indeed good advice, if a little ironic coming from an information rights activist. If they maintained they knew nothing, they could claim the whole incident was a misunderstanding. Even if given a dose of the truth drug *feer*, they might still be able to muddy the waters and sow the seeds of doubt in the minds of their prosecutors. As things unfolded, however, it soon became clear that the Administration was less interested in their possible innocence than he had expected. Their fate had already been decided. Within days, the pair were in confinement state and on their way to a 'new' life.

Ever since, Kane had retained that memory of his companion's defiance. When things were hard in the initial stages of his incarceration on Korb-1, he liked to think of Strauss's courage in the face of overwhelming odds. For Kane, this would be his inspiration when the dark days hung over him in the form of a deep dark purple cloud.

The Technician intervened: "Kane, do you think *you* were to blame for Strauss going down? After all, she was far more experienced than you, far more motivated as well? Only for you, she probably would have succeeded – but you messed up, you left her exposed – and she was caught."

Kane thought of that cheeky confident face, those beguiling green eyes that looked right into his soul. He remembered the first time they met, the first time they talked, the first time they made love. He remembered the lake where they had gone to be alone. He remembered the rain the day they were there.

"You destroyed her life, Kane. She relied on you but you let her down."

Twisting high upon the wire, his brain in turmoil, Kane's conscience weighed heavily upon him, pulling him down. Was it really his fault that Strauss and he were caught? Surely not? Everything had been planned down to the last and everything had gone according to plan. How could it have been his fault? Kane delved deep into his memory of those last few days, examining in detail the couple's every move. Nothing had gone wrong – nothing – until the agents pounced. There had to have been another force in action then – there had to have been – somebody else who had observed their movements along the way. But who? Deep inside Kane's memory stood a shadowy figure, a blurred form standing – watching – in the darkness. In the office, in *The Colony*, even in their apartments, that form seemed to be always there. But no matter how hard he tried, Kane couldn't see a face. Every time he approached the spectre, the darkness grew deeper and the figure was submerged into the gloom. Kane chased the image through his memory, through his imagination, through the empty, abandoned streets of the past, but the figure remained elusive. Sensing the futility of his pursuit, Kane was about to concede when he suddenly found himself in *The Colony*. It was the Presidential Room and the crowds were dancing slowly, almost in slow motion. Glancing, looking for Strauss, Kane spotted his stalker in the dark corner. Pushing his way through the crowds, the young man kept a constant eye on the figure. His movement through the crowd was tantalisingly slow, but he continued to maintain his focus on the form as he waded through the crowd towards it. Finally, Kane reached the edge of the mass of tangled dancing bodies and realised he was only a few feet away from the face he so eagerly wanted to see. Arriving beside the figure, he found it had its head bowed down. Kane shot out an arm to raise its head and reveal its face. On doing so, the young man recoiled in horror. Stunned, he discovered that the face before him was his own. Suddenly, a jab of pain shot through Kane's head as the Technician moved his hand over the console. "Why bother, Kane?" the Technician asked. "As you can see, you were the one ..... The guilty one is you!"

ON THE OTHER SIDE of the viewing wall, Kontroller Windsor, awaiting news of the missing novo, smiled. Although impatient at the slow methodical approach adopted by the Technician, he liked the manipulative aspect of the technique. Seeing the prisoner squirm and turn on the wire while the interrogator played games with his mind appealed to a basic element in Windsor's nature. In some ways, the scene reminded the kontroller of the barbeques he and his friends used to have in their youth. Seeing the animal on the spit had always given Windsor a strong sense of achievement. It symbolised for him the end of the chase, the conclusion of the matter. For Windsor, that was the only way to bring events to a close – the prey on the skewer. Kane's plight in the Interrogation Room was a powerful image for the kontroller – it was the sign that the hunt was coming to a climax. Windsor was eager to enjoy every minute of this chase, but at the same time was conscious that the clock the Master had set was ticking away. An impatience to see the pursuit brought to an end began to race through Windsor's veins.

WITH CHAOS REIGNING IN the prisoner's head, the Technician decided to spread his wings. "Nevin", the Technician said. "Nevin". Just one word – "Nevin" – and then he sat back in his chair, watching the response monitors closely. The prisoner said nothing but the mention of the veteran prisoner's name was enough to attract a response in Kane's brain patterns. The response was not a major one, but significant enough in the eyes and ears of the Technician to warrant further probing.

"Is Nevin the leader of the plot or is it you that calls the shots now?" He paused to observe. "Nevin tells all around him these days that you're a loudmouth, someone who can't be trusted. He says you botched the only job you were every given to do on the mother planet and can't be allowed near another one." The Technician paused once more.

Kane's first inclination was to be angry. How dare Nevin speak of him in that way! Kane wasn't the only one to end up on Korb-1. Nevin was here too. What did that say for *his* abilities? Then Kane began to think. Whatever Nevin might say or do, Kane would not rely on the Administration to report it to him. Anyway, he thought, if the phantom in his head was really himself, maybe Nevin was right! This audacious thought served to stabilise Kane's mind. Despite his physical and mental discomfort, the thought brought a brave smile to Kane's cheek. At that moment, it occurred to the prisoner that he might yet survive.

The Technician noticed the upturn in Kane's graphs and prepared to intensify his approach. Almost simultaneously, though, the viewing screen became transparent and the Technician saw Kontroller Windsor watching outside. When the kontroller spoke into his communicator, his message appeared on the Technician's screen: "This is going nowhere! We need to move faster!" the message read, "Put him in the Void!" Stung by the abruptness of the kontroller's intervention, the Technician paused, about to argue for more time but, realising that to debate with Windsor now would be futile, he merely replied: "Very well." Then, reluctantly, he set about closing down the interrogation session. Before the screen mirrored over again, however, the prisoner managed to catch a glimpse of the face outside, a face that conveyed a primitive expression of loathing and disdain.

25 THE VOID

THERE WAS SOMETHING ABOUT the Void that everyone subjected to it *had* to fear. The recipe was simple – deprive the subject of all sensory perception and, when the spirit was at its lowest, pounce with the probing, clinically thrust, question. Kane was three days in the Void now. Floating around for that length of time with no contact with the outside world, it wasn't easy to keep a grip on one's sanity. With hunger pangs and all other possible distractions neutralised by a jab before the prisoner was cast into the chamber, the prisoner's only external stimulation was the occasional self-inflicted slap or pinch or even a splash of urine to remind him that he indeed had a corporeal existence. In total darkness in a weightless atmosphere designed to deny the subject any physical contact with any other object, the mind was inclined to sink gradually into a languid state, sensing that it existed in a world devoid of physical dimensions. In that situation, other, normally subdued, areas of consciousness opened up and the unpredictable nature of the complex thought processes that gradually developed in a situation of stress created a general sense of disorientation and insecurity. Without the assuring certainties of the physical world, the mind expanded in different, unexpected directions in order to fill the Void. It was in these unpredictable directions that the subject would be taken – stretched as if on a mental rack – until he had passed a threshold he had never even imagined before.

Floating in the Void, Kane struggled to keep his concentration and prevent himself from sinking into what the experts called 'the void of consciousness'. He decided to choose a thought that he could develop in his mind and to which he could return when he was losing his anchor. Kane chose a day he had spent with Strauss by the lake. The prisoner realised now that that day was probably the pinnacle of his personal happiness in his old life – before his path crossed with that of the Administration to such devastating effect. The incident with the *r-rav* later on that same day was probably a portent of what was to come in the young people's lives. How ironic, the prisoner thought, that the happiest times in many people's lives often immediately precede their nemesis. There was something cruel about that, Kane believed. Just when happiness had been finally attained, it was cruelly snatched away. If he could choose a moment in time from which to launch his life again, Kane would choose that afternoon. Given the chance again, the prisoner would certainly follow a different path to the one which had led to his banishment to prison servitude for life on a korb kolony.

This was the memory to which Kane would return when the emptiness of the Void was about to pull him down. He would regard that day as a continuous present in the continuum of his life. Nothing that had happened since or that threatened to happen in the future would dislodge the memory of that day from his mind. It would be his anchor in the Void, the only certainty in a sea of drowning insecurity. With that rock of assurance to cling onto, Kane would take anything the Void could throw at him and smile the smile he had given Strauss so many years ago.

Strauss was someone with whom Kane had shared an earth-dream. They had both had a vision. Strauss was a committed activist, clear in her mind as to what she wanted to achieve. Kane, on the other hand, was someone who would have liked to have made the world a better place but who could never really identify the issues he wanted to address. Strauss was the catalyst that brought about the transformation of the liberal with a social conscience into the radical who was willing to act – and act they did.

Drifting in the darkness, Kane thought he was losing the feeling in his body. It wasn't that his limbs were becoming numb, it was more that his body was becoming irrelevant, fading from his consciousness as his mind became the only active part of his being. Kane sunk further and further into himself.

IN THE CONTROL AREA, the Technician studied the various screen and hologrammatic representations of the subject's mental and vital signs. Applying himself with a cold enthusiasm to the job in hand, he poured his eyes over all the incoming readings. The subject's brain patterns showed a strong mental state that was only slightly impaired by the physical disorientation he was feeling. As in the Chamber the previous day, the object of the exercise for the Technician was to carefully engineer and monitor a sensation of crisis in his subject and then recognise and exploit the subject's weakest moment in order to gain vital information. The challenge for the subject was to devise a strategy whereby he or she could still function in a normal mental state despite the almost total sensory deprivation they endured. Once the hatch was sealed on the large chamber, the contest between the two began. The Technician had the support of the Security Unit at his command. The prisoner was entirely alone. Or so it was supposed to be.

The Technician had impressed upon Security Officer Simpson the importance of this crucial information-gathering procedure and requested that her most capable officer be assigned to assist him. Simpson was eager to participate but the job of coordinating the search for the Ferret and his assailants prevented her from adding another pleasant experience to her lifelong collection. Windsor himself had impressed upon her that not only the future of the kolony but, more important than that, their own future depended on their resolving that issue effectively and speedily. Unable to take the opportunity to enjoy the event herself, Simpson decided to delegate the task to her Assistant Security Officer – McKenzie.

Thus, the Technician, confident in his mind that he held all the advantages in this critical game of *War-Raok!*, was unaware that he carried a weak flank. The Prisoner, attempting to gather all his mental strength to withstand the inevitable assault alone, had – unknown to him – a vital ally in the midst of the enemy's forces. The game was as neither competitor suspected. A challenging contest lay ahead.

The Technician was a professional. Everything he did as part of an assignment was properly prepared and thought out. Nothing that could be controlled was left to chance. This thoroughness and the results it achieved gave the middle-aged man immense satisfaction. He regarded himself as the best there was in the area of interrogation techniques and indeed was highly regarded in the security echelons of the NC Administration.

One would have thought that the Technician's task of breaking down decent people and reducing them to a state in which they would divulge information that could cost them their lives or liberty, or cause their friends or associates to lose theirs, would be a source of some regret to the interrogator. This was not the case. In the Technician's experience, his subjects could be divided into two groups. One – the criminal variety – was composed of those whose criminality was combined with a peculiar cunning that meant the ordinary security devices of the Confederation were unable to deal with them. They were few in number and generally difficult to break down. They were people who had no conscience and therefore had little to offer their interrogator in the line of useful material with which to bend them.

The second group, on the other hand, were the politically motivated people who opposed the regime. Most of these were idealistic in what the Technician regarded as a naïve way. The Technician had no political opinions of his own but regarded any regime that existed and operated on a widespread basis as being legitimate enough for him. The higher ideals of democracy, freedom of information and expression, and human rights didn't interest him, and belonged, he believed, in the domain of theorists and people 'with no bills to pay'. The politicos who passed the Technician's path were generally those who, despite their idealism, had a hard streak and had consciously developed an outer tougher skin. These were people whose combination of idealism and realism was a difficult package to handle, but the Technician had almost always found that deep in their subconscious these prisoners had a sensitive area which had nurtured their idealism in the first place and made them what they were. It was his job to uncover this 'weak spot' and exploit it to the full.

For the most part, the Technician respected his subjects, privately regarding them as his 'opponents'. For him the cause of their incarceration was irrelevant, except in as much as it might help him to break them down. How they came to be in the game didn't interest him either. They were there, that was all. However they came to be there, the interrogator gleaned immense pleasure from his jousts with his opponents. He took great pleasure in that vital moment when he realised he was going to make the move that would give him the game. Those who withstood the assault the longest, he respected most. Those who broke early, he did not regard as worthy opponents. What befell his subjects after he had caused them to divulge devastatingly damaging information did not concern the Technician. The game was over then.

THE TECHNICIAN HAD LEARNED to respect Prisoner 313. His failure to break Kane during the earlier interrogation had disappointed him greatly. Having studied 313's file, he was convinced the prisoner was a hothead, whose volatility would prove his weakness. That Kane turned out to be a tough opponent with patience and the ability to move thoughts around in his mind to hide them from the Technician surprised him. Kane seemed to have the ability to deliberately mix up his thoughts in order to confuse his interrogator. Too often the Technician pursued an idea he found in the subject's head only to find himself chasing a falling star into a black hole. The Technician thought Kane was able to sense this confusion on the interrogator's part and capitalize on it. 313 was an admirable opponent and the Technician would need to harness all his skills if he was to bring him down.

The Technician eagerly monitored the information being fed back to him by the Void. After three days, the subject seemed to be holding up well. There appeared to be no serious diminution in his resolve and, unfortunately for the Technician, in the vital area of confidence and self-respect the prisoner was holding the line. The Technician decided to increase the concentration of splinter rays on the subject's inner brain, a move similar in impact to the spaghetti band in its distortion of brain patterns and generally effective in reducing resolve in the subject. He would check later to see if the assault was having the desired effect. Leaving McKenzie to monitor events, the Technician withdrew.

Composing herself in front of the monitoring station, McKenzie lost no time in taking over the system. She first examined the feedback information and immediately set about identifying those areas in which Kane was weakening. To her delight, all signs showed positive returns on the part of the prisoner, though McKenzie noted that a strong concentration of splinter rays was being directed on the inner lobes. McKenzie became alarmed. The security woman was all too well aware of the inevitable consequences of an approach of that kind. If not counteracted, the result would be the disintegration of the prisoner's resolve. McKenzie decided to act fast. Touching the screen to convey a series of commands, she directed a phased application of soovnus rays at the lobes. This intervention would neutralise the effects of the splinter rays and leave the prisoner in more or less the same state as he was before they were applied. Nevertheless, McKenzie realised that if the returns showed no reduction whatsoever in the prisoner's resolve they would arouse suspicion and lead the Technician to a detailed investigation of the circumstances in which that had occurred. In order to allow a limited reduction in resolve but not enough to threaten Kane's survival, the woman placed a time limit of one hour on the application of the soovnus rays. She then sat back to monitor her friend's ordeal, a line of worry on her brow.

ONE OF THE DEVELOPMENTS the Assistant Security Officer noticed was the appearance of pleasure ripples in the left hand area of the subject's brain. A pleasing thought was apparently visiting the prisoner's mind. As the source of the pleasant thought seemed to be the archive area, it was more than likely a memory that was being enjoyed by the prisoner. Instinctively, McKenzie wondered was it to do with her.

Kane was a long way away from Korb-1, however. He was sitting beside a lake in another world with his former friend, lover and accomplice, Sheena Strauss. They were talking and laughing, and Kane was noticing how the sun ran its golden fingers through the young woman's red hair as the pair enjoyed being alive together.

Looking out over the lake, Strauss asked Kane did he want to go for a swim. Kane readily agreed. Then the young woman asked him one of those unexpected questions she often used to spring, questions that made the young man feel uncomfortable: "What would you do if I vanished in the lake, Kevin? Would you look for me?"

The question made the young man uneasy for a moment. Then he replied: "I would search forever until I found you!"

With that, the memory faded from Kane's mind.

McKenzie noticed the change in mood on the monitor.

26 TO THE BRINK

THE TECHNICIAN CARRIED A look of comfortable determination on his face as he entered the Central Security Area. He was eager to examine the returns from the Void monitors to see if his opponent had been weakened enough to be finished off. His first port of call was to check the reading from the inner lobes. Expecting to see a major deterioration in the prisoner's resistance, the Technician looked at the colour graph – it was mostly a pale blue with patches of light red. The Technician was surprised. Having been subject to a continuous attack of splinter rays, the area in question should have been almost totally red by now – the colour assigned to stress. Instead, the predominant colour was blue, the colour of calm.

The first thing the Technician did was check to ensure that the splinter rays had actually been applied and, indeed, the record showed that, not alone had they been applied, but that they were still being directed at the subject. The Technician was perplexed. This level of reaction was unusual and totally unexpected. He thought for a while, experiencing contrasting emotions. His initial reaction was to be disappointed – the high regard in which he held his own ability was being challenged by his apparent inability to assess the opposition properly. Could he be losing his touch? The Technician dismissed that silly thought immediately and looked at the latest development another way. Maybe 313 was, indeed, a worthy opponent? The Technician experienced a slight buzz of excitement at the thought that his talents were now being tested by a formidable adversary. 313 was indeed proving to be a foe worth fighting. He had stood his ground in the standard interrogation during the week and now he was withstanding what was a considerable assault in particularly difficult circumstances. The Technician sensed his adrenalin begin to flow and realised that a stimulating contest lay ahead. Invigorated by the unexpected challenge, he set the system to administer a 30% stronger dose of splinter rays at a faster rate. Satisfied that this adjustment should make all the difference, the Technician sat back to monitor events and choose his moment. Confident that he would soon have the situation under control, he was also aware that he could not continue the process beyond five days, as this was the limit fixed on this form of interrogation by NC statute law. Of course, there were many ways to get around this technicality, but the Technician was aware of his reputation in all of this. He prided himself on getting the job done within the agreed parameters. Asking the authorities to bend the arrangements was an admission that he had failed. The Technician would have to play a good game from now on in.

McKenzie was worried as she watched the Technician scan the returns. She hoped she had not left any loose ends that would lead her senior associate to suspect sabotage. If she had, there would be only one suspect. Immediate indications seemed to suggest the interrogator had not yet considered the possibility of third party intervention. The likelihood was that, although surprised, he would accept the readings produced and take steps to ensure that an extra application was sufficiently strong to have the desired effect. The challenge for the Security Assistant, of course, was to find a way to counteract that. She knew that if she didn't get an opportunity to intervene again soon, Kane would be in big trouble. The question was *how could she do it?*

Oblivious to McKenzie's machinations, Kane floated in the Void like a piece of human space debris, unwanted and unclaimed. Most of the time, his thoughts were of happier times – days and nights when his troubles were far far away – days of golden youth and innocent expectation. But those days were gone and, gradually, as the Technician's latest assault began to take effect, the prisoner's thoughts grew darker and eventually a cloud of doubt began to form in his mind. It began with a memory of his first date with Strauss and a strange feeling that had come over Kane shortly after the pair had entered a restaurant together. He didn't think much of it at the time but remembered thinking about it the next day. When being served by the waiter, a refined shorthaired clean-shaven type, Kane sensed an unease that seemed unwarranted in the young man's behaviour. It was as if the waiter was aware of something going on that Kane had missed. But, enjoying the company as much as he did and intoxicated with Strauss's company, Kane soon forgot the incident and went on to enjoy what turned out to be an extremely pleasant night. When he mentioned all this to Strauss the following morning, all the young woman did was raise her shoulders and throw out her hands, proclaiming "They must have little to do!" When Kane enquired as to who *they* were, the young woman merely replied "Ah, you don't want to meet *them*!" and then proceeded to introduce some other topic into the conversation.

Over the following months, as the liaison between Kane and Strauss developed, for Kane the strange sense of being followed, watched or monitored became almost a permanent feature of the relationship between the two. The feeling of continuously being the subject of some form of remote surveillance almost became acceptable to Kane, who put it down as a feature – albeit an unwelcome one – of his relationship with the unusual young woman. Why it was there at all became almost irrelevant. Strauss had obviously *done something* to warrant this attention, the young man believed, but it was the nature of that attention that concerned Kevin Kane.

Drifting in and out of the past, Kane was grappling with a memory that had been buried deep in his mind until now. It concerned a holiday he had spent with Strauss at an adventure holiday centre in NCR 15 on the west coast. The week had gone very well and Kane and Strauss had a great time. Towards the end of the week, however, a number of unfortunate events occurred which marred an otherwise pleasant stay. First of all, Strauss's consumer card went missing. This was strange as Sheena hadn't taken it out of her pocket bag at all since she arrived, the pair having agreed to pay all the bills off Kane's. Then they noticed that someone had been rummaging around in the Strauss's *prt*, which the couple had been using to travel around the area. Nothing seemed to be missing, but the documents in the left glove, which Strauss kept in a certain order, had been moved around. Then finally, Kane, having left Strauss in the hotel bar in order to leave his disk viewer into the room, was surprised and bundled over by an intruder running out of the room as he opened the door. Shaken, Kane reported the incident to the hotel management and checked the room to see if anything was missing. Nothing seemed to be gone. The strangest aspect of all of this was that Kane thought he had recognised the intruder. He was convinced it was a man who had served the couple in the hotel bar a number of times – a quiet sullen type who didn't speak much. Kane and Strauss volunteered to identify the man from staff files. The hotel manager who dealt with the complaint was shocked and promised to investigate the incident. But that turned out to be the end of the matter. From then on, any time Kane and Strauss sought to speak with the manager to whom they had reported the incident, nobody could find him. Before the couple left, they were told by hotel staff that there was no record of a reported break-in that week and that they must have been the subjects of a practical joke. The bartender concerned was never seen again. Surprisingly, Strauss didn't appear perturbed by these events and advised Kane to "just forget it", as they sat into the *prt* to head home.

While Kane's thoughts and memories wandered through his mind seeking a place to rest, his opponent was preparing his assault. The Technician's approach to his work was thorough. Anything that might be of relevance in pinning down a subject was collated in a database through which the interrogator skimmed with amazing speed and dexterity. The slightest utterance by a subject – no matter how trivial – was cross-referenced in order to identify a context, a link, a weakness to be exploited. When the finale approached – the moment when the Technician sensed his opponent's resolve weakening – the database was utilized in a feverish frenzy, as the interrogator sought to identify the clinical weapon with which to bring his adversary down and claim the prize. Kane was not yet ready to divulge that vital element of information to his tormentor but the Technician was a patient man.

GOING DEEPER INTO HIS memories of his days with Strauss, Kane wondered why the Administration was so interested in her then. If she was only planning her information assault at that stage, two questions arose. First, why the security attention *before* she struck and second, if they were on to her, why didn't the authorities move to prevent her attempt at 'information liberation' as the movement termed making classified information available? Kane struggled with these thoughts in his head in an attempt to identify events that had occurred then and since, and even words that had been spoken, that could someday clarify why events had panned out as they did.

Kane concentrated on the first question first. It had occurred to him during his time with Strauss that the security interest she seemed to excite was unusual in that if the authorities had any doubts about the woman they would hardly allow her to continue to work in an informationally sensitive area. Why would they spend their time spying on someone while at the same time allowing them daily access to information systems that contained a myriad of sensitive files?

The prisoner travelled down many avenues and pathways in his efforts to make sense of his memory of that peculiar time. Some of these paths crossed and crossed again, leaving Kane with a spaghetti-like collection of strands of thought, none of which seemed to bring him to the conclusion he felt he needed so badly to identify. But, like a child playing a game of *trace the line*, he followed his leads one after another until finally he was left holding one thread between his trembling fingers. The realisation that he may have at last solved one of the continuing mysteries in his life unnerved Kane. He knew full well that the answer towards which the thread was leading was not going to be a pleasant one. The prisoner hesitated before following it through.

Kane asked himself one more time. Why were the authorities interested in Strauss and why would they stand back and allow someone they suspected of 'something' to work in a sensitive area, rather than arrest them immediately or at least dismiss them from their position? Kane now sensed that there could only be one logical answer to that question and that that would also provide the explanation for another mystery that had bedevilled the prisoner's mind in his loneliest hours: how come both he and Strauss had been caught so easily, despite their careful preparations?

The answer was becoming clear now: the authorities knew what Strauss was planning from Day-1 – the reason being that she had already carried out this kind of operation before! Strauss had stung the security people already and they weren't going to allow her to do it a second time. They watched her walk into the trap and then pounced, getting Kane into the bargain. The woman was playing with fire, and both she and Kane had got burned.

The realisation that Strauss had been playing on short odds shocked Kane. But if that was true – and it certainly appeared to be the case now – then another chilling realisation had to be confronted: if Strauss knew that she was being monitored because she had stung the regime before, she must have realised that they would be less than enthusiastic about her doing it a second time. In shock, Kane spoke these words slowly and reluctantly in his mind: Strauss must have known that the likelihood of getting away with their intervention was very slight and the possibility of being caught and banished to a korb kolony conversely high. Strauss had not only gambled with her own freedom but with Kane's!

The thought that Strauss had been reckless with their future – *his* future – horrified Kane. How could she have been oblivious to the possibility that the operation she was planning could so easily deprive them of their liberty forever? What was the point of jeopardising everything for an enterprise that could at best only embarrass the regime? How could Strauss have been so blind to the risk she was taking, not only with her own life but with her partner's? Kane struggled with the questions that now filled his mind. Could it possibly be that Kane's partner, the one he had mourned for so long, was the one who was responsible for putting him in jail in the first place?

The other troubling question for Kane was could it be that the face that had haunted him for so long had really been his own? Kane delved deep into the depths of his mind. How could that have been? It *had* been there, watching, staring, spying. He hadn't imagined it. It couldn't have been his own. Kane thought and thought and thought. Gradually the face began to come together again, floating as usual, malformed, ethereal, nebulous. But Kane kept at it. This time he pursued the face, staring back until it began to take a new form. Slowly, it began to change shape, adopting a new appearance until, eventually, it became clear. Kane watched with fascination as the face confronting him was finally revealed – it *was* the bearded novo – 1319!

Kane's heart began to race as he realised he had unmasked the figure that had been in the shadows during all that time – the one who had most probably betrayed the two young idealists in the prime of their lives. And now he was here – here on Korb-1 – to continue his dirty work. But he was unmasked at last, and retribution would not be far away. Vengeance would be swift and sure, and delivered by the prisoner's own hand.

Monitoring events on the outside, the Technician's face betrayed a slight smile. The colour modulation on the scanner was moving to a distinctly prominent red. Kane was succumbing and possibilities were opening up. The Technician's spirits rose.

McKenzie was becoming alarmed. The Technician had been plying his trade unhindered for well over four hours and the inevitability was that sooner or later his subject would succumb to the assault. When that happened, anything was possible. A confession that would leave Kane deprived of any privileges and render him useless in bringing down the kolony was a possibility. So was the chance that he would confess to something of a serious nature that could even lead to his execution. The possibility that he could implicate *her* was not far from her mind either as she observed the Technician at work and wondered how she could prevent him driving home the fatal blow.

Slowing down the process so that the interrogator ran out of time was the most effective way of preventing him retrieving anything of use from the process, but McKenzie felt she had already shot her bolt on that one and that, with only three hours left, the opportunity to do so again was unlikely to arise.

McKenzie thought hard and racked her brain. Maybe there was a way ......

As Kane began to talk, albeit initially in an incoherent fashion, the Technician sensed that at last the game was on.

"Strauss ..... Strauss .... How could she? .... Why did she? .... Throw away our lives for nothing? How? How?"

Rapidly consulting his database, the Technician decided to intervene.

"She did it for the cause....... Not for you, for the cause...... You were just a tiny pawn in a bigger game............... You were dispensable!" he whispered in a pseudo-sympathetic voice into the button microphone.

The Technician's words were received in the prisoner's ears via a transmitter that fed sound into the subject's head at will, controlling the tone, volume and speed of the input.

Kane didn't respond to the intervention, but continued to verbalise his realisation of possible betrayal by someone he had always believed to be beyond reproach.

"How could she?.................... Only a pawn, only a pawn .... How could she? Only a pawn ...."

As the Technician prepared for what he expected to be the final battle in his campaign with Prisoner 313, Assistant Security Officer McKenzie was on her way back to the Void Resource Room. Although the use of the facility was under the sole control of the interrogator, the chemical, medical and environmental resources were stored in the VRR. So, while the interrogator controlled the use of these support elements, the elements themselves were situated in, and could be accessed only in, the VRR. Entering the room, McKenzie was fully aware that what she had to do was a gamble that could backfire and have fatal consequences for the prisoner in the Void.

The Technician could barely subdue his glee at the turn of events. Prisoner 313 was as clear as a lark as he openly revealed out the innermost thoughts in his mind. Accepting the carefully introduced comments of his interrogator, he was soon responding to a comment here and a word there to the extent that his thoughts were being skilfully manipulated and directed down a path chosen by his enemy.

"McKenzie wasn't the only one to treat you as a pawn, was she? .... Nevin takes you're for an absolute fool .... Why doesn't he respect you, anyway? .... Does he think you're not trustworthy? What is it?"

"Nevin .... Nevin .... We'll find out what he's made of soon enough .... soon .... He'll have to show what he's made of."

"Will he look for your opinion, though? He seems to take you for a fool ...... why? ...... Who does he think he is, anyway?"

"I'll show Nevin .... He's supposed to be the leader ..... but where is he leading us? .... Nowhere .... Nowhere!"

"But what can he do? .... He has no plan and no support............ What can he do? .... He's on his own."

"He's not on his own .... He's not ...."

The Technician stiffened as he realised that 313 was about to venture into what could be a fertile area for his interrogator.

"But who has he got? .... He's no support .... He hasn't," the Technician declared challengingly.

"Yes, he has", Kane confirmed, "Yes, he has."

McKenzie had to work fast. Judging by the vocal interactions she was monitoring, things could unravel rapidly if she didn't intervene soon. Uncovering the valve outlets for the main intrusive gases that were released into the atmosphere of the Void by the interrogator, she loosened them, one by one. This was a simple enough task but it did involve a high degree of fine judgement. It was totally up to McKenzie to decide how much higher she could inflate the inputs so that Kane's life signs became unstable, but at the same time ensuring that the situation wasn't allowed to get out of control.

Looking at the screen, McKenzie tried hard to concentrate in order to make the correct decision in each case. One by one, the output valves were adjusted until finally McKenzie stood back to overview what she done and hope that the consequences for Kane would not be fatal. In the back of her mind, however, she was aware that if matters had been allowed to continue in the direction they were going, the consequences would not alone be fatal for the prisoner but for her as well. Kane's life had to be gambled. If not, then both lives were at stake. Her intervention complete, McKenzie returned to the Void Monitor Station.

McKenzie was nervous when she returned to the VMS but the Technician was too immersed in what he was sure was the final assault to notice. He was feverishly manipulating his database and feeding more leading information to his subject in the Void. Many of his interventions produced responses. All of the responses were fed into the database and produced more suggested interventions. Although more than a few produced blanks, the Technician was pleased with the general direction in which the exercise was going. Aware of the time factor, he moved with speed to carefully construct a dialogue in which revealing information might emerge. McKenzie's heart stopped on hearing the Technician's latest intervention.

"What have you got that Nevin hasn't? .... Surely he's a leader and you're not?"

"We'll see", Kane replied, reluctant to attack his theoretical leader.

"But let's be honest .... He's a leader and you're not .... That's the truth of it, isn't it?" the Technician suggested.

"He hasn't got what I've got ...."

The Technician impatiently awaited a further comment but none came. McKenzie tensed in her chair at this latest turn in the dialogue. Was Kane about to spill the beans and reveal her efforts to support his escape? Tensed, she watched the vital signs returns to see if her latest intervention was taking effect. Levels were falling across the board.

"Maybe he has, though?" the Technician suggested. "What could you possibly have that a leader like Nevin hasn't? .... Let's be realistic here!"

The Technician waited for a reaction, anxious to move his subject further towards the abyss. The seasoned campaigner smelt blood. McKenzie feared that Kane was about to cave in. Observing the vital signs readings, she saw that they were still heading down. Immediately, she logged a vital signs warning on the system. Taken aback, the Technician checked his monitor. Vital sign warnings were there. Deciding immediately to ignore them, the Technician intervened again, sensing that something valuable was about to emerge.

"You have nothing, Kane. .... Isn't that right? .... "You have nothing ...."

"Haven't I?" Kane asked in response, this time his breath heavy as the pressure on his mind and body rose to a new high.

McKenzie logged a vital signs warning again. The Technician scowled in her direction, all the time his fingers bouncing on his touch screen like demonically possessed digits on a ouija board.

"I don't think you have", the Technician replied in a sympathetic tone, "He's a leader, you're not."

Silence.

The Technician awaited a reply, like a snake waiting for the right time to pounce on its prey.

Silence.

McKenzie awaited the next move, her heart pounding like a drum in her ears.

"I'll tell you what I have", came Kane's feeble reply. .... I'll tell you what *I* have ...."

The Technician waited, his eyes concentrating on the monitoring screen.

McKenzie looked once more at the vital signs readings. They were heading down too low.

The Security Assistant hit the warning button a third time. Again, the Technician ignored her and continued.

"Tell me!" he asked in a reassuring voice.

As the Technician uttered his invitation to Kane to share his secret, the time signal on the monitoring system emitted a slow continuous beep. The statutory interrogation period had passed.

"Tell me!" the Technician asked again.

McKenzie looked at the vital signs monitor once more. The red lights of the monitor reflected in her eyes. Kane's life was in danger. The young woman jumped to her feet.

"Stop! Stop now!" she demanded.

The Technician turned to glare coldly at the Assistant Security Officer.

"This man's life is in danger", she roared, in an effort to bring the Technician to his senses. "You can't continue!"

The Technician cast his eyes over the monitor one more time, like a wild animal reluctant to accept that his prey was about to escape.

McKenzie continued: "We must get this prisoner to the medics immediately. Anyway, our time is up. You will need a new certificate to continue.

The Technician sat back dejectedly in his chair and stared blankly through the glass at his luminous subject floating slowly in the darkness of the Void. MacKenzie left, rushing to the VRR to return the support element inputs to default. The game was over.

27 THE DARK KORB SKY

A TYRON ON EACH SIDE held Kane's arms to keep him on his feet. The prisoner was groggy as the escort accompanied him out of the Security Area and back to his cell. Feeling physically sore as a throbbing headache filled his skull, Kane was till relieved to be released, particularly as he was certain his adversary hadn't managed to extract any meaningful information from him. On arrival at his cell, Kane stumbled inside and the tyron escort departed.

Lying on his bunk, Kane thought of his ordeal at the hands of the Technician, particularly in the Void. Despite his satisfaction at not having divulged any information that could be of use to the Administration, he was disturbed at the ease with which his interrogator had managed to penetrate his mind. Kane felt as if his innermost emotions had been violated by the skilful questioner. It was as if a stranger's eye had peered into an area that should never have been revealed. He felt ashamed that his personal feelings, down to the very detail of his relationship with his parents, had been defiled by an intruder – an enemy. The prisoner experienced a combination of shame and anger, but also a sense of relief that he had managed to conceal the information the Technician really wanted to know.

Staring deep into the darkness above his head, Kane was unaware that his experience was not unique and that a number of prisoners had been taken in the swoop. However, it took the arrival of Dayton to apprise him of the scale and extent of the arrests.

"Molumphy, Bennor, Martin, Puzedski, Cassini .... Al-sari, French, McGrath .... dozens were brought in. They'll all being released now – but God knows what the Regime has learned from all of this. Novo 1319 was arrested in one of the Generation Chambers. Seemingly it took an almighty struggle to take him in. Apparently, the tyrons were out to get him after he rubbed their noses in it. It took nearly twenty of them to get him and then only after he had been trapped under a feeder belt. Only the intervention of the crew saved his bacon, the tyrons wanted him so bad."

Kane considered the significance of all this. 1319! The spy whom he had believed had engineered his banishment to Korb-1 and ruined his life! It was obviously a stunt – just like the novo's attempt to gain his confidence in the incident in the corridor. The regime had realised that Kane was on to their man and had constructed an elaborate hoax in order to 'arrest' him and get him out of circulation. The bastards! They were even going to deny Kane the satisfaction of revenge!

As well as all that, if the regime had interrogated so many people, they must have gained at least some useful information. If they had, well then the chances were that they had some knowledge of the planned revolt. Time would tell – but, on this abandoned rock, on whose side was the clock ticking?

Dayton interrupted Kane's thoughts: "I'll leave you to relax and recover. I know it'll take time. Back to work in the morning, of course. Maybe we'll talk then."

Dayton left the cell with a wave of his left hand and left the prisoner to ponder the meaning of this burst of activity by the kolony administration. 'What about Nevin?' Kane wondered. 'Had he been taken too?' Because of his status amongst the prisoners, Kane didn't think the Administration would drag Nevin in – not unless they really had to. Warts and all, Nevin was the leader of the prisoners in the kolony – even the Regime itself accepted that. Soon, however, Nevin would have to show his hand and there would be no going back then – for anyone!

His mind racked with post-interrogation trauma and guilt, floating in a continuous void of uncertainty, the prisoner fell into a disturbed asleep.

NOVO 1319 WALKED DEJECTEDLY towards the Security Area, surrounded by tyrons and led by Kommander Krantz. Krantz walked arrogantly with his prize, like a cat with a mouse, proudly bringing it back to its master to show what a great hunter he was. There had been an air of uncertainty and even tension in the kolony recently. Things were happening that shouldn't be happening in a well-run prison. People were missing, prisoners were challenging the authority of the regime, mysterious deaths were taking place, and rebellion was in the air. Krantz was of the view that Kontroller Windsor's analysis of the situation was right – the Master's leadership was too soft. He was giving the wrong signals to the prisoners. Lenience breeds insolence, he had been told in the Security Academy, but the Master wouldn't understand that – he had no real security experience at all. Despite his misgivings, however, Krantz would say nothing just yet. Windsor could do the running on that. If he succeeded, he would need trusted lieutenants, if he failed he would be on his own.

It was well into KC10-1's midnight period as Kane's Korb-1 night began to fall. The prisoner still lay on his bed, resting his weary body and soul, and attempting to see the future through the thick korb cloud that hung threateningly over his head. The burst of intense security activity by the Administration was unexpected. Maybe there was an informer amongst the conspirators, there always was in these situations – very little could be done about that. On the other hand, perhaps the clampdown was the result of the disappearance of the Ferret. It was an open secret that the Ferret was a controlled creature that did his owner's bidding and that spying for the Administration was the only thing he had going for him. But was he that important?

Kane drifted in and out of sleep, thinking as he did on his options for the future. The revolt would have to proceed, but did the Administration already know too much? Perhaps the conspirators' plans should be shelved until the heat died down? Maybe the opportunity had already passed? Initially, Kane felt he should talk to Nevin and see what he made of all this. On reflection, however, he decided not to approach him just yet. Immediate contact between the two men would be monitored and taken as confirmation of a conspiracy involving them both. Kane would be patient and wait.

In the L+S Area, a tough game of hurling-ball was taking place. It was a robust encounter with no quarter given – and none asked. Despite the intense nature of the competition, the players couldn't but notice the presence of an unusually high number of tyrons, a presence that created an air of tension usually absent from such events. The tyrons looked on grimly as the game progressed, none of them displaying any great interest in the action on the field of play. Rather they watched in vain for any signs of subversion. Had they watched a little more closely, however, they would have noticed that the close encounters were a little more frequent and slightly slower than what one would have been accustomed to see.

As the ball bounced into no man's land between the two teams, Kelvin, a large stocky man from KC7-3, with a light black beard, and Jarvic, a tall thin fair-haired type from GC8-3, raced together to gather it. Kelvin shouldered his opponent. Jarvic shouldered him back.

"Have you been talking to Nevin?" the bearded man asked.

"He doesn't want anything to happen yet", his opponent replied.

"When?" Kelvin enquired.

"When things cool down, he says", was the reply.

Kelvin swung the ball away from Jarvic with an adept flick of his stick.

MANY AEONS AWAY, LYING on a bunk in a lonely Korb-1 cell, prisoner 313 was a tired and lonely man. Looking back over his life, it appeared that he was destined to be a loner. All of those who had ever been close to him had been hurt by the experience. The Technician may have been trying to weaken his resolve, but there was some substance in what he was implying. The faces of those who had meant so much to him floated in front of his mind's eye, reminding him of happier times, times when the past and the present combined to promise a future of content. In Kane's life, those times had never lasted long, and the faces that passed before him were a reminder of that. Any moment of happiness in the prisoner's life had almost always turned to tragedy – this was a fact that he found it hard to deny.

Maybe, someday, Kane's fortunes would turn. With Strauss and later with Thorsen, he had believed a new beginning was possible in his life. They were full of the hope and confidence that he had always felt himself to lack. They had a vision of their own future, and they had a hand in writing the script. That their futures had turned out to be as bleak as his own was an obvious fact that escaped Kane's torturous examination of conscience. To him, they were bold, daring individuals, brave enough to look the future in the eye and challenge it to single combat. Their lives would always be an inspiration to prisoner 313. It was for them, as much as to vindicate himself, that he would survive Korb-1 and someday leave it all behind.

Overhead, the perpetual purple korb sky loomed threateningly. The prisoner sensed its intrusive presence and felt as if it was watching him and reading to his every thought. Even though he couldn't see it from his cell, he sensed that it could always see him. He felt its cold vicious eye focused on him at all times – listening, watching, stalking. Its eternal eye was a continuous presence in his mind, sometimes making the hair on the back of his neck stand on end. It cast a dark cloud on his life on Korb-1, a cloud that would never clear, a cloud that made its presence felt every minute of the prisoner's day and night. Thorsen had been the sun that had shone for so long during his years on the kolony, brightening the atmosphere with her positive glare and leaving the cruel korb sky in the background. Now, with her light extinguished, the dark ether was in control again.

Drifting asleep, Kane thought he heard the slight *beep* of a message coming in on his computer. Taking a few seconds to become fully conscious again, he opened his eyes and jumped from his bunk. The prisoner dropped into the chair in front of the pc. Orange letters floated across the screen "Hello – you alright?" was the welcome message.

28 RED

KANE SAT ALERT, EAGERLY watching the monitor before him. Contact! "Hello – you alright?" McKenzie wasn't just a pre-interrogational dream, after all! She was for real. And the recent spate of arrests hadn't frightened her either – she hadn't run away. Heartened by McKenzie's concern about his welfare after his ordeal, Kane felt a real boost to his confidence as he placed his hands on the keyboard His fingers moved swiftly as he replied: "Just about! My head needs to be tightened on again though!"

"It always seemed well screwed-on to me", McKenzie replied, reassuring.

"Screwed-*up* now, maybe!" Kane replied humbly.

"Don't think about it", the soundless voice advised, "walk away as if it never happened. They want you to feel low, to feel violated. They want you keep their dark and dirty little thoughts in your head. Just close the door on it – think about brighter things – the things that make you happy. If you can do that, then they've failed."

Kane thought for a moment. What McKenzie said made sense. At the end of the day, if he kept them out of his mind, they couldn't influence his actions. If he ignored what they were trying to do to him, then mentally he would be in a position to survive. Kane appreciated the advice.

"I'll try – thanks!" Then he added: "When can we meet?"

"It's going to be dangerous to make contact for a while", McKenzie warned, "but I'll do my best. We'll have to let things settle a bit first."

"It's up to you", Kane signalled, eager not to pressurise.

"Keep a low profile for a while – they're still watching you. And don't make contact with anyone suspicious! One mistake could be fatal now. .... Maybe we'll have a game tonight. It would be good to ease the tension."

"O.K. I'll be here!" Kane replied.

As the screen returned to its green blue mist, Kane felt a degree of disappointment that McKenzie hadn't agreed to an earlier meeting. Although he realised that avoiding contact in the immediate future was probably the most sensible approach at this stage, he couldn't escape the feeling that another meeting would help to move things forward, particularly after he had had a chance to study the Kolony Plan.

Kane sat back in his chair, peering deep into the recesses of his mind. His left hand rubbed the stubble on his chin as he turned his entire experience over in his head. It was strange, he thought, how there always seemed to be an inspirational woman in his life who guided him through the tougher terrain when his resilience was ebbing. First there was Strauss, then there was Thorsen, now there was McKenzie. But, in many ways, McKenzie had still to be really tested. Unlike the other two, she hadn't travelled through the firewall yet. Maybe she would, but then again maybe she would let him down.

Maybe the whole thing was a charade, carefully constructed to let him down big time. Maybe it was the Master's pet project. He still couldn't be sure. Granted, McKenzie *appeared* to be genuine – and her words were certainly reassuring – but maybe she was just a good actor. Maybe there was no end to the resources the regime had at its disposal to infiltrate the minds of its victims. One thing was clear in *his* mind, however – he was determined to find out.

Novo 1319 sat on the wire waiting for the game to begin. He didn't appear too worried at the prospect of a grilling from the regime's notorious Information Technician. If anything he looked relaxed as his interrogator entered the chamber.

"Pedersen! You look pleased to see me!" the Technician remarked as he approached the prisoner.

1319 ignored the figure in the brown uniform of the security service, though the unwelcome familiarity unnerved him a bit. The Technician noted the response as he made his way towards his control chair.

"I notice they've fitted you up for me. That should save time."

The prisoner still ignored the dark figure while sensing the suggestion of threat in his seemingly innocent comment. The Technician sat down in the interrogator's chair.

"Oh, I'm bored today, Pedersen. Life sometimes gets drab here, doesn't it?"

1319 remained silent.

"Anyway", the Technician continued, "life must go on, mustn't it – and we must do our work, mustn't we? You, producing korb. Me … well …." The Technician's voice tailed off, leaving the thought swinging in the wind in his subject's mind.

Pedersen settled himself for the impending session. He know things were going to become uncomfortable. But he was ready. After a considerable silence, the Technician began. "Well, Pedersen, are we ready – we've so much to get through. Where should we start, do you think?"

The captive didn't reply, merely listening intently for an indication of what was going to happen next. He steeled his nerves once more. "Maybe with your earlier days ....Tell me about Kennedy?"

1319 was taken aback. Stunned. Kennedy! God! How could he bring Kennedy up so soon? 1319's body temperature suddenly lowered.

Balancing on the wire, the prisoner's mind swept back many years to his youth in NC City 12 of NCR 41. It was around ten o'clock on a Saturday night in mid-summer and there was a clammy heat as he and all the other young bloods in NCC 12 were gathered at the Dree Memorial in the centre of the town, throwing back alcohol tablets and playing their music disks loud. It was a fun night like any other, the usual antics going on. Murphy, Tom Pedersen's best friend, was doing his regular party-piece of pretending to make love to the memorial and his boisterous colleagues were egging him on. Pedersen was clapping his hands in encouragement when suddenly he noticed two new girls had joined the group. One of them had short black hair and wasn't too tall. The other had roaring red hair and a freckly nose – that was Pedersen's first view of the Margaret Kennedy, 'Red' to her friends. Pedersen felt a cool breeze against his face.

"Ring a bell?" the Technician wondered, dragging the prisoner back to his unpleasant present.

1319 didn't reply. He knew what was going to come next.

PEDERSEN WAS IMMEDIATELY ATTRACTED to Kennedy. There was something about her that made him want to be with her all the time. She seemed to reciprocate but always carried an air of aloofness that even he sometimes found it hard to penetrate. They soon became a team, however, and after that the Dree Gang, as they were known, wasn't complete without the eager young Pedersen and his confident vivacious companion. Although the pair were regular attendees at the Gang's events for a number of months, they eventually realised that they each preferred the exclusive company of the other rather than the frenetic goings-on of the Gang. Soon Saturday nights were spent, not at the Dree Memorial with the Gang, but elsewhere. Kennedy had a particular interest in nature and liked to spend long hours observing the surviving species of birds in NCR 41. It wasn't long before Pedersen was enticed into participating in these expeditions and soon learned to enjoy a feature of the environment to which he had previously been blind.

Kennedy had a link with the Earth that Pedersen had never really felt and, as he got to know his new companion, the young man had a sense of learning something new about himself and his place in the natural world. It was a far cry from the buffoonery of the Dree Gang and the young man felt as if he was maturing, becoming somebody new. Soon the two young ornithologists were almost inseparable, their trips outside the city becoming regular events.

Anytime Red's parents were out of town, the two young people would enjoy one another's company in their house. Pedersen liked being alone with Kennedy. He liked her composed style – the way she seemed to have it all together. The two would share theories on the origins of the universe, the concept of time, the possibility of time travel and a myriad of other challenging subjects. Kennedy would never bring Pedersen to her house when her parents were there and, as a result, the young man had no idea what they were like. When he asked her what they did for a living, he was told they both worked for the Administration and that they were fairly well paid.

After more than a year together, Pedersen was sure that his relationship with Kennedy was the best thing that had ever happened to him. He no longer hung around with the Dree Gang and lived every day waiting to meet Red as soon as they had both finished work, him in NC College of Aeronautics and her in NC College of Physics. Although they rarely discussed their own future together, Pedersen felt they had a kind of understanding that they were meant to be together.

It was in the late summer of their second year with one another that an incident occurred that was to change their lives forever. They were out in the Corn Fields, an area southwest of the city where most of the sectors cereal requirements were produced. It was a golden sunny day and an expansive blue sky crowned the crusty brown of the abundant crop that stretched out in every direction as far as the eye could see. Kennedy and Pedersen were looking for rare birds that Kennedy had catalogued in the region, but not having any luck in spotting them. After a long trek through the crops, they decided to lie down and rest. The sun's heat warmed their eager bodies as they lay together amongst the tall strong stalks of wheat making love. It was a perfect day and, after a session of youthful passion, they both fell asleep. Kennedy was the first to wake and nudged her companion, who awoke to see the sun getting low. As Pedersen began to talk, his companion placed her hand over his mouth and nodded her head to draw his attention to something. The young man stopped and listened. He could hear voices in the distance. They both listened intently. There seemed to be three individual voices, all talking in an excited manner. The two young people looked at each other as if unsure as to what they should do. Peeping out through the stalks, they saw three individuals – two in NC security uniform, the other in casual civvies – in animated conversation. Pedersen and Kennedy's facial expressions suggested that they both agreed they should stay put and not make their presence known. They listened awhile as the voices got louder – the word 'baggage' was being mentioned a lot, but the rest wasn't too clear. They decided to get closer. Crawling through the stalks in the direction of the commotion, the two were careful not to move the corn and attract attention. Along the way, Kennedy spotted a particularly large beetle and pointed it out to Pedersen, smiling. When the two got close enough to the scene of the altercation, they stopped.

"I'm only going to ask you one more time!" one of the security personnel, a large man with a tight haircut and a big round face, roared at the civilian – "Where's the baggage?"

"Look, I already told you it was left in the usual place. There was nothing unusual about this drop. I don't understand why it wasn't there when he arrived to collect it", the civilian replied turning his head in the direction of the other security man.

"Was it there?" the angry one asked of his security colleague, his eyebrows raised to indicate disbelief.

"No!" the other replied, shaking his head.

The civilian, a thin man with drawn unhealthy features, looked at the others, with a defensive expression on his face. The animated one raised his eyebrows again and, looking the thin man straight in the eye, said slowly "Last chance!"

The thin man appeared to be lost for words. Holding his open palms out, he shrugged his shoulders. The noisy one moved his head, adjusting his sun visor as he casually cast a glance around him. Then suddenly, without warning, he produced a small *fencer* weapon from under his sleeve and fired a blast straight into the face of the unsuspecting man in front of him. The civilian slumped to the ground, dead. In the brief few seconds after the blast was fired, the second security man looked at his companion.

"Why did you sear him? Now we'll never know what happened!" he bellowed.

"It was him or us", the man with the fencer calmly replied.

"What are you talking about?" the second man countered, "What's Walker going to say now?"

While the second man argued and gesticulated, the big man began to search the victim on the ground. The dead man appeared to be carrying very little. The card to his *ptv* was all the big man discovered. "Look, he wasn't even armed!" the second man exclaimed, his tight crop of black hair failing to hold back a stream of perspiration. "Walker will have your balls for beads for this!" he declared.

Suddenly the big man stopped and, looking the other in the eye, said calmly: "Hey, look, he had a searer after all!"

The second man froze, sensing that something was wrong. The big man produced a second *fencer* from his back pocket. The second man stood back. "Wait a minute!" he pleaded, his eyes moving nervously from the big man to the *fencer* and back. Tzzzz! The big man released a shot from the *fencer* and, without as much as a sigh, the second man fell to the ground, crushing the corn stalks that attempted to break his fall.

"Aw, pity I didn't get him before he got you!" the big man exclaimed, with an insincere drawl.

Kennedy and Pedersen looked at one another as the blood froze in their veins.

29 AFTER THE CORN FIELD

K ORB CHAMBER 10 WAS unusually subdued this morning. Although, with Kane's release, the KC10-1 team was now intact and seemed to have survived the recent spate of arrests, there was a sense that the purges might not yet be over and that a difficult period lay ahead. For most of the prisoners, life on Korb-1 had been monotonous and repetitious. The continual shifts in the chambers and the almost claustrophobic atmosphere on the kolony created a sense of tedium that was only dispelled by the social activities pursued by the prisoners. A good game of spaceball or squash or hurling-ball in the L+S and the high-spirited banter engaged in by the prisoners in the Dining Hall, in their cells and in the korb chambers were the only mechanisms the prisoners had to allay the darker, more negative, effects of life on the kolony. The recent burst of activity by the security forces had threatened the thread of order that ran through the prisoners' lives and endangered their sense of having, at least in some respects, a normal, healthy existence on Korb-1. The activities of the tyron snatch squads were an unwelcome reminder that the prisoners on the kolony would always be at the mercy of their jailors. This thought was enough to render transparent the veil of normality covering everyday life on Korb-1. In the back of their minds, the prisoners of KC10-1 were well aware of that depressing fact.

1319 SAT ON THE wire, staring in front of him, his mind's eye focused on a face he had once thought he could not live without.

"Yes", the Technician continued, "Kennedy – now there was an interesting lady!"

1319 heard the Technician's voice as if it was a long distance away, maybe even as far away as the scene he could now see unfolding in his memory. Thinking back now, his most immediate recollection of the incident in the cornfields was the dry smell of the soil and the corn as they bleached in the sun. This dryness had almost overcome himself and Kennedy as they lay together that afternoon. When the two young people knelt amongst the stalks having witnessed two dreadful murders, the dryness intensified, to such an extent that it almost desiccated them to their very innards. Like parched prisoners in a cell, the two stared at one another, hoping the other would know what to do and would make the right call. To both of them, it appeared that the safest thing to do was to remain where they were and not to budge until the murderer had left the scene. Sweat rolled down their bodies as they knelt amongst the corn stalks and the dry heat swelled their throats and tongues.

For what seemed like an eternity, they crouched in amongst the stalks, afraid that the slightest move would give them away. Pedersen decided to peep through the stalks to see if the big man was gone. He wasn't. Standing beside the bodies of his victims, he seemed calm and totally composed as he looked around to see if there were any witnesses to his foul deeds. Then, bending down beside the second security officer, he went through the victim's pockets, examining the contents closely before standing up again. His work done, the murderer again surveyed the immediate area before scanning the horizon in every direction. Then he raised his communicator to his mouth and roared in a feigned voice of breathless terror: "407! 407! Officer down! Officer down! Cornfields, south-west NC12! Officer down!" Having listened to the response to his call-in, he replied: "Shooter down too! Shooter down! Site secured! Ok, will do!" After disconnecting, the fat man sat back on the bonnet of the *ptv* and relaxed in the sun.

Both Pedersen and Kennedy sensed that the appalling event wasn't over yet. Security were obviously on their way and would soon be scouring the area. In whispers, they both drew the same conclusion – nobody in security would take their word against an officer and they would probably end up regretting ever getting involved. Having agreed it was time to leave, the two moved as quickly as they could without drawing attention and, eventually, after what felt like an endless crawl through the corn stalks, were safely ensconced on their electric speed bikes and leaving the scene of the crime in their wake.

"Yes, an interesting lady", the Technician continued. "Interesting, but slightly pre-occupied – don't you think?"

1319 remained silent, still reeling at the re-appearance of a face he hadn't seen for the last four years – and would never see again. Despite his concentration on the interrogation, nothing could have prepared him for this.

"Yes, pre-occupied – obsessed, even. Don't you think?"

The novo said nothing, preferring to immerse himself in remembrances of times past. It was only a few short years ago that he waved goodbye to Kennedy for what was to be the last time. Having made their way out of the cornfield, the pair sped as fast as they could to a quiet location, well away from the scene of the terrible crime they had witnessed. There they wondered what they would do next. Should they report the incident to the security services? How could they? It was a member of the security services that had committed the crime. If they reported what they saw to them, they could become the next targets. It was then Kennedy revealed that her parents were connected to the security services. Pedersen was surprised, but only mildly. He had always felt her parents were secretive, even reclusive. In fact, he had only seen them once and that was when they were getting into their *ptv* to leave for a few days as he was arriving early to see their daughter.

Kennedy decided she would tell her parents what she had seen. They would come with a plan to report the murders. They might be able to have the matter investigated without endangering their daughter's life. Once reported, the situation could easily get out of control, though – they both knew that. For that reason, Red told Pedersen she wouldn't mention his presence in the cornfield at all and would pretend she had been there alone. If anything went wrong, Pedersen would still be safe. The young man didn't like the plan at first, believing it to be cowardly of him to allow his companion to endanger herself alone, but Kennedy insisted, assuring him that she would be safe because of her family's security connections and that, anyway, if anything happened to her, he would be free to take whatever action was necessary. The young man reluctantly agreed.

THE SUBDUED ATMOSPHERE THAT had prevailed in the korb chambers was evident in the Dining Hall. Nevin and Kenning sat down to dine with two of their colleagues who were about to begin their KC shift.

"How do you think the production of korb is progressing this year?" enquired one of them, as the four sat at a table in a corner of the seating area.

Nevin smiled. "We're always anxious to reach our targets in the kolony", he replied, understanding the code perfectly, "even if it takes a while to get there."

"How long will it take to achieve them eventually, do you think?" asked the young man, whose eyebrows matched his bright yellow hair.

"There's no point in expecting to maximise production until all the resources are available", Nevin replied, raising his eyebrows and looking the young man in the eye in order to emphasise his point. The questioner understood and left the matter there. There would be no uprising until everything was ready and there was a real chance of success. He would pass that message on to his people in KC39-3.

There was silence for a while as all those around appeared to consider the seriousness of the challenge they would eventually face. So many things had to come right, Nevin thought, as he sat moving his korb kolony kurry around on his dish. It only needed one thing to go wrong and there would be disaster – and the stakes were very high. Nevin felt the weight of responsibility for so many lives lying heavily on his shoulders. It wasn't a burden that was easy to carry. As silence reigned, it appeared to Nevin that everybody around the table was being troubled by the same heavy thoughts as him.

"Anyway," said Nevin, trying to escape from his sombre thoughts, "how are your guys getting on? You've more than your share of novos, I hear."

"Yup", the yellow-haired man's companion ventured. "They don't seem too eager to learn the ropes." Nevin smiled. "Not that I blame them!", the young man added. Laughter all round.

"Hmm – not bad!" the yellow-haired man emitted a sound of pleasure as he finished his plate of spaghetti. "By the way", he continued, "how's your hologram going? I believe it's mega!"

"It's getting there", Nevin replied, casting a good-humoured glance at Kenning. She forced a smile.

"When are we all going to see it?" the bearded man asked. "It sounds fascinating."

"All will be revealed in good time, won't it, Karen?" Nevin announced.

"Sure!" was Kenning's brief reply.

IN THE CONTROL UNIT, the sound engineers sat watching panels of video screens. Faces from all over the kolony appeared before their eyes. Nevin, Kenning, the yellow-haired man, the bearded man and others filled the screens, their lip movements monitored and verbalised into screen script as they spoke. The engineers were totally silent, assiduously reading the titles that appeared before their eyes continuously. It was their duty to monitor and interpret every word and log anything that might be useful to Kolony Security. This was done by simply touching a button as soon as something questionable was said. The dubious sequence and the time it was uttered, down to the last millisecond, would be noted immediately.

As Nevin and his companions discussed the production of korb, the technicians watched the screen intently. One of them, his black tunic a perfect fit, screwed up his eyes to focus on the faces of the subjects as they spoke. When Nevin arched his eyebrows to end his discussion on korb production with the yellow-haired man, the operative, with a sense of satisfaction, hit the logging button.

High on the wire, 1319 hovered perilously between an uncertain future and an equally unpleasant past. The Technician carefully monitored the changes in his subject's wave patterns, waiting for the right time to intervene. But 1319 was far away, remembering a face, a beautiful face – as beautiful as it was the last time he had kissed Margaret Kennedy goodbye.

It was a nervous time, a time of great worry and uncertainty. Pedersen was very much aware that witnessing two murders was bad enough but seeing them committed by a member of the security police was about as serious as it got. The idea that Red and he could avoid the consequences of what they saw now seemed so naive. Two innocent young people in the wrong place at the wrong time. Two innocent young people who couldn't walk away. Two innocent young people whose lives would never be the same again.

At first, Pedersen thought that maybe things would work out alright. Kennedy had told her parents and they had warned her not to say a word to a soul. Although obviously concerned, they didn't seem to be alarmed. After a few days, Pedersen called Kennedy on her *per-com*. She assured him everything was under control – but it wasn't.

A few days later, Kennedy rang to say that her parents had been called away on an assignment. They would be back in three days. Pedersen wanted to meet but Kennedy said it would be too dangerous until things blew over. It would be a month or more before they could be sure. Pedersen was perplexed. Uncertainty for a few days was bad enough – for a month or more, it would be intolerable. But he had no choice.

Almost a week passed and no word from Kennedy – not a whisper – and no response on her *per-com*. Pedersen couldn't bear the pressure anymore. He decided to go across the city to Kennedy's place. As the young man drove down Trans-City Passage 4, the sweat rolled down his temples. Using the cuff of his tunic, he wiped it off, but it still came pouring.

Soon, the perspiration was gathering on his eyebrows and eventually rolling into his eyes, like tears.

The Kennedys lived in a well-to-do part of town. Theirs was one of the bigger homes in the Lyndon Estate, a collection of luxurious houses built less than ten years previously. Driving slowly down the tree-lined roads, Pedersen watched anxiously for a sign of anything unusual. There was nothing.

Arriving at Lyndon Drive, the young man parked his *ptv* around the corner, deciding to take a cautious approach. Although his concern for Red drove him on, a voice in his head told him he shouldn't go any further. But, as he would do again and again in his troubled life, the young man ignored the warnings and kept going, his heart pounding in his chest. Turning the corner, Pedersen saw a posse of security vehicles at Kennedy's home. Most of the personnel were standing around talking, but two more came rushing out of the house just as he arrived at the corner. Pedersen's heart stopped – something serious had happened. At that moment, he felt an overpowering sense of loss, knowing full well that Red had paid the price for what they had reluctantly witnessed on their last sunny day together. He felt guilty that he had left her to carry their terrible secret alone.

30 REVEALING THE PICTURE

PEDERSEN'S LIFE AFTER LOSING Kennedy was to become a long chase – a dangerous hunt with him as the prey and agents of the security services as the hunters. Standing outside her house that evening, the young man realised that his life was about to change dramatically and that things would never be the same again. Powerful forces that operated *behind* the law were at work and individuals who opposed them had no chance. It wouldn't take them long to discover that Kennedy hadn't been alone in the cornfield and then he would suffer the same fate as his companion.

Pedersen observed the large security presence swarming around Kennedy's house for a while, saw the security ambulance arrive and take her body away, then moved away slowly and headed home. The young man was well aware of the seriousness of the situation. Kennedy – his first and only love – was gone. The security services would soon establish

Pedersen's connection with her — and then *he* would become the object of their interest. He knew he had to act soon. His father had died two years previously and his mother wasn't in good health. His final year exam was to take place the next day and already he realised what he would have to do. That night he explained to his mother that he had received an offer of a job in NCR 731 and would have to go there immediately to take up the offer. The social health service was good and there would be no problem having her looked after. He would visit regularly and, when he had sorted things out, he would come home.

Pedersen often thought about those days as he lay awake at night many many miles from NCR 41. He could see the disappointment in his mother's eyes when he announced he had to go, but she pretended to be happy for her son and hoped that things would go well for him in his new job. When he kissed her on the cheek as he left that morning, he knew he would never see her again.

The fugitive spent almost two years moving from place to place, using false identities he had learned to produce in his college information technology course. They were only good for so long and a two-minute check on the NC DNA Grid would blow them almost immediately. He would regularly check the local databases for NC City 12 for news from home and sometimes even send his mother notes and some money telling her how well he was getting on and that it wouldn't be long before he returned. He realised how dangerous that could be if the security services were really interested in tracking him down and he would travel a long distance to communicate or wait until he was about to leave a locality to send a note. When he discovered a death notice for his mother accompanied by an appeal sponsored by the security services, for his return for the departure ceremony, he decided that his links with NCC 12 were now cut forever.

It was while working in a microchip manufacturers in NCC 4 in NCR 731 that Pedersen met two young men called Gerson and Hovendon. Having shunned social contact since his departure from his home region, Pedersen found his two new associates interesting. There was something about them. Sitting in his apartment at night, he wondered what it was. When the two invited the newcomer out for a few drinks after work one Friday, he decided to go. Having talked workplace politics for a while, it wasn't long before Pedersen realised these two young men were interested in more than attractive ladies and strong liquor. Time after time, the two brought the conversation back to a single theme.

"D'yever think, Raven, how much 'bout *you* the Administration knows?" Hovendon asked as they sat at a back table in a cave – slang for an underground drink 'n dance venue.

"Never thought about it much", replied a cautious Raven, Pedersen's assumed name.

"Ev'thin', boy. Ev'thin'!" said Hovendon, answering his own question.

"They know what'ya have fur yur breakfast, boy!" Gerson added. "They sure do!"

Pedersen nodded weakly in agreement.

The two continued. "They got information on ev'thin' you do – what'ya like, what'ya don't like, what'ya think, what'ya don't think. They got it all. You' just a number on their big screen – tha's all."

"Probably true", Pedersen agreed, "but what can we do about it?" His two companions looked at one another, as if it was time for a break, and went out to dance with two ladies dressed in space cadet gear.

Watching the two boys out on the floor, Pedersen wondered were they silly amateurs or the real deal.

Observing Novo 1319's brain patterns, the Technician decided it was time to intervene.

"Was it the loneliness that drove you to become a terrorist, Tom? Was it Kennedy's suicide that drove you over the edge?"

1319 startled when he heard the word 'suicide'. He became angry. How low of these people to even slur the memory of the dead to achieve their ends.

The Technician observed his monitor as the prisoner's thoughts became clouded with anger. Moving his hand over the screen, he could see the prevalent green colour that indicated that the prisoner's emotions were overcoming his reason. He decided to continue.

"Well, Tom, was it the thought that she had mutilated herself because of you that caused you to become a criminal?"

The prisoner's mind focused on a scene upon which his eyes had never set and one which he hoped he would never have to see – Kennedy's face shot up, her beautiful features torn forever. The anger that the suffering of the innocent raises in the heart of the just boiled up inside the prisoner. A dark hatred filled his mind.

The Technician continued: "I've seen the images – they're not a pretty sight!" Silence. "How a pretty young thing – no matter how disturbed she was – could do something like that to herself I'll never understand." Silence. The Technician knew he was hitting raw emotion. His animal instinct told him that the subject was about to explode. "I can get them for you, if you like. We were only looking at them the other night."

"You bastard! You slimy bastard! I'll see *you* cut up if it's the last thing I do, you slimeball!" the prisoner exploded.

"Just like you did Leonard, I suppose?" the Technician queried mildly, as he watched the subject's brain patterns reach dark green.

The prisoner continued to seethe but said nothing. The Technician continued to press. "You did Leonard in revenge for Kennedy, didn't you?" he asked, raising his voice. "You did, didn't you?" As he shouted the question, he tilted the wire ever so slightly. The prisoner, expecting to lose his balance, tried to realign his body.

"You did, didn't you – in revenge for the slut Kennedy!" He raised his voice even further. "In revenge for Kennedy - a little whore who gave a piece to every man in a uniform. In revenge for a little slut, you killed Leonard!"

"The bastard! The fucker! He got his. The lowlife."

"How did you do it, Tom? How did you exit the little ferret? The little bastard!"

"You'll never know – you scumbag – you'll never know! And you'll be next!" the prisoner roared, in a frenzy.

"Tell me, Tom, tell me – we must know!" the Technician harried.

On the wire, 1319 became conscious of his angry state and realised it was time to pull back. Almost like a boiling pot being reduced to a simmer, his anger peaked and calm returned to his mind and body until he was in control again. In the distance, he could hear the Technician prompting him, hoping he would fall again. Changing the balance to leave the prisoner attempting to regain his physical composure once more, while sending hostile waves through his brain to confuse him, the Technician tried all his tricks. To his surprise, however, he noticed a clear change in the subject's brain patterns. The dark green was fading back to a lighter colour. The pattern was changing. The Technician was losing his grip and the prisoner was regaining control – Novo 1319 would make no more mistakes.

ON THE OTHER SIDE of the viewing wall, Kontroller Windsor smiled. He knew now he had his man. 1319 had exited Leonard. Although he hadn't admitted it straight out, he was the man. But Windsor knew his work was only beginning. Who exited Leonard was irrelevant to him really. The little spineless ferret was useful to the Administration in bringing in information but there would be more Leonards where he came from. Windsor's interest was the *bigger* picture. Who was running the show amongst the prisoners? Who was planning? Who was directing operations? Only when its head had been severed would the monster be laid low. Only when he, Windsor, could burst into the Master's Chamber and throw the monster's skull on the table in front of him would he have won the war and proven himself to be the natural leader of Korb-1.

The prisoner on the wire, struggling to maintain his composure and wrestling with a troubled past, would be the sword he would use to behead the conspiracy. 1319 would have the honour, he thought, to atone for his crimes and bring anarchy to an end for once and for all in the kolony. It was *his* blood that would cleanse Korb-1 and bring it at last within the power of the one whose destiny it was to lead it. Displaying a smirk of satisfaction, Windsor turned and walked away.

IN KOLONY KONTROL, THE Master was lying back in his chair, reading a holodisk that was displaying in the ether in front of him. Record after record appeared before him as he read the background information on every single prisoner in his care. 'Kare' was a word used frequently by the Master to describe his role in the kolony. He was so fond of the idea that his was a caring role that he had recently taken to spelling the word with a 'k', as if it was an integral part of the Korb brand package. His was the duty of a caring paternal figure, one who would be firm when the situation demanded such a response but who would never lose sight of his obligation to reform the men and women under his care. As the faces and details came up before him, the Master occasionally breathed a sigh. How sad, he felt, to see such young and talented people throw away the opportunities afforded them as citizens of the Confederation to become determined criminals. How misguided was it possible for someone to be? If they were subjects of the Saladdan States, he could understand. But citizens of the prosperous Northern Confederation! Bizarre! These thoughts troubled the Master as he sat back, drinking a glass of arctic ice juice. In comfort, he reassured himself that he was not unaware of the enormity of the challenge before him – 1,332 prisoners – and twenty more due soon. But he was convinced that he would be successful in his task and would produce a happy and contented community in the kolony, one that would be a shining light for all to see. Sipping his drink, the Master regarded the variety of faces that peered at him through the thick warm air of his studio. Reading their accompanying records, he tried to imagine what had gone wrong in their lives to have left them so misguided. For the most part, they *looked* like intelligent people. Most of them came from settled respectable backgrounds. Most of them had good educations. Most of them had been in good employment. Yet they had all fallen into crime and, worse than that, crime against the very Administration that had educated them and given them every opportunity. What was the factor that brought them all to their present sad state? Perhaps if he could identify this factor, he could devise a programme to correct it. Then he could publish the results of his work from which other prison Masters could learn and by which thousands of prisoners could be redeemed and helped to live useful and productive lives. Comforted by this positive thought, the Master scanned the life stories that flashed before him.

In the Security Detention Area, 1319 was disappointed at his performance on the wire. The Technician had set out to get him riled and he had fallen straight into the trap. Annoyed with himself for dropping his guard so easily, he tried to establish what exactly he had said and how much he had given away. Although he had given the impression that he had had a hand in the disappearance of the Ferret, he wasn't sure he had actually admitted to anything in particular. But maybe he had said enough to convince the Administration that he was the man to get talking.

With his hands behind his head, he lay back thinking of the dreadful things the Technician had said about Kennedy. In calm recollection, he now realised that the Technician's claims were not to be taken seriously but, in the heat of the moment, it wasn't easy to listen quietly to his vicious words. What exactly happened to Kennedy had yet to be established, he knew well. As time had passed, doubt had grown in his mind as to her fate. It was in order to clear that doubt that Tom Pedersen had decided to listen a little more to his two new comrades, Gerson and Hovendon, back in NCC 4 that night – a decision that had him now dangling on a wire in Korb Kolony One.

The afternoon in the cornfield so long ago still cast a long shadow over the life of Prisoner 1319.

31 REST DAY

It was Rest Day. The 24 hour period every ten days when all korb work shifts ceased and everyone on Korb Kolony One could relax. On Rest Day, prisoners were entitled to unwind in the cells or enjoy any of the many sporting and leisure activities available on the kolony. Leisure pursuits were delayed this morning, however, by the hologrammatic broadcast of an address by the Master. As prisoners sat down waiting for their Rest Day morning meal of 'wheat biscuits with milk and honey', they were treated to a lecture on the value of industry and cooperation in the attainment of an agreed goal. For twenty long minutes, the assembled captive audience listened sporadically to the Master's analysis of the need to pull together "to achieve our great goal here on Korb-1". Eyes glazed over as the Master outlined the excellent production figures that the kolony had enjoyed since its establishment. These were remarkable figures, the Master opined, compared to those of the other korb kolonies and must be a source of great pride to everyone on Korb-1. The contribution of the kolony to the energy requirements of the Old World was phenomenal and was greatly appreciated by the population there, he reassured the prisoners. The Master seemed to be totally enthralled by his subject and appeared to look into the distance when speaking as if experiencing a vision of the wonderful place in the development of civilisation that the kolony enjoyed.

Despite his obvious enthusiasm, the Master's countenance took on a slightly worried look towards the end of his contribution as he informed the prisoners that "despite the unparalleled success" that the kolony had enjoyed, "there were those who were intent on promoting strife and dissension" and who, "being committed to notions rooted in the past", were unable to appreciate the significance of the collaborative success that was Korb Kolony One. These "misguided individuals", the Master warned, were in danger of jeopardising the continued success of the Korb Project and would have to be dealt with firmly. He was convinced that "the vast majority of right thinking prisoners" would shun the activities of these "thoughtless people" and help the kolony authorities to prevent them from "causing damage" and "poisoning the atmosphere" for everybody else.

To ensure that Rest Day fitted neatly into the Korb-1 working week, there were three breakfast, lunch and evening meal sittings. These catered for all work shifts but served to limit the social intercourse between the various shift teams, particularly that between the 1 and 3 shifts. On all three occasions that it was broadcast, the Master's speech was received by a spontaneous round of applause by the prisoners. That this was a sarcastic gesture aimed at ridiculing the pompous contribution wasn't lost on the security personnel watching the proceedings from various vantage points. The Master, watching from the viewer in his suite, got a different impression, however, and felt that the reception his speech received was indicative of the genuine desire of the prisoners to see harmony in the kolony, a harmony based on respect for the individual roles everybody had to play to keep Korb-1 on the path to success. Wallowing in a mire of self-congratulation, the Master sank back into his padded chair and sipped his favourite arctic ice juice.

When the feigned show of adulation after the Master's address had been played out to the full, Dayton smiled at Kane and nodded his head, pretending to be impressed. "Now, that's what I call drama!" he said emphatically. The other prisoners around the table hesitated for a while and then a howl of laughter erupted. Some of the more exuberant in the party stamped their feet and clapped their hands, shouting "More! More! More!"

Two tables away, Nevin looked disapprovingly at the boisterous behaviour of the KC10-1 Team. His experienced mind was uncomfortable with indiscipline – it was a factor that couldn't be controlled, and lack of control in a sensitive situation could mean disaster. The greying leader cast his eye slowly around the Dining Hall, observing the demeanour of the prisoners present. Most of them were under forty with a few, like himself, the wrong side of the big 5-0. There were three, Peters, Maartens and Fleming who were over 60. He wondered how they would fare if things got rough. All in all though, Nevin reflected, the bulk of the prisoners were young, fit and able-bodied. If push came to shove, they should be well able to defend their territory. But what was that territory to be? Despite his best efforts, his team had still failed to come up with a complete map of the entire kolony, and without that, it would be impossible to draft a comprehensive escape plan.

Nevin tapped the table with the metallic fingers on his left hand provided for him by the Kolony Administration. Following weeks of careful intelligence, he now had a complete plan of the prison area in the kolony. That was the easy bit, though. His information on the Administration Area was patchy, to say the least, and the Accommodation and Recreation

Area for the Administration was almost totally unknown. The Oxygen Generation System was probably in the core of Korb-1 as it would have to be protected from all hazards. If he could locate that, he would have a fair idea of the extent of the kolony and be in position to set about filling in the blanks. How, though? Security was very tight and nobody on the Administration side was spilling any beans. He would have to find some way of getting information from the official side. He tried to come up with possible information targets amongst Administration staff but those even 'slightly likely' were few and far between. After all, what could the prisoners in an isolated space colony have to offer their guards that would be sufficient to elicit useful information – and, more important than that, how could any information given by them ever be verified? It wasn't going to be easy.

"A penny for your thoughts!" Kenning ventured, interrupting her partner's reflection. Slightly startled, Nevin smiled and replied, "Oh, I was just reminiscing", and set about enjoying his Rest Day Kolony Breakfast.

"Nevin seems depressed!" Dayton opined as the KC10-1 Team relaxed.

"Maybe Kenning is losing her touch", O'Hara said smiling. "Maybe she's into tyrons now!"

"No way", said Kane, "even the tyrons would be too scared to go there!"

Laughter all round.

KONTROLLER WINDSOR LOOKED SECURITY Officer Simpson in the eye. "How soon can we have it?" he asked.

"Within minutes – unedited", she replied.

"And edited?"

"Give us half an hour", the Security Officer replied confidently.

"Do it then!" Windsor directed.

Simpson nodded in the direction of McKenzie, and passed the instruction on.

On her screen, the younger woman began busily collating every piece of information relating to the disappearance of the Ferret, from transcripts of interrogations to intercepted conversations to extrapolated security sequences. Bit by bit, McKenzie pieced together what was called a 'logical conclusion' based on the evidence fed into the program. After less than twenty minutes, the logical conclusion was that GC9-3 Operating Assistant Leonard had never left Generation Chamber 9 and had been killed and disposed of in the Generation Tank. The probable culprit was Prisoner 1319, Thomas Pedersen, a conclusion supported by the prisoner's own admission.

McKenzie hesitated when the result of the evidence sweep appeared on the screen before her, as if considering what course of action to take. Her concentration was broken almost immediately, however, by the appearance at her shoulder of Simpson.

"Have we a result?" she asked curtly.

"I'm transferring it to you now", McKenzie replied coldly.

Simpson touched a yellow spot on her tunic on the inside of her cuff and a narrow screen, which extended from her wrist to the tips of her fingers, emerged from under her sleeve. Touching the corner of the screen twice to choose the file she wished to view, she observed the logical conclusion as it filled her screen. Having read the file, the surly lady with a serious expression uttered a slightly audible grunt and left the room.

THE GAMES AREA WAS the main part of the L+S Area in the kolony. On Rest Days, large groups of prisoners gathered there to hang out, exercise and play games on the various playing areas provided. Pre-arranged tournaments between korb teams would take place and excite the interest not alone of the participants but of their supporters and other interested parties. The grudge match today was a hurling-ball encounter between KC44-1 and KC18-1. 44-1 were seasoned campaigners and played a hard game. 18-1 were a younger team, fitness being their main asset. The two teams had played a draw twice already this season and were now pitched together in the quarterfinals of the Korb Kolony Kup. 18-1 wore a scarlet vest with a yellow explosion on the right shoulder. 44-1 played in black with no logos – just the figure 44-1 on their chest. Playing gear was provided by the Administration, as was the trophy. The fixture excited a lot of interest and there was an enthusiastic turnout to enjoy the impending battle.

Nevin and Kenning were among the large attendance, accompanied by a number of prisoners, mostly from the KC27-1 Team. As predicted, the game was a hard one with the fit and skilful KC18-1 team attempting to move the ball around fast and set up scores before the slower but stronger 44-1 side could catch them in possession. The veterans did gain possession from time to time and then the challenge for 18-1 was to prevent the 44-1 'juggernaut' forcing its way inexorably into the younger team's goal. The juggernaut did get through once but it was balanced out by 18-1's speedily taken scores, leaving the score at the first quarter 1 net goal / 5 over points (a total of 8 points) to 1 net goal / 4 over points (a total of 7 points) for the younger team. Despite the excitement of the close challenges in the second quarter, Nevin and two of his companions appeared to lose interest in the game and become engrossed in deep conversation.

"We can get nothing on the overall layout of the kolony – nobody has ever been outside the prison and hospital areas – and there's nothing coming from the other side", a serious red-faced man with dark eyes and a bandana reported.

"What about that hologram of yours?" Hasn't that got detail?" he asked.

Nevin gave a frustrated laugh. "That's a work of imagination to stop me going insane – we wouldn't get far on that!"

"What about you?" Nevin enquired of the other prisoner, a woman with a fuzzy Afro.

"Same story – no space walk!" she added, a disappointed look on her face.

Nevin was frustrated, almost annoyed. He hesitated as if about to say something, then stopped.

"Alright, it looks like we're up against a brick wall here. We'll have to come up with something ourselves." Nevin hesitated again, as if looking way into an uncomfortable future in which there were no easy choices. Then he continued: "O.k., we can't fight our way out of here on spec. The stakes are too high to play Russian roulette. There's only one other choice then."

The two others listened carefully, eager to hear what Nevin take was going to be. The older man hesitated again, then spoke.

"The only areas we really know are the prison, including the L+S, and the Treatment Unit. We know they are both accessible from the Security Area. We know the Security Area is accessible from the Administration Area. There is certainly a way out from there. That's the way to go."

The other two remained silent, taking in the import of their leader's words. Getting into the Security Area would be no easy task. At the same time, escaping from a custom built space kolony was never going to be simple either and, on the other hand, if the prisoners did manage to gain control of the Security Area, they would be in a commanding position. In fact with no reinforcements available to the Administration, the fight for control of the Security Area could be the decisive battle. Nevin's idea seemed to make sense. The two nodded their agreement.

"Keep it under wraps", Nevin urged, "we don't want the slightest hint of our strategy reaching the other side. If it does, we're korb kake." The other two nodded agreement, then all three returned to the game.

They were just in time to see a Team 18-1 break on goal result in a bone-crunching tackle by one of the 44-1 defenders. The ball broke lose straight into the path of an 18-1 attacker who first-timed a shot into the goal net to leave the score at 3 net goals / 11 over points (a total of 20 points) to 2 net goals / 11 over points (a total of 17).

Tension mounted as the game entered the closing minutes of the last quarter. The 18-1 offences grew slower and less frequent as the young legs eventually began to tire after a frenetic attacking game from the throw-in. Team 44-1, sensing an opportunity to turn the game around, pressed forward in strength. 18-1 decided to fall back in an attempt to hold on to their slender lead and block their opponents by sheer weight of numbers between them and the scoring zone. Attack after attack was repulsed as the experienced 44-1 bore down again and again on their opponents' goal. Then, following a shemozzle on the edge of the scoring zone, a 44-1 attacker found the goal at his mercy. Raising his stick almost as in slow motion, the helmeted forward slammed the ball into the bottom right corner of the goal zone. The buzzer immediately signalled a goal. The 44-1 attackers didn't waste time celebrating the score, regrouping immediately to defend their hard-earned draw. With the scores now level, it was 18-1's turn to attack. Attempting to break down the left wing, their attackers found their way blocked by a solid phalanx of 44-1 defenders. A quick switch of the ball to the centre seemed to offer a break but the 44-1 defence regrouped with remarkable speed and 18-1's path to glory was blocked once more. As the ball was switched to the right wing for a final assault, the hooter sounded and the game ended in a hard-earned draw for both sides. A replay would be necessary in a week's time – another big day for the spectators. Nevin and his cohorts moved away, the crowd cheering.

32 DESERT ENCOUNTER

KANE WAS LYING ON his bunk with a disk viewer in his hand surrounded by a variety of skin disks obtained from the Kolony Entertainments Depository. To the casual observer, he was a captive, denied the pleasures of a normal relationship in a prison far from his former reality, relaxing and fantasising about what could have been. A security scanner, which Kane believed was probably operating in his cell, would have shown Prisoner 313 to be enjoying his experience to the full, feasting his eyes on every view and then closing them to imprint on his mind the pleasurable experience he had just enjoyed. Even the security extremists would admit that there were times when security was not threatened by a solitary prisoner dreaming of things that were never going to be – but sometimes even the security experts make mistakes.

Surrounded by skin disks of every description, Kane lay back devouring the scenes that spread in front of his eyes on the viewer. With each new view, he took in every aspect of the pleasant sights that unfolded.

Then, closing his eyes to aid his memory, he memorised in minute detail what he had just seen, as if his life depended on it – and, in many ways, it did. For Prisoner 313 wasn't enjoying the 'healthy' delights of a skin flick, rather he was viewing the Kolony Plan presented to him by McKenzie. Like a child experiencing a new flavour of ice cream, Kane savoured every detail on the screen, studying again and again the minutiae of the kolony layout and committing it all to memory. Wonder showed on the prisoner's face as he observed what he thought he would never ever have been allowed to see – actual dimensional images of what lay beyond the walls that had delineated his world for so long.

The prisoner thought his first task should be to get an overall impression of the Kolony Plan, knowing what areas were close but unconnected, what areas led to others and what permutations and combinations were applicable in terms of movement throughout Korb-1. Already, he had learned that beyond the L+S Area was a vast chamber called the Mobility Area where large quantities of equipment of some sort were stored. Beyond that was an area called **KEKU** - the Korb Environment Kontrol Unit.

Kane worked at the same pace for over two hours, observing and storing details that could possibly make the difference between success and failure when the big day came. When the prisoner was content that he had at last an overall picture of the layout of the kolony, he decided to rest for a while and let the invaluable information he had just devoured settle into his brain. Besides if he were to continue feasting his eyes on the viewer without taking some kind of a break he would sooner or later attract the unwelcome attention of Security.

The prisoner put the viewer away and lay on the bed reviewing in his mind everything he had seen. Testing himself, he decided to move through the kolony east to west on the upper grid, then west to east on the lower grid, then back west to east on the central grid, then south to north on the central grid, and so on until he could automatically set out a path from any one place in the kolony to another.

Sitting up on his bunk, drained in one sense and exhilarated in another, Kane couldn't believe his luck. Out of the blue – just when everything had seemed so black – his saviour had arrived, in the form of an officer of the Administration! Unless the Kolony Plan was a hoax, the woman in the tunnel was the real thing. And as it would take an incredible amount of time and expense to create a fictional layout – and Kane didn't consider himself important enough to warrant such an investment – he had to conclude that Zeena McKenzie was for real. At long last, it appeared to the prisoner that his dream of freedom could, some day soon, come true.

Kane was conscious of the fact that McKenzie hadn't been in touch since, not even for that game of *War-Raok!* that she had promised. He resisted the worrying feeling that something had gone wrong and contented himself with her own advice that lying low for a while would be the best thing to do. As for him, it was time to go back to the skin disks that given him such delight all afternoon!

DOWN IN THE RECEPTION Area, another twenty novos were arriving in Korb-1. Dressed in their bright blue body vests, all shared the same sullen expression as they were marched out of the Reception Area and into the main Welcome Chamber. Defeated souls frowned upon by a purple sky, they followed the path laid out for them by the Master and his tyron guards and trekked hopelessly along towards a bleak future, the Master's brief welcoming address still ringing like a dull bell in their numbed crania. The prisoners' representative carried a bored expression as she marched along with the troupe.

The Master carried his usual smug smile on his well-preserved features. Every Arrival was an important moment for the kolony, bringing as it did new blood and new abilities. Although he understood that none of the prisoners was arriving of their own volition, he always nurtured the hope that they would soon come to terms with the reality of their situation and settle down to make a meaningful contribution to the welfare of Korb-1 and to its essential goal – the production of korb. Earlier, as the novos passed through the Registration Tunnels and received their 'plug', as the security staff referred to the identity microchip inserted under the skin, the Master had looked on with admiration at the fine physique that paraded before him, confident that the new arrivals would indeed make excellent Generation and Korb Chamber workers and team members.

In contrast to the Master's unchallenged air of superiority, the tense expression on the face of Kontroller Windsor as he observed the new arrivals revealed a different view. Windsor's beady eyes watched closely as the prisoners passed through the Chamber. To him, each and every one of these miscreants was a potential threat to the security of the kolony. In Windsor's mind, these prisoners were sent to Korb-1 for good reason. They were hardened criminals, bent on destroying the security of the Administration. They had made a global alliance with the enemies of the Administration and had used and abused the freedom provided by the Regime to attack its very existence. Anyone associated with such treacherous activities could never be trusted and, when caught and dispatched to Korb-1, must be treated as what they were – treacherous criminals bent on the destruction of the Administration. These thoughts were never far from Kontroller Windsor's mind and, for him, every new Arrival in the kolony reinforced the necessity for a strong security capability. Windsor would always ensure that KK1 was in a position to deal resolutely with any threat posed by its enemies.

Standing observing the novos, Windsor presented his usual pompous countenance. His squinting eyes and sharp features gave the former ASA (Active Service Abroad) Colonel a determined look which was made more intense by the scar he carried on his right temple, a yellow scab that extended as far as the top of his right eye. Windsor was proud of his battle scar. He remembered with no small measure of pleasure his encounter, years before, with the Saladdans. The Saladdan States had completed a period of rearmament and had taken a large swathe of territory from the African Alliance. Security briefs suggested that they were now bent on testing the reaction capabilities of the Northern Confederation. Considering themselves yet unprepared for a direct attack on the Confederation, security sources reported that the Saladdans had decided to do two things. The first was to prepare a major assault on the Confederation's communications and information networks with a view to disabling the NC's defences. The second was to send an assault force to test the defences of the NC Moon Base network.

The Moon Bases had been set up in the latter part of the 21rst century and numbered twenty-three in all. Their original purpose was to explore the possibility of locating an energy source to prepare the way for large-scale settlement programmes for NC citizens there. The search for energy proved fruitless – the dust ball yielding nothing of any exploitative value – and the colonisation programme was eventually confined to manning the bases themselves.

When news of the Saladdan plan reached Administration Security, they dispatched some of their finest tyron divisions to the Moon Bases to buttress their defences. Windsor was the Colonel in charge of Moon Base 13. A full year Windsor and his force spent on MB13 but nothing happened. The status of the alert was then changed from *alert 1* to *alert 3* and most of the tyrons were sent home. Windsor was bitterly disappointed. He had long been looking forward to a chance to score against the Saladdans. The Colonel was firmly of the view, as was his want, that the Saladdans were a major threat to world security. It was time they had their wings clipped. He had spent an entire year on MB13 waiting for his opportunity and now he was being called home. Reluctantly, he packed his bags and joined his tyrons on an *ipc* (interplanetary personnel carrier) to return to the Confederation.

But then fate took a hand. As it entered the Earth's gravity field, Windsor's *ipc* was hit by a meteorite. The object was too small to cause any great damage, but broke against the engine exhausts of the machine. Most of the debris fell away, but some was sucked up into the carrier's engine, causing it to falter. As the pilot crew tried to retain control of the craft, the vessel lost course and veered in another direction. After twenty frightening minutes on board, the *ipc* landed in an arid region in the north east of the African Alliance. With the crew scrambling out and assembling outside, the pilots contacted NC Military Traffic Control to agree coordinates, only to be told that they had landed in the Saladdan-occupied part of the African Alliance. On hearing the news, Windsor became invigorated with excitement. At last, contact with the enemy!

Control told *ipc* 56567-sd to prepare emergency defences, assess damage, carry out repairs and leave as soon as possible. Windsor dug six defence positions around the *ipc* at a distance of 50 metres from the vessel and waited. Projected repair time was 2 hours 50 minutes. As the engineers worked on the damage, the tyrons sat tight and waited for the Saladdans to arrive. A timer in each bunker displayed the projected time remaining for departure. Tense eyes looked at it from time to time and then looked away deep into the desert at shapes in the distance.

Twenty minutes before departure time, word came that repairs were nearly complete and that the vessel would leave on schedule. Windsor, disappointed that no encounter with the Saladdans had materialised, ordered his forces to prepare to return to the ship. Methodically, the

NC forces organised their withdrawal. Suddenly, however, as the tyrons abandoned their positions to return to the *ipc*, a voice shrieked over the communicator system "Vessels! Large! Nine! Two minutes! North-east approach!"

Windsor froze. The majority of his tyron force was clambering over the sand between their abandoned bunkers and their ship. If they returned to their bunkers, the possibility was that they would be pinned down there and eventually wiped out. If they returned to the ship, they at least stood a chance of leaving the arena in one piece. But what about the scramble across the shifting sands to get to the ship? Anybody caught there would be a sitting duck. Windsor's lieutenants were calling into his ear – "Orders awaited! Orders awaited!" Windsor made his call – "Ignite bunkers! Deploy smoke bombs. Return to ship immediately!"

Three tyrons from each group returned to their bunkers and set incendiary devices, then rejoined the rest of the force heading for the ship. Those on the flanks scattered smoke bombs as they went in order to impair the enemy's visual contact with the force. As the main body of tyrons was approaching the vessel, three large Saladdan Spectral Craft appeared over the dunes northeast of the *ipc*. These were followed swiftly by three more, and another three followed them in equally quick succession. Panic ensued as the craft immediately opened fire on the retreating force. Within seconds, the entire area was the scene of total chaos, with the smoke bellowing from the bunkers and from the smoke bombs creating a cloud of cover for the tyrons and the Spectrals firing blindly into the general area. The Spectrals' explosive beams tore through the sand like a knife through sugar as the tyrons raced towards the ship. Time and again, the Spectrals swooped over the throng of retreating tyrons and cut swathes through them until almost all of those capable of running were on the ship or about to board.

As the *ipc* couldn't release its boosters to take off until everyone was aboard, it sat on the sand firing salvos at the passing enemy ships, that had now turned their attention to the stationary craft. Standing at the gangway onto the ship, Windsor oversaw the scramble on board, shouting directions and orders, most of which went unheard in the din of battle. With the last of his tyrons boarding, Windsor ordered a '7-3' – 'gates closed, immediate departure'. With the main gate closing, the angry Colonel stood inside, aware that he was about to leave a lot of personnel dead or – worse still – injured and in the hands of the Saladdans. Ordering all available firepower directed at the attacking vessels, his anger was assuaged at the sight of two of the Spectrals being downed before his eyes. A third vessel, following on close to the two stricken craft, pelted the *ipc* with laser fire. One of the blasts lanced a metal support beam on the boarding door beside Windsor and a splash of molten metal hit the Colonel on the temple.

THE COLONEL AWOKE IN the main military hospital in NC City 2, with a rocking headache and an injury that, after some fancy skin surgery, would mark him for live. Not that that have troubled Windsor. A scar received in battle with the enemy was the epitome of honour for a soldier, he believed – a sign of valour, a receipt for something given to the Confederation in its hour of need.

After a few weeks, Windsor was right as rain and looking forward to rejoining battle with the Saladdans. Initial inquiries, however, regarding plans for retaliation against the enemy brought evasive responses from his superiors and soon Windsor realised that honour was once again going to have to take second place to politics. The Saladdans had made a big show of the fact that a "Northern Confederation invasion" had been repulsed and displayed the bodies of fifty four tyrons on the state communication system before consigning them to a cesspit. Thankfully, no live prisoners were produced. The Confederation denied the incident had ever occurred and claimed the Saladdans were merely attempting to impress a population on the verge of revolt with stories of victories against non-existent enemies. Windsor was horrified and protested in the most strenuous manner possible against this "policy of denial and non-confrontation". His immediate superior, Ludmilov, explained the situation in simple terms: "We need the Saladdan threat, Bob. It concentrates the mind. What we don't need is a war with them. We're not ready for that yet."

Eventually, Windsor accepted reality, but not before contacting an NC Senator he knew to complain. When his friend communicated elements of the 'confidential security briefing' he had received to the indignant Colonel, the gung-ho hero felt the dull heavy sensation of betrayal deep in his bowels – the official line given to Senators was that the entire disaster was Windsor's fault! It was "suspected" that he had deliberately engineered a crash in Saladdan territory to provoke a war, and that, when in enemy territory, he had dug positions too far from the stricken craft, thus exposing his personnel to a long march over difficult terrain to get back to their ship while under heavy fire. On hearing the official line, an apoplectic Windsor decided to go to NC Court of Justice to defend his reputation but when every lawyer he talked to advised him to forget about it and get on with his life or the baseless allegations would end up as fact in the public domain, even the unyielding Windsor knew the game was up and reluctantly accepted a new assignment offered to him by the Confederation. The NC Administration's view that Korb-1 was the place for a man with the undeniable talents of Robert Windsor went unopposed. As one insider quipped – "at least he can't take on the Saladdans single-handed there!"

Ever since that event, a burning desire to vindicate his actions and achieve his true destiny consumed Kontroller Windsor. On Korb-1, it was clear to the angry man what he needed to do.

33 HUNTED

KANE HAD ONLY A few hours sleep time left. He knew he had to sleep if he was to think clearly. Clear thinking was an effective weapon in a war of wits, sometimes the main one. At the same time, he was eager to finish his reading of McKenzie's Kolony Plan. Kane felt groggy as he drifted in and out of sleep. The tiredness he was experiencing he put down to the total concentration he had been giving to memorising the Plan. He believed the Plan was his ticket out and he had every intention of using it. The Plan could give the prisoner access to any place in the kolony – the security sector, the Despatch Port, even the Master's Suite! At long last, Kane now had a weapon that would make a difference. The prisoner revelled in the fact that the information in his possession now was of a kind the Master would never expect him to have. When he had memorised the layout of the kolony, he would have the advantage of not playing blind anymore. He would be able to identify and study weaknesses in kolony security and devise his tactics accordingly. With these thoughts in mind, Kane was reluctant to put the Plan away and go asleep but, having decided he could take in no more, he put the reader safely hidden away and lay back in his bunk.

The prisoner soon fell asleep but, after only a short while, heard a noise outside his cell. He decided to get up and have a look. Moving slowly, and rubbing his tired eyes with the fingers of his right hand, Kane went outside to see what had attracted his attention. Looking up and down the corridor, he could see nothing, yet sensed a presence somewhere. Walking slowly along, Kane thought it strange that there seemed to be no movement at all in the area. *Where was everyone gone?* he wondered. Had there been a mass arrest of prisoners? Were they all being interrogated now? Or had there been a mass escape? Maybe everybody was gone and nobody bothered to tell him? A feeling of anger and frustration overcame the prisoner as he realised he may have been left behind. Running along the corridor he began to shout the names of his friends – Dayton! Nielsen! Gibney! O'Hara! Suddenly, the prisoner, hearing a noise behind him, stopped in his tracks and looked around. Behind him, only a few metres away, stood a group of tyrons, sneering at the prisoner and holding their zennors at the ready. Kane stood staring at the tyrons, wondering what his next move should be. Tensed, he focused his eyes on the armed gang, his nostrils dilating as he sensed a very real threat. Suddenly, one of the tyrons called out: "Get him – now!" Instinctively, Kane turned on his heel and ran as fast as his legs could manage.

The prisoner ran as he had never run before. With searer shot blasting all round him, he realised his chances of escape were slim unless he could shake off his frenzied pursuers. All kinds of questions bounced around in the prisoner's head as he ran like an old world gazelle trying to shake off a pack of ravenous hyenas. Where was everybody gone? What had happened overnight? Had the rebellion begun without him – unknown to him? How would he find the rest of the prisoners? And more pressing than anything else, how was he going to escape the hunting pack?

Kane's brain worked overtime as he attempted to figure a way out. Stopping was not even an option as his pursuers obviously had no interest in taking prisoners. If he kept running, he would eventually be caught or seared. Raising a hand to wipe the sweat rolling down from his brow and blinding him, Kane sensed his pursuers breath on his neck.

Turning the corner towards the L+S, Kane saw the entrance to the tunnel where he had met McKenzie. The prisoner thought fast. If he could manage to get into the tunnel before the tyrons turned the corner, he might be able to put ground between him and them before they realised where he was gone. Swerving, Kane bounded towards the tunnel, palmed it open and rushed in, hearing it closing reassuringly behind him.

Kane stopped for a moment, gathering his breath and waiting for the tunnel entrance to open behind him. But nothing happened. He listened intently – nothing. The prisoner composed himself for a few seconds, then took stock of his surroundings in the red-lit tunnel. If his recollection of the tunnel system was correct, he could make it to the Dining Hall and see if there was anyone there. If there was no one there, he could try the L+S Area, another place where large groups could assemble or be held captive. Kane decided to start moving, as the tyrons could soon figure out his whereabouts and be on his trail again.

Kane walked fast, hoping to be able to conserve as much energy as possible. Recalling the Kolony Plan in his mind as he moved along, Kane tested himself by attempting to predict the landmarks he would meet along the way. A service duct here, a tunnel exit there, a junction ahead. To the prisoner's relief, he called it right every time. This, and the absence of any sign of his pursuers, gave Kane, if not a sense of confidence, certainly a feeling of relief, and gradually a slight mood of hope settled into the prisoner's mind.

But Kane's positive mood didn't last too long. Hurrying along the tunnel and past the first junction, the prisoner's heart missed a beat as he heard a commotion in the distance behind him. The sound of tyrons boots moving with speed in his direction was the last thing Prisoner 313 wanted to hear. Kane quickened his step and began to run again. The noise behind him told him the posse were gaining on him and getting closer. Kane decided to leave the red tunnel at the next exit point. Running along the tunnel, he reached the exit point and turned right. Kane stopped suddenly. To his dismay, the prisoner found himself facing a blank wall. Horrified, Kane stopped momentarily, then turned and continued on his way up the red tunnel. The prisoner was disappointed at having failed to recollect the Kolony Plan as he had hoped he would, but knew that the intersection with the yellow tunnel wasn't far and a turn there would soon bring him to another exit point. Kane's tunic was soaked in sweat as he ran like a quarry that knows its hunter is only one step behind. Seeing the red-yellow intersection ahead, Kane became confident again that he was back on the right track. The prisoner's pace quickened as he spun around the corner into the yellow tunnel and headed straight for the exit point. His eyes welcoming the yellow stringer bulbs that confirmed his location, Kane moved speedily. Turning into the exit spot, however, the prisoner was again stopped in his tracks. Astounded, Kane stood once again before a blank wall. Thinking he was perhaps forgetting a code or energy point to exit the tunnel system, Kane frantically moved his palm around the wall, hoping to see it melt away and expose the exit point he had so clearly remembered from the Plan. Nothing happened.

At this stage, Kane was a very worried man. The tunnel system was of limited use to the prisoner if he was merely to run blindly through it hoping for a lucky break. If Kane couldn't plan his escape from the pursuing tyrons, he was unlikely to escape at all, and his capture and murder was inevitable. He placed his forehead against the wall in a stupor as he tried to work out what to do next.

Suddenly, the wall against which the exhausted prisoner lay his weary head opened before him and the prisoner found himself falling – not out into a corridor or a room but downwards. Continuing to fall, Kane sensed he was descending into an abyss, a void, blackness – his hands and feet flailing out to stop his fall.

On his way through the blackness, Kane tried to make sense of it all. *What had happened? How had it all come to this? Had all his plans come to nothing? Had he wrongly placed his faith in McKenzie? Was she part of this cruel trick relentlessly carried out until there was nothing left but abject failure? Was it all to end now, like this in a free fall through infinity?*

Unexpectedly, Kane's fall came to a halt, not with a splatter or a physical spaghetti-isation but rather with a minor thud. He opened his eyes slowly, the light burning his pupils as he tried to focus on his new environment. Gradually, the prisoner got a fix on his surroundings. Stunned, and covered in the cold perspiration of a terrified man, he realised he was in fact on the floor beside his bunk. To Prisoner 313's confusion and fright was added an element of embarrassment and shame as he realised the Master had managed to get into his head and now even dictated his dreams.

Kane clambered back into his bunk and attempted, albeit with a certain reluctance, to go to sleep once more.

After his horrifying night, during which the prisoner got little sleep, Kane was tired and mentally exhausted. The reader file would expire in half an hour – 27 minutes, 51 seconds to be precise, and the prisoner was concerned that, despite three days of hard work, he still hadn't managed to memorise the detail of the Kolony Plan in its entirety. The complex security tunnel system was the most difficult part of the exercise. The tunnels network was designed in such a way as to enable the tyron guard to access any area in the kolony within minutes. The system was apparently totally soundproofed and was serviced by a freestanding ventilation system, independent of the main kolony air system.

Carefully studying the network of tunnels, Kane was convinced that if they provided the security forces with speedy access to all areas of Korb-1, they could equally provide anyone else who had an in-depth knowledge of the network with the opportunity to move swiftly through the kolony. Kane carefully studied the most direct route from the L+S Area to the Despatch Port, for example. If an escapee was going to make a run for it, that would be the obvious direction in which to go. The question then would be could they stow away on a *korb transporter* before the Administration realised there was somebody missing – but there were no sleeper trays on *korb transporters*. Hijacking a transporter involved the same problem, though a shorter course to a destination rather than Earth might be an option there. That option was an unlikely one, however, due to lack of flight expertise on the prisoner's part and the rapid reaction training of the tyrons. An attempt to run for it in that fashion would almost certainly be doomed to failure …….. unless, of course, the tyrons were otherwise engaged. The tunnels could be used to create a diversion in another area of the kolony while an escape bid through the Despatch Port was attempted. The tunnels from the location of the diversion towards the Despatch Port could be blocked in some way to prevent the tyrons getting there in time to prevent an escape. How to block them was another question, of course.

Kane was methodical in committing the Plan to memory. He would study an Area in the kolony and note the positions of the tunnel entrances there, plus the direction in which it was possible to travel through them.

He would then close his eyes and attempt to find his way around the network in his mind. Section by section was memorised in this fashion and the prisoner sensed he was making real progress. Kane sat on the floor in the corner of his cell in one last effort to master the system. The reader's life span was quickly running out. Nine minutes to go, eight, seven, six ...... The tension as the clock ate away his time was almost unbearable for the prisoner. Suddenly, with only three minutes to go, Kane noticed with the side of his eye somebody standing at the door of his cell — the Master, accompanied by two tyrons!

"Ah, Kane, relaxing I see! Don't get up! This is only a social call!" he declared chummily.

Kane, alarmed, glanced nervously at the reader. The Master, noticing Kane's discomfort, walked over and, taking the reader from the prisoner's hand, remarked that he hoped the prisoner was broadening his mind. Horrified, Kane glanced at the hologram clock above the Master's head – forty seconds left! The prisoner's blood froze in his veins as he watched his enemy take his only real hope for escape in his very hands. Thirty seconds, and the Master smiled as he prepared to see what the troublesome prisoner was viewing. Sweat rolled down Kane's brow as he prepared to take what would be a mortal blow. Twenty seconds. Noticing Kane's perspiration, The Master hesitated.

"Kane, my friend, what's wrong with you?" he asked, adding "This must be exciting stuff!"

Kane forced a smile – and an answer: "It's poetry from the soul of the cosmos!" Flummoxed, the Master raised an eyebrow and looked at the screen. As he did, Kane looked at the korb klock – one second! Still worried, the prisoner looked anxiously at the Master's face for a reaction.

"Kane!" the Master announced dramatically, " – a blank screen! What's wrong with you at all? I thought you'd been getting your act together!"

Experiencing a huge sense of relief, Kane felt he could afford to be flippant now.

"I was just beginning to write some poetry but you broke my train of thought."

"Oh, Kane, I *am* sorry. But don't worry – there's lots of inspiration in Korb-1!"

Then, turning on his heel, his purple cloak swinging after him, the Master headed for the door.

"You must keep me apprised of your literary efforts, Kane. The kolony is not just a place of industry, you know. There is an important place for the arts here too," he announced and then departed.

34 HOW DEEP IS THE KEY?

As Kane knew only too well, sleep was no refuge for the prisoner. For others, he thought, slumber was a welcome escape from the tyranny of the present – and the future. In sleep, one could find old friends and places and feel at home. For them, reality was the nightmare. For Kane, however, sleep meant the continuous churning of his mind to see clearly the events that had destroyed his life. Time after time, he relived those moments. After a night spent fleeing in a cold sweat from the ghosts of his past, awakening to a Korb-1 'morning' wasn't that bad after all.

This night wasn't to be any different for Kane. It started when he met Strauss in the Silverweed Cafe. She had a mint and vodka, he had a beer. They talked about the latest *ptv* released by the Siskin Corporation. She liked its shape, he thought it was too small. She said she planned to get one and trade in her *t-and-t* model she had had for the last three years. He said he'd stick to his *purtawn*, which had served him through thick and thin. It would cover any terrain and had never let him down. As the two young people talked and enjoyed one another's company, Kane had the distinct feeling someone was watching them, that they were being observed, though he had no idea who the observer was. Looking around the large room, he couldn't identify anybody in particular displaying an undue interest in him and his companion.

After leaving the Silverweed, the couple were still talking as they passed a shadowy figure on the steps. Strange to relate, although Kane hadn't really looked at the person's face – a man – he felt he had somehow seen it with the side of his eye. Why this was important, he didn't know. But that face seemed to haunt him ever since. Over the next few days, it seemed to be lodged in the back of his brain as he and Strauss went about what were to be their final days of freedom in the Old World.

Even now in the darkness of the Korb-1 night, that face, obscured in the ether of the galaxy between then and now, old and new, past and present, seemed to still be observing him from afar, listening to his every thought, waiting for him to make his move, waiting to pounce once more. It was always just as this shadowy figure was about to pounce that Kane was snatched from his tortuous sleep. In this way, awakening under the dark purple sky of the kolony had become in a strange way a welcome respite from the torment of the past.

But on top of Kane's usual difficulties with the Korb-1 night was the added factor that the prisoner had had little sleep or indeed sustenance for the last three days. From the moment he opened the disk reader to its timely demise three days later in the very hands of the Master himself the prisoner had fed his insatiable eyes on a sight he had thought he would never see. Kane's total focus had been on viewing, comprehending and memorising as much of the Kolony Plan as he possibly could, and now he felt drained.

As the Kolony Plan file revealed itself to a prisoner starved of information for years, Kane had been almost overcome with delight. The Plan presented the kolony as a massive five level building in the shape of a dome. The bottom level, referred to as the Source Level, was where the raw deposits of korb were dug out of the solid base rock by the core mining operation. The base was bombarded by smither rays and when an area disintegrated, a gathering system identified and sucked up any korb rock there. This rock was channelled upwards to the second level – referred to on the Plan as the Generation Level. On this level – as novos were aware – the huge korb rocks were loaded into Generation Chambers (30 in total) and broken down to smaller, more manageable sizes. Once this process was complete, the korb rocks were fed through funnels up to another floor – the Production Level. It was at this level that most of the prisoners worked, in Production Chambers. The Central Atrium, with its stairways and elevators, connected all levels. The plan showed there to be 100 korb chambers at the Production Level. Kane was aware that at present there were just 44 KCs in operation and 10 GCs, leading him to the reasonable conclusion that the kolony was far from working to its full capacity. With eight prisoners on each team, the Administration would obviously require the labour of many more prisoners in order to bring its operations to full capability.

Above the Production Level was the Accommodation Level. This consisted of cell accommodation for 3,000 prisoners – way above the present population and again an indication that *korb kapacity*, as the Master liked to call it, was far from being attained. Large areas of empty accommodation were walled off and out of sight. On the same level, but at a lower stage, was the Dining Hall and at a higher stage the Leisure and Sports Area, with its various game centres and pitch areas. The next level – the Security and Administration Level – was the one that interested Kane most. This Level had dormitory accommodation and training and association areas for 200 tyrons and housed the security and administration nerve centres. An interesting facet to this was that the Treatment Unit was linked to the

Administration Area and vice versa – this, Kane realised, would explain his arrival in the Administration Area when fleeing the tyrons on the night of Thorsen's death. A more important detail presented itself to Kane's eager eye, however, and that was that the Security Area – and its 200 tyrons – was linked to every other area on every other Level by a series of access tunnels. McKenzie's Kavern, as Kane now familiarly referred to the scene of his various trysts with his once mysterious contact, was shown as part of this series of interconnecting tunnels. Kane's blood raced a little faster as he realised the significance of the tunnels. The top Level of the kolony consisted of the Arrival Area (the first glimpse of the new kolony afforded to the novos' weary eyes), the Despatch Port – from where kanned korb was dispatched to Earth, and – surprisingly – the Kitchen Area.

Nice and simple, Kane thought, as his eyes once again poured over the Plan in his mind to keep his recollection sharp. He had striven over the last three days to make every element of the kolony layout a permanent feature in his memory and eventually forge it into a weapon to be used to devastating effect. He was now confident he would succeed.

"LONG TIME, NO TALK!" The message woke Kane from a light doze on his bunk. For some reason he couldn't really figure out, Kane didn't respond immediately. Instead, he sat up on the edge of his bunk, staring at the screen, wondering how important this message was going to be.

"Well?" The impatience implied in the second message woke Kane from his lethargy and he bolted over to the media station, sending a rapid reply in case his correspondent decided he wasn't there or just couldn't talk.

"I'm here. What's the story?" was his brief response. Kane's sense of relief that McKenzie had finally contacted him was conflicted by a sense of annoyance that it had taken her so long.

"No story – I'm just checking in", came the rejoinder. Kane relaxed a bit, realising he had no right to demand anything from his accomplice that she didn't want to give.

"It's nice to hear from you, anyway!" Kane sent, regretting already that he might have seemed abrupt.

"Same here!" McKenzie replied. "How's the courage?"

"We're o.k." Kane confirmed, shrugging off the question. "And you? Are you enjoying the wonderful atmosphere on the beautiful rock? I suppose you folks live in the Garden of Paradise!"

"Got it in one", was the unrevealing reply.

While Kane considered his next comment, another one arrived.

"Do you want to meet?"

Kane was pleasantly surprised. A meeting was the very thing he needed now, something to boost his spirits.

"You make the call. I'll be there", Kane reassured.

"I think we should talk – I'm sorry it's been so long, but it wasn't possible".

"Don't worry about it – I understand", Kane replied, trying to conceal his enthusiasm, and already feeling ashamed of his original annoyance. "When?"

"Be ready for K3-2hrs — I'll contact you shortly before then".

"Can't wait!" Kane quipped. Two hours into the third shift was o.k. for him.

KANE WAS ALL SET as he watched the hologram clock in his cell. It read K3-1:54:07 in the Master's perfect world. Kane marvelled at this world in which everything was neat and tidy and organised like clockwork. What a wonderfully ordered ship the Master ran! All hands on deck and everybody making a contribution to the voyage under their jolly captain! What a happy crew! Kane wondered did the Master really delude himself into believing that everything was rosy in his little space garden. Did he really mistake the sad fatalism of the majority of prisoners for a form of happiness with their lot? *What a sad bastard!* the prisoner thought. Lying on his bunk, staring at the ceiling, Kane wondered how much closer it would be to the truth to regard that same fatalism as a sign that the prisoners were merely marking time – waiting for their chance. When the opportunity arose, they would rise up and grasp it. Fatalism was a dangerous condition, in the prisoner's view. It sapped the vital juices of motivation and left the subject in a lifeless state. Acceptance of an intrinsically unacceptable situation – even as a tactic – was not an ideal foundation for rebellion. The vital question to be answered if there was to be a real chance of a mass uprising was how deep had the culture of acceptance permeated the bones and spirits of the prisoners? At the end of the day, the belief that you could *never* escape was the most effective lock of all, the key to which was deep in the recesses of the mind. If the majority of the prisoners had buried that key so deep as to render it irretrievable, he could do nothing for them. In that case, they would ultimately become their own jailors.

Bleep! Kane leapt to his feet on hearing the bleep of a message bounce off his screen. "Same place – five minutes!" the message on the screen read. "It's good!" Kane replied.

PASSING ALONG THE ATRIUM Balcony, Kane looked down at the Dining Hall staff cleaning up. Dining Hall staff were prisoners specially selected on good behaviour to serve out the food. There were six dining sessions in the korb day. Every shift had a breakfast and dinner, each of which lasted one hour. Every breakfast session for one shift was followed, half an hour later, by a dining one for the previous one, shift-finishers being allowed a half an hour to tidy themselves up. Breakfasters were given a standard lunch pack to eat during their half hour break in the shift day. Dining Hall workers had a relatively easy existence and were generally chosen from the more docile among the prisoner population. There was no cooking to do at all as the food, hot and ready to go, arrived in a counter of separate trays that travelled, the Dining Hall workers presumed, from a Kitchen Area elsewhere. The counter stretched all around the inside of the circular service area. A green light flashing on the serving tops signalled the arrival of the trays while, almost simultaneously, an inner platform containing the plates and utensils was ushered up behind the workers. When the meal had been served and the utensils returned, the now emptied food trays and the utensils were spirited away again.

With the serving tops opened, an array of korb 'specials' was to be seen. Most of these were korb reproductions of Earth meals. Meat was always minced or squared – so were the vegetables. Korb stew was by far the favourite meal on the kolony and almost all but the contrary were agreed that for flavour it would be hard to beat – even back on Earth. Soups were generally good too, with almost every conceivable recipe included. In the quality stakes, drinks and juices were no exception, with almost every taste catered for — bar alcohol, the lack of which took the good out of the rest of the menu for some of the prisoners. Novos were always pleasantly surprised to discover the high standard of food on the menu. Senior prisoners would explain that the Master was of the view that a well-nourished prisoner was a good worker. All were thankful for small mercies.

The meals over and the supplies spirited away, the prisoners would leave the Dining Hall to go to their various destinations. Then, almost immediately, the Hall would be transformed. The large service counter and the seats and tables all around the large room would sink into the floor, to return later when meals were to be served again. The Hall was then free to be used for other purposes – concerts, plays, departure ceremonies – all the 'normal' activities of a space labour prison.

35 THE HOLLOW

A PRISON COLONY TEEMING WITH prisoners can still be a lonely place, and for every prisoner on Korb-1 there was a multitude of ghosts. Ghosts feed on loneliness. Despair is the medium that draws them to the feast. Sandra Nielsen was lying on her bunk, her short yellow hair a beacon of beauty in the dimly-lit cell. It was one of those silent times for the young woman, with her shift finished, another one started and the third shift people safely ensconced in their beds. It was strange, she thought, how easy it was at one level to become used to an imposed environment. On another level, she was sure the soul never really lets go of what it had once embraced. When Nielsen first arrived on Korb-1, the novo felt that life would be unbearable in an outpost from which there could be no escape. The prospect of hard labour on a prison rock in space left the young woman in a depressed, almost suicidal state. But soon the cloud that hung over her head began to lighten as she got to know the other prisoners and saw how they coped with their lot and maintained generally high spirits.

Nielsen was on a par with Dayton – with whom she had recently become romantically associated – as one of the main sources of fun and humour in the circle of friends that was KC10-1, and her three years on the kolony appeared to have failed to dampen her zest for life. Time and again, the smiling Nielsen would lift the blanket of gloom that would occasionally descend upon Korb-1, with her endless supply of jokes and funny stories. Most of the team looked forward to hearing her comical twist to the latest serious event and she never failed to deliver. Like her partner, she was an expert at imitations and occasionally treated her fellow prisoners in the KC and in the Dining Hall to extempore performances.

Nielsen's story was really no different to that of most of the other 'political' prisoners in the kolony. A star pupil in Deever College in NCC 3 in NCR 40, she, along with three others, had established an *e-zine* for students. An excellent publication, the *e-zine*, called *The Hollow*, quickly developed a reputation for concentrating on issues the college authorities would have preferred ignored. Championing students' complaints against the administration of the college, *The Hollow* gradually became the voice of the student body on campus. As its popularity grew, it became more daring in its challenging view of the college administration and was soon regarded by the authorities as a promoter of discontent and dissatisfaction and an unwelcome intrusion into matters which officialdom felt should be of no concern to the student body. The Chief Registrar was of the view that *The Hollow* should be immediately and unapologetically shut down. The Governing Body, however, considered that a rather extreme reaction and ruled that, unless the law was broken, no action should be taken.

But then it happened. One of the four student publishers came across some information regarding an unusual arrangement between college authorities and the military. This arrangement involved experimentation in genetic re-engineering using low-ranking members of the forces. The subjects were deliberately kept uninformed of the potentially devastating effects of these experiments on their health. The arrangement – a commercial and security one – involved military funding in the form of a grant to the college, while the results of the research and any potential product was to be used and exploited exclusively by the military. Nielsen remembered well the night the four publishers sat up into the early hours as they struggled to reach a decision on whether to publish or not. Eventually, having overcome their fear of a backlash from the college authorities, they decided that the students had a right to know. The following evening, the latest edition of *The Hollow* went on-line, with the heading "College profits from illegal experiments!"

The reaction was swift. Before midday the following day, all four had been picked up by military intelligence and were being questioned on their relationship with "agents of a hostile power". A number of NC security police gave evidence of shadowing suspected Saladdan agents as they visited the college campus and stated that there could be no legitimate business for these people in that area. The latest visit, they claimed, was on the evening the new edition of *The Hollow* went on-line. The four denied any involvement with enemy agents but as the charges related to 'information terrorism in the cause of a hostile power', the onus was on the defendants to prove their innocence. After two hours, the judge found the four guilty, adding that he felt a particular reluctance to bring in such a verdict as all four youths came from respectable backgrounds.

The following day, another edition of *The Hollow* appeared. This contained a retraction of the story by the four editors and an apology that their youthful enthusiasm for a good headline and their "inexperience in confirming rumours, no matter how potentially attractive to readers they might appear to be" had led to a seriously misleading story being published. They informed their readers that they had now investigated the story fully and had discovered that there was no substance in the allegations at all. They expressed themselves to be embarrassed by the whole episode and hoped that their "unintentional error" would not damage relations between the college and the military and indeed between those two important institutions and the student body. The four announced that they had been offered student placements by the NC Strategic Publications Unit, which in the context they greatly appreciated and would be immediately taking up. A caption under an image of the four being shown around SPU headquarters contained a promise that they would return after their two-year placement was up and re-commence the publication of *The Hollow*.

As students read the final edition of *The Hollow* and dismissed the four editors as unprincipled opportunists who had probably invented the story of the experiments in order to draw attention to themselves and used the student *e-zine* to further their careers, the four hapless students, oblivious to their 'apology' and subsequent 'placements' by the military, were in a limbo tray heading for a rock 37 years away.

Nielsen experienced a flash of cold anger when remembering that time but always managed to pull herself up by the bootstraps when her mood was heading south. Springing from her bunk, she took up a palm-reader and began to read a comical story she had been writing recently.

Outside, Prisoner 313 passed by as silently as possible.

SIMPSON SAT IN HER apartment watching a film on her wall screen. She had dimmed the lights and was relaxing in her wrap-around couch, sipping some wine. These were lonely times for the lady who had once been a hot commodity in the security area of the NC Administration. A string of affairs with some of the most powerful men in the Administration had inevitably followed the same familiar course. The first contact and the realisation that something was there. The initial exciting stages of courtship, during which expense was never spared on 'the dark lady', as she was known in Administration circles. Then came the buzz of being close to decision makers, close to power. Being in on the big hits, the crunch calls, the late night deliberations gave the woman from rural NCR 122 a feeling of having made it to the top. The greatest satisfaction for Laura Simpson, though, was the way the other women regarded her, the looks and whispered conversations that greeted her arrival with x or y at an event. The looks of admiration from the younger women, the looks of envy from her own generation and the look of optical assassination from the wives and partners who wondered would their man be next. Simpson's relations with her fellow female officials were a different matter, however. Most of them, like their male counterparts were happy enough to do whatever it took to make upward progress in the organisation and didn't pass judgement on their ruthless sister, but all of them watched her carefully, always monitoring what pillow she lay her head on in case it impacted on them in any way.

In all of her many relationships, there always came the days when the 'the dark lady' realised her calls weren't being answered, that her present 'friend' (as she euphemistically termed her beau) was rumoured to have been seen with younger 'friends' of his own. Simpson's reaction was always to shrug her shoulders and move on. There was always another powerful figure looking for a companion, particularly one who spoke their language and had the reputation of 'the dark lady'.

Nonetheless, as the years passed, Simpson found herself drifting into that category that doesn't like to be alone but realises the inevitability of it all. The chemistry was wearing thin, the midnight meetings were going ahead without her, and she soon became yesterday's commodity amongst the powerful security elite. Facing a boring career and the probability of ending up a spectator in a game in which she had once been a main player, Simpson decided to accept the invitation from one of the few men she *hadn't* had a relationship with and joined the Master in his new Korb-1 Kolony.

The intervening years had been lonely but had given 'the dark lady' the opportunity to re-invent herself as 'the hard lady'. Enjoying every minute of her power trip on the kolony, she had become somebody who could live without the powerful men to whom she had once been so attracted but, at the same time, if the possibility emerged she wouldn't say no to another 'alliance' as she had always described her relationships in the past. The Master was not the kind of man any woman would find attractive and most of the male kontrollers were weak men running away from their failures in the past. Windsor, however ..... mm .... now he was his own man. One who had not shied away from challenges in the past, he was the kind of leader who could take the kolony and turn it into a real prison, a place where those who had power wielded it and those who hadn't respected those who did.

Mm ... Simpson pulled her legs up on the couch and made herself comfortable, sipping her wine and looking beyond the screen on the wall.

THE MINUTE HE ENTERED the tunnel and felt the portal close behind him, Kane sensed that his progress towards freedom had begun to move to a new phase. McKenzie had proven herself to him by providing him with the Kolony Plan – he was sure of that. Now, he was convinced he had an ally in a high place on the other side, something unimaginable until recently, and something that would give the prisoner a distinct edge in his battle with the Master. His access to the Kolony Plan was a good example. If the prey now knew the route of the chase, he would be harder to corner and pin down. Kane already felt a feeling of empowerment he had not experienced since his arrival on the kolony. It was a good feeling, a feeling of recovery from the debilitated state of the weak into which so many of the inmates of the kolony fell on their arrival on the rock. Kane walked strong and tall in the tunnel, like a man who had turned the corner and left a bad period in his life behind.

Kane wondered what else McKenzie could do. If she was sufficiently high up in the Administration, perhaps she could sabotage and manipulate the kolony's security system so as to facilitate a breakout – or a revolution and a prisoner-controlled regime on the kolony. Kane knew it was all to play for when he sat down beside his guardian angel in the tunnel.

"Well, hello, 313!" was McKenzie's welcome, the officer smiling as she used the prisoner's Kolony Identification Number to greet him.

"Hello, officer!" was Kane's attempt at retaliation.

Inviting Kane to sit down with a wave of her open hand, McKenzie sat and activated her security sensor, placing it beside her, as usual.

Without further ado, Kane produced the Reader from inside his shirt and presented it to McKenzie. "Thanks", he said, "best present I ever had!"

"Delighted!" McKenzie replied, an enticing smile gracing her attractive features. "Hope you found it interesting."

"Fascinating!" remarked Kane.

A silence followed, loaded with smiles and grins on both sides.

"O.k.!" said McKenzie, "I'll test you!"

Kane concurred with a wave of his hand.

McKenzie put on a serious expression. "From sector one, Level One to Treatment Unit, using tunnel system."

Kane sat back, reflected, then rattled off the following route: "Tunnel access adjacent right to GC7. Follow right over three turns till t-junction. Go right over two turns. Stairs access first stop left. Up four levels, then exit stairs left. Progress over two turns, then take third …" Kane hesitated, thought a while, then recovered. "Take third left, followed by immediate right. Access TU outside main panel".

McKenzie listened intently, following Kane's progress through the system with her mind's eye. When the prisoner finished his imaginary iteration through the tunnel system, she sat back, genuinely impressed.

"What can I say? Star pupil!" she remarked, a look of pleasant surprise on her face.

Kane was pleased, and looked at his companion challengingly.

"O.k!" McKenzie began again. "From Dining Hall to Korb Despatch Port."

Kane took up the challenge. "Enter system right of main rear door. Follow red corridor until it meets junction with green and blue. Take sharp turn up blue and proceed over seven left turns. Take eight and immediately enter stairs on right. Up one level, then exit stairs left. Continue up tunnel over five right turns. Take the next, just before junction. Proceed down red 1over eight turns. Access KDP just inside main entrance."

When Kane was finished, he emitted a sigh of achievement, then looked at his companion for a reaction. McKenzie was in awe. "Unbelievable! Unbelievable!" she uttered in amazement. "If the Master ever loses the Plan, I'll tell him to contact you!"

After a giddy silence, things settled down. McKenzie reflected for a minute. "We're making progress, Kane", she announced.

"Thanks to you!" Kane replied simply, anxious to record his appreciation of the support he had received.

McKenzie smiled, then reflected again.

"It must have been hard, Kane, coming to terms with this place."

"Have been! 'Is' is the word, I think! Especially when the phantoms come."

"I know," McKenzie replied in a compassionate tone.

"I'm not sure you do, or ever will. Don't get me wrong, I know you sympathise but you'll never know the loneliness in the middle of the night and the ghosts that won't go away. They're always there, waiting to look me in the eye, waiting to remind me …"

A sympathetic silence followed.

"Then there's the face!" Kane confessed.

"The face?"

Kane explained the background to his most regular 'visitor', how it was the most painful reminder of Strauss, his happiest times and a past that was never going to return.

"For years, I have believed that if I could only recognise the face, I could leave it all behind – draw a line and leave it all behind. And now I know who it is!" Kane announced with an air of satisfaction. "Now I know!"

"Who?" McKenzie asked, interested.

"Pedersen, the novo!"

36 FATEFUL DAY

THE MASTER WAS A serious man – a man with a purpose. Ever since he first devised the Korb Project and presented it to his superiors, the development and success of the project had been an intensely personal matter for him. Many in the Administration had scoffed at the rather pompous middle manager's proposal. Others, though, despite seeing *some* merit in it, regarded the proposal as too ambitious and hardly worth the return in terms of energy production. Line after line of management knocked the serious man's proposal to the ground – some on grounds of cost, others for reasons of 'security', others for a variety of reasons and some basically because it was his idea and not theirs. Eventually it appeared that the proposal to build a series of space colonies to mine for korb was never going to be acceptable to the dull upper echelons of administration management. It appeared that the serious middle manager would have to accept that lack of imagination amongst those in power would probably result in what he regarded as one of the most far-seeing and positive investments in the future of the Confederation being dispatched to the ethereal regions of the "Possible Long Term Projects Area".

But the serious man regarded himself as being possessed of a more forward-looking mind than the visionless functionaries who were attempting to block his imaginative proposal. There had to be a way to convince these small-minded creatures that the Korb Project was the future, even if it meant modifying it to accommodate their limited intelligence. He thought long and hard and then, as often happens to the visionary who has the patience to wait, an opportunity arose.

The Saladdan scare, although provoked and orchestrated by the Administration, had resulted in unexpected unrest in many areas of the Confederation. This unrest had ranged from public reaction to the information laws in the form of mass demonstrations to the more serious and threatening activities, in the eyes of the Administration, of 'information terrorists', those who felt strongly about the information restriction laws and were willing to act to frustrate them. The Administration reacted as those with power usually do and a major clampdown on 'information terrorists' and 'Saladdan agents' ensued. The result was a large prison population of highly motivated and capable people – mostly young and angry, and desperately seeking a way to strike back at what they saw as a dictatorial and corrupt regime. The serious man recognised his opportunity.

Word was siphoning down through the multitudinous layers of Administration management that the regime was wondering what to do with its new Class A prisoners. To hold them in public prisons would be to openly admit that the regime had a major political problem on its hands. To release them would be political – and security – suicide. A way would have to be found to deal with the problem of the 'new prisoners' and contain the threat to the security and political future of the Administration itself. It was then that the serious man sensed that his destiny was about to be fulfilled and stepped forward with a revised proposal.

The reaction of the Administration to the serious man's proposal was one of great interest. A plan that involved a solution to the 'prisoner problem' and the production of a continuous supply of korb just couldn't be ignored and the serious man soon found himself at the centre of attention and the composer of a series of memorandums requested by senior policy people. Slowly but surely the serious man convinced the various lines of command that he encountered along the way of the value of his idea and, one by one, they put their stamp of approval on the plan. The serious man knew his time had come and was convinced that it was now only a question of time before his dream would come to fruition. There was one more barrier to surmount, however, and soon the views of the Financial Control people became clear – the cost of the project was, in their view, prohibitive. The planners would have to think again.

The serious man was taken aback and even *he* felt at that stage that his project might be smothered in the red tape of Financial Control, bur serious men don't wilt at the prospect of a challenge and, after three days of intense concentration, a master plan was devised. Even the Financial Controllers were impressed with the sheer ingenuity of the new proposal and soon the Korb Project was on stream as a priority administration project.

The Master often thought of those days when it appeared that his greatest ever idea was to be discarded by moronic functionaries. Sitting in his office suite in the heart of Korb Kolony 1, he looked admiringly at the hologram of the kolony in the corner of his room. How narrow, he often thought, is the line between success and failure, between recognition and dismissal, between victory and defeat. How easy it is to be beaten down by the negativity of the ignorant and be forced to abandon what history must judge as monumental.

Now the serious middle manager had become the Master of his own domain, a domain created by him from the ingenious depths of his own imagination, a domain nurtured and protected until it had become a reality. That reality, it had often occurred to him since, had also become reality for many others in the intervening years – their only reality. For them, the Master's kolony was their universe, one whose limits were defined by the nature of the world he had designed – for them Korb-1 was home. This thought pleased the Master immensely. That his creation had become the new world for so many who had found the rules of the old one too hard to obey was an irony that brought a smile to the Master's lips. He also felt great pride that a plan conceived in *his* mind had become one of the main flagship projects of the Northern Confederation. That he had served his Administration in a manner in which no ordinary traditional servant of the regime could possibly have done was a badge of honour. When asked what his reward should be, he had no hesitation in seeking an appropriate prize for such sterling service. To be made Master of the biggest of the Korb Kolonies – Korb-1 – would be his crowning glory.

Putting a glass of arctic ice juice to his lips, the Master felt the liquid caress his palate. Closing his eyes, he wallowed in the pleasure of a man who had been proven right.

HEADING FOR HER WORKSTATION in Kolony Kontrol, Zeena McKenzie, Assistant Head of Security on Korb-1, was thinking of Kane. A strange feeling concentrated in her whole being as she thought of the relationship she had developed with the prisoner. Foremost in the mixture of feelings that teased the young woman as she walked quietly along the security corridor was not, as she thought it might be, the fear of being discovered and punished by the Kolony Administration but the fear of failure – the fear that, despite all the thought and planning so carefully invested in her scheme, it might somehow fail and that her efforts would come to nought. Making her way towards the Central Security Area, she vowed, as she had done time and time again, to ensure that, whatever happened, failure would not be the end-result of this particular project.

Entering the CSA, the young officer passed the offices of the kontrollers who, under the supervision and guidance of the Master, ran the kolony. McKenzie had nothing but disdain for these people, regarding them as idiots dressed up in fancy uniforms, pretending to be powerful and influential, but really frightened of taking a decision on anything for fear they would get it wrong. But, as in most things in life, there was the exception. In this case, it was Windsor. Windsor, McKenzie found particularly pompous. A sweating, serious type, he was a regular visitor to McKenzie's boss, Security Officer Simpson, one who fed the obnoxious kontroller's desire for 'involvement' in the minor detail of the security programme – or the *Kolony Protection Programme* as it was officially styled – by providing him with behavioural monitoring disks – essentially video close-ups of members of the prison population together with a voice over analysis by a kolony psychologist. Windsor would discuss the latest batch of these disks with Simpson, and ask her opinion of the mental state of some of the prisoners, and whether this behaviour signalled a threat to security. Sometimes Simpson would surprise Windsor by producing a digitally enhanced video clip of some prisoners talking in the Dining Hall or the L+S and discuss what she would call "key words" in the dialogue. Together they would read all sorts of potential threats to security into the prisoners' conversations and bemoan the smugness and blindness of the Master in failing to recognise the "immediate security menace" in the kolony. Their discussions would generally end with the expression of the shared belief that it would not be long before the "old fool" was forced to recognise the reality of the situation and act accordingly.

McKenzie watched the series of monitors in the panel in front of her. On these, prisoners could be seen coming and going along the corridors, seated in the Dining Hall, working in the chambers and indulging in a variety of other activities. It was an accepted part of the life of the kolony that all areas would be monitored by Administration Security. Even if the Administration denied that, the prisoners would operate on the basis that it was true anyway. One area which was not monitored automatically, however, was the prisoners' personal quarters. Following discussions with Nevin shortly after the establishment of the kolony, the Administration agreed not to monitor these areas but sought an assurance from the prisoners through Nevin that "no actions that could be regarded by the Administration as a risk to security" would take place in personal quarters. The prisoners agreed to this arrangement and the practice of monitoring personal quarters was discontinued – except, and this was the bit the prisoners never heard about, 'when the security of the kolony was threatened'. This meant that whenever a kontroller certified that the security of the kolony was under threat – and Windsor could always be relied upon to sign on the dotted line – a monitor eye, as small as the head of a pin, would be strategically placed in a prisoner's cell and a three dimensional audio-visual feed of the prisoner's activity in that area obtained.

The Assistant Security Officer never liked viewing this material but was often given the task by Simpson. The young woman felt this kind of activity was an unnecessary invasion of what little privacy the prisoners on Korb-1 enjoyed, as everybody knew full well that surveillance of this nature had never turned up anything of significance anyway. Simpson and Windsor, of course, were of another view. They regularly poured over this material, agreeing that behaviour observed was suspicious and warranted continuous monitoring. McKenzie concluded at an early stage that the two security fanatics were very dangerous people, imbued with a perverse sense of morality, and addicted to security in the same way that others were fanatical about other spectator sports. She was convinced that both of them got their rocks off watching the more intimate moments of the prisoners in their cells.

On one occasion, McKenzie herself had experienced a strange mixture of shame and excitement when asked by Simpson to analyse coverage of two prisoners in a cell together. Watching the two naked in one another's arms and listening to their intimate conversation, she felt both stimulated and contaminated at the same time. On finishing the monitoring of the take in which both prisoners were clearly discussing possible escape from Korb-1, McKenzie had sat and thought long and hard about how to handle the situation. She had no desire to bring the full weight of kolony security on the two, particularly if they *were* serious about their plans but, at the same time, if Simpson or anyone else saw the recording, they would conclude that an escape bid *was* being planned and that McKenzie's failure to bring this plan to the attention of the authorities demanded an immediate explanation. Having watched the recording a number of times, McKenzie decided on a course of action. Editing the take meticulously, she turned the two prisoners' conversation into a harmless one about the more intimate parts of their relationship. She was convinced that this fictitious element would be so attractive to the voyeuristic instincts of the two securocrats that they would find it immediately credible and never suspect any third party intervention. Working feverishly, the Assistant Security Officer finished editing the piece, wrote her report on it, declaring it "of no security value", and filed it away in Simpson's directory.

That night, in her bunk, McKenzie had thought of the two prisoners on the tape and wondered what their backgrounds were. What had they done to be banished off the face of the Earth and hidden away like this? What was their offence? Had they actually succeeded in damaging the Administration? She thought that unlikely. The Administration was so powerful now that 'information terrorism' as they called it could never really be anything more than a minor irritation.

Surrounded by images of young lives, plucked from the welcoming soil of friendship and companionship and tossed into the barren hole that was Korb-1, McKenzie found it difficult to keep her sense of morality intact. In the sordid reality that surrounded her, it would have been so easy to slide into an automatic acceptance of the inevitability of it all. McKenzie's response was to take every realistic opportunity provided to thwart the Administration. This she did by engineering interventions to frustrate the regime at every hand's turn. It was ironic that the beneficiaries of the quiet young woman's involvement would never even suspect there was a helping hand playing a role in their lives – but that was the way it had be.

McKenzie thought about the day Kane's path and hers had crossed. It was remarkable, she thought. She knew something big and unusual was happening in the security area because Simpson had told her to take the day before that off. As Simpson wasn't the warmest of creatures, McKenzie concluded that something was going down that Simpson didn't want her to see. The following day, Simpson gave the air of someone who had pulled off a mighty stroke, smiling a reptilian smile that suggested the beast had just devoured its prey. As soon as she got the chance, McKenzie scoured all the data and takes from the previous twelve hours. Some of the takes were so uneventful as to suggest that they had been doctored and some bland file piece put in their place. Nothing seemed to be emerging.

The back-up files were the same. Then it occurred to McKenzie to look at the archive back-ups, a system devised by her to automatically store back-up files in case one got lost or was corrupted. What the Assistant Security Officer saw shocked her.

The young woman had just made an extra copy of the file and hidden it away when she heard a commotion outside her office. Laser shots were searing everything in sight. Alarmed, she opened her door slightly to peep outside. As she did, a prisoner came careering down the corridor, two tyrons in hot pursuit. Just as the prisoner got to her door, he took a shot in the shoulder and collapsed in to the room. McKenzie rapidly closed the door behind the hunted prisoner and stood over him in the knowledge that only her intervention could prevent the tyrons from finishing the job. As she did, the door burst open and the tyrons aimed at the fallen prisoner. "Don't shoot!" McKenzie roared. It's o.k. He's my prisoner now." The tyrons stood back, visibly disappointed.

McKenzie knew she had to act fast. Using the security frequency – all calls made on which are logged and recorded – she called a doctor she knew in the Treatment Unit. "Rodriguez – McKenzie here", she said, "I've got a prisoner here in my office with superficial wounds. I repeat: prisoner here with *superficial* wounds." The message received, McKenzie looked at the fallen prisoner on the floor. One glance confirmed what she had thought at first – this was the male prisoner whose intimate conversation she had doctored only days before.

As the tyrons stood by, like predators deprived of a meal, the medic team arrived and the prisoner was carried away. Just then Simpson came on the scene. "What's going on?" she demanded. "What happened?" McKenzie gave her superior an account of what had taken place, but it was clear to the young officer that Simpson already knew.

McKenzie was sure something unwholesome was happening in the kolony and was equally certain that, whatever it was, Simpson and

Windsor were up to their necks in it. Perhaps it was a power struggle between the kontrollers, maybe even the beginning of a push against the Master. Perhaps it was bigger than that. She decided to find out. What she had on file already was enough to sink their sorry skins but she wanted more – she wanted to sink the entire kolony. That fateful day, McKenzie became convinced her path would cross with that of the prisoner again but, in the meantime, she would have to find out more.

37 HARMONY AND COOPERATION

IT WAS GETTING HOT in Kane's cell. The prisoner felt the temperature rise with almost every breath he took. He sat in front of his personal communication station, sweat running down his brow, at times checking for messages, at times beginning a game of *War-Raok!* but always exiting after a few rudimentary moves. Sometimes he paced up and down in the cell, other times he lay nervously on his bunk. The hologram clock above his head moved slowly, almost reluctantly, forward as if held back by some unseen hand. Kane was restless and had been so since McKenzie told him he might be wrong about the Face. Her reaction to his suspicions regarding the bearded novo, Pedersen, had been that she would be very surprised if *he* was an agent as he had been targeted by the Technician and thrown into the Void by Windsor! If he *was* an agent, the authorities seemed to be going to extraordinary – and unnecessary – lengths to disguise that fact. Why subject an agent to the Void? What would be the point? If it was to depict him as being regarded as a dangerous threat to the regime, it was an odd move, considering the only way the general prisoner population would be aware he was in the Void in the first place would be if the authorities let the word out or he himself announced it on his release. But as no prisoner could verify such a claim as fact, it would be sufficient for the authorities to merely make the announcement without carrying out the deed. In short, McKenzie just didn't buy into Kane's theories on Pedersen.

McKenzie's reaction took Kane by surprise. Having been traumatised twice by the revelation of the identity of the Face in recent days, he was fearful of what could be in store for him next in that regard. Consequently, when McKenzie offered to conduct an exploration session with him, using the *feer* drug, Kane became nervous. If Pedersen wasn't the Face – then who was? He would be back to square one if he couldn't identify the one who had been in the background during those troubled final days in his former life. But what if he did succeed in identifying the unseen hand that he believed had been manipulating events at that time? What if it turned out to be someone close, someone dear, someone on whose positive memory he relied in the depth of his nocturnal despair? What then?

Kane paced up and down. McKenzie had made it clear that the decision to proceed would be his and if he decided not to go ahead with the session, that would be ok with her. If, on the other hand, he decided to take his chances with the truth drug, she would be available the following evening to carry out the session in the tunnel. It would be his call. Kane moved around his cell uneasily, turning over in his mind the possible consequences of action or inaction in tackling the Face again. One thing was certain, though – when McKenzie contacted him again, he would have to decide. Even if his decision turned out not to be a wise one, Kane hoped he would eventually learn to handle that and move forward.

Kane sat in front of the station and waited. He waited an hour and then 2, and then, disappointed, lay on his bunk to rest. Lying on his back, staring at the stringer bulbs on the ceiling, the prisoner found himself sinking into an unsettled sleep, over time and space, and moving once again amongst those he loved. Magically, Kane was in the Old World again, enjoying a life of guiltless bliss, ignorant of the machinations of the Administration, and interested only in the kind of information that made his life more pleasant – the times of the sports on the networks, the days off he would earn in the coming month, the nights Sheena would be free to spend with him in the coming week. Life would have been so simple if Kane had been given a second chance. Blissfully, he would ignore the cause of 'information freedom' that had eventually come to destroy his life. After all, the mass of the population in whose interest he and Strauss had destroyed their own lives were oblivious to the patriotic sacrifice of the two young ideologues. In fact, most people would probably hand them over to the Administration if they ever managed to escape and make their way back to Earth.

Yes, if Kane got the chance to live his life again, he would not make the same mistakes a second time. If only there *had* been a second chance. If only there had been a warning sign that he could have heeded. Wallowing in a sea of regret and despair, Kane felt something pulling him back. Gradually, he left his lost world of old friends and imaginary new ones and returned to his real one with its stringer bulbs and plastic walls. Perverse as it was, he knew this was his only reality now. If he were to escape from its suffocating grasp, the prisoner would have to accept that reality, stare it straight in the face and challenge it to mortal combat. Only then could Kevin Kane hope to become a free man again.

Suddenly, Kane heard the message receiver on his contact station beep. Leaping from his bunk, he jumped into the seat in front of the pc. A message flashed on the screen:

"How are things?"

"O.k. I thought you'd abandoned me!" Kane replied limply.

"Man of little faith!" McKenzie replied.

"What's next?" Kane enquired eagerly.

"Well, that's up to you. Do you want to go ahead with the session or leave it? It's decision time!"

Kane waited a moment, then to his surprise found himself keying in the words "Let's go!"

"Enthusiasm!" remarked McKenzie, "I like it – it turns me on! We meet .... ten minutes .... same place!"

"I'll be there!" Kane assured.

Kane sat back in his chair. Tired, drained, worn out – but ready to take on the challenge that would, he hoped, be another milestone along the road to his ultimate liberation. Composing himself, the prisoner left his cell.

WALKING DOWN THE CORRIDOR to meet McKenzie, Kane felt a strange sensation. If anyone had told him only a month ago that Thorsen would be dead and he would be wandering through the kolony in the middle of the night to meet a member of the Administration, he would have thought they were mad. So many things had happened, and events had taken so many unexpected turns, that nothing would surprise him now. Whatever way events panned out, he felt there would be no turning back at this stage. The present cycle would run its course – no matter what the result.

Passing through the security rays, he couldn't help worrying that the alarm would sound and his association with Zeena McKenzie would come to a sudden and painful end. Every step of the way, he expected a team of tyrons to swoop out on him from behind another secret panel and drag him away to receive vengeful retribution for daring to think he could escape. But the tyrons never appeared and Kane soon found himself at the entrance that had opened at his first meeting to reveal the graceful apparition that he had had the pleasure to view regularly ever since. As soon as Kane approached the panel, it opened and the prisoner entered.

IN HIS OPERATIONS CENTRE, Windsor was studying the lists of suspects provided by his minions. Going through the files on screen, he studied the physiognomy of the faces appearing in front of him. In Windsor's dark mind, these were the enemy – a criminal subspecies of subversives – individuals who had displayed an inability to play a productive role in society. They had now been sent to the kolony to be punished and make a constructive contribution to the Administration. But because of the Master's ineptitude, Korb-1 had been turned into a holiday camp. Prisoners who had failed to live a fruitful life in the past were now being rewarded in what was turning out to be a leisure centre. But that was all about to come to an end. Windsor believed that the insolence of these ungrateful good-for-nothings, whose villainous characters were evident in their unrefined features, and the inability of the Master to appreciate the threat these criminals posed to the welfare of the kolony were now about to combine to create a dangerous situation, one which would ensure that Windsor's destiny as saviour of Korb-1 would soon be fulfilled.

As the identity files flashed on the screen before him, Windsor studied the synopses and the faces.

Wilson, Harper. Male. D.O.B.: 20.01.2104. P.O.B.: Urban 13, NC Region 2271. Offence: Information Terrorism.

Kerwin, Donald. Male. D.O.B.: 01.07.2118. P.O.B.: Urban 2, NC Region 188. Offence: Acting as Agent for Alien Power.

Cronan, Fletcher. Male. D.O.B.: 11.11.2121. P.O.B.: Rural 32, NC Region 286. Offence: Pathological Larceny.

Denny, Sonya. Female. D.O.B.: 30.06.2125. P.O.B.: Urban 71, NC Region 111. Offence: Industrial Espionage.

Deschamps, Louise. Female. D.O.B.: 19.09.2127. P.O.B.: Rural 152, NC Region 71. Offence: Information Terrorism.

Merriman, Bernard. Male. D.O.B. 12.09.2122. P.O.B. Rural 9, NC Region 7. Offence: Information Terrorism.

.... and on and on through faces and facts that told stories that Windsor could never understand.

The kontroller looked with distaste at each and every one of the mugshots on the screen. One or more of these, he was certain, if not them all, was actively involved in planning insurrection right now and he was going to stop them. By the time he was finished with them, their loose mouths would divulge their imbecilic plans and he would destroy them all – soon, very soon.

WHEN KANE SAW MCKENZIE in the tunnel, his first reaction was to feel he was meeting an old friend. She smiled as their eyes met and he responded with a friendly nod. After the initial glance, however, Kane sensed a slight tension in his friend's demeanour that refocused him on the decision he now had to make.

"Are we going ahead?" McKenzie asked immediately, a serious expression on her face.

"Looks like it!" Kane replied, with a smile, relieved at having at last taken the decision.

"I think you're right", McKenzie returned, "let's get into it!"

The woman in the smart security uniform set her security scanner down beside her, as was her wont on these surreptitious occasions, then, in an equally business-like manner, she produced from the leg pouch of her uniform, a jabber, a cartridge, a small circular device and a small box.

"Um, impressive! You'd make a great doctor!" remarked Kane.

"What till I'm finished with you!" McKenzie warned, a wicked smile on her face.

When everything was ready, McKenzie appeared to suddenly remember something else and produced a mini-zennor baton from another pocket.

"Oh, expecting trouble?" Kane enquired, eying the weapon.

"Just in case you get too excited!" McKenzie responded, smiling. Kane returned a quizzed expression.

"O.k. – ready to roll? If things get complicated, I can pull you out."

"Ready!" Kane replied, a determined expression on his face. Kane sat back against the tunnel wall, closing his eyes momentarily and taking a deep breath. At once, the smell of the tunnel, a neutral plastic smell, and the scent of his companion's perfume mixed to remind him of his first visit to this now-hallowed meeting place. Although not that long ago, it seemed in a strange way to be almost a lifetime away, so many things had happened in the meantime. Kane attempted to relax.

"Right! Let's go!" announced McKenzie. Immediately, she placed the circular device on Kane's forehead, as he lay back against the wall of the tunnel. Opening the small box, she touched a button and immediately a red line, moving in a circle, lit up on the object on Kane's forehead. "This is to monitor your vital signs and mood patterns," she re-assured. Kane nodded. McKenzie then inserted the cartridge into the jabber, nodded to Kane and administered the measure into the back of the prisoner's right hand. Kane was ready once again to travel into the past.

THE Master sat alone in his office, looking at the Korb-1 hologram. Admiring it, adoring it, he wondered was he the only one who *really* appreciated the achievement that was Korb-1. His political masters seemed nowadays to be taking the kolony for granted. It continued to serve them well but yet they insisted on providing him with second-rate support staff, people whose understanding and feeling for the project was less than was desirable. They had even saddled him with a psychopathic megalomaniac who suffered from delusions of 'leadership'. But he knew how to handle Windsor. Enough rope – and then exit krazy kontroller stage left. As for the prisoners, he was certain that his strategy would be successful, as it always had been – once a prisoner realised there was no escape, he or she considered themselves part of the kolony and carried out their role like everybody else. Goading the prisoners, as lunatics like Windsor would demand, would result in only one thing – resentment and revolt, and nobody wanted that.

The Master wondered was it time to act on Windsor. On his screen, he called up the staff files. Going through them, he tried to figure out the reasons these people had joined the service. Was it the status of being on top in a prison situation? Was it that they had nothing else to do with their lives? Or was it that they were all running away from something?

Whatever it was, he had indeed been presented with a motley crew. He closed the files in disappointment. His examination of the records led him to the conclusion he had always suspected. He was alone in his awareness of the onerous responsibility resting on the shoulders of the Korb Kolony team, alone in his appreciation of the importance of the project, and alone in his understanding of how to defend it. It was a heavy burden, he felt, but he would carry it through. If he didn't – if he couldn't – it would fall.

He decided it was time for the kolony, both prisoners and administration, to return to basic values. It was in the interest of everyone on Korb-1 to make the project work. They were all, in their own way, part of this great experiment. Everyone must work together for the success of the project. The production of korb was the primary reason for the establishment of the kolony. It was better that this aim be fulfilled in a spirit of harmony than in an atmosphere of tension and mistrust. Prisoners were prisoners and labour was labour, but if those whose future lay in imprisonment and work on Korb-1 realised that they had no other future, he was sure they would see it in their interest to make the whole project proceed as smoothly as possible.

This policy of cooperation and common purpose would remain the cornerstone of the Master's approach to governing Korb-1. No matter what Windsor or anyone else tried to do to upset this approach, the Master would remain true to his vision of the productive harmonious korb kolony. It was *his* idea and it was *his* duty to protect it.

38 WAVES ON THE SHORE

Waves. There was always something about the sound of waves, slowly, incessantly falling on the strand. Since the time she was a little girl, McKenzie had always been fascinated by the waves. They soothed her when she was afraid, they relaxed her when she was alone, they gave her hope when all seemed lost. Time and time again, she would sit on the beach or on the dunes overlooking the cove beside her home and listen as the waves kissed and kissed and kissed the shore. She remembered that it was at Traw Beach that she had first met Ruyan – Ruyan Kendrick, First Officer in the Confederation Guard of NCR 18.

He had been out surfing off the beach the day they first met. She had been watching him, interested, and when he passed by and let his bag fall beside her, their first conversation had begun. He was an attractive figure – great physique and friendly relaxed personality. Getting to know him better, she discovered that the handsome young man was a dedicated soldier with a determined sense of duty, a young man who believed in the system and was ready to serve. She had been working two years, at that stage, in the Systems Area of the NC District Administration and they both felt that their work with different areas of the Administration gave them something in common – two young people serving the public good. Both of them took their security duties seriously – him on the military side, her on the information one. Together they felt their respective roles supported one another, like two sides of the same coin. They even kept their respective occupational secrets to themselves, as all good NC servants should, though she always knew when he was working on something big because he seemed to tense up, almost unconsciously. Her area of responsibility didn't, as of yet, allow her access to sensitive or highly confidential projects, but anytime she came across something 'interesting', she never succumbed to the temptation to share it with Ruyan.

Waves. She remembered the sound of the waves on Traw Beach the day they decided to live together and the day when, having been vested with the authority of the Northern Confederation to form a union, they set up house in an apartment close to the strand.

Life was idyllic for the young couple for almost a year, then, suddenly and tragically, it all came to an end. McKenzie remembered so clearly the horrible afternoon when District Intelligence officials arrived at her office and asked to speak to her. "A terrible incident", they said. "Cruel and heartless", was how they described it. "These people have no feelings – they're not like us!" one of them declared, referring to the Saladdans. "They will stop at nothing to damage us", they said, "even when it comes to murdering fine young officers like Kendrick." They said that Kendrick had been working on a sensitive project, the details of which could not be revealed, and had uncovered two Saladdan agents in the course of his duties. They had incinerated his *ptv*, leaving nothing remaining of the young officer.

McKenzie had proudly carried First Officer Kendrick's personal banner at his farewell ceremony. Even now a tear would touch her cold eye as she reflected on the short time they had had together and the cruel manner in which their union had been brought to a tragic end.

The young woman continued on in her position with the Administration, and the fact that she was essentially a war widow brought her 'Special Trust' status within the system. Soon she was promoted to Assistant Systems Manager and then to Systems Manager. After that she became an Assistant Systems Executive and then Systems Executive. McKenzie trusted the system and the system trusted her. But trust is a delicate piece of equipment – damage it and it can't be repaired, break it and it will remain broken forever.

McKenzie remembered well the day that trust was shattered. She had been routinely archiving backup files in the District Security Area when she came across a single file, obviously dislocated, containing a date. To many, a date would be just a date, but to McKenzie this was no ordinary date – it was July 2, 2169 – the date First Officer Ruyan Kendrick had died. Instinctively, the Systems Executive opened the file.

What McKenzie discovered that day was to change her life forever. Sitting in front of her work unit in her apartment near the beach, she analysed thoroughly the file she had copied and brought home. Much of it was encoded but as McKenzie had access to almost all the encoding principles used by Security, it didn't take her long to break in. The most intriguing part of the file was a document called "Special Project – Terminations". This was followed by a series of code numbers and words and corresponding dates. The date 07.02.2169 corresponded to the number FO88976 and the word *ark*. All the other dates on the list were within the time span 2166 to 2169. McKenzie sipped a fruit juice and looked out at the setting sun on the sea, thinking.

McKenzie recalled the day she had decided to check the files on the prisoners she had been monitoring in their cell for Simpson. Prisoners 313 and 393. It was the day that Kane had literally fallen, a wounded and hunted man, into her lap. The files showed the two to be Kevin Kane and Andrea Thorsen. Kane was classified IT2, a classification that signified less than total motivation to Information Terrorism, whereas his accomplice was IT1. Both their files showed that they had recently become the subject of cell monitoring, as a result of her expressed interest – shared with other prisoners – in gaining information that could infringe security. What this information was wasn't specified nor was the identity of the prisoners she had discussed these matters with. Her psychological report indicated that she was a dangerous prisoner, and likely to become involved in subversive activity. Thorsen's file ended there.

McKenzie listened to Thorsen's voice identification tape. Once more she heard the husky voice of the woman whose most intimate moments with Prisoner 313 had now become an object of interest to the Securomaniacs in the kolony. It made her sad to think that, after what she had seen on the archive file now in her possession, Prisoner 313 would never hear that voice again. McKenzie copied both prisoner records, deleted all evidence of a copy transaction, and closed the Prisoner Records Database.

Just then, the communicator buzzed. McKenzie answered. It was Doctor Rodriguez, her contact in the Hospital.

"That headcase you sent in here is sure screwed up", he informed the silent McKenzie. "He's mad as a hatter – but he's got good reason to be. His woman just died from injuries received in a chamber accident today. It was awful, she's was burned all over."

McKenzie was shocked. She thought immediately of the recording in her possession.

"Are you still there?" Rodriguez enquired.

"Yes .. yes", McKenzie confirmed, weakly. "It's sad, isn't it? Though he's lucky to be alive himself, another few minutes and the tyrons would have sent him packing too."

"Tough guys, aren't they – really rough", was the young doctor's reply.

When the conversation finished, McKenzie sat at the control panel again. In her mind, she played back the video file she had stashed away hurriedly that day. The first scene was straight from the chamber back-ups. She remembered the scene as a young woman prepared for another gush. The signal light had turned green as she approached the funnel for inspection. Just as she opened the funnel door, however, the light turned red again and the prisoner, attempting desperately to get the door closed fast, was struck on the left shoulder by a small gush. Falling to the ground in pain, the prisoner's face registered the agony and fear associated with korb exposure. Surprisingly, four tyrons arrived on the scene almost immediately and the injured woman was taken away.

The next scene was one McKenzie remembered very clearly. The prisoner was seen being taken away down the corridor – in the opposite direction of the Treatment Unit! Somehow realising that her escort's intention was not to save her, the young woman started to wrestle with the tyrons in an effort to escape. Brutally the soldiers pushed her back down onto the stretcher. McKenzie could clearly see the terror on the woman's face as she realised what her captors had in store for her. McKenzie recognised the face as that of Prisoner 393 – Andrea Thorsen.

Inside GC1, closed for maintenance work that day, the prisoner's fate was sealed. Strapped to the open door of a feeder funnel, a small gush of korb was released. McKenzie could still see the mixture of dread and defiance in the young woman's expression as the gush approached. In a few moments, the deed was done, and having been placed in a sealed container tray, in which the patient is suspended over an air current, she was moved away by two tyrons wearing korb protection suits. The final act of the carefully choreographed drama had been the one carried out in front of Thorsen's soul mate in the Treatment Unit.

McKenzie was still horrified to think of the events she had witnessed. It was merely more proof, if more was needed, that the regime would stop at nothing to achieve its aims. The question remaining to be answered now was why – why was Thorsen so dangerous that she had to die. What had she done or what had she discovered? The Assistant Security Officer swore that, whatever it was, she would find out.

TRUTH, MCKENZIE THOUGHT WRYLY. What a marvellous concept! Since time immemorial, human interaction has been governed by the communication of messages between individuals and between groups. This continuous interaction soon begged the question as to whether a communication was truthful or not and to what extent. In other words, who told the first lie? One could never ever be sure, of course, when anybody was telling the truth and the basis on which information was imparted and received was one of trust or levels of trust. We all craved for truth, for the facts, but we ourselves never had a problem being economical with the truth. 'What you don't know doesn't hurt you' is a proverb as old as human interaction at its most basic and the entire art of politics is based the economy of truth at best or on the huge lie at its very worst. The information services in all the major global political conglomerates were now in the hands of the Administrations. In many cases the concept of truth no longer existed. Perhaps it never had. Truth was a word rarely used now. Most people regarded facts as things produced by the regime and most people trusted the regime – so there was no problem. Granted, there were a few hotheads who wished to make an issue out of these things, but they were not taken seriously by the majority of citizens anywhere.

Ironically at the same time that the outdated concept of truth was fading into the distant past, the *feer* drug had been developed – by the Administration. The *feer* drug was the supreme weapon of control in the hands of the administrator. Available in a variety of forms, the new drug, following a small dose, would result in the inability of the recipient to tell anything but the truth as he or she knew it to be.

NC Public Order 887987883290 granted the Administration the power to administer the drug to anybody held in legal custody. This meant that anybody and everybody, no matter what the accusation levelled against them, could be placed in a state in which they could not conceal or disguise the facts. Initially, the Administration was delighted at the success in crime detection and the conviction rate soared. But two developments muddied the waters somewhat. First, the Administration decided that in some exceptional cases it might not want the truth to emerge. This led to NC Public Health Order 887987883290-2, which stipulated that only the Administration could decide in what cases and in what circumstances *feer* was to be used. This was done in the interests of "the functioning of the judicial system". Second, almost everyone in society got their hands on the easily, and unnoticeably, administered drug. This led to the break-up of social, business and sexual relationships, and damage to the fabric of society. NC Public Order 887987883290-13 attended to this matter by banning the sale, distribution or possession of the truth drug. Matters became even more complicated for the Administration, however, when an anti-drug for *feer* – *shayna* – was produced. This diluted the effects of the truth drug and allowed the subject to convince themselves that whatever they said was actually the truth!

NC Public Order 887987883290-41 banned the sale, distribution and possession of *shayna*.

In the heart of the Korb-1 Kontrol Centre, Zeena McKenzie wondered what it meant to be truthful anymore. She wondered did it matter. The incident of 2 July, 2169, and the events that followed that fateful day had dispelled from the young McKenzie's mind any ideas she had once harboured that one of the main responsibilities of the civil authority was to protect the truth. After that harrowing time, McKenzie realised that truth, just like oil, korb and water, was just another important resource that the regime needed to be able to control, manage, and administer when it suited *them*.

39 OPERATION OPPORTUNITY

IN MCKENZIE'S TUNNEL, UNKNOWN to the prisoners and tyrons passing by outside, a strange scene was being played out. Prisoner 313, propped up against the wall, a critical signs monitor on his forehead and a jabber-full of *feer* in his veins, was describing in a trance-like state events that had happened, depending upon the perspective, forty years ago or perhaps only three or four. Sitting across from the entranced prisoner, monitoring his vital signs and mood direction and listening intently to his every word, was Assistant Security Officer Zeena McKenzie.

The observer would have assumed that some form of torture or interrogation was taking place. But that was not the case here. Kevin Kane was making a journey, a journey back into himself and into the events that had changed his apparently happy life and created for him the new identity of Prisoner 313 on Korb Kolony One. It was a journey to make one last desperate effort to discover if the events of those days, which seemed so far from the prisoner's present reality, were the sad result of a botched idealistic attempt to change the world or something else, something more sinister, involving some unseen hand.

The detail of Kane's recollection impressed McKenzie. Where the Development Sector employee and his work-partner girlfriend went at night, who they encountered, what he said, what she said, how they were dressed – everything came out with undiluted honesty to recreate an apparently average relationship in a seemingly normal environment. But this was no average relationship. Before it had gone very far, Kane's young companion had convinced him of the moral duty they bore, because of the opportunity their employment represented, to strike a blow for information freedom. Soon, the couple's association was transformed from the usual boy-girl romance and sexual relationship into a liaison of intrigue, bonded by secrecy and danger, as theory and planning moved into the realm of practice and execution. Kane's recollection of the relationship now was characterised by the excitement of the clandestine more than the normal thrill of chemical attraction. Increasingly since those days, however, he had become convinced that the conspiracy that shrouded the young couple's lives involved more than the two idealists.

Time after time, Kane would tense when recounting an event as simple as a visit to the Cave Club and begin to form a recollection of some other individual watching, listening, waiting somewhere in the hazy backdrop. But time and time again, the image would fade just as the disturbed prisoner was about to peer in its direction, in an attempt to formulate a face or identify a feature. McKenzie was beginning to lose hope that Kane would ever recognise his illusive phantom and free himself of its accusatory stalking presence — but then it happened! Kane had just managed to identify what he thought were the colours associated with the shady figure as it hovered in the background of the Tumbleweed Restaurant – purple and yellow – when it drifted out of his consciousness again. It looked as if that would be the only glimpse Kane would ever be allowed of whatever or whoever it was that stalked him. Then suddenly, as Kane was using the spray room on the way out of the john, a man came in, passed him by and headed for one of the cubicles. Kane didn't take much notice, choosing his perfume and getting sprayed being his main priority, but he did throw a glance in the stranger's direction as he passed.

"What's he wearing?" McKenzie asked, willing to look in any direction to discover a link.

Kane looked dreamlike into the distance, sometimes squinting his eyes as if to focus on some unseen event taking place behind McKenzie's shoulder. Hesitating, he looked again as if to clarify something he thought he had seen. Then the answer came: "A purple suit with a yellow tie."

McKenzie tensed slightly on hearing her subject's response, her face taking on a serious expression. Somehow, she sensed this could be the chance they'd been waiting for for almost an hour now.

"Kevin, look carefully, very carefully at the man's face as he passes you by. Can you see his face? Is it clear?"

"Yes!", Kane replied with a swiftness that caused McKenzie's pulse to race.

"Kane, look at the man and tell me: do you recognise his face? Do you recognise the man's face?"

Kane again looked over his companion's shoulder into a distant past, his eyes blinking lazily. Then suddenly the prisoner's expression began to take on a viciousness that McKenzie had never seen on her friend's face before. His head, which had been bowed down slightly, moved up slowly, his eyes fixed on an apparition from another life. As Kane's face began to turn a dark angry colour, the monitor beside McKenzie began to emit slightly audible beeps. The beeps rapidly became more frequent as a fuming Kane began to rise to his feet. McKenzie was worried. What was Kane seeing? What was he going to do next? As the beeping on the monitor became one continuous alarm-call, Kane was on his feet. McKenzie watched in shock as a base hollow sounded began to emanate from deep in the prisoner's throat. She moved back nervously and the monitor on her lap fell to one side. The sound from within Kane began to grow like a bellowing roar of rage as the prisoner threw himself in fury at an unseen foe only to smash into the wall of the tunnel. Aware that the racket Kane was raising could attract the attention of the tyrons and leave their plans in ruins, McKenzie grabbed the zennor baton and delivered a zap into the raging figure beside her. Kane immediately slumped to the ground, uttering a harmless "uh!" as he fell.

Kontroller Windsor was content as he marched down the corridor towards the Security Centre. For the first time ever, he felt absolutely convinced that his presence in the kolony was going to make a difference. Ironically, it was only a few weeks before that he had experienced the unprecedented low of having the Master, in front of low-ranking security officers, literally laugh in his face when he had read out his list of security breaches in the kolony. On that occasion, as so often before, his efforts to beat Korb-1 into shape had been thwarted by the old fool and his carefully prepared list of infringements of prison discipline had been ridiculed, the Master even making a mock salute as the wounded kontroller left his office, a snide reference to Windsor's demand that prisoners be compelled to salute security staff as they passed. Then came the infamous showdown when Windsor had decided to openly challenge the Master on the direction his policies were taking the kolony. Bereft of support, the angry kontroller's efforts had failed miserably but now, on reflection, he was convinced he had grasped victory from the jaws of defeat. The Master, in his attempt to humiliate the brave kommander, had in fact bestowed upon him a weapon with which to inflict the final mortal blow on the ineffective ruler of Korb-1. Windsor would not only find the missing Ferret but also those responsible for his abduction or murder, and that would lead him to the identities of those plotting the overthrow of the kolony regime itself. After that, no-one could dispute his claim to possess the natural qualities required to replace the 'old fool' and become Master of Korb-1. The kontroller allowed a slight smile to cross his serious countenance as he pondered the stupidity of the man who, in attempting to destroy him, had given him his greatest opportunity.

There was an atmosphere of excitement in the Security centre when Windsor arrived. Security Officer Simpson, her Assistant McKenzie and two other members of security staff were examining a list of prisoners to be arrested. Simpson was coldly efficient as she went through the list, highlighting those she felt merited particular attention.

"Golden, make sure these three are brought in but don't allow them to communicate at any stage!" she ordered.

Golden agreed, with a nod of her head.

"Smolak, these two here are to be brought to the Technician the minute they are taken in!"

"Affirmative!" the solemn looking young man responded.

The Assistant Security Officer remained silent throughout, carefully noting the direction in which her superior's orders were about to move events. Large-scale arrests were rarely successful in producing useful information and merely created an atmosphere in which nobody trusted anybody and information dried up accordingly. Successful intelligence gathering involved tactical use of agents and clinical operations aimed at the arrest of individuals based on sound information received. But the young woman held her counsel. The further off-target this operation was, the better as far as she was concerned and, as long as Simpson's main aim was to impress the lunatic Windsor, nothing would come of this ham-fisted effort.

As these thoughts went through McKenzie's head, she noticed a sudden change in Simpson's demeanour, a sweet smile spreading over her serious features. Looking up, she saw Kontroller Windsor enter the room.

"Dismissed!" was Simpson's immediate order to the others, as she prepared to welcome the kontroller.

Heading down for breakfast before his korb shift, Kane was in good form. Things were going well. Only a number of weeks after Thorsen's death, he felt had made significant progress in his bid for freedom. An important contact in the Administration, the Korb Kolony Plan accessed and memorised, the possibility of escape becoming more of a reality, and the icing on the cake – the Face identified! The prisoner felt that things were really going his way now. The recent incident with the Master served to illustrate that point to Kane. When he barged into Kane's cell while the prisoner was holding what was one of the most incriminating objects possible, it could have been curtains for 313. A few seconds earlier and Kane's goose was cooked – not to mention McKenzie's. But luck had smiled on Kane. The prisoner had stood only moments away from detection and ruin, but the Master was too late and, rather than discovering Prisoner 313's vital secret, had actually been impressed with Kane's newly discovered literary interest. That had to be a good omen, Kane believed. Everything had been going the Administration's way until recently but now the wheel seemed to be turning his way. Kane had a confident bounce in his step as he made his way down to the Dining Hall.

Dayton joined in along the way – "Well, 313 – what's the story?"

"Nothing really, Tom. Just looking forward to a challenging day's work on behalf of the kolony", was Kane's sardonic reply.

"That's the right attitude," Dayton smiled, "there's too much cynicism on Korb-1! It's time people knuckled down to the task at hand and started producing!"

Both men were laughing heartily when Nielsen met them at the foot of the stairs.

"Nice to see we've got some happy space warriors on board! Any particular reason for the jolliness?" she enquired.

"We've decided that as long as we're alive, they haven't beaten us yet!" Kane declared.

Nielsen looked quizzically at the other two, and the three entered the Dining Hall.

IN HIS OPERATIONS CENTRE, Windsor was discussing the progress of the security operation with his officers. Forty more prisoners had been brought in and were now being interrogated about Leonard's disappearance and 'related matters'. As 1319's semi-admission to having despatched the Ferret was being concealed from the Master until it suited Windsor and Simpson to reveal it, Windsor had every intention of using the task entrusted to him by the Master to arrest as many prisoners and gather as much information as possible. With the interrogations taking place in various holding cells, Windsor's teams made use of the official array of 'medicines' available to them, including *feer*. Soon, his team began to prise open the minds of the arrestees. Those earmarked for special attention were awarded a 'personnel audience' with the Technician. Although it soon became clear to the interrogation teams that no one else seemed to have anything to offer on the question of the disappearance of the Ferret, a number of prisoners had broken down and suggested Nevin might be involved in organising 'something'. The fact that the Master and his entire security team already knew this did not weaken Windsor's firm belief that he was about to crack the whole investigation.

In the Security Centre, Windsor, accompanied by Simpson, was being shown a myriad of screens by a team of operators. All of the screens showed a different view of an area in the kolony. Prisoners' cells, leisure areas, corridors, korb chambers, assembly areas, loading bays, the Dining Hall – all were displayed on a wall of monitors. Prisoners and tyrons could be seen coming and going and all chamber operations were under observation – all kolony life was here.

Viewing the monitors with his officers, Windsor was deciding who should be targeted next in order to locate Leonard.

"We have his entire GC team in now." The kontroller spoke as if thinking aloud. "We must get anyone who had dealings with Leonard in the last two weeks. I want to know who was the last to see him. If it wasn't for that imbecile Deltare, we'd have it all on screen. He'll be the first one to go when I ......"

The kontroller stopped in mid-sentence, looking around for a reaction to his half-spoken threat. So wound up was he with the chase that he had started to utter thoughts he had intended to keep to himself. Windsor was convinced that when this operation had been successfully brought to a close, the Master's position would be untenable and the vindicated kontroller would assume the mantle of power that was destined to be his. Then those who participated in the slide into inefficiency and irresponsibility that now choked the operation of the kolony would be severely punished. Deltare, the security official who had failed to carry out the "simple responsibility" of maintaining the surveillance equipment in the kolony and left non-functioning monitors un-repaired, would be one of the first to pay the penalty for his carelessness. The assembled security staff pretended not to notice the kontroller's outburst and continued with their various tasks.

40 LIPSERVICE

"WHEN CAN WE TALK again?" a male prisoner with long red hair in a ponytail asked a female with oriental looks sitting across the table from him.

"As soon as you like – after work this evening", was the enthusiastic reply.

The male smiled an intimate smile and then both moved the food around their plates with their forks, her with her left hand, and him with his right. With their free hands, the pair touched slightly in the middle of the table, casually glancing occasionally to see if they were being observed. Little did the nascent lovers know that their most intimate conversation was not only being monitored but was also being recorded for further examination.

Assistant Security Officer McKenzie felt a pang of guilt at viewing this private moment. It had been recorded by the monitors who followed to the letter their instructions that *"any contact between prisoners that could* be construed as being of a conspiratorial nature should be recorded for further investigation". This meant that almost any conversation between prisoners involving an arrangement to meet again or any discussion that was vague in nature (which many romantic conversations are!) could be recorded.

Generally, McKenzie would experience a feeling of revulsion at having a part in this intrusion into what was a personal encounter in the lives of two young people. That the victims of this invasion of privacy had only recently been plucked from their friends and loved ones without any prior warning and cast alone into an unpredictable future made the deed all the more odious. A romantic encounter in the kolony was probably, apart from establishing a close friendship, the only thing to look forward to for most prisoners. That the Administration should not only intrude on these special moments but record them for further desecration was despicable, an added indignity of which, fortunately, the prisoners were unaware. Marking the take "10", the code for "not considered relevant", McKenzie moved on.

Apart from the intimate scenes she found distasteful, McKenzie nearly always found viewing the day's lip-takes a boring occupation. There would be at least three hours of takes – mostly harmless – to be examined. Nothing of real value to the Security Team was likely to turn up – and, even if it did, McKenzie would ensure that it would be valueless by the time it got to Simpson's desk. The only 'interesting' captures would be the intimate conversations of Korbers who were about to 'click' or the conversations of those who just had. The saving grace in all of this, McKenzie always felt, was that *her* listening in rather than somebody else would ensure the safety of the subjects for another while. A few days before, she had stumbled on a breakfast conversation between two prisoners who had just become lovers. Despite her misgivings, McKenzie found the take strangely entertaining, involving as it did a combination of silent admiring looks, half-finished sentences and over the top complimentary remarks. McKenzie giggled to herself as the young woman praised her lover's virility, only to break into laughter when the young man clumsily attempted to return the compliment. The innocent lovers were a joy to behold as they surreptitiously held hands under the table while trying to eat their Korb Kream Kakes with their free hand. Of such feelings was the alternative universe comprised, McKenzie thought sadly.

Back in the real world, the Assistant Security Officer went automatically through her workload, hoping for some entertainment or a real-life conspiracy to brighten up her day or even to ensure for her the satisfaction of sabotaging the system. The other Assistant Security Officer, Jacinta Gomez, was always eager to come up with something to report but McKenzie noticed that Simpson was inclined more and more to disregard the simplistic theories Gomez would concoct around a lip-take or an observed conversation – an *obcon* in security-speak – and file them away under 'inconclusive'. McKenzie herself would occasionally produce an *obcon* that seemed to be conspiratorial but would, on examination (McKenzie ensured), be revealed to be innocuous.

McKenzie was of the view that for the Administration to regard the detection of subversion in a prison camp designed for subversives as an achievement was wonderfully comical in a black sense and a reflection of the paranoia that had long since eaten away the heart of the Northern Confederation's Administration. At the end of the day, what exactly did these idiots expect? A holiday centre full of happy campers with no interest whatsoever in attempting to escape and make a life for themselves somewhere else? At any rate, if people were actually going to try and effect an escape, they were hardly going to discuss it openly – and, if they did, they weren't particularly good conspirators. Despite her feelings on the matter, though, Assistant Security Officer McKenzie realised that if any conspirator was silly enough to reveal themselves to the

Administration in an *obcon* she could intervene to save them from the Void or from a mysterious 'accident'.

Still, even if her role was to sabotage the Administration's efforts to gather information, the work had to be done. With the middle finger on her right hand, she casually set the viewer in motion again.

KANE HAD ALWAYS FOUND Karl Streever an interesting kind of fellow. Although his background was completely different to Kane's, Prisoner 313 always had a healthy respect for the ex-soldier and the two always got on well. Streever was the ultimate loner. If you didn't make conversation with him, he didn't talk to you. If you wanted to talk, he would too. Although participating successfully in every sporting event on the kolony and mixing well with whoever crossed his path, the young military man actively sought the company of nobody and paddled his own canoe through the narrow water that was life on Korb-1.

Streever was an unusual prisoner. Of all those on the kolony convicted of Information Terrorism, he was the only one with any kind of military experience. Having been a strike commando in the Confederation LSA (Land, Sea and Air) Force, he decommissioned and went abroad, selling his expertise to the highest bidder. Most of his time had been spent in the employment of the African Alliance aiding their defence forces to withstand the Saladdan invasion of their northern territories. This successful operation inspired the thrill seeking Streeker to go further with his activities and he soon found himself defending the Libertad States against the Northern Confederation itself in a dispute over mineral rights in the Caribbean Sea. Confrontation was minimal, comprising a number of minor skirmishes off the coast of Cuba. Although the NC won most of these, the tenacity of the LS forces in confronting the NC at every hands turn prevented the NC forces from consolidating their victories and a stalemate situation developed in which the LS refused to allow the NC to pursue mineral exploration in the area. The NC noted with stern displeasure the activities of Streever and the other former NC personnel involved in the conflict on the side of the LS and waited patiently to get their hands on their treasonous citizens. When Streever eventually returned to his home in NC Area 6611, he was tracked down by NC Security personnel and immediately arrested. Streever based his defence against a charge of treason on the very Constitution of the Northern Confederation itself, which enshrined in NC law freedom of action for all citizens in the area of economic activity. He claimed he had been paid for his services to the LS and that, as a decommissioned soldier, he was entitled to sell his services to anybody. The court reluctantly accepted Streever's imaginative defence but, as the right of the NC to tax from the economic activity of all its citizens was also enshrined in the Constitution, the successful defendant was immediately charged with failure to declare his earnings from his various activities abroad and ordered to pay tax to the NC on his entire income. When the NC Finance Department demanded an account of all the mercenary's income from his foreign exploits, Streever reluctantly obliged. Almost immediately, Streever was arrested again and charged with 'being an agent of a hostile power'. This was based on the 'fact' that, according to the Confederation's Intelligence and Policy Institute, the Libertad States' military was bankrolled by the Saladdans, who were therefore Streever's real paymasters. The rest was a foregone conclusion. Within days, Streever was in a confinement tray and heading for Korb-1.

Many of the prisoners didn't trust Streever and felt that as a former soldier in the service of the Administration, he was 'suspect'. Streever knew this but couldn't care less. His military training and his nature led him to be patient. Mentally and physically he kept himself fine-tuned, believing that some day his chance would come and when it did he would be ready. Many of the prisoners were interested in the former soldier's stories about his military activities in the service of the Administration and elsewhere, but getting him to talk wasn't easy.

One of the prisoner's most interesting stories involved his secondment to the DSF (Deep Space Force) to investigate the triggering of a messaging device on the planet Ark-1 in the Nayal Sector. This beacon had been intended as a pager by means of which other civilisations could contact Earth. When the device was triggered, 23 years after it was planted, NC replied immediately and awaited the response. But there was no reply – nothing. After six months, NC decided to send a DS team to investigate. When the beacon was activated, the probe was positioned deep in the Golden Sea on Ark-1, having been dropped with a number of others from the air. Streever, whose expertise was in amphibious exercises, was invited to join the team. The mission turned up nothing – no clues whatsoever as to who or what had activated the device. Despite intensive research, no explanation for the beacon call could be discovered. In the absence of any obvious reason for the contact message, a number of theories began to circulate. These ranged from the accidental triggering of the message mechanism by an alien force, which left immediately it realised its mistake, to a mechanical error – strongly denied by the Administration, to the theory that the whole episode was a scam by the Administration to re-inflate flagging enthusiasm amongst the NC public for the space programme. Whatever the reason, the story of the Ark-1 beacon excited all kinds of imaginative theories when recounted amongst the prisoners of Korb-1.

Kane walked along the corridor to the Dining Hall with his disciplined friend, discussing various theories on the Ark-1 incident. Kane wondered was it possible to set off beacon devices of that kind from a remote location, far away. Of course it was, Streever assured, but only if the system source code was known. When Kane asked was it possible to carry out an operation like that without the signal being tracked, Streever opined that a meteor shower, a bacanite concentration or nuclear activity could cloak the operation. A bacanite concentration could cloak almost anything, he added.

"Interesting!" Kane noted.

The soldier glanced at Kane, raising an accusing eyebrow, but remaining silent.

IN THE DINING HALL, Dayton and Gibney were waiting for Kane to arrive. As they enjoyed their morning diet of home grown orange juice and porridge pudding, they wondered what the next development was going to be.

"When is Nevin going to make his move?" Gibney asked.

"I don't really know", Dayton replied. "He's biding his time."

"Is he going to involve Kane?" Gibney continued.

"I doubt it – a lot of them think Kevin is too volatile at the moment."

"Who will he involve then?"

"The ones who are advising him to exclude Kane, I suppose", was Dayton's conclusion.

"What's Nevin strategy going to be? Will he go full frontal?"

"It's hard to see that succeeding. It will need something special – but where do we find that?"

"Here's Kane!" Gibney interrupted.

Kane was tired but cheerful as he sat down beside his companions. A group of tyrons marched through the Dining Hall, observing the diners. Some of the prisoners, particularly the novos, reacted nervously as the guards passed through, but most just ignored them.

"What's happening?" Gibney enquired.

"Ask Nevin", Kane responded, "He hasn't got back to me yet."

"Why don't you talk to him?" Gibney suggested.

"Maybe I will", Kane confirmed.

As the prisoners dined, far above them near the dome that roofed their strange little world, hostile eyes were focused upon them. Windsor and his friends looked down upon the assembled group below and watched for any signs of unusual activity.

"Watch the ones on the list. We'll pick them up today. Note who they're talking to – we'll take them too. If you see anything changing hands, note it and arrest the recipient the minute he or she leaves the Dining Hall."

The minions nodded unenthusiastically as the kontroller issued his orders. Then they got to work, directing their remote distance monitors towards the Dining Hall and studying the various views afforded by the devices. Nevin was seen in deep conversation with Lambert and Blinker from KCs 12 and 13. Daner, Jerson and Kilroy, from KC 71 were together but not saying much. Kane, Gibney and Dayton could be seen, relaxing over their breakfast, Gibney occasionally speaking a few words. As the remote monitors panned around the Dining Hall, stopping here and there, the operators occasionally soundfixed on a conversation. One of them homed in on the KC 10-1 trio:

Dayton: *Nevin's an astute man.*

Gibney: *But his choices are limited.*

The operator pricked up his ears.

Kane: *What's wrong, John, don't you like your porridge?*

Dayton: *John's on a diet. He needs to lose some weight.*

Gibney: *Yeah, yeah. All you guys can do is joke.*

Dayton: *Who's joking?*

Dayton and Kane laugh.

The operator, disappointed with the useless nature of this boring banter, moved on, and then homed in on a group from KC 19-3, who seemed to be having an animated conversation.

Male: *I don't think it's going to succeed. We'll need to have a more unified approach.*

Female: *If we pull together, we can do it.*

Other male: *What do we do if it doesn't succeed?*

The operator sat up in her seat, tensed. She was on to something.

Female: *Don't be defeatist - we can do it.*

Other female: *We haven't enough manpower.*

The operator smiled to herself. She had hit the jackpot.

Male: *It's a question of timing.*

Other male: *Timing, my grand-daddy's arse! We can't get an extra gush if we haven't got the supply coming in from the Generation Chamber. What happens your Production Prize then?*

The operator stopped in her tracks, disappointed, like a cat that had just lost its hold on a mouse.

Still, the machine scanned the huge hall, watching, scrutinizing, listening, monitoring. It fixed on the KC 17-2 group. There were discussing Leonard.

Male: *Where do think he went?*

Female: *He can't be gone far. There's no way outa here!*

Male: *But he must be gone somewhere.*

The female: *I think he's just been demoted from low life form to Administration staff.*

The operator scowled.

Other female: *Impossible, he'd have to become a tyron first and then work his way down.*

Laughter all round.

The first male: *Maybe he remembered he'd left the light on in the Old World and had to go back and turn it off.*

Laughter again.

Female: *There's only one way to go back to Earth.*

Male: *That's right - become a korb particle. Hey, maybe Leonard is coming in useful after all!*

Hysterics.

Disappointed, the operator moved on as the Chamber group got up to go to work. When the operator moved to Nevin's group, a conversation was just ending.

Nevin: *You know what you've got to do, then?*

Others: *We do, don't worry.*

Nevin: *Worrying's o.k. – as long as things get done!*

Smiling nervously, the group got up to leave.

LIKE A BALL OF self-important smoke, Windsor moved around the monitoring centre, eager to see results.

"What have you got?" he demanded eagerly.

None of the monitoring staff replied. Instead they looked at one another as if hoping that someone else would answer the difficult question. Windsor asked again. A small round-figured officer gathered the courage to respond:

"Not a lot, Kontroller."

"Not a lot!" Windsor repeated mockingly. "Not a lot! What the hell have you been doing? You monitor a hall of almost six hundred people, and what do you get? Not a lot!"

The man replied: "We think this group", pointing to the KC 17-2 group on the screen, "know something about Leonard's disappearance."

Windsor looked at the screen. "Show me", he demanded eagerly. The man obliged.

Windsor squinted, in an unconscious effort to see into the minds of the prisoners. He paused for a few seconds and then, with a commanding air, gave the order to his officers: "Arrest them. I want them all in now!"

Without a moment's hesitation, the security officers nodded to the tyron officer, who left immediately to carry out his mission. Windsor moved his head slightly, as if involved in a conversation with someone unseen, and announced in a quiet but determined voice: "This is it. The time for retribution has arrived."

41 OUTBREAK

Team 17-2 were about to get up to go to their shift when they noticed the team of tyrons heading in their direction. Instinctively, they stopped their conversation, eyed one another and looked anxiously at the approaching sea of red. The tyrons moved swiftly in unison through the Dining Hall. As they got closer, 17-2 stood up together and prepared themselves for whatever was about to happen. On reaching the group, the tyrons quickly surrounded the prisoners and ordered them to move.

The group moved reluctantly away from the table, the other prisoners in the Dining Hall looking on with concern. With the entire assembly in the Dining Hall on its feet, the tyrons led the team away. On the way, one member of the group, Aidan O'Flynn, stalled to look back at the tyrons behind him. Delaying a little longer than was advisable, he soon became the object of a harsh glare from the military escort. Instinctively, O'Flynn decided to meet stare with stare. When one of the tyrons produced his zennor baton to move the prisoner along, the prisoner reacted, somewhat foolishly, by swinging around and pushing the zennor away. Immediately the tyron used his stun gun to immobilise the prisoner. O'Flynn fell to the ground like a falling star in a dark night sky and two tyrons picked him up unceremoniously to carry him away. The assault on O'Flynn brought a loud roar of disapproval from the onlooking prisoners, and some of them began to throw abuse and the nearest solid objects at hand at the tyrons. Almost immediately, all the prisoners joined in and began to pelt the invaders with anything at their disposal. Retreating with their captives, the tyrons used their armour-plated arm-pieces to fend off the shower of objects raining down on them from all sides. Any prisoner daring enough to get too close received a taste of zennor and hit the ground fast.

With the arresting party attempting to make their way out of the area, the 17-2 prisoners tried to break loose. In the ensuing chaos, zennors were used generously and soon all the proposed captives were immobilised and lying on the floor. As there weren't enough tyrons to carry them all away, one of the arresting party messaged on his wrist communicator for reinforcements. As he did, a novo from GC 3-1 jumped on the tyron's back and brought him to the ground. With the tyron falling, his zennor slipped from his grasp and slid across the floor, stopping at the feet of Karen Koomer, a member of Nevin's new organisational committee. Koomer grabbed the weapon instinctively and looked around. As she did, a tyron fired a deadly blast into her chest. Koomer fell immediately, stone dead. No sooner had she fallen then another prisoner took the weapon and floored the tyron who had shot his companion. The fallen tyron's zennor was immediately grabbed by another prisoner.

With a wave of more daring prisoners throwing themselves on the tyrons, both tyrons and prisoners fell like tenpins with zennor rounds flying in every direction. Kane and Dayton took the opportunity to grab a zennor and a stun gun respectively. As chaos reigned in the Dining Hall, the kolony security alarm went off, an eerie grating sound that produced nausea in those unlucky enough to be exposed to it too long. Almost at the same time, another wave of tyrons poured into the scene of the battle, firing at any prisoner unwise enough to show their heads above a table.

Kane and Dayton, crouching behind a seat, looked at one another. "Time to go", Kane quipped to Dayton, a serious look on his face, and the two men slipped out of the Dining Hall and headed towards the korb chambers. Others followed as the prisoners, realising they could not resist the greater numbers and superior arms of the tyrons, retreated. In the ensuing pandemonium, prisoners ran in every direction, zennor rounds giving the unlucky an immediate and sudden exit.

The kolony alarm droning in their ears, Kane and his companion ran down the corridor in search of an empty KC. They looked behind them as they moved swiftly, expecting a tyron unit to follow, or some zennor rounds to speed them on their way. None materialised and they soon located an unused chamber. Entering the KC, the two placed the windfall weapons on the ground inside the door. With the korb tunnel empty, Kane opened the door and Dayton immediately proceeded to press the gush control. A large burst of steam from the tunnel filled the Chamber with heavy purple smoke. Under cover of the dense cloud, the two men placed the weapons inside the control panel, behind the control levers.

Their task complete, the two left the KC and returned in the direction of the Dining Hall. As they did, they were met by a fiery group of prisoners carrying a disarmed tyron. The prisoners were in a state of frenzy and were emitting a mixture of roars and cheers while the helpless tyron struggled to get free. On reaching KC 12, the throng entered and in matter of minutes had despatched the helpless tyron in a korb gush. As the light flashed to indicate a successful operation, the mob released a deafening roar and rhythmically bashed the equipment with their assorted selection of weapons.

Kane and Dayton looked at one another gravely, both realising that events were taking a very serious turn, one from which there would be no going back. Leaving the Chamber, they were met by Nevin, in the company of Gibney and others.

"What's happening?" The two asked Nevin.

Nevin seemed confused, slightly disorientated. "Things have got out of control. We may have to act. Tell everyone to regroup in the L+S."

"But we're unarmed. We'll be annihilated", Kane protested.

"What choice have we got?" Nevin asked, genuinely looking for an answer.

"What about the Master Korb Chamber. We can keep them out of that. Then maybe we can do a deal", Kane offered.

Nevin hesitated for a minute, then nodded agreement. "Get the word around", he said to the others "The Master Korb Chamber!" The others moved off immediately.

THE SHOOTING AND SHOUTING was fading to a hum as the bulk of the shocked prisoners headed for the MKC. Those involved in KC shifts or resting in their cells when the riot began were now beginning to arrive into the corridors to swell the numbers heading for the rendezvous point. Groups of prisoners carrying makeshift weapons of every description were on the move.

At the gate of the Master Korb Chamber, Nevin welcomed the throngs of arriving prisoners with a word of encouragement or an instruction to position themselves in various areas in the large Chamber. Some of the fleeing prisoners even carried food that they had grabbed from the Dining Hall as they left.

The Master Korb Chamber was one of the largest chambers on the kolony. It was positioned in the centre of the network of korb chambers in which most korbeans carried out their daily labours. There were twenty individual korb processors in the MKC but, as the kolony wasn't yet working to capacity, all twenty were never functioning simultaneously. Four were in use when the mass of prisoners arrived in, their crews watching in astonishment as the excited prisoners gathered to begin a frenzied exchange of information and opinions on what was taking place.

THE IMMEDIATE FLASHING OF lights on Zeena McKenzie's security panel signalled the sound of the kolony alarm. Surprised, the young woman stared at the signals to establish the source of the alarm. Dining Hall flashed in red on the screen in front of her as she did a security scan on the entire kolony. Almost immediately an array of lights lit up, forming a path from the Dining Hall to the Master Korb Chamber. Almost simultaneously, Master Korb Chamber flashed on the screen. McKenzie moved her hands over the touch panel and viewed the scenes in the Dining Hall, the MKC and a variety of locations in between. The Dining Hall was quiet, the only activity being the medics tending to the wounded, particularly the tyrons who had come off second best in the skirmish there. The MKC was a different matter. There, it appeared, chaos held sway, with hordes of prisoners arriving from every direction, carrying a motley array of objects that they obviously intended to use as weapons. Nevin could be seen directing operations as the prisoners arrived. The scenes in the corridors leading to the MKC showed the same picture of mass movement of prisoners towards the Chamber. McKenzie examined all the views available in an attempt to locate Kane but, before she could get a sighting of Prisoner 313, Security Officer Simpson came rushing into the Unit.

"Security Situation Red 1!" she roared. "Red 1! Alert all areas. Kolony Revolt in progress! Red 1 – Hurry!"

Reluctantly, McKenzie send out an all-Kolony alert.

Simpson spoke into her communicator: "Security Situation Red 1! Repeat – Security Situation Red 1! All kontrollers to Master's Centre immediately. All security staff to assigned Response Areas! Security Situation Red 1!"

"Get visuals of all effected areas – live and recent archive!" the excited Security Officer roared at her assistant. "Get all key personnel here within five minutes!"

McKenzie followed orders, as the athletic form of her superior left the Unit with speed. But, having sent out the alert, the young woman immediately returned to her own mission of locating a man who had been a stranger only a few weeks before. His role in helping her make the future a vengeful fulfilment of a tragic past demanded he survive whatever was taking place now.

Ideally, a code dialled into the keyboard would have brought up Prisoner 313's electronic code. This could then have been fed into the electronic search system and the whereabouts of the prisoner quickly ascertained. McKenzie knew, however, that a search carried out using the electronic coding system would be recorded, thus leaving the security official open to the fairly obvious question of why she was interested in the location of one particular prisoner in the middle of a mass revolt. McKenzie continued to scan the visuals with her trained eye, her eyes pouring over the scenes of chaos on the screen as she frantically searched for Kane. Eventually McKenzie experienced an immense sense of relief as she caught sight of Kane and Dayton leaving a korb chamber and making their way towards the MKC. Satisfied that Kane was safe, at least for the moment, McKenzie breathed a sigh of relief. At that, the first of the security personnel called in by Simpson began to arrive.

McKenzie was concerned. Everything was happening so fast. A major riot like this could totally derail her plans to spring some of the prisoners and instigate her campaign of revenge against the Administration. If events continued in this vein, anything could happen. The security profile would certainly change immensely, setting back her preparations months if not years. Worse still, Kane could be a casualty of all this, be consigned to the detention block, or be injured or even killed. Anxiously, she followed the prisoners to the MKC on her surveillance equipment, only to find shortly after they arrived there that the monitoring equipment in the Chamber had been put out of action.

The atmosphere in the Security Area reflected the situation throughout the kolony. The assembled security personnel were in a state of confusion and agitation, many of them hurling questions and even accusations at one another. Against that background, McKenzie tried to think clearly and form a view as to what needed to be done to protect Kane. As she did, Simpson re-appeared on the scene and, positioning herself beside McKenzie, began to relay instructions to her assistant that she was receiving from the coordinator at the kontrollers' meeting.

"*Status report – surveillance capability – MKC!*"

"*Status report – surveillance capability – 100 metre radius MKC!*"

"*Status report – missing weapons!*"

"*Status report – prisoners in cells!*"

"*Status report – prisoners at large!*"

McKenzie responded reluctantly to the directions passed on by the Security Officer in her usual cold but efficient manner. Simpson was too close for the younger of the two to attempt to sabotage any of her information requests but the reluctant securocrat comforted herself with the observation that, so far, nothing that could cause real damage to the prisoners was being collated.

THE MASTER WAS IN his office when news of the eruption in the Dining Hall reached him. Immediately turning on his monitor to view the scenes of mayhem being acted out in the kolony, the usually smug administrator was horrified at the sight of the running battle unfolding before his eyes. After a moment of inactive astonishment, he roared into his communicator:

"All kontrollers – Master's Centre immediately!"

Placing his hand on his forehead in disbelief, the Master wondered what had caused this unbelievable outbreak of violence. Was it a deliberate action on the part of the prisoners? Surely not! If it was, it had been very badly thought out. It certainly didn't have the appearance of a planned uprising. What had caused it then? He hoped the tyrons had not over-reacted and provoked this security problem themselves. Anyway, what were they doing in force in the Dining Hall, where incidents of a serious security nature never occurred?

Soon, the kontrollers began to arrive. Rushing into the Master's Centre with what they regarded as an appropriate air of urgency, they positioned themselves in front of their superior. He had only one question to ask, one repeated with vehemence: "What's going on?" One or two of the kontrollers offered the opinion that it looked like an arrest operation had gone wrong, but it was too soon to say. Relieved that the incident appeared not to have been planned by the prisoners, the Master simply moved to the next question, again a simple one: "Who ordered the operation?"

"I did," Kontroller Windsor announced boldly, as he joined the assembled group.

The Master glared at the man who had been a thorn in his side for so long and the other kontrollers tensed. Realising that, at last, his opportunity to deal with the troublesome kontroller had arrived, the Master took the initiative.

"You what?"

"You wanted Leonard found. I was just about to ascertain his fate, when a riot was instigated by those responsible. The situation has been brought under control, however, and the culprits are in retreat", Windsor responded assertively.

"In retreat?" the Master asked. "To where?"

"They're assembling in the MKC now. We can take the area without any great difficulty."

"You fool, the MKC is one of the few areas in the entire Kolony that you *can't* take *without great difficulty*", the Master exploded, emphasising sarcastically the last three words. "With korb tanks all over the place, the whole Chamber – even the kolony itself – could go up. Tell your tyrons – all of you – to back off!"

The Master thought for a minute. Then, looking around, he picked two kontrollers, Dixon and Kembledon, and told them to secure the area around the MKC. The others were to ensure that order was restored in the kolony in general.

"I want ten-minute update reports on the situation. We'll meet again later! Dismissed!" the Master ordered firmly, turning away from the kontrollers as they left the room.

42 SIEGE

The tyrons were soldiers – trained and clinical. Recruited into the Confederation's defence training academies at the age of fourteen, they were the perfect professionals. Bound to serve until the age of thirty and barred from personal relationships until they left the force, they spent a life in the front line. Knowing no other existence, they accepted the limits of their military career without question. Most of them had seen action of some intensity or other in the various campaigns generated for that purpose by their masters in the Administration. From minor campaigns in remote parts of the globe, like the Patagonian campaign to aid its once close ally, the Union of Latin American States, against the threat of infiltration by the Saladdans, to full-scale war with the Mesopotamian Republic, before that state was eventually lost to the Saladdans, the military masters had always been successful in finding a theatre of combat in which to blood their latest recruits. The tyrons enjoyed a long-established reputation as the best fighting force on the planet and indeed beyond, having taken control of three Mao Republic space bases, when that power had attempted to block NC communications satellites.

When the korb kolonies were established, the tyrons were chosen to police them. This was decided in the context of the threat of Saladdan attacks, a not unrealistic prospect considering the value of the kolonies in terms of energy production. Initially, it was proposed that the tyrons merely provide a guard to protect the kolonies from external attack, but the argument was then advanced that, as many of those banished to the kolonies were in fact jailed for their activities as Saladdan agents, the Saladdan threat was not only an external one. It was therefore decided that the tyrons would provide all the security requirements of the kolonies and that a permanent garrison of tyrons would be posted in them all.

The tyron soldiers accepted their new postings without question, as one would expect from professional combatants. Their recruitment and training at an early age and their service conditions, involving as they did isolation from the general public and a ban on relationships, resulted in a unique culture of absolute acceptance of authority, and a posting to a korb kolony was just another mission, as far as a tyron was concerned. It had been rumoured in the kolony that the tyrons regarded some of their duties in the jail area as being inappropriate for a military force but, apart from that, there was never any suggestion that the tyrons would refuse to carry out an order of any kind.

The tyrons were a formidable fighting force. Their early introduction to the military way of life ensured that they would be a highly-skilled, finely-tuned fighting machine with an unquestioning attitude to authority. Because of their unique training in arms-handling techniques and marksmanship skills, they were to the forefront in the use of the latest weaponry developed by the armaments industries for the Confederation – thus giving the NC a significant advantage over its rivals in any potential theatre of war. The tyrons also possessed state of the art personal protection.

The *pps*, personal protection suit, was developed specifically for the tyron, and was far and above anything in the armoury of the other players in the game. The *pps* was the direct result of the development, by a scientist called Merthyr, of a metallic alloy called named merthyrite. Merthyrite was one of the strongest and most solid materials in existence. When its internal molecules were heated to 200 degrees centigrade, however, it became pliable. The development of merthyrite heralded a new era for the NC defence service, and the material was used in the production of a variety of new weapons and supports. The most important of these was the *pps*. In the creation of the tyrons' coat of armour, a thin layer of merthyrite was sandwiched between two equally thin layers of heat resistant material. Imbedded in the merthyrite were heat emitting diodes which could be triggered on and off by a button on the sleeve of the suit. In diode-on mode, the armour was supple and pliable, but resistant. When off, it was a solid defence against almost anything. The result was a light, comfortable and highly manageable suit which could be transformed, in a millisecond, into the hardest and most protective piece of armour ever invented. It turned the tyron into a virtually invincible opponent in close combat.

On the korb kolonies, the sight of tyrons as a welcoming party was enough to depress even the most stout-hearted novo and their presence throughout was a guarantee that indiscipline among the prisoners would be kept to a minimum. The prisoners' awareness of the history of the NC's elite army ensured that utter euphoria greeted the sight that now unfolded in the MKC. A massive cheer greeted the arrival in the Chamber of a group of prisoners that carried not one but three tyron guards! What had been unimaginable for the inmates of Korb-1 for so long was now taking place – and before their very eyes! The prisoners stared in amazement. Kane and Dayton looked at one another in wonder.

"Looks like we've got ourselves some insurance", Dayton remarked, smiling broadly.

Kane, watching the assembled prisoners moving around like a kolony of ants, didn't reply.

"We've got to get organised", Kane suddenly erupted, hit by a sudden sense of urgency. "Where's Nevin?" he asked.

Dayton pointed across the Chamber and the two headed for their leader. As the duo approached Nevin, he was sitting on a chamber direction kiosk with Kenning, talking to Nielsen and three prisoners from KC 39-3 – Gagarov, Guivarc'h and O'Grady. The discussion seemed to be animated but stopped as the two newcomers approached.

"We've got a great show going here, Nevin. What's your game plan?" Dayton enquired.

"I honestly don't know", Nevin replied. "The capture of the tyrons gives us some leverage, but we must be careful."

"Why not get people together to decide?" Kane suggested, "One representative from each KC should do. Then we can go through all the options."

Nevin reflected for a moment, then agreed. "O.k.", he nodded. "First of all", he said, speaking to Dayton and Guivarc'h, "find out what weapons we have. Give them to those who know how to use them and ..." he continued, "those we can trust!"

Then, speaking to Gagarov and O'Grady, he ordered them to "secure all exits and entrances, and post our armed people at them" before directing Kenning and Nielsen to organise the selection of KC leaders.

"Come on, Kane," he said, taking the younger man by the elbow as the others left, "We've got to discuss this thing first." The two sat down inside the direction kiosk. "What do you think our chances are?" Nevin asked, his face adopting a serious expression.

"Not great, as I see it," Kane replied, frankly. "There's no way out of here. But maybe we can cut a deal."

"There's no way they'll let us go," Nevin interjected.

"At the very least, we'll have to get an assurance that there'll be no repercussions for the riot, and no limits on privileges", Kane suggested.

"What about getting some people out?" Nevin wondered.

"I can't see that happening", Kane replied, "We'll be lucky if they don't annihilate us all in here."

Nevin seemed depressed. "We'll form a prisoner defence committee", he decided.

Kane nodded in agreement, but added a cautionary note: "Whatever you do, don't let people get carried away. Make them realise our options are few and far between. If hopes get too high, people will be devastated if things go wrong."

Looking over Nevin's shoulder, Kane observed a scene of chaos. Prisoners were streaming in from all directions, some of them wounded. With hundreds gathering, the gravity of the situation began to dawn on Kane. In a matter of minutes, the kolony had been brought from a situation of extreme tension to outright revolt and he wondered if there could be any going back now. Some of the prisoners were cheering as if a major victory had already been achieved and, in a way, it had. The tyrons had been taken on for the first time ever – and not unsuccessfully. The prisoners had proven they could challenge their tormentors and not necessarily come off second best. But, watching the buoyant group assembling, Kane knew in his heart and soul that taking possession of the MKC was not the solution to the prisoners' problems and could even set back the real event, perhaps irreversibly.

"We'll talk again later", Nevin interjected, waking Kane from his reflection.

THE MASTER SAT AT the top of the table at the resumed Kontroller Kouncil meeting, observing his team of inefficient henchmen around the table. Looking around, he found it difficult to conceal his disappointment at the fact that splendid korb kolony kontroller uniforms were being worn by what amounted to a bunch of incompetents.

"First of all", he began, "the latest security status report indicates that 713 prisoners are unaccounted for – presumably all holed up in the MKC. It would not appear that any have managed to locate themselves elsewhere. There are 31 tyron guards injured – seven seriously – and four missing. There are 23 zennors, 25 stun-batons, 190 stun grenades and 13 helmets unaccounted for. Surveillance in the vicinity of the MKC is 100% but visual capacity inside the MKC has been reduced to three electronic eyes, though the presumption is that, like the rest, it is only a matter of time before these are taken out as well. A two-way monitor can be activated in the Chamber." There was silence as the Master scanned the faces around the table, challenging those present to comment on what was for all of them an unprecedented disaster.

"Well, what are we going to do now?" he asked challengingly, as if relying on his kontrollers for advice.

"We must have a show of strength – that will leave the criminals in no doubt as to our abilities – and our intentions", Windsor replied immediately.

"And what if they realise we can't fulfil that threat of force, that to attack the MKC is to endanger the entire kolony – have you thought of that?" the Master rejoined impatiently.

"These are criminals!" Windsor retorted, "They haven't got the intelligence to come to that conclusion. All they'll be concerned about is saving their own miserable skins!"

"Windsor's right", a worried looking little man ventured. "An all-out assault won't be necessary when they realise the consequences of their actions."

"Oh, I'm not too sure about that", the Master rejoined confidently, casting a glance at Windsor in the process. "There are people in there with excellent organisational ability – just read their files. We're going to have to talk them out."

Windsor spat a response: "Talk them out! These criminals can only organise riots – creating mayhem and chaos is their sole talent. They're …"

The Master interrupted: "A large force of tyrons will be positioned at all entrances to MKC immediately." Windsor grimaced. "They will take no action, however, and will only be used to generate disquiet amongst the prisoners. This will be done by displaying their mobilisation on the monitors in the MKC." Windsor's pursed his lips in anger – the old fool was vacillating again.

"After a full day has passed, communications will be opened up with the prisoners inside and I will talk them into surrendering. By then, they should be feeling the pangs of hunger and regret." Windsor scowled. "No action of any kind will be taken by anyone without my explicit command. Understood?"

The Master's question was answered positively but feebly by the kontrollers. Windsor remained silent.

AN UNEASY CALM HAD descended on the MKC as the Defence Committee, as named by Nevin, deliberated. After the leader had given an appraisal of the security situation, including the fact that three more electronic eyes had been located and disabled, a general discussion took place.

"Most of the prisoners realise we're in a serious situation but few, apart from those optimists who expect to be given their personal belongings and a ticket back to Earth, can see any clear way out", Ciara Sweeney of Team 35-1, reported.

Fortune Imbuna of 21-1 agreed: "Nobody is clear on what our objective is at this stage. Are we going to try and get ourselves out of this situation with some kind of a reward or do we believe we can actually sail away into the galaxy from here?

"Yes, we need to identify our objective and then see how we're going to progress it", Nyran Panvi of 13-3 enjoined. Others agreed, by nodding their heads or adding a monosyllabic note of agreement.

"O.k.!" Nevin concluded. "Are we agreed that our minimum objective must be to get everybody out here safely with no reprisals against anybody?"

The group agreed.

"Very well." All our efforts will be directed at achieving that aim. Are we also agreed that, failing that, our aim will be to obtain any positive advances that appear possible – from better privileges to release from the kolony?

Again, an agreement of voices and gesticulations signalled support.

"Right", Nevin summarised, "tactically, our initial demand will for a mass release, but the least we'll accept will be no retribution for the riot, and no victimisation of prisoners in the future."

As the Committee considered its tactics for what all expected would be a long siege, many of the members were confident that the tyrons taken in the fray would be a major asset to the prisoners in any negotiations. Nevin wasn't too sure. "They may be a pretty sight", he warned, casting a glance at the captured tyrons surrounded by prisoners, "but their value shouldn't be overestimated. After all, they're only tyrons, dispensable people sent to the front line – like us, in a way". A disappointed silence was the committee's response.

Before breaking up, the group accepted Nevin's suggestion that the audio-visual connector be activated and monitored in order to facilitate communications – and negotiations – with the Administration. The look of worry on the committee members' faces as the meeting ended said it all – a testing period lay ahead.

43 STAND-OFF

THE LOOK OF LOATHING on the faces of the captured tyrons said it all as they were hoisted up on chains and suspended above the main door of the MKC. To the injury of being captured by mere prisoners was now to be added the insult of being hung up on display for all the kolony to see.

"If the tyrons make a move, it's their swinging buddies who'll be the first casualties!" a female prisoner with red hair observed, smiling wide as the captives were slowly raised above the assembly.

"Yeah! I'll do it with my own hands!" declared a muscular male with a ponytail.

When the tyrons were finally hoisted, a big cheer filled the Chamber and objects of every kind were thrown at the helpless captives swinging in the air.

"Take it easy!" Nevin implored, moving towards the hoist operators. "We need some discipline here."

Nevin told the more excited prisoners to sit down and rest, that the time might not be far off when they would need all their energy. Respecting their leader's leader's judgement, the prisoners moved away and began to sit down in groups all around the Chamber. As they did, some began to sing and, before long, the massive chamber was echoing to the sound of songs and ballads of every variety: love, patriotism – and resistance.

"What a sight!" Dayton remarked. "That'll give them something to think about."

Kane didn't reply, unsure in his mind as to how the authorities – or the tyrons – would react to seeing their finest strong up on display, like a gaggle of turkeys for Christmas. His thoughts were interrupted by Nielsen who arrived to announce that Nevin wanted the committee to gather over by the monitor.

NEVIN WAS NERVOUS. THE siege had now moved into day two and there was still no contact from the Administration. He looked at Kane questioningly and the pair cast their eyes over the assembled throng.

"Will they be up to it?" he asked.

"Two days – no food. They'll have to break sometime. Only for the water and the latrines in here, we'd be in huge trouble", Kane replied.

"It can't go on forever, though. Something's going to give. I'm afraid that ..". Nevin's words tailed off as an apparition appeared before his eyes on the communications monitor. To the dismay of the prisoners, hordes of tyrons were displayed marching around in formation outside the MKC. When the prisoners had been left in no doubt as to the numbers rallying against them on the other side of the MKC gate, the military scene faded away to reveal the smug well-fed countenance of the Master. The buzz of conversation in the MKC rapidly tailed off as everybody sat up to listen to what the vision had to say.

The Master appeared calm, even relaxed. He addressed the prisoners in general, rather than Nevin or any other individual. On this occasion, his plummy tones, usually a source of major irritation to the prisoners, were balm to their ears. At last, contact was being made. At least they weren't being ignored and left to rot on a heap of raw korb.

The Master expressed the wish that the prisoners were not too uncomfortable in their temporary accommodation and hoped that they would be reasonable and allow him to resolve the difficulties that had brought about this "unfortunate situation". He treated the prisoners to his usual party piece about their common interest in making the kolony a success, and went on to deliver his perpetual mantra of there being "no way out of Korb-1". The Master announced that, even as he spoke, the tyrons were being withdrawn from the entrance to the MKC and would return to their garrison. When this withdrawal had been completed, the prisoners should return to their cells and allow the kolony to return to normality.

The unexpectedly relaxed address was treated with a wary silence tempered with an occasional guffaw. As the prisoners looked at one another searching for reactions, Nevin got up to speak. He thanked the Master for his welcome, if belated comments, and welcomed his "suggestions" but then went on to explain that the prisoners could do nothing without an agreement between them and the Administration on a number of key issues. If the Master wished, he would open up "discussion" – he chose the word carefully so the Administration could not claim they were 'not in a position to *negotiate*' – and he was confident that "agreement could be found soon on the principal issues". Nevin and the prisoners waited patiently for the Master's response to his comments but, if they did, they waited in vain. All the screen showed was the tyrons marching away from the immediate area of the MKC. When it was clear that no reply would be forthcoming, Nevin turned away. "Stay calm", he told the prisoners, "Just relax."

Turning to the committee members, he asked them to gather together to discuss their reaction to the Master's address. Meeting in the corner of the MKC, the group wondered what to do next. All were agreed that the prisoners had no option but to ignore the Master's address and hold out for negotiations.

"We trust you, Nevin", Dayton declared, a broad smile on his face, "We know you'll get us all out of the kolony – plus a year's supply of korb to keep us warm as we float in space!"

Most of those present laughed, happy to find a release for the tension. Nevin merely said "Thanks!" displaying an embarrassed smile.

HOURS HAD PASSED IN the MKC since the Master's chubby countenance had graced the communication monitor – and long hours they were too. Six long hours, in fact. Prisoners took the opportunity to rest or to play games of cards or dice, but Nevin sat with Kenning, sometimes talking quietly, other times in silence as if contemplating a heavy responsibility. Time hung above the prisoners' heads like a dark cloud of poisonous purple korb vapour. Then, as if to scatter the cloud before it intoxicated all those unfortunate enough to lie under its threatening gaze, the communication system activated again, and the Master's face appeared once more. Looking gloomy, the man on whose shoulders the weight of the kolony lay announced quietly and in semi-reverential tones:

"I'm disappointed. I had hoped reason would prevail, but my humble efforts have been spurned. I must now warn you that if you do not vacate the MKC immediately, the full force of the kolony will be mobilised against you. This is not as I would have wanted things to be. It is not as I would have expected you to act. You have disappointed me."

The prisoners, tense with hunger, looked to Nevin for a reaction, but Nevin didn't even bother to reply. With a nonchalant pre-arranged nod, he indicated to a prisoner by the monitor to disconnect the machine.

In the Security Centre, the kontrollers viewed the footage of the MKC from the takes of the Master's addresses. All they could view, however, was the scene directly behind Nevin and there wasn't much to be seen there. Nevin had cleverly cleared the area directly in front of the monitor and, when the broadcast was on, had peopled that area with a handful of prisoners who acted out a scene of animated conversation and enthusiastic interplay with the intention of convincing the Administration that energy and sprits were as high as ever in the Chamber. Nothing could be gleaned from the footage that would be of use in a military sense and Kontroller Windsor ordered it switched off.

"This revolt has gone on long enough!" he announced, puffing up his cheeks, "We must act!"

"A full frontal?" Kontroller Dixon suggested.

"Precisely!" Windsor concurred. "We should attack the main entrance first and then, when the prisoners' attention is distracted, direct two assault teams at the smaller entrances. When we force an opening in one of the doors, we can pump in the syrus gas and it will be all over."

The others nodded. They would have a meeting with the Master in ten minutes and that would be their proposal.

With the seconds and minutes ticking by almost audibly, the tension was palpable in the MKC. The prisoners could do nothing but wait. Sooner or later, the Master would return with a more conciliatory approach – or military might would be used to end the standoff. In the event of the latter, Nevin was determined not to be caught on the wrong foot. If an attack took place, the prisoners must be ready to respond effectively, he believed. Immediately, he arranged his forces into ten groups. Three of these were posted at the entrances to the Chamber. The rest were spread around the MKC. If an attempt were made to break through at any point in the perimeter, the three groups nearest to the assault would converge on that point in an attempt to smother the attack. Most of the armed prisoners were posted with the groups at the entrances, while those in possession of the captured weapons were to the front. Prisoners holding makeshift weapons gathered behind them and those whose only weapons were their fists and their wits took up the rear. A small group of armed prisoners were positioned in the middle of the Chamber and ordered to be prepared to move at speed to support any of the defences at the point of an attack. With the preparations in place, Nevin told the prisoners to wait and remain alert.

The three tyrons, still hoisted above the entrance, although occasionally lowered and given water, viewed their captors' preparations with disdain. Swinging above the entrance in their red suits, they looked like nasty cocooned insects eager to break out of their moulds and devour whatever fell into their clutches.

Preparing for the meeting with his kontrollers, the Master wondered if a quick clinical assault could put an end to the siege. It would not be the ideal solution, in his view, but equally he was sure that time would heal any enmity that had been caused by the unprecedented events taking place in the kolony. He had every confidence in the tyrons and their ability to bring the situation to a conclusion and was veering towards the view that perhaps the sooner that happened the better. But his belief in his own ability to save the day was still strong and he was certain he could still utilise his impressive array of skills to bring the whole sorry mess to a conclusion.

When the meeting began, Windsor was gung-ho. He told the Master that everything was in place for a quick assault that would bring "this intolerable situation" to an end. The tyrons would force an entry in one if not all of the gates and the crisis would be rapidly brought under control. The prisoners would be returned to their cells and those responsible for the revolt would face the consequences of their "evil deeds".

"What if the assault was slowed down and the korb tanks were exploded by the prisoners? Or what if stray fire caused them to blow? Or what if the assault was repulsed?" the Master wondered, signalling a note of caution that merely confirmed Windsor's view of him as a useless coward.

Windsor answered instantly: "There is no way the tyrons can be repulsed by this rabble. We should have gone in earlier and sorted this out. There are four tyrons missing – probably murdered by this foul mob. This situation should not be tolerated for another minute. Also," Windsor added pompously, "there will be no stray fire from the tyrons. Every shot will count!"

The Master looked at the other kontrollers for a reaction to Windsor's outburst. He knew that if he were to deal with his strong-headed kontroller he would need the support of the others. The Master noted no great reaction amongst the assembled kontrollers to their colleague's display of temper. Thinking quickly, he decided to be led by his instincts.

"Good. The assault force will be lead by Kontroller Windsor. Kontrollers Dixon and Kembledon will hold two support forces in readiness, in case they are required. The assault will take place tomorrow – but *only* on my instruction. This matter may be sorted out sensibly yet." Then he added: "Beforehand, I will attempt to impress upon the prisoners the absolute impossibility of their position. If they fail to understand the situation adequately, we will be left with no choice. That is all."

Despite being irritated by the Master's continuing inclination to talk to the rebels rather than act immediately to cut them down, Windsor felt a stir of contentment in his bones. At long last, he would have the opportunity to show how to deal effectively with insurrection. He would not be slow to use this situation to impress the other kontrollers with his resolute action and clear military thinking. Marching down the corridor from the Master's office, his helmet under his arm, Windsor had the bearing of a man whose time had come.

THERE WAS AN AIR of apprehension as Nevin's committee gathered around their leader at the monitor and when Nevin gave the word to switch on the communicator, anxious eyes perused the atmospherics fizzling on the screen.

Moving his palm over the communication activator, Nevin spoke: "Nevin here. This is a message from the prisoners in the Master Korb Chamber. We wish to speak to the Master." A tense silence followed and Nevin sat motionless, eyes fixed on the communicator. With the seconds ticking by, the hush around the Chamber was such that only the beating hearts of the worried prisoners could be heard. Then, exhaling audibly, Nevin announced while looking at the screen: "We will turn this communicator on every half an hour. If you want to communicate with us, you may do so. We will talk to no-one but the Master."

Having waited a few moments, Nevin nodded to Nielsen to switch the machine off. Just as she was about to, however, an image began to take shape on the screen. It was a dark blue eagle on a crimson background chasing a comet above the planet Earth, with a banner in its beak, and the letters NC – the emblem of the Northern Confederation. With the prisoners' eyes peeled to the screen, the loathed emblem gradually gave way to reveal an equally detested image – that of the bald crown and well-puffed face of the Master nestled on a purple cape. Nevin waved his hand towards Nielsen. She left the machine on and every eye and ear in the Chamber focused in as the Master began to speak.

"My dear Nevin, I speak to you as a friend. Indeed, in my role as protector of the Korb-1 Kolony, it is my duty to be friend and protector to all who reside and labour here. It pains me greatly to see the dreadful turn that events have taken. Such unnecessary upheaval and, indeed, destruction on the kolony is a reflection on us all. I must ask you, even at this late stage, to respect my legitimate authority and return to your cells. Although a great amount of damage has been done, I am sure that, with good will on all sides, we can resolve our difficulties and return once again to the harmonious spirit of cooperation that has sustained us all in our various roles on Korb-1. Please, please, return to your cells!"

The assembled prisoners waited in anticipation for their leader's reaction to the Master's appeal. What approach would Nevin take to the apparently reasonable request to return to a peaceful existence? Nevin remained silent for a while, as if aware that his first comments could set the direction in which future events would turn, leading perhaps to a previously unimaginable liberation or to death and punishment for many, if not all.

"Thank you for your kind and conciliatory comments, Master", Nevin commenced, his features relaxed as he spoke, though his respectful approach disappointed many of his assembled supporters. "However,

I feel that the behaviour of your security personnel has not matched the positive nature of your comments, either now or in the past. You have always spoken of cooperation but the heavy-handed approach of the tyron guard has constantly led us in a different direction. Now, it appears they have shattered even the one-sided peace that has reigned on the kolony since its inception. I'm afraid that, at this stage, confidence in your administration has been destroyed and the prisoners now have only one desire – to go home!"

"To go home!" the Master repeated with a sigh of exasperation, "to go home! Are you all mad? I have told you again and again from your very first moments on the kolony that it is not physically possible to leave Korb-1. The atmosphere out there would kill you in a millisecond! What would be the point in that?"

"If it is possible to arrive, it's possible to leave", Nevin interjected calmly.

"No, no, Nevin! Not so!" the Master insisted. The chemical make-up of the atmospheric shield around the kolony is the opposite to that of Earth – so that exiting objects can heat up to as high a temperature as 1,500 termons – only a custom-built korb cargo ship can survive that. You all know that – I have told you so many times! Why deceive yourselves into thinking otherwise?"

"Why not let us see for ourselves, then?" Nevin asked.

"Within the confines of kolony discipline, I have no problem with that", the Master replied, then, without hesitation, moved on. "We are all in this together. The Korb-1 Kolony depends on us all. I am sure that if we can sit down in a spirit of cooperation, all outstanding issues can be resolved. Please, return to your cells and both you and I can discuss the situation tomorrow to see what can be done to restore our confidence in one another."

"The prisoners want to go home – it's as simple as that", Nevin interjected simply.

"Good Heavens, man! Why can't you listen to what I'm saying – it's not possible to leave – you all know that! Think about what you are doing! The tyron guard are massing outside the Chamber even as we speak. If you will not be reasonable, then they must do their duty. Let it not come to that!"

The Master emphasised the word 'that' as the screen changed from a view of the Master to one of the tyron hordes marching in formation outside the Chamber, before returning to the Master's concerned visage.

"I will give you some time to think this out", the Master returned. "But, please, please be realistic and come to your senses!"

The Master's image faded away and the NC badge soon reclaimed the screen before giving way once more to atmospheric spots. Nevin turned to the Defence Committee. "Well, where do we go from here?" he asked, raising his eyebrows in frustration.

44 NOTHING TO LOSE

As the view faded on his monitor, the Master considered the position. The prisoners were obviously well organised, in good spirits, and ready for the long haul. Their demands were at the extreme end of the spectrum and Nevin was obviously intent on playing hardball. At the same time, the Master was sure that only the most foolish amongst the prisoners would consider departure from the kolony a realistic possibility and that Nevin knew this well. He was sure that whatever arrangement was arrived at, it would be cosmetic enough to allow 'normality' to return to Korb-1 once more. But it was early days yet and, when the pangs of deprivation struck, the prisoners might end up happy to return to what they now were so eager to leave behind.

Using his wrist communicator, the Master contacted the Systems Kontroller.

"Monitor all oxygen and other chemical levels in the MKC continuously. When oxygen falls below comfort levels, I want to know."

"Done! What about the temperature, Master?" the Systems Kontroller replied.

"That too – and any other critical information."

The Master wondered how long it would take to sweat the prisoners out of the Chamber. He knew that some of them would stay there forever if they had too, but they would be a small minority when the time came. As soon as the conditions in the Chamber – no food or drink, falling oxygen levels, uncomfortably high temperatures, and slipping morale – started to hit home, he was certain tensions would develop amongst the prisoners. Then he would let them simmer and it would be time to act. When the prisoners fully understood that there really was no escape – no way out – they would come to their senses. Admiring the hologram of the kolony in his studio, he still considered Korb-1 to be in safe hands – despite the challenge thrown up by the MKC siege.

Moving across the room, the Master sat into his astral centre and closed the door behind him. Seated inside, he inserted his favourite disk – Astra 2137 – and waited for the experience to begin. Inside the centre, a musical composition encapsulating the year 2137 – an extremely happy and successful one for the Master – began and the darkness of the centre gave way to a gradually emerging all-embracing light that carried with it hologrammatic images of Earth-2137 – and Korb-1. The Master relaxed to glide gracefully through the galaxy. Sights, sounds and other senses changed as the vain man indulged himself in a journey through time and space. The realism of the simulation was such that the temperature, sound and images in the centre transformed as various parts of the galaxy were visited. The journey complete, the music came to a close and the lights in the cabin came on again. The Master was a relaxed man.

Everyone looked closely for Nevin's reaction after the Master's image had vanished from the monitor, and questions began to develop in their minds. How was this encounter working out? Who, if anyone, was getting the upper hand? How realistic were the prisoners' demands at this stage? What should the next step be?

Nevin, having called the Defence Committee together to gauge reactions, sat down on the floor with his comrades. First to offer an opinion was Tina Penner of KC31-2:

"I think they're bluffing – I think we can still get out!" she contended.

A brief silence followed, then Guivarc'h agreed: "Yes. I think they've got themselves into such a mess that anything is possible".

Nevin looked around for other views. Sweeney responded to the leader's questioning look: "I don't agree", she ventured, "I think they've got all the cards. They can leave us here to rot and get away with it."

Imbuna concurred. "They could seal this Chamber and forget we ever existed", he lamented, looking his fellow conspirators in the eye.

"Yes, we need to be realistic", Panvi suggested "even with the tyrons here, we've very little to bargain with."

The mood of the committee was shifting away from the idea of escape. Nevin looked at Kane. "What about you, Kane?" he asked.

The prisoner looked around at his colleagues and sighed. Then, brushing his hair back with his right hand, looked Nevin in the eye.

"My gut feeling is that there is no way these people are going to let us walk home. Even if they agree to let us go, you can be sure they'll be waiting around the block to jump us and get us back inside as soon as they can – and then make sure there isn't a second time." Prisoner 313 looked around for reactions. His colleagues carried serious expressions. Kane continued: "The only way to get out of here – if there is a way – is by surprise. The element of surprise is gone now. It will take a while for it to return. I think we should use whatever bargaining power we have here to improve our position in the prison – maybe obtain better mobility in the kolony – and build on that. When the time is right to strike in the future, we can be ready to surprise."

Guivarc'h reacted with a negative shake of his head.

"I think Kane is right", Sweeney ventured. "Although we can still pursue our demand for release, we should be focused on winning something meaningful for all the prisoners from this. The future will throw up new opportunities".

After everyone had spoken, Nevin presented his own conclusion.

"We will press our demand for release but, if it becomes clear that release is not an option at this time, I propose to attempt to find out from the Master what *he* is willing to do to resolve the situation. In the meantime, I want all of you to communicate to Sweeney what you think our objectives in that case should be. Sweeney, please have that ready for me within half an hour. Meeting over!"

At the conclusion of what had been a remarkably calm discussion, anxious glances were exchanged by people with nothing – or maybe everything – to lose.

WHEN SIMPSON CONVEYED THE Master's instructions to her deputy, McKenzie listened intently as the Master's intentions became clear. He was going to wait until the prisoners were at their lowest ebb before negotiating an end to the occupation. In a way, McKenzie was relieved to hear that. At least there wasn't going to be a full frontal attack yet, an event that could result in the deaths of hundreds of prisoners, including Kane. But she was well aware that the Master's plan would be more effective than an open slaughter. His objective was to get the prisoners back working in the Chambers. In order to achieve that return to normality, he would probably be willing to relax a rule or two but there was no way that anything radical would be countenanced either by him or his more hawkish kontrollers.

McKenzie herself preferred this option. She was as aware as anyone else that mass escape or release was a sad non-starter. In her mind the only way an escape could be effected was by waiting patiently and picking the right moment to strike. Then, and only with a carefully prepared plan, a small number of prisoners might manage to break free. It was McKenzie's intention that, when that time came, Kane would be among that chosen few.

In the meantime, the reluctant Assistant Security Officer had been given the task of monitoring the vital signs in the MKC. Immediately, McKenzie wondered how she could intervene at a critical juncture to ensure a safe and reasonably satisfactory outcome to the siege. As she did, her mind wandered back to other dark days in her life. Inevitably, she remembered the day she had stumbled on the terrible truth about the death of Ruyan Kendrick.

The young woman had spent hours that day going over the file she had just discovered. Every single item of information was studied, analysed and cross-referenced, as her heartbeat thumped louder and louder in her ears. Although eager to continue her efforts to make sense of the information she had stumbled across, McKenzie reluctantly decided to call it a day at seven o'clock, the normal time for those working an extra period to leave the building. Anytime after that required an overtime sanction notice to be despatched to the section head. That would only attract attention that McKenzie could do without in her unsettled state.

After a sleepless night, McKenzie arrived into work early the following morning to continue her search for an explanation of the devastating discovery she had made. For a woman engrossed in establishing what the terrible truth behind the termination of 02.07.2169 was, the day passed quickly. As time moved on, the security information expert used every element of her experience and expertise to connect a trail through the jungle of files and databases at her disposal.

One thing she noticed was that the letters *ark* regularly occurred against a number of dates. Others apparently in the same category were *ran*, *kep* and *pel*. Another feature McKenzie noticed was that the reference numbers in the files were not in exact sequence. Carrying out a minimum of official duties, she spent most of the day bent over her work station, only the odd *uipr* (urgent information processing request) distracting her from her task of identifying the pattern she was convinced lay behind the mass of figures and entries that lay before her on screen.

When the end of the day arrived, the Systems Executive reluctantly closed up shop to go home, have the slightest of meals and a disturbed night's sleep and return early the next morning to continue her quest. For days, McKenzie feverishly went through the system —always covering her tracks — in search of the key that would unlock the door. Behind that door, she was increasingly convinced she would find a horrifying vista, the details of which she could at this stage only imagine. Time and time again, she pursued an item of information only to come up against a stone wall. But unfailingly she would return to follow another lead. Every step of progress made along the way was greeted with a suppressed sense of elation, every last minute disappointment immediately overcome.

It was on the fourth day of her quest for the truth that Zeena McKenzie eventually realised she was gradually piecing together a picture – albeit a cryptic one – of an operational network functioning behind the legitimate information gathering and management system. It was a structure of operations that appeared to involve the systematic use of assassination. What the objectives of this assassination apparatus were remained unclear, but one of its victims was unquestionably Ruyan Kendrick, First Officer, Confederation Guard, NCR 18.

The realisation that the only one she had ever loved in the world had been done to death by the very administration he had faithfully and courageously served caused a numbing effect on the young servant of that same administration. A chill set into McKenzies's bones as she sat at her workstation, a chill she remembered to this very day. As time had passed since her devastating discovery, that chill of horror had gradually transformed into a numb determination that would drive her towards her sole aim from then on – revenge.

Despite her best efforts since, however, two objectives had eluded the determined avenger – the opportunity to exact the price she so wished to have the administration pay, and an explanation of the reason Ruyan Kendrick had died.

A number of months after McKenzie's discovery, with her spirit waning, the young widow was surprised to be approached and invited to join what her supervisor described as an exciting new project that was then in train. It was to be a unique project, one demanding a particular dedication and skill, one offering an exceptional opportunity to make a contribution, one involving a new start. McKenzie asked for time to consider the invitation. She was told that would be fine but not to take too long as the position might be offered to someone else if it looked as if she wasn't interested. After some thought, and in the hope of gaining an opportunity to achieve her ultimate aim, Zeena McKenzie decided to accept the invitation and was soon embarked on a new life as Assistant Security Officer on Korb-1.

45 A WORRIED MAN'S OPTIONS

Following the clearly implied threat in the Master's last address, a mixture of tension and fatigue hung heavily in the atmosphere in the MKC. This energy-sapping mood was compounded by a noticeable deterioration in the oxygen supply and an obvious rise in temperature and humidity. The prisoners were assembled in their appointed positions, nervously awaiting the assault the Master had warned them was being prepared. On top of korb mixing machines to the side of each of the doors, prisoners with zennors were waiting anxiously to use them on the first tyron head to appear through the gates. Directed at the doors from each side were the funnels of the korb feeding machine, which had been fixed at the entrance in an effort to provide a defence against an attempted forced entry by the tyrons. An operator was at the ready on each machine to power the appliance into action. Whether this would prevent the tyrons entering the Chamber or merely slow down their approach was an academic argument – it was the only defence that Nevin and his committee could think of. It was Nielsen who had pointed out that any breach in the gates or walls could be sealed up immediately with a dose of korb, but the risk of contamination to those in the front line was in high percentages. If it stopped the tyrons in their tracks, however, everyone believed that was a risk worth taking. Without a degree of accuracy that only intense training, innate talent or uncanny luck could produce, the seized weapons would be of limited use against fully armoured tyrons – the zennors could not penetrate the tyrons' *pps*, merely knock them down with the force of the blast. After a while, the tyron could get up again and continue his or her inevitable advance. The only way to down a tyron permanently was to hit them in the face. This area was less protected, in the interests of sight and communication, by the electro-magnetic cushion that defended the body and head. Karl Streever knew this from his own experience, and had taken great pleasure in sharing his familiarity with the tyron defence armour with everybody in possession of a weapon.

Nevin had warned the prisoners that, whatever happened, the tyrons couldn't be allowed to open a breach in the gates. If they did, they could gas, bomb or even dehydrate the prisoners with *de-h* grenades.

"Lodge the heaviest wedges you can find and place them at each side of the gates. If they won't move, the gates won't either", the leader ordered.

Weak and weary as they were, the prisoners had done as Nevin suggested. Long girders were removed from the korb conveyor belt systems and prised in between the edge of the gates and the machinery on each side. It was hard to see how the entrances could be forced open now. If they were, clearly the prisoners' minutes would be numbered. Their work done, the prisoners took up their positions as directed by their leader.

Despite the small beads of sweat on his brow, Nevin seemed to be his usual mixture of relaxed concentration. Tapping his metal fingers off the edge of the seat on which he sat, he appeared to be ready and willing to take on the might of the tyrons. Behind the calm exterior, however, the usual series of doubts were traversing Nevin's worried mind. What would be the repercussions for all those who had placed their faith in his judgement if they were to be overrun and subjugated again? Whatever regime replaced the present one would be markedly more oppressive – of that there could be no doubt. The regime that had developed over the years under the Master would seem like a paradise in the distant past if things went wrong. But a victory over the tyrons would change the situation considerably. There would be everything to play for after that. Nevin knew in his heart and soul that such an eventuality was unlikely. The regime had all the aces in this game of bluff and the best the prisoners could hope for would be a negotiated return to their cells. It would be in such negotiations that Nevin would hope to make his most valuable contribution. It was in the area of strategy and planning that the veteran had made his most telling contributions to the information freedom campaign in the NC. His unique ability to see into the adversary's mind had helped ensure the success of many informational release operations in his freedom years. It was that quality that had placed the seasoned campaigner high on the NC's list of the most wanted and had made his arrest a cause of celebrations in the shady corridors of power. It was in the final intellectual joust with the Master, not in the battle with the tyrons, that Nevin planned to play a decisive role. But, in order to get to the negotiating table, the battle with the tyrons had to be won.

Nevin ranged his options on a scale of one to five. One was total freedom for everybody – "with a picnic hamper to boot", as Kane had described that extremely unlikely eventuality. Two was freedom for a select few with no guarantee of survival – but who would select the ones to go? Three was democratisation of the kolony, with prisoner representatives, elected by prisoner committees, participating in the running of the Korb-1. This would enable prisoners to look forward to relative freedom, living out their lives as free men and women in a democratic society. Four was surrender and a return to the status quo, with little or no repercussions for the prisoners, and five was defeat followed by a new regime of unprecedented oppression. Kane was convinced that most prisoners would prefer death to option five and that was why they had chosen to make their stand here and now. Facing down a tyron attack would almost certainly mean that option five would be the least likely at that stage. It would also ensure that the other, more appealing, choices became more real. If the tyron attack came, the prisoners, quite simply, could not afford to lose.

Nevin was impressed at the farsighted nature of the prisoners' analysis so far. The simplest thing in the world to demand was release and departure from the Korb-1. It was also the easiest to refuse. Option two wasn't much better. The challenge in the third option was twofold. First, the Master had to cede at least some real freedom to the prisoners or lose his credibility as a partner in the resolution process. This would involve facing down the hawks in his camp for once and for all and proving his commitment to partnership. Second, however, was the challenge for the prisoners themselves. Accepting a stake in the system meant revising their view of the future to include a lifetime on Korb-1. Nevin was impressed by the prisoners' willingness to gamble and call the Master's bluff. In the meantime, though, it was imperative that they overcome what could turn out to be an insurmountable obstacle – the capability of the tyron guard to end the revolt in one foul sweep.

Nevin's thoughts were broken by the arrival of Kane and Dayton.

"Ready for the negotiations?" Kane asked, smiling a relaxed smile.

"It's what might have to come before that that worries me now", was Nevin's honest reply. "And even after that, we haven't got a great hand of cards to play. If they decide to play hard, what can we do really? Ice the tyrons above the gate? Then what?"

"Maybe it *will* work out", Kane reassured. "The Master's no fool. He will know that he must give something to get 300 prisoners to walk out of here peacefully. Unfortunately, he may know how little he needs to give as well. That could be the real problem."

"We can only do our best, Nevin. Go for it – there's nothing to lose!" Dayton added.

The conversation was interrupted by a signal from O'Hara over at the monitor – The Master was about to appear.

SETTLING HIMSELF DOWN IN front of his monitor, the Master was confident he was now about to make progress. Security Officer Simpson had already assured him that the temperature, oxygen and humidity levels in the MKC were at "uncomfortable" levels. "Good!" was the Master's simple reply. Always one to keep his plans to himself, he was certainly not going to share his thoughts with Simpson. Although he held the *dark lady* in high regard because of her record of service and valuable experience, the Master was also aware that she was not a woman to be trusted. Simpson's loyalty was unquestionably to herself and the less she knew of his plans the less likely she was to reveal them to others. "Good!" the Master repeated, as he turned to switch off his communicator, adding "keep me posted. I'm going to talk to the prisoners now."

Taking a deep breath and ensuring his purple cape of NC authority was visible, the Master palmed the monitor on and was greeted by the relaxed visage of Tom Nevin.

"Well, my dear Nevin. Are we in a position to sort this business out?"

"That really depends on you, Master", was Nevin's restrained reply.

"Are you ready to lead your people out of the Chamber and back to their cells? I'm sure we can work everything out in that event."

Nevin responded immediately and clearly: "We have considered our position carefully and this is what we propose. First: Those who wish to leave the kolony are allowed to go and are assisted in so doing. Second: Those who wish to remain are given the opportunity to participate in the administration of the kolony, to which they would then give their allegiance. What is your reaction?"

The Master's features momentarily appeared to betray alarm at the prisoners' proposals, but the experienced negotiator almost immediately regained his composure. Displaying a sympathetic smile, he expressed surprise at the prisoners' demands, particularly their request to leave.

"Nevin, how many times do I have to explain that from Korb-1 there can be *no* departure? The chemical composition of the atmosphere here is such that departure alive is not physically possible." The Master stressed the last two words of his pained statement, then continued "If I was to assist anybody in leaving the kolony, I would be directly responsible for their deaths! This is a position I could not – in all conscience – accept. As for your second proposal, I am a firm believer in the irrepressibility of human nature. With a little bit of give and take, I am certain we can find an even more meaningful role for all in the future of Korb-1. Perhaps we can discuss some ideas on that after this unfortunate situation has been resolved."

Nevin listened carefully to what the Master had said. His inclination was to take whatever could be enticed from the other side and build on it in the future but, first, the main demand of the prisoners must be addressed.

"I welcome your positive reaction, Master, but it is the wish of all the prisoners that the opportunity to leave the kolony be afforded to anybody who wishes to depart. After that, the future of those remaining can be discussed. Even if departure from Korb-1 does mean death, there may be those of us who would still choose that course. As for future prisoner participation in the administration of the kolony, I would be delighted to discuss that with you at the earliest opportunity but that could only be done on the basis of certain principles to be agreed beforehand."

"I must assure you once more, Nevin, that departure from the Korb-1 Kolony entails certain death and there is no way I could allow such a suicidal path to be followed. It is my duty of care to you all to prevent such madness from taking place. On the other issue, however, you will find me a very practical man. As soon as prisoners have returned to their cells, I will talk with you about the future. We will speak again soon. But I must warn you – there would be others who would wish to act differently to resolve the situation in the way they know best. Let us both ensure that good sense will prevail. I will talk to you again shortly. Though, at that stage, decisions must be taken."

With that, the screen returned to the banner of the Confederation and Nevin and his fellow prisoners turned to analyse the latest interplay with the Master.

IN THE SECURITY AREA, Windsor winced as the Master finished his latest bout of negotiations with the rebels. How could matters have been allowed to come to this? he asked himself angrily as he considered the appalling scenario opening up before him – those responsible for the murder of kolony personnel, the destruction of kolony property and the loss of hundreds of hours of korb production were about to be rewarded with a role in the administration of their own prison! The very thought of those whose treason towards the NC had led them to be incarcerated in Korb-1 in the first place being given the slightest recognition beyond that of disgraced convict was more than the veteran soldier could take. The situation was out of control, he now believed. Somebody must take decisive action to rescue the kolony from chaos and anarchy. Windsor knew that *somebody* was him.

46   HEAT OF BATTLE

For the briefest of moments, a niggling doubt crossed the Master's usually untroubled mind. Was he making the right decisions in this extremely serious situation? Could his approach be too restrained? Was it possible that the tiresome eruptions of vicious rage from the maniacal Windsor were in reality a crazed representation of the essential truth? Unsettled at the thought, the Master immediately retreated back into the sanctuary of his smug self-belief. Although aware that the kontrollers would expect to be allowed to act if things dragged on, he would continue to believe in his ability to talk the prisoners out of the corner into which they had painted themselves. The Master knew that his appointment of Windsor, Dixon and Kembledon to lead the assault on the MKC was a gamble and that gambles sometimes didn't pay off. But he was also aware that if his troublesome kontroller failed, then he would be in a position to rid himself of the fool for once and for all. In the unlikely eventuality that the demented kontroller succeeded, he would expect his achievement to be recognised. The Master was confident, however, that in that case his superior political skills would enable him to outmanoeuvre his delirious subordinate. With ease, the acclaim would be skilfully shifted to the others involved in the escapade, leaving Windsor cast as a minor figure in the event. Comfortable once more in the certainty of his natural leadership qualities, the Master stepped into his astral centre and closed the door.

Assistant Security Officer McKenzie had taken up her duties in the korb kolony with less than total enthusiasm. The world she had once believed in had been blown asunder by the shattering discovery she had made one fateful evening as the sun went down on Traw beach. Everything she had taken for granted – loyalty, the common purpose of citizenship, the very legitimacy of the state – had been called into question in the painful days that followed. The certainties upon which she had hung the routine of her life had proven to be hollow totem poles, empty structures that supported a system of deceit. When the death of the only one she cared for in the world was followed by the shocking realisation that he had been murdered by the very regime he had given his life to defend, the young woman was left with nowhere to go. A total nervous collapse leading to a likely institutionalised existence in an NC mental care facility was a distinct possibility. This was a risk of which the young woman was painfully aware and something she would have to avoid at all costs. When the invitation to join the kolony arrived, it was couched in terms of tenderness and concern, that a "new challenge" might be just what she needed following her "recent tragic loss". All the time, though, McKenzie sensed something more sinister behind the official concern at her plight. There was even something in the body language of her supervisor when he spoke to her that led her to believe there was a lot more on his mind than he was revealing.

McKenzie spent the few short days she had been given to consider the offer wondering if there were any other options open to her. She considered leaving the service altogether but this would be frowned upon by the authorities and would require special permission, as those who had spent more than three years in the system were regarded as being 'attached', having had access to security files. In the back of her mind, the young widow sensed an element of threat in the 'invitation' issued by the Administration. The phrase "it would appear to be your best option at this stage" meant only one thing in the mouths of those who would lie and cheat to achieve their aims – whatever those were. Eventually, McKenzie decided to accept, but settled her mind by making herself a promise: that, after a period of normality during which she would familiarise herself with the security apparatus of the kolony, she would concentrate on wreaking her revenge on the Administration. When the moment was right, she would deliver a major hit on the NC Security Structure that would leave them reeling. The day the fleeing Kevin Kane landed at her feet in the Security Area of Korb-1, McKenzie realised her opportunity had arrived.

WINDSOR PACED UP AND down in his suite. Since viewing the latest 'shameful episode of capitulation' to the prisoners, he had almost worked himself up to a frenzy. It was becoming clear in his mind that the time for decisive action had arrived. The Master's 'pathetic' efforts to cajole a 'vicious criminal element' into accepting his authority was below contempt. His action in even speaking to the 'criminals holed up' in the MKC was itself an act of 'unforgivable treason'. No security officer 'deserving of respect' could countenance such a 'demeaning deed'. 'Immediate and decisive' action was needed to 'salvage the reputation' of the kolony. These were the thoughts that disturbed the securocrat's mind as he attempted to decide what form of action he should now take. Using his interconnector, Windsor spoke to Security Officer Simpson. He then contacted Kontrollers Dixon and Kembledon, ordering them to come to his office immediately. As he waited, Windsor put his plan together and, when Dixon and Kembledon arrived, the Kontroller was ready.

Using an audio-visual collage compiled for him by Simpson, he treated the two kontrollers to a speech by the Master outlining the discovery of a serious security threat from the prisoners in the MKC. This involved releasing a large quantity of korb into the ventilation system, thus endangering the entire kolony. Immediate action was required and the Administration was depending on them, under the direction of Kontroller Windsor, to take the MKC and prevent the rebels from carrying out their deadly plan. In the meantime, the Master would be involved in careful deliberations with the NC authorities.

On receiving the Master's analysis from Windsor, Dixon and Kembledon were struck by a feeling of immense responsibility. The future of the kolony depended on their immediate and effective action. Oblivious to the fact that the entire crisis was a clever stunt, staged by their fellow controller and arranged by his collaborator, Simpson, they were instantly filled with a determination to fulfil their instructions to the best of their ability and save the kolony – and in the process, of course, win recognition for their decisive action.

WINDSOR WASN'T LOSING ANY time. Having been informed by Simpson that the Master was indulging himself in his favourite pastime, he knew he had two hours in which to break the prisoners' defences down and take the MKC. His plan was simple and typically 'tyron' in the arrogant confidence it illustrated in the ability of the NC elite to master any challenge. Windsor would use a 'shock force' to stun the rebels and rapidly 'breach their rudimentary defences'. The tyrons would have a code red direction permitting them to eliminate on the spot anybody daring to resist their legitimate authority. The rest of the 'rabble' would be frogmarched off to their cells to await 'retribution for their crimes'. When the 'old fool in the nostalgia chamber' awoke, the balance of power in the kolony would have shifted to the one figure of authority deserving of the title 'Master' – Windsor himself!

On Windsor's instructions, the tyron force was initially drawn up in the Dining Hall. The muster of tyrons was an impressive sight and the entire manoeuvre was carried on the internal broadcast system, timed to be the first sight to greet the prisoners when they reactivated the monitors in the MKC. Windsor's aim was to frighten the prisoners into considering surrender and then, at their moment of doubt, to send his shock troops in to take control of the Chamber. In tight ranks, the tyrons presented arms and gave out their individual unit war cries in turn. It was a scene intended to set the hair standing on the back of the necks of even those amongst the prisoners who had experienced the heat of battle in the past.

Windsor was happy things were going to plan. In their red suits and helmets, the tyrons presented arms and marched to and fro. The Kontroller exhibited a tightly controlled smile as his formidable forces marched by in clockwork waves.

"Bah, toy soldiers!" a prisoner beside Dayton jeered as the prisoners in the MKC watched the manoeuvres on the screen.

"Yeah, we can handle them!" exclaimed another.

"I wish I could share their confidence", Dayton confided to Kane.

"It's better than low morale any day", Kane ventured. "Anyway, maybe they're right!"

Nevin smiled a weak smile. "If we have to face those bastards, we'd better have more than a few zennors and stun batons to our name."

No one responded as those within earshot reflected on the truth in Nevin's statement. After all, how could a force of unarmed prisoners resist the best fighting force in the galaxy? Keeping the entrances well guarded seemed to be Nevin's only option.

"Looks like the Master has decided he doesn't want to do any more talking", Nevin quipped as the entire body of prisoners in the MKC viewed the mechanical soldiers on parade.

Nevin decided not to waste any time. He called the Defence Committee together.

"We can't afford to take any hits here", the leader informed his tense colleagues. All of them sensed a strange look in the veteran's eyes. They all interpreted it to be the look of destiny, that particular moment when the realisation that you must swim hard or sink deep hits home — the recognition that action as never before is required to save the day and that that action in itself might not even be enough. The committee members understood exactly the emotions going through their leader's mind as he tried to take the decisions that would make all the difference for those under his control and command.

The prisoners were in their appointed positions, ready to add the weight of their bodies, diminished though they were after three days of fasting and fatigue, to block any surge of tyrons that might breach the first lines of defence.

The heat that had built up in the Chamber over the last three days was almost unbearable, despite the fact that the ventilation system was still in operation. In fact, it had occurred to many of the prisoners, in an inspiring example of gallows humour, that a minor breach in the gate would in fact be a good thing, as it would allow some of the hot air to blow out on the tyrons!

Untidy, dishevelled, unwashed and dripping with sweat, the prisoners were by no means a lean fighting machine, but their determination and their will to resist created a dynamic amongst them that would have to make any invading tyron's task that much harder. Men and women of various ages stood shoulder to shoulder to face the impending onslaught, made more threatening by the uncertainty of its timing.

As the minutes passed, the prisoners remained in their positions, most of them hunkered down in the spot in which they were expected to make their stand, a low hum of nervous conversation floating above their heads. Tension and temperature mounted in the Chamber as the clock moved on and no approach had been made by the Master. Time weighed heavily on the minds of the besieged. Some thought they could hear the seconds ticking away. Others thought they could feel them throb away in their very bones. With the passage of time, the throbbing became more intense until it felt almost as if it was coming in through the walls. Gradually the sensation became stronger and stronger until the very walls themselves began to reverberate. With the throbbing slowly became a pounding, the prisoners looked nervously at one another as a realisation set in.

"It's starting!" a young man with short yellow hair and a red face announced, and the prisoners rose to their feet as one to face their destiny.

The main gate of the MKC shook and vibrated until a shrill drilling sound was heard near the centre of the main door. "They're using a pounder drill!" Nevin announced – a factual statement, devoid of emotion. Just then, the slightest crack appeared in the middle of the gate. "Get ready to seal the breach if it opens up!" Nevin ordered. The prisoners watched anxiously as the pounder drill hammered and drilled its way through the gate.

The pounder mechanically carrying out its task, Nevin turned to Kane, Dayton and O'Hara who were standing beside him:

"They're trying to split the gate. They'll be through within fifteen minutes. Unless we can stop them or block the fissure, they'll gas us out. Korb operators at the ready!" the leader ordered. "Release korb at the signal!"

The prisoners had worked frantically to direct a korb feed towards the gate. They knew that accuracy would be the key to success. If the feed were to fall short, it would solidify where it fell, leaving the cleft in the gate wide open. With the drilling of the pounder becoming more intense, the funnels were finally manoeuvred into place, inspiring a confidence of sorts amongst the prisoners facing the gate. Eventually, the throbbing became almost unbearable as the drill achieved its objective and its ugly steel tooth appeared in a cleft in the right gate. The prisoners operating the korb funnels waited anxiously for the sign from Nevin to direct their gush on the gate. Nevin waited.

Suddenly, the drill stopped and a spooky silence descended upon the Chamber but, as quickly as it stopped, the drill started up again, this time in reverse motion as it withdrew from the split in the gate, its work done. Nevin signalled to the operators to hold their fire. The pounder fully withdrawn, a narrow robotic tentacle was introduced from outside the gate. As it appeared through the cleft, it was seen to have a camera eye and was obviously intended to reconnoitre the area before an assault began. As soon as the tentacle entered the Chamber, one of the prisoners, a well built crazy from 37-3, ran forward and jumped on it. Everybody watched in amazement as the courageous prisoner wrestled with the unwieldy piece of equipment. At first, it looked as if the machine would be too powerful for the dehydrated prisoner, but soon the muscle-bound man's motivation added to his undoubted strength and, with an almost primordial cry of victory, he forced the tentacle to the ground, smashing it on the solid floor. Almost immediately, and apparently in response to the prisoner's brave intervention, loud bursts of zennor fire were directed in through the cleft. With that, a fierce exchange of fire took place between the frontline prisoners and the tyrons. The tyrons, obviously not expecting to come under zennor fire from within, fell back. In the crossfire, the giant hero was hit in the leg and fell to the ground, still clutching the camera tentacle. "Move! Now!" Nevin shouted to the hero who immediately released the tentacle and rolled away across the floor. Displaying a look of urgency, Nevin signalled to the korb operators to release their load. Suddenly, a lava-like flow of korb hit the gate just above the cleft. Streaming down the large metal door, it solidified, closing the gap as it rolled treacle-like towards the ground. The camera tentacle was cemented in the middle of the gate, its limp head lying aimlessly on the Chamber floor.

The realisation setting in that the tyrons' initial assault had been fought off, a huge cheer went up in the Chamber. Prisoners hugged one another and danced as they celebrated. Nevin looked at his cohorts and smiled. Even as the prisoners' cheers died down, however, it became clear that their celebrations might be premature. A commotion being heard at the right side entrance to the Chamber, the prisoners turned around to see their comrades involved in a desperate struggle to keep the gate closed as a wedge drill was being forced between the doors. The other prisoners charged down to the gate to assist their comrades, but as they did, a similar commotion broke out at the left gate.

On hearing the uproar, Nevin leapt up on top of the nearest korb direction station and, standing on the roof, surveyed the situation. One glance made it clear that if the tyrons were not stopped immediately, they would be in the Chamber in a matter of minutes. Nevin was joined by Kane and Dayton.

"We've got to wedge those gates closed right now!" Kane announced. "The cooler pipes are our only choice. If we can rip them out, we can wedge the door closed." Nevin didn't hesitate. "Do it – now!" he concurred. "Kane – organise the left one! Dayton – the right!"

Both men jumped down from the roof of the direction stand and ran towards the action, screaming directions as they arrived on the scene. On Kane's arrival, the prisoners in the left gate area proceeded to rip out all the korb cooler piping they could find and wedge it on either side of the gate. With that, the tyrons' wedge machine stalled and seemed to be making no more progress. The prisoners used all the energy at their disposal to keep the piping wedged in place. At the other gate, however, progress in getting the piping in place was slower, and the wedge drill seemed to be advancing alarmingly. Suddenly a gap appeared between the two gates and red searcher lights streamed in, creating an eerie image through the smoke and dust. As the prisoners attempted to cover the gap, a stream of zennor rounds burst through and a number of the defenders were hit. With Dayton and a large group of prisoners getting the piping wedges ready to be pushed into place, a fierce exchange of zennor fire took place through the gap in the gate. Then the nose of a zennor appeared in the opening, firing wildly, followed by a second and a third. A breach seemed inevitable. With prisoners scattering for cover, and the wedges in place and ready to be pushed in, urgent action was required. But just as Dayton was about to give the signal to wedge the gate shut, the figure of a tyron appeared, squeezing in through the gap. Dayton was horrified – was it too late? The tyrons struggled to clear himself through the gap but was finding it difficult to squeeze through, as zennor shots bounced off his armour like pebbles off a wall. If the tyron wasn't removed from the gap, there would be no possibility of sealing the entrance again. Sweat ran down Dayton's brow, his worried eyes watching the scenario unfold. With the prisoners backing off, defeat was suddenly becoming a distinct possibility.

Suddenly, however, a figure came running in the opposite direction. It was Nielsen. Carrying a zennor, the nimble woman ran directly to the side of the gate. Then, steadying herself and taking a deep breath, she ran straight towards the invading tyron, approaching him on his blind side. On noticing the prisoner beside him, the tyron immediately twisted towards her, attempting to turn his weapon in her direction. But Nielsen's reaction was immediate and obviously premeditated. Placing her weapon under the tyron's chin, she delivered a devastating and fatal blow. For a split second, all activity on both sides of the gate ceased. Then, as the import of what had taken place sunk in, Nielsen pulled the tyron inside, shouting to Dayton to "Do it! Now!" Dayton didn't need a second message to seize the initiative. Ordering the prisoners to push with all their strength, he watched with pleasure as the gate wedged shut.

At once, a strange silence descended on the Chamber. Nobody dared celebrate another victory lest they be proven premature once again, and end up rueing their enthusiasm, so the prisoners waited, looking at one another nervously, hoping against hope. As the moments passed by, eventually the situation became clear. The tyrons *had* been repulsed and the Chamber was secure once more. At last, the prisoners allowed themselves a howl of delight and some, despite their lack of sustenance in the last three days, even danced a victory jig. Kane, Dayton and Nielsen smiled at one another and embraced in celebration before hoisting the hero of the hour onto their shoulders to accept the acclaim of her besieged peers. Nevin smiled a smile of relief.

On the other side of the main gate, unseen by Nevin, Kane and the other prisoners, Kontroller Windsor's face was ashen with anger.

47 SETTLING THE SCORE

THE MASTER EMERGED FROM his astral centre flushed with satisfaction. His visits to his favourite year always recharged him with energy and enthusiasm and this trip had been no exception. Re-energised, the old fox was fully confident again in his ability to handle any situation and emerge unscathed. With his newfound motivation, he decided to draw up a clear plan for the ending of the MKC siege. Filling himself a glass of arctic ice juice from the dispenser on the wall, he sat back in his chair to admire his hologram of Korb-1 and bask in his unshaken belief in himself. Sipping the wine, the Master decided he would be firm on the question of departure as this was a core issue. In regard to the role of the prisoners in the kolony in the future, he would be more conciliatory there because, at the end of the day, the happier the prisoners were the more industrious they would be in the production of korb. At any rate, he would be the final arbitrator, in practical terms, on how best to implement anything agreed. As for Windsor, the Master was coming around to the view that it would perhaps be best not to allow the thick-skinned toy-soldier to play any role at all in events, lest he be successful and raise his stature amongst his peers or fail miserably and drag the kolony further into the morass than before.

Content that he could rely on his ingenuity to resolve every issue that would arise, no matter how complex, the Master palmed his monitor on to view the general situation in the area around the MKC. Initially he looked blankly at the view that unfolded in front of him. Then, as his eyes and mind gradually took in the events that were actually taking place, he stared in disbelief at the screen. A loud crack echoed in his suite as his fingers released his glass of juice and the glass bounced off the floor beside his chair.

SIMPSON AND MCKENZIE WERE both monitoring the events at the MKC when the Master ran in to the Security Unit, his eyes glaring madly at the teo women.

"What's going on? What's happening?" he demanded in disbelief.

"The situation is under control, Master!" Simpson replied coolly.

"What do you mean 'under control'? What happened?"

The Security Officer appeared totally composed as she responded to the Master. "A probing operation was carried out to ascertain the defence capabilities of the insurgents in the Chamber. The operation is now being brought to a successful conclusion."

"What successful conclusion? Is the Chamber taken? Are the prisoners recaptured?"

"Not exactly, Master. The operation was of a probing nature and has been successfully terminated."

"Not exactly?" the Master queried sarcastically. Then, regaining his composure somewhat, he asked the question Simpson knew would come sooner or later: "Who ordered this operation? Who was it?"

"The operation was a subcode 2 – a probe in preparation for a code 1 assault. It was carried out by Kontrollers Dixon, Kembledon and Windsor on foot of your order 112-188-u8", Simpson delivered her prepared reply without faltering, deliberately placing Windsor's name last in the order of responsibility and referring specifically to the Master's decision at his last meeting with the kontrollers.

The Master thought for a moment, then issued an order to Simpson: "I want a background report on this in ten minutes and a status report in twenty minutes – including all audiovisual takes!"

Rushing back to his suite, the Master contacted Dixon by communicator and asked what was going on. The disappointed kontroller's answer was brief: the probe element of the operation had been a success but the thrust operation had not been so and tyrons forces were being withdrawn from assault positions.

"Who ordered the operation?" the Master asked bluntly.

A puzzled silence ensued, followed by the simple response: "You, Master!"

After a slight pause during which the realisation of what was taking place dawned in his mind, the Master simply ordered: "Be in my suite in fifteen minutes!" Then he sat back in his chair to await the reports from the Security Unit.

The Master knew he was facing a serious deterioration in the situation. There was little doubt that Windsor was the one behind what appeared to be a botched effort to take the MKC. It was possible that Dixon and Kembledon were involved in the plan as well, but the Master expected that they had merely gone along with their intellectually challenged colleague. Either way, that didn't really matter at this stage.

What was important was to establish if the assault had in fact been a fiasco, apportion blame to the guilty party – which would ultimately be Windsor, remove the fanatical fool from his command, admonish the others, then move on to negotiate a deal with the prisoners, in the hope that they would not have been hardened in their resolve as a result of the attack. The Master's game plan was now clear in his mind and he would act effectively to move on from this unexpected but hopefully fortuitous turn in events. With that, the first report came in.

THE MASTER BANGED THE table. Such an exhibition of emotion by him was rare – extremely rare. Generally preferring mind games to zennor blasts, he was used to getting his way in that fashion. As he looked at the faces of the kontrollers around him, he banged the table again.

"Failure! Total failure!" he exploded. "Hundreds of tyrons. Three kontrollers. Result? Total failure! Total abject failure." He repeated those three words for maximum effect.

The kontrollers remained quiet, though the Master sensed that Windsor was champing at the bit already. In a further attempt to goad his disturbed underling to react, the Master repeated his depressing mantra one more time.

Windsor took the bait. "You withdrew the tyrons too soon!" he roared. "Another push and we were through! When we withdrew, we gave them the opportunity to regroup. We had them reeling, and you withdrew!" he bellowed, thumping the table in front of him and looking his despised Master in the eye.

The Master calmly watched the other kontrollers as Windsor spewed out his criticism. None betrayed any inclination to support their colleague. Recognising that the time of reckoning had come for the irritant kontroller, the Master decided to make his move.

"You fool!" he glared, "you stupid, stupid fool! I laid the entire military capacity of the kolony at your disposal, including the finest fighting force there is. Your objective? To retake a Korb Chamber from a gang of unarmed and starving prisoners. Result? Total failure! Total abject failure!" The Master continued: "It was you who drew up the tactics for the assault, you who organised the forces placed at your disposal, you who failed miserably to achieve the objective. Your failure was such that your fellow kontrollers had no option but to try to save the situation by attempting an incursion at the back gates."

Windsor started at the mention of his fellow kontrollers, while the Master did not fail to notice the ovine expressions on Dixon and Kembledon's faces, betraying their relief at being spared the burden of responsibility for their involvement in the disaster. It was clear to all that the failure of this operation was being laid squarely at the feet of Kontroller Windsor and no one else. That the excitable kontroller was bearing the brunt of the recriminations was, in their minds, if not fair, at least justifiable as he was the one who had turned up the temperature on the Master all along. Listening impassively as the Master skinned Windsor to the bone, they were already beginning to convince themselves that they had been merely inactive observers of events. That the Master had obviously already come to that sensible conclusion himself was, both men believed, greatly to his credit and a mark of his stature as a natural leader.

On realising he was being left alone to face the music, Windsor could not resist the urge to have at least some of the blame laid on his fellow kontrollers' shoulders. "It was Dixon and Kembledon who failed to take the initiative that I had handed them. It was I who created the opportunity for a surprise action at the other gates. They signally failed to take advantage of the chance that I had created for them."

Alarmed, the sheepish two wracked their brains to come up with a response to their tormented associate that would not entail admitting their deep involvement in the fiasco in the first place. Before they could utter a word, the Master intervened.

"I find it reprehensible that your only defence for your abject failure is to attempt to heap the blame onto your fellow kontrollers. Dixon and Kembledon did their best to make your stupid plan a success. That they failed is not their fault but the inevitable result of your stupidity. Is it not in your character to accept responsibility for your own actions? Shame! Shame!"

As the craven pair sat meekly in silence, every syllable of the Master's tirade against Windsor was music to their ears. None of the other kontrollers showed any reaction. The Master continued, with a grave expression on his face. "Kontroller Windsor, you have shown very poor judgement, both in your failure in the field and in your ill-considered defence of your conduct. I am left with no choice but to withdraw your commission until a final decision is taken on your future." The Master concluded: "I must ask for you badge of appointment."

Windsor's face turned white with anger and a sense of betrayal. His eyes burning with rage, he searched vainly around the table for a sign of support. The other kontrollers merely looked blankly ahead as they waited for the Master's command to be obeyed. In disgust, Windsor jumped to his feet, removed his badge of commission from his chest and banged it on the table in front of him. Then, without comment, the fuming kontroller turned away and left the room.

In the shocked silence that followed Windsor's abrupt departure, there was a sense of relief amongst the remaining kontrollers that retribution for the dismal failure of the assault had not involved a drop of their blood, but this was tinged with a slight apprehension that perhaps the bloodletting wasn't over yet. Their fears were allayed, however, as the Master merely stood up and stated that the meeting was now over and that they would meet again later to discuss a "return to sanity and an immediate resolution of the siege". Relieved, the kontrollers left the suite.

THE MASTER WAS HAPPY with his performance at the kontrollers' meeting. His gamble on giving Windsor charge of the assault force had paid off handsomely. The madman was now where he wanted him and, as soon as the crisis passed, the disgraced kontroller would be dealt with appropriately. The Master looked forward to considering his options on dealing with Windsor. He smiled as a number of possibilities came into his head. One was to retain the troublemaker in the 'kolony kadre' at a reduced rank – the humiliation option. Another was to convict him of insubordination and make him spend the rest of his days amongst the prisoners he despised so much – this was the 'revenge supreme' option. A third option was to give him a jab of suan gas, place him in a confinement tray and forget all about him. This was the postponement option – passing the problem on. The Master was well aware, however, that Windsor could easily have an 'accident', as others had had at his hands, and be a problem no more. Whatever he decided to do with the defiant incompetent, the Master was sure it would give him immense pleasure.

The Master was also happy with his handling of the other kontrollers. His decision to exonerate Dixon and Kembledon from any blame for the fiasco would ensure that they would be firmly in his camp from now on. They realised full well that if the Master chose, he could easily associate them with Windsor's debacle and demand the same price of them that he had exacted from their more prominent accomplice.

The pressing question now, of course, was how to resolve the situation. The prisoners would be ecstatic following their successful tussle with the tyrons but, at the end of the day, they were in a no-win situation – no food, no way out, no future unless they came to an agreement with him. If he showed some generosity now, he would have the vast majority of the prisoners back in their cells and the kolony back producing korb in a matter of days. There were limits to his generosity, of course. Release for prisoners was obviously out of the question, as was any large-scale diminution of korb production duties. Apart from that, he was sure he would find a way back to Korb-1 tranquillity.

The Master wondered what exactly the prisoners would want. The lunatic fringe would obviously demand to leave the kolony, but he was sure that once it was made clear that departure was not on the agenda – that in fact, given the location of the kolony, there would be no point in even attempting to leave – the prisoners would become more realistic in their approach. He felt that if he concentrated on the question of conditions, he could do business. There was a thorny issue, though, from which it would be hard to escape, and that was the question of the deaths of tyrons. Casualties inflicted on tyrons in a battleground scenario were part of the hazards of the tyron's existence. They were trained from an early age to accept casualties and move on. The missing tyrons could be a problem, however, in that if their bodies were not to be found, it could only be concluded that they had been done to death and vaporised, as Leonard had obviously been, in a cold blooded manner. Somebody would have to pay for that. Maybe, that somebody would turn out to be the crazed Kontroller Windsor, a man who had placed tyrons in the line of fire without proper preparation and adequate planning. Maybe it was him rather than the wretched prisoners who would carry ultimate responsibility for all casualties, tyrons included. As he thought more about it, the idea of pinning everything on Windsor began to give the Master immense pleasure.

But before all of that, discussions would have to begin. Then, it would become clear what the important issues would be, and he would deal with them as they came along. Hopefully, his skills as a negotiator would help bring the whole sorry business to an end and make it clear to any independent observer that it was his abilities that had brought to a satisfactory conclusion a situation that had been created by lesser beings. A glass of arctic ice juice helped the Master relax as he thought of the challenge ahead.

48 THE IRONY OF CONFLICT

THE PRISONERS IN THE MKC were ecstatic. Despite the hardship they had gone through in the last three days, not least of which was their lack of food and sustenance, they had faced down what no one could deny was the finest fighting force the administration had ever possessed. This feat was made the more remarkable by the fact that they had done so almost totally unarmed. Their victory in repelling the tyron attack was a major psychological boost for the prisoners. It was now reasonable to believe that if they stuck together they could play a part in determining their own future, a thought many of them had abandoned so long ago.

The big question now, as of ever, was how? Thanks to their victory over the tyrons, Kane was happy that the prisoners' fate was still in their own hands, but being cooped up in the MKC meant that their room for manoeuvre was extremely limited. He was aware that the tyrons might try again, and again and again until they found a way in. Once inside, they would mop up any resistance in a matter of minutes. On the other hand, the regime might decide to try and talk the prisoners out now, as it was apparent that the tyrons would not manage to take the Chamber without a huge loss of life, and a huge loss of life was something the Master couldn't countenance. Why? Because that would result in a smaller, not to mention, less motivated workforce – and that would entail a huge fall in the production of korb. There was also the fact that a huge loss of life is hard to conceal, even on a rock in space under the control of an information-controlled society. No, the probability now was that the Master would want to talk soon

With those thoughts in his mind, Kane sat down with his companions on the Defence Committee to talk through the likely course events might take. He wondered what they could really hope to achieve now. He knew the prisoners were not going to walk out of the kolony and on to a ship. There was no way the regime would agree to that. Whether they would agree to the release of some prisoners was another question, but he had his doubts about that too. Looking at Nevin, he was sure the prisoners' leader was well aware of the limitations that reality would put on any optimistic expectations. It was probably time for the committee to agree on the minimum they would have to achieve in order to call off the occupation.

As the meeting progressed, some of the reps were ecstatic at their success in holding off the tyrons. They were convinced that the regime would be in disarray after their defeat and that a sudden push out of the Chamber could take them by surprise and allow the prisoners to take over the entire kolony. Kane, Nevin and others tried to explain that such a proposal was unrealistic and that the minute a square metre was opened in the MKC's defences, the tyrons would be in like lightening to overcome the prisoners and, in the process, exact terrible revenge for their earlier defeat. Revolt was not out of the question for the future, Kane maintained, especially as the prisoners had shown they had the bottle to go for it, but it could only succeed when the kolony was organised and ready. That time had not yet arrived. Most of the other reps agreed with Kane, and eventually Nevin was delegated to get as good a deal as possible from the Master. This would have to involve an amnesty for all prisoners and no reprisals against anyone. The rest was for negotiation and anything else would be a bonus.

In a positive frame of mind, the prisoners rested to conserve their dwindling energy, and Nevin waited for the Master to call. Some of the prisoners played cards and dice games, others sat and talked, and others slept the uncomfortable sleep of the hungry and the trapped. Kane and Dayton talked.

"Well, Andy, what's the verdict?" Kane asked his comrade, half in jest.

"We've a good chance of getting everybody out of here safely, but I don't see much of a chance of getting anything else", Dayton judged.

"I think you're right", Kane replied. "We should be looking towards establishing some sort of normality, so that we can go about doing it right the next time."

"The battle was good, though," Dayton added, with a smile. "At least our people know what it's like now. Some of them are even eager for the next time!"

"Let's hope so! Nevin is doing o.k., isn't he? Looks like he hasn't lost his touch."

"Yeah. Dead on. His lover isn't too happy, though", Dayton added, nodding towards Kenning, who sat beside the sleeping Nevin, with a sour expression.

"Maybe she just misses her hologram!" Kane replied and the two laughed, before putting their heads back against the wall to relax.

Time passed slowly in the Chamber, as it always does for those whose stomachs remind them that they haven't eaten and who are not likely to in the foreseeable future. The prisoners lay in weary groups around the MKC, waiting, and wondering what the next step was going to be. The heat was almost overpowering and had left many of the prisoners in a torpid state. While the weary though victorious prisoners rested, however, the defences of the Chamber were not neglected and armed prisoners watched and listened for the slightest movement or sound that would indicate a threat.

Kane lay against the wall, his mind and his heart far away in a world that had died long ago and whose spirit had sought refuge in a lonely man's heart. In his mind, he saw Strauss, sitting on the balcony of his apartment on a warm balmy summer's night. He saw her eyes inviting him into her world – teasing, tantalising, tempting him to follow her. It was an irresistible invitation, one born in the heat of the night and destined to have devastating results. Kane experienced a mixture of emotions when he revisited those days – the passion of his bond with Strauss had been explosive and the conspiratorial nature of their relationship stimulating but the price they had had to pay had been far too high. And it was a price the prisoner paid every morning he opened his eyes on Korb-1 and realised he was waking to another's day's labour in a prison in space. If only there was a way to go back and do things differently. If only there was a way to avoid what had come about. If only. In his reverie, Kane began to hear a voice. It seemed to be in the distance. The prisoner couldn't quite hear what the voice was saying and strained his ears to listen. Suddenly, he felt himself being pulled and shaken. Opening his eyes, he could see Dayton, trying to tell him something.

"Wake up, wake up! The Master's broadcasting!"

Kane shook his head and stared, as he awoke to find the Master's pompous features on the screen, surrounded by the purple background of his office. The prisoners listened intently to hear the Master's message.

Was it to be war? Was it to be negotiation? Was the siege to continue? The Master spoke.

"Today, I speak with a heavy heart. The kolony into which we have all put so much fruitful effort is in crisis. The cooperative relationship which has, since the inception of Korb-1, been the basis for the resounding success of our venture has broken down and been replaced by anarchy."

The Master's voice displayed a note of sadness as he repeated the word – "anarchy". The prisoners smiled accepting the Master's verdict on their conduct as a fine accolade. The Master continued.

"There is no way to adequately express my sadness at this sorry state of affairs. People have died, valuable equipment has been damaged, the production schedule of the kolony, for so long the envy of the other kolonies, has been totally disrupted, and the actions of a few have been allowed to destroy for everybody the harmony that once existed on Korb-1."

The prisoners looked at one another, not knowing whether to laugh or cry. "Pass me a tissue!" Dayton asked Kane, feigning tears as he listened mockingly to the Master's address.

"This dreadful situation cannot be allowed to continue. It is in all our interests to bring it to a close now and return the kolony to the harmonious state in which it has for so long flourished and prospered. There is only one way to achieve that objective and that is through dialogue. Together we have built this wonderful kolony and together we shall save it from the insanity that has attacked it. To this end I shall make myself available to listen to any reasonable proposals that are made. I suggest that Prisoner Nevin contact me for confidential discussions by using the communicator in the MKC direction kiosk. I look forward to hearing from you."

With that, the screen faded and the Master's smug visage and viscous voice faded away. The prisoners looked at one another for reactions. The Master was ready to talk. In fact, he sounded quite restrained and conciliatory. There was a feeling that a reasonable resolution to the siege could be at hand. Nevin stood up and was immediately applauded by the prisoners, many approaching him to shake his hand. As they did, he glanced at Kane and Dayton, and they nodded in support. It was time to negotiate.

THE PRISONERS WEREN'T THE only ones focussing on the negotiations ahead. In the heart of the Administration's Security Centre, deputy security officer McKenzie was thinking hard. When the prisoners had activated the monitor, McKenzie had studied the scene eagerly, as did everyone in the Security Centre. But her focus was different to the rest of the security personnel. McKenzie's eyes scoured the scene to locate the man who had literally fallen into her life only a few weeks previously. His welfare was now her primary concern. Eventually spotting Kane to the left behind Nevin, she was happy to note that he seemed to be holding up well and, happily, wasn't a casualty of Windsor's debacle. Having ascertained that Kane was o.k., McKenzie tried to establish what the mood of the prisoners in general was. Watching for signs of a change in their disposition since the last time she observed them, she was pleased to see that spirits were still high. But how long would that last, she wondered? It appeared as if the Master's intention was to come to an arrangement with the rebels that would restore what *he* regarded as normality in the kolony. He had faced down Windsor and was now in a position to come to terms with the prisoners. But her one fear was that if the prisoners' demands were unreasonable, the Master would be forced to adopt a harder stance that could eventually lead to a long-term stand-off and serious consequences for the prisoners. McKenzie found herself praying that the Master's negotiating skills would prove to be up to the job of convincing the prisoners to end the occupation and return to their cells and korb chambers. How odd, she thought, that she now found herself relying on the Master to sort things out. But the young woman was clear in her mind on the priorities for her – if a planned escape was to succeed, the present rebellion would have to fizzle out. Such was the irony of conflict, she assured herself, as the monitor shut down.

49 TALKING YOUR WAY OUT!

THE MASTER WAITED IN his chambers for the communicator to sound. He had gambled on Windsor playing into his hands and the gamble had paid off. For his strategy to be a success, however, his attempts to settle the dispute with the prisoners would have to succeed. Only then would his defeat of the idiotic soldier be complete and the suspended kontroller's miserable effort to dislodge him a total failure. To achieve that success, he would have to *talk* the prisoners back to their cells where Windsor had failed to *force* them.

If his plan worked, he would be hearing Nevin's voice soon and 'discussions' would begin – the Master didn't like the word 'negotiation'. Anyway there was very little to negotiate. One could be harsh and say that this was a korb kolony in which the inmates were compelled to work, and from which there was no possible escape, but the Master preferred to see it as a joint venture in which all the participants had a stake.

If he could convince the prisoners that their interests lay in cooperation and in the avoidance of friction, that in fact they actually had a future in the kolony, he would soon have things back to normal, and the prisoners back to work. That he might not succeed was unthinkable.

The Master didn't expect failure. After all, he was the one whose intelligence and vision had built Korb-1, his was the ability that had developed and shaped the kolony into the success it had become, and his was the skill that would rescue it from its worst ever crisis and deliver it from its darkest hour. Relaxing with a glass of his favourite arctic ice juice, he surveyed the Korb-1 hologram on his cabinet with admiration. Looking at its clever intricate design through the liquid in his glass, he knew he would not fail – Korb-1 was his destiny, and he the kolony's creator and saviour. His eyes closed to savour his own conviction, the Master heard Nevin's voice on the communicator.

The prisoner leader's voice was weak, as one would expect in the case of a man who had spent three days without food, leading a band of prisoners in two battles and resisting a siege.

"You want to talk?" he enquired with the calm assurance of a man who knew what he was doing.

"Talking never did anyone any harm!" the Master replied in an effort to set the right tone.

"I'm listening, then" Nevin confirmed, his weariness concealing his eagerness.

WITH THE NEGOTIATIONS TAKING place in the chamber direction kiosk, the prisoners lay exhausted and weak on the floor of the MKC. Expectations were high that Nevin would achieve a 'good deal' and ensure that the prisoners' stand would be vindicated. Kane and Dayton talked.

"It's now or never! How is Nevin going to talk us out of this?" Dayton wondered aloud, his cheerful smile unaffected by the hardship of the past three days.

"We'll see what he can conjure up", Kane replied, seeming almost uninterested.

"You don't seem too enthusiastic!" Dayton remarked.

"If we can get out of this and return to normality, as the Master says, I'll be happy!" was Kane's response.

"Oh!" Kane's cheerful companion quipped, "you're a disciple of the Master's now!"

"Normality is good", Kane declared, "– because normality is the cloak of intrigue!"

Dayton was impressed. His companion's facility for revolution had in no way been diminished by the siege. He decided to joust.

"And for whom does chaos provide a cloak?"

"For the revolutionary, the poet – and the scoundrel", Kane replied.

"Maybe those three are one and the same?" Dayton pondered cheekily.

"In injustice, the revolutionary sees an opportunity to achieve his destiny, the poet sees an opportunity to bring down the heavens in lyrical vengeance, and the scoundrel seizes the opportunity to sell them both to the highest bidder."

"Where is the scoundrel in this revolution?" Dayton wondered.

"In the heat of battle, he will be nowhere to be seen. In the aftermath – if you win, he will be the first to congratulate you – if you lose, he will stand behind a screen, receiving a NC Universal Dollar for every unfortunate he identifies for his master. The same night, he will be the only one to sleep well."

Kane's response depressed Dayton somewhat and for a moment his cheerful smile evaded him. He looked around the room crammed with prisoners and wondered who the traitors and informers were, and what could possibly motivate them.

Kane noticed his idealistic friend's discomfort. "Don't worry, Andy", he reassured his colleague, "scoundrels are a natural part of our world. Like insects, they are part of the food chain. Anyway, if it wasn't for them, against whom would we judge the just man?"

"That's it", Dayton quipped, smiling once more, "let's be positive!"

"Good", exclaimed Kane, "now I'm going to have a nap. Annoy some else!"

Dayton smiled and lay back to rest.

THROUGHOUT THE MAIN KORB Chamber, an atmosphere of quiet anticipation descended, as if those present realised their future was now in the hands of others. Most relaxed, but some gathered together to gamble. In one of the corners, a small group played pitch and toss, tossing pieces of korb against the wall to see who could get them to land closest to the base. All the time, however, the armed prisoners kept a vigilant eye on the doors and anywhere else from which a renewed attempt at invasion by the tyrons might come.

Some of Nevin's closest lieutenants waited outside the direction kiosk while the veteran campaigner negotiated with the Master. Time hung heavily as the minutes slowly passed. Inside through the light green glass, they could see their leader involved in dialogue – sometimes animated – in front of the screen. They regarded his energetic movements as a sign that the Master was not getting things all his own way. When Nevin was still, apparently listening intently to the Master's response, they wondered what exactly was on the cards. As the minutes became an hour and then two, they grew concerned that the Master hadn't come to an agreement yet. Some thought the protracted nature of the negotiations was a good sign, others the opposite. Then, with time approaching the three-hour mark, Nevin turned away from the screen and emerged from the kiosk.

When their leader appeared, the prisoners immediately moved forward to see what the talks had produced. His lieutenants insisting the crowd remain orderly, Nevin moved silently towards his perch at one of the korb docks in the Chamber. He looked pale and tired, and had the appearance of a man racked with doubts. In silence, he sat up on the edge of the dock and ran his hands across his face in an attempt to summon up the energy required. He had every appearance of a man about to reveal the results of his efforts to those whose future depended so much upon them. As the defence committee sat around to listen to Nevin's report, the rest of the prisoners waited anxiously for the news to filter through. Dayton asked Nevin "Is it good?" "It's never as good as it should be!" the older man replied cryptically.

Nevin's 'inner cabinet' listened intently as he outlined the proposals for a settlement agreed between himself and the Master. Tense and weary, the prisoners paid close attention as the tired veteran revealed the points he had agreed with their oppressors. The agreement was that all prisoners would be allowed to return unhindered to their cells, all those injured or incapacitated would receive immediate medical attention, food would be served in the Dining Hall two hours after the prisoners left the MKC, there would be no punishment for anybody involved in the revolt; there would be no work in the Chambers for a week, all weapons would be gathered and returned to the authorities, a Kolony Kooperation Kommittee would be formed, to be jointly chaired by Nevin and a Kontroller nominated by the Master, to examine any issues that might arise in the future to jeopardise harmonious relations on the kolony – that was it. Nevin looked closely at the faces of those listening to his report, searching for reactions that would reveal an initial verdict on the success or failure of his efforts. Though his revelations were not received with tumultuous acclaim, most of the negotiator's comrades seemed relieved that the siege could now be brought to an end. Only one, a 21-1 member named McClennon, signalled his instant rejection of the deal, claiming a return to normality with no release for anybody would be a victory for the Administration. Nevin didn't respond, leaving it to the others to argue the point with his critic. When he had finished his report, the jaded leader held his palms in the air, stating simply: "That's it! That's all! They won't countenance any releases – he claims it's not physically possible".

"Let's break the news!" Kane suggested, and offered Nevin a hand to stand up and mount the dock. Nevin grasped the younger man's hand, accepting his offer as a gesture of moral as well as physical support.

From his vantage point, Nevin surveyed the assembled prisoners, men and women, young and not so young, some of them injured, most of them weary, all of them starving. For a few moments, he merely stood and watched, sad in the knowledge that what he had to report would probably disappoint most of them. It was that understanding, rather than any fear of a violent rejection, which most made the seasoned revolutionary apprehensive. Used to disappointment himself, he wondered how difficult a lesson in *realpolitik* this was going to be for the majority of the prisoners. Then, looking at the hopeful faces below, he spoke. Outlining the deal through which he expected to achieve at least some of the prisoners' aspirations, he watched the facial expressions before him, as he had done with his lieutenants a few minutes earlier. The disillusion that follows high expectations like a spectre was evident on the faces of the majority of his audience. At the same time, there didn't appear to be any open hostility to the proposed deal. When the exhausted leader concluded his address, a brief silence followed – then a round of applause and cheering began which eventually turned into wild celebrations.

As celebrating supporters helped Nevin down from the korb dock, Gibney shoved out his hand to Nevin and congratulated him warmly.

Kane added his congratulations and posed a question: "Well done – but can we trust them?" Nevin replied, almost apologetically: "We've no other choice." All around, the celebrations continued.

WHEN THE PRISONER REPRESENTATIVES came together to formally confirm acceptance of the deal, the defence committee officially ratified it. It was now up to Nevin to convey the prisoners' decision to the Master. The agreement was that within half an hour of conveyance of acceptance to the Master, the prisoners would allow kolony engineers to open the gates unhindered, and would then march out in a dignified manner and return en masse to their cells. A ragged bunch at this stage but with spirits high, most of the prisoners were apprehensive when the moment to leave arrived, wondering what awaited them around the next corner. Moving slowly out of the MKC and through the neighbouring area, they sensed that every empty corridor they entered was adding to the eeriness and unease. Where were the tyrons? Was there treachery afoot? What kind of breach of trust would they encounter as soon as they had left the safety of the Master Korb Chamber?

Kane and Dayton walked slowly together towards their cells. They were silent and nervous, expecting something to happen at any time as the weary procession of prisoners plodded their way back to what passed for normality on a rock in space.

"Do you think they'll keep their word?" Dayton eventually asked his companion.

"Don't be surprised if they don't", was Kane's simple reply.

"We're at their mercy now. If they decide to renege on the deal, we can do nothing about it", Dayton continued.

"We'll always be at their mercy as long as we're here", Kane explained logically, "and there's only one way to change that!"

Dayton was quiet for a moment as he interpreted what his colleague had said. Kane had obviously made up his mind. Now he had to make up his.

"You won't be on your own when that time comes!" he assured his companion, "You won't be on your own!"

On reaching his cell, Kane gave his fellow traveller a friendly punch on the shoulder and entered, leaving his companion to continue alone.

50 AFTERMATH

THE KONTROLLERS LEFT THE Master's suite following a briefing on the ending of the prisoner revolt. There was a sense of relief all round that the situation had been resolved peacefully, and the Master had smiled unctuously as he received the congratulations of his kontrollers on his successful resolution of the crisis. Ambling down the corridor towards their sectors, the group of functionaries also felt a sense of relief that the only casualty in their ranks had been the obstinate Windsor. Privately, some of them recalled with a sense of relief how close they had come to voicing support for the renegade in his opposition to the Master. Many had genuinely felt that Windsor's way *was* the only way, that the Master really had gone soft on control of the kolony and that his appeasement policies would result in disaster. But Windsor had failed, failed miserably, to drive home the initiative and the ball was now firmly back in the Master's court. Windsor was on his own.

At the meeting, the Master had told his kontrollers to keep a discreet security presence over the following few days and to remember that the production of korb was the *raison d'être* of Korb-1. A return to normality and to the high production levels enjoyed by the kolony would be the primary goal now and the kontrollers' role in maintaining normality would be crucial. Any kontroller deviating from this policy would pay the price for endangering the success of the Project. As for the "irresponsible Windsor", as the Master called his former irritant, his actions had caused "unprecedented turmoil" and placed the Master in the position of having to make the very "arrangements" (the Master's euphemism for 'concessions') of which the kontroller had been so vociferously complaining. Removal from the ranks of the Administration and imprisonment followed by "return to the Earth Zone", as the Master termed it, would be the only fitting punishment for his reckless behaviour. It would not be appropriate for the Master himself to impose these penalties, he informed his compliant minions, rather it would be the function of the former kontroller's peers to meet in the Kouncil of Kontrollers to impose the appropriate punishment on the mutineer. This proposal was greeted with silent acceptance by the kontrollers. Windsor had raised his head above the parapet and it was now going to be cut off.

Heading for their own sectors, the kontrollers were keenly aware that they could easily have had the bad luck to have been caught on Windsor's side of the divide and find themselves facing the same fate as their troublesome associate. Whatever doubts they had privately held or expressed in confidence to the former kontroller, Windsor was now clearly on his own.

For the prisoners, the days after the ending of the siege were a mixture of delight at having survived the onslaught of the tyrons and uneasy feeling that perhaps the episode wasn't over yet, that the forces of law and order were really only biding their time before acting to avenge their embarrassing defeat. This feeling that retribution could yet be handed out tempered the celebratory mood prevalent amongst those who had seen off the administration and its fearsome fighting machine. Celebratory messages were passed on in a restrained manner – smiles replaced waving fists, chuckles replaced cheers and small groups replaced large gatherings. But, despite the apprehension, the mood was still unmistakeable – the prisoners had taken on the might of the administration and survived. For those who had passed that test, there would be no going back.

The korb 10-1 team, assembled in their korb chamber on their first day back at work, were in cheerful form. Theirs was a team spirit second to none and, following their survival of the siege, that communal spirit was now forged into a stronger affinity, moved to a higher plane of intensity. All of them sensed the new bond between them, but none expressed it openly. It was understood.

As before, Dayton took the lead in providing the amusement, rattling off a series of jokes about tyrons, kontrollers and the Master himself. Nothing could suppress the young man's wit and soon the entire team were laughing aloud.

"Why are tyrons' suits red?" the comedian asked. After a variety of imaginative responses from his comrades, he delivered the coup: "to disguise their red faces after the galactic battle of the MKC!" Everybody laughed, imagining the embarrassed expressions of the serious soldiers as they wrote an account of the MKC debacle into their CVs.

"How do tyrons get high?" was the young man's next contribution. After a series of 'dunnos', came the punch-line "You hoist them on chains!"

On a roll, Dayton's next question arrived on cue: "What's the latest special in the Korb-1 kitchen?" Inspired by the news filtering down through the kolony of Kontroller Windsor's demise, the answer delighted everybody: "Windsor's head on a plate!" Laughter rocked the chamber as the first korb rush in almost a week was initiated.

KANE WAS IN HIS cell, reflecting. The last few days had been incredible. The kolony had been blown inside out. The prisoners had courageously resisted an attempted arrest by the tyrons. An all-out assault had been repulsed and a siege upheld, and a more liberal regime was about to be put in place in the kolony. There was an invigorated mood amongst the prisoners, an atmosphere of confidence. Despite the mistrust and the unease, most prisoners hoped a new era of cooperation would emerge. But where did all of this leave Kane's own little war? What now of his campaign to avenge Andrea Thorsen? What now of his plan to escape from Korb-1 and start a new life somewhere else? What now of his unprecedented alliance with Assistant Security Officer McKenzie? Would the new entente on Korb-1 signal the end for the prisoner's own plans for liberation?

All of these questions bounced around in Kane's head. One of his objectives in supporting Nevin's efforts to bring the siege to a successful and peaceful conclusion was to regain a sense of normality on the kolony. Kane's experience of life was that normality was the cloak under which most abnormalities in society occurred. Normality was the comforting smokescreen that enabled most people to live their daily lives oblivious to what the conspirators in their midst concealed with ease. The routine of life was the perfect backdrop for every nefarious deed imaginable – and a few more besides. Kane was determined to use it to achieve a noble objective – liberation from a prison labour kolony and the attainment of some form of human happiness in what remained of his life. When the veil of normality had been draped once more over Korb-1, Kane could return to his objective since Thorsen's departure – escape!

But the success of Kane's endeavour depended entirely on the continued cooperation of someone else. Zeena McKenzie had restored to Kane his belief in himself. She had returned to him his hope and his will to survive. Kane believed that the determination to be free was the first step everyone must take in order to go about achieving liberation. McKenzie had revived that motivation in the prisoner. As long as she remained by his side, his desire to be free would be a realistic one – not the frustrated hope of a prisoner unable to release the bonds that tied him down but the concentrated effort of a man who would not be shackled. Kane now knew the way out of the prison that was intended to hold him forever. When McKenzie contacted him again, he would be ready to move on to the next fateful phase in his deliverance.

A knock on the door woke Kane from his deep thoughts. It was Pedersen, Prisoner 1319.

For McKenzie, this was a time of contemplation and relief. That the MKC stand-off had been ended peacefully was a major release from the anxiety and worry that had plagued the conspirator since the trouble had begun in the Dining Hall almost a week before. She had invested and risked a lot in her relationship with Kevin Kane. If things went wrong, she knew she would pay a high price. She had been bold in choosing Kane and preparing him for the task that lay ahead. At the same time, she had been careful in what she had let him know and in laying out the timetable of events. For her, this was more than helping a prisoner to escape

— this was personal. For that reason alone, McKenzie could not allow anybody to jeopardise its success — not even Kane himself.

But now, she hoped, the danger of the past week had passed and, as was usual in these circumstances, a period of calm and reflection was expected. During that time, she hoped that a regime would emerge in the kolony that would promote a culture of harmony and cooperation. In such a calm environment, McKenzie would be in a position to concentrate on the only objective of importance in her life — revenge for the deaths of Ruyan Kendrick and Andrea Thorsen. She would be in touch with Prisoner 313 again soon.

KANE WAS SURPRISED TO see Pedersen. The last time they had spoken, they had agreed to meet again but since then both had been arrested and Kane had even become convinced — though he now realised he had been wrong — that Pedersen was the demon that had been persecuting his subconscious for so long.

"Want to go for a walk?" the stranger asked, with the air of someone who was a regular visitor and was making a customary call.

"Why not?" the surprised Kane replied. "I thought we'd never see *you* again!" he quipped, warming to the man he had been convinced at one stage was an agent for the Administration.

"Thought I'd never see outside the Void, myself! But whatever you folks did to the tyrons, it certainly shook this place up! Apparently, it's amnesty time for everyone!"

"Yeah, we gave those guys a bit of a fright alright", Kane replied modestly. "Things seem to have changed, but whether the new world lasts or not is the big question."

"It all certainly happened at the right time for me — so I'm not complaining!"

"Well, welcome to our new society!" Kane announced. "How long it lasts is probably up to the securocrats and how soon it takes them to organise some kind of destabilisation."

"That's the world we live in!" was Pedersen's realistic response, "It's never the ordinary folks who write the script. It's usually the unseen hand that does that – generally a hand carrying a big stick and a flashy cashcard. We just react and try to stymie them along the way."

"Pretty pessimistic take on the game of life", Kane observed.

"Just telling it like it is", was Pedersen's simple response.

The more Kane listened to the bearded novo, as he used to call him, the more he liked him. Pedersen appeared to have a fatalistic view on things but his fatalism didn't seem to have diluted his idealism or blunted his desire to take a stand and make a difference. When Pedersen told Kane about Red Kennedy and the events in the cornfield, about his life on the run and his arrest following his involvement with Hovendon and Gerson, Kane understood what his companion's motivation had been. Once arrested, the fact that the young man hadn't even carried out *one* action with the pair of conspirators had become irrelevant. Being recognised as a 'fugitive' was enough to have him despatched to Korb-1. In a strange way, his banishment may even have saved his life and prevented him falling into the 'wrong' hands. In Pedersen, Kane saw something of a mirror image of himself – an unintentional revolutionary, the wrong man in the wrong place at the wrong time. Kane felt a new bond with his former adversary and, when he and Pedersen shook hands after two hours, he knew he had met someone who wouldn't run away when the time came to take a stand. Before they parted, Pedersen made an unexpected request. He asked that Kane, if he ever got back to Earth, would try to establish what had happened to Kennedy. Kane was aware that such a promise wouldn't be easy to fulfil but gave his word that he would try, promising he would help his comrade find out the truth when they *both* got home.

Returning to his cell to be greeted by Kenning, Nevin was a happy man. Having just emerged from a particularly cordial meeting with the Master, the prisoners' leader was convinced that a new era lay ahead for the Korb-1 kolony. The Master's attitude had been extremely positive and already a number of issues had been identified as priority resolution issues. Although consciously anxious to avoid over-optimism, Nevin told his partner that a series of radical changes were about to take place in the kolony. Going into the meeting, Nevin was unsure as to what the Master's approach would be. Had the old man announced that nothing was really going to change, Nevin would not have been surprised and would have been left to hope that at least the situation would not deteriorate for those who had placed their trust in him. After all, the Master held all the cards. If he had chosen to spurn magnanimity in favour of the crude assertion of authority, there was really nothing Nevin could do to stop him.

But clearly that was not the route the Master wanted to go. Throughout their hour-long meeting, the recurrent theme in his speech was 'cordiality and harmony in the interests of all, so that the work of the kolony – korb production – could continue unhindered into the years ahead'. Anything – within reason – that accommodated or accelerated that achievement would be considered.

Nevin was relived to hear the Master's position. He had always really believed that obtaining the release of prisoners, on any scale, was a non-starter. Therefore, the aim had to be the improvement of the living conditions of the prisoner population in the kolony. Nevin had a wide range of plans to achieve this and the Master had already shown himself willing to accommodate reasonable proposals. Nevin was confident a positive future lay in store for the prisoners of Korb-1.

51 THE LONELINESS OF DEFEAT

It was quiet – deadly quiet. Windsor sat alone in his plush office suite, surrounded by diplomas and citations received during what he was proud to proclaim had been a glorious career. A dim light lit the room, sufficient for the observer to see the sombre figure of the defeated kontroller, the worry lines on his face accentuated by the cruel shadows. The gloom couldn't conceal the deep hurt experienced by the fallen war hero, his mind filled with dark thoughts of rejection and defeat.

The crushed kontroller tried to rationalise how a disaster brought about by the stupidity of the Master had resulted in him – a four-eagle kontroller – being relieved of his commission. Throughout his security career, he had taken a strong stand on behalf of the important principles he saw as underlying the highest standards in his profession. Without these, there could be no real control of any situation and no real security for the Administration. In Korb-1, these principles had been flaunted and thrown to the wind by others, but somehow it was he, the one who stuck steadfastly to these fundamentals, who was taking the blame for the breathtaking incompetence of others. Windsor wondered how this incredible turn of events had come about.

No matter what way Windsor looked at the situation in which he now found himself, there was no way he could bring himself to accept that he had in fact been outwitted at almost every turn by the Master and eventually hoisted with his own petard. That one he had deemed to be an idiot could get the upper hand on a professional of his calibre was a conclusion that Windsor could never countenance. In his neatly ordered little world, such things didn't happen and, if the kontroller now found himself on the edge of the precipice, there was no question of any of the blame attaching to himself. History had regularly shown, he thought in the gloom of his studio, that great men had been brought down by the stupidity and low treachery of lesser beings. If such was to be the mantle that he must now wear, he would do so, but he would not rest until his side of the story – the true facts – had been heard by a higher authority. Then, his own principled and honourable approach would be clear for all to see against the background of the calamitous idiocy of others.

Every time Windsor reached that conclusion, however, other darker thoughts would enter his head again. Amongst them was that, in situations of this gravity, the word of the Master would generally be accepted above that of his subordinates – unless a significant proportion of those under his command put an alternative version of events forward. Windsor knew well that this would not be the case here, as the other kontrollers, to a man and woman, were spineless cowards who would say or do anything to save their worthless skins and would certainly support the Master in whatever fictional version of events he wished to present.

Despite his consuming anger, Windsor could not avoid facing cold facts. Relieved of his command and certainly about to face serious charges to be levelled by the Master – who was probably at that very moment hatching a plot with his pathetic minions to deliver the *coup de grace* to Windsor's career – the future looked particularly bleak for the kontroller. Time and time again, the angry soldier turned over all his options in an effort to find a way out of his plight, but there was no escaping the inevitability of his destruction. No silver lining brightened up Windsor's dark korb kloud and his options, like his command, had evaporated.

Windsor sat back in his chair a defeated man. He wondered should he end it all now before the Master had a chance to add ignominy to what he had already suffered. At least then he would not have to tolerate the sniggers of lesser beings delighted at the fall of one who had had the courage to confront an intolerable situation rather than join the herd and pretend that nothing was wrong. Windsor was beginning to realise that, in the darkness of defeat, there was only one way out for the man of honour. To the faithful servant of the Northern Confederation, there appeared to be only one honourable course to follow now. Windsor's face took on a dark grey complexion as he walked slowly over to his cabinet and took out a phial of green-coloured powder. Pouring out a cup of water from the dispenser beside him, he dropped a few grains of powder into the cup.

IN THE SECURITY CENTRE, Simpson was studying footage from the surveillance beams in the Dining Hall and the area surrounding the MKC during the revolt. The Security Officer's face betrayed an expression of distaste as she watched the scenes of mayhem that unfolded before her eyes. The eruption in the Dining Hall clearly began with the arrival of the tyrons and their attempts to arrest the KC 17-2 prisoners. The reaction of the other prisoners seemed to take the tyrons by surprise, and the prisoners' subsequent refusal to back off in the face of the tyrons' superior arms was surprising. The pitched battle that ensued seemed to be spontaneous, with the prisoners using whatever makeshift weapons they could lay their hands on to fight back the tyrons. Following the tyrons' retreat from the Dining Hall, scenes of anarchy and chaos were captured on the beam returns from many areas of the kolony, as prisoners and tyrons participated in local battles in the corridors surrounding the Dining Hall.

As the mayhem continued before her, Simpson sat up in her chair, her eyes piercing the screen in order to focus on a battle taking place near the korb chamber corridors. Three tyrons confronted a group of about twenty prisoners. With the tyrons firing indiscriminately, the prisoners dived for cover wherever they could. Those unlucky enough to be in the line of fire fell instantly. As the tyrons advanced through the corridors, however, they were suddenly set upon by a group of prisoners who had lain unseen inside a korb chamber door when they arrived. Suddenly jumping the tyrons from behind, the prisoners quickly overcame their surprised opponents, bringing them to the ground. Then, in an act of terrible revenge, the three soldiers were carried shoulder high down the corridor by the prisoners. Other security footage showed the unveiling story as the frenzied prisoners carried their powerless captives to the korb chamber door and bundled them inside. The beam footage from KC 15 revealed the final act of the dreadful event, as the prisoners bundled their captives into a korb tunnel and in a matter of seconds had them vaporised in a korb gush. When the visual showed the prisoners celebrating their successful despatch of their enemies, Simpson was so appalled she jumped up and exclaimed in a low venomous voice: "The scum! They won't get away with this!" Then, in shocked silence, she sat down at the screen again as McKenzie entered the room to see what had happened. Noticing her arrival, Simpson calmly ordered her to "copy this segment – we must show it to the Master."

A SMILE BURST ON Kane's lips. The message was simple yet re-assuring:

"It's time for another game. Do you want to start first?"

Kane lost no time in replying. McKenzie was his only link with an alternative sense of the future – one that didn't involve korb chambers, tyrons or the Master. She was his only possible ticket out and he wasn't going to keep her waiting.

"I'm game – if you are!" was his brief reply.

A ferocious game of *War-Raok!* ensued, with no prisoners being taken and no quarter given. After a sly ruse on the second dimension, McKenzie stole in to take Kane's HQ.

"Looks like you're out of practice!" the woman quipped as Kane realised what had happened. ,

"I've been occupied with different battles recently!" Kane replied.

"I noticed", McKenzie responded, "and you played a good game there!"

"Thank you!" Kane responded before moving on to the issue that exercised his mind. "What about the final game that we must play?" he asked purposefully.

"It won't be played for a while", McKenzie replied, "For the present, it's important to keep a low profile. The circumstances must be right for the final move and we can't afford to get that wrong. When the time comes to play the end-game, nothing can be left to chance. Until then, we must be patient. When conditions are right, we'll know. Do your best to keep everybody calm and out of trouble because efforts are afoot on this side to raise the temperature and bring things to a head again. I'll do my best to prevent that but you must strive to keep heads cool on your side. If things get out of hand, the consequences could be immense. The tyrons are spoiling for a re-match. Whatever happens, they mustn't be given a second chance. Maybe we can meet soon to talk. In the meantime, everyone needs to stay calm – whatever happens. The stakes are too high!"

Kane read intently every word that came and went on his screen. Although he found McKenzie's advice unexpectedly negative, he decided to take her at her word without any probing questions.

"Alright!" he replied, "I'll wait for word from you. While I'm waiting, I'll promote peace and understanding between humans and tyrons!"

"Good! I'll be in touch", McKenzie replied, "In the meantime, work on your game!"

THE MASTER WAS SITTING at his desk looking busy when Simpson arrived at the door. The visitor was greeted with a businesslike "Enter!" before proceeding to approach her superior's desk. The Master busied himself with a file on his desk screen before raising his eyes towards the Security Officer.

"Well, Simpson, what's this vital piece of information that's come to light?", he enquired, his slightly patronising tone and the emphasis he placed on the word 'vital' suggesting he expected the reason for the intrusion to be on the 'trivial' end of the spectrum rather than the earth-shattering.

"I think you should look at this, Master", the dark lady imparted as she handed the disk across the desk.

Accepting the disk from Simpson without comment, the Master thumbed it into his machine, while casting a cautious eye towards his visitor. As the disk played, however, it was the Dark Lady who observed, patiently waiting for a reaction on the Master's face to the dreadful events being acted out before his eyes. If Simpson expected to see signs of shock and abhorrence in the Master's expression, however, she was to be disappointed. When the piece had played, he merely commented on the shocking nature of the material, adding his congratulations to her for having discovered it.

"This is shocking, shocking indeed! Appalling!" he added.

When Simpson asked would she forward the material to the kontrollers so that they could view the material and express their views to the Master on the action required as a result of her discovery, the Master demurred.

"No! No!" he uttered, "There's no need for that. I'll look after this myself. This is a serious matter." Then, casting a stern glance towards the dark lady, he added: "I trust no one else has seen this?"

"No, Master", Simpson replied, immediately forming an opinion on the likelihood of the Master taking any action at all. "No one!"

The Master's reaction was telling. "Good!" he said, "we don't want something like this getting into the wrong hands now, do we?"

Suppressing the temptation to enquire as to the identity of these "wrong hands", Simpson merely added a note of agreement. "No, Master, we don't."

"Good", the Master concluded, again thanking the officer for her excellent work. "Do keep me informed of any other developments", the Master added with a smile, as Simpson rose to leave.

Emerging into the corridor, the dark lady smiled a harsh smile – a smile that many of her adversaries had seen to their cost in the past – and moved on.

NEVIN WAS IN GOOD form. Things were settling down nicely and there was no sign of any negative reactions from the tyrons, despite their humiliation at the hands of the prisoners. The general body of prisoners had been maintaining a low profile and had been refraining from any action that could be misinterpreted as being a challenge to the security forces. Although there was obviously a long way to go, Nevin was hopeful that a more humane regime was about to evolve in the kolony and that someday the prisoners would look back with satisfaction on the role they had played in bringing that about.

The arrival in his cell of a group of prisoners he had invited to organise a sports event for the next rest day brought the leader's daydream to a conclusion.

"Welcome, friends", said Nevin. "Let's hear your plans for the big occasion!" as the men and women given the task of organising the 'healing event', as Nevin termed it, sat down.

MEANWHILE, IN THE BLEAKNESS of his studio, Windsor was diverted from raising his glass by the sound of a call on his communicator.

52 NORMALITY

GLIDING AROUND HER APARTMENT as if carried on a cloud of contentment, Security Officer Simpson was a happy woman. A tall female whose good looks were clearly withstanding the passage of time, Simpson was impressive in her bright green uniform tightened with a black belt around her slim waist. Her black curled hair was at neck length and she proudly displayed the NC emblem on her left shoulder. A barely suppressed smile poised on her lips, she removed a set of *pv* (personal video) disks from the breast pocket of her uniform and, choosing one, inserted it into a black *pv* viewer on the comfort table in front of her.

The light from the screen reflected in the woman's dark green eyes as she squinted slightly to take in the display. While the disk played, dark shadows were cast on the purple walls of the room. The walls were bare but for the Security Diploma proudly displayed at eye-level facing the door, positioned evenly between two electro-light windows that attempted to lend an air of earthly normality to the setting. Sitting calmly in front of the screen, Simpson was like a cat studying a mouse before it pounced, watching the events on the screen with unconcealed glee. Every frame was savoured, every development lapped up. Eventually, the Security Officer's thin polished lips broke into a broad smile as the on-screen happenings came to a close. Smirking, she touched the display to a halt and sat back in her wrap-around armchair, clearly pleased at the impact she imagined her newfound possession would have on the guest she was expecting to call soon – and on others when she chose to reveal it.

Rising, Simpson went to a grey cabinet on the wall beside the door and took out a bottle of olive brandy and two glasses. Placing the glasses on the table, she filled them to the brim from the twin-handled bottle. Returning to the cabinet, she took out a blue freeze box and popped two freeze cubes into each glass. Just then, she heard a slow and deliberate double knock – a simple code – on the door and, pursing her lips in expectation, touched a button on the wall to open the door.

THE MASTER WAS ENJOYING a glass of arctic ice juice. This had probably been the most momentous week in his entire life. He believed that only he understood how close to oblivion the kolony had actually been during the chaotic days that were now thankfully over and that it was his unique ability that had rescued the entire enterprise from the brink of disaster. His beloved brainchild – the biggest of the korb kolonies – had been in utter turmoil and even perhaps on the brink of extinction but, due to his own extraordinary intellect and ability to muster cogent logical argument, the situation had been resolved and the kolony brought back from the edge of the abyss. Those who had felt aggrieved, for whatever misguided reasons, were clearly now content in the knowledge that the proper management of the kolony was in everyone's interest, including their own. It was evident to the Master from his meeting with Nevin that the prisoners had finally realised that their future lay in harmonious cooperation with those charged with the effective governance of the kolony. The Master prided himself in being a man of give and take, live and let live, and remained convinced that even the most hardened of cases would eventually see the sense in an argument based on evident truths. This would logically lead to the abandonment of extreme positions shown to be founded in the realms of unreality. That this was coming to pass on Korb-1 was beyond doubt and, he believed, was yet another unprecedented achievement on his part.

The Master was not as understanding in relation to those who would imperil the future of his wonderful and productive venture in order to promote their own deluded sense of importance. They had been seen off and would now pay the price for their treachery. Again, it was the Master's 'exceptional powers of reasoning and tactical superiority' that had seen this 'sinister threat' to the future of the kolony evaporate. The Master believed that egotistic mavericks like Windsor would always rush into the trap if it was prepared carefully for them. They believed they must be right, even if the sky must fall, and they could always be relied upon to stick to that clear and simple principle. The destruction of everything he or she purports to defend is a price the insane narcissist is always willing to have everyone else pay. The lunatic Windsor was now where he belonged – in his chambers pondering his fate.

The past week had indeed been momentous. Yet, until future years when his memoirs would be published and the upper echelons of the establishment made aware of his incomparable contribution over the decades, nobody would yet appreciate how close to the edge Korb-1 had actually been and how critical a role the Master's unique qualities had played. Normality had been restored to Korb-1 and the man who had brought that about was enjoying his achievement to the full.

WINDSOR HAD THE APPEARANCE of a condemned man when he entered Simpson's apartment. His face carried the scowl of one whose arrogance has been rejected and spat back in his face. The sacked kontroller's battle scar completed the appearance of one who had been to hell and back as he entered the room. Stepping into Simpson's lair, therefore, the tormented functionary was taken aback to find a cheerful face awaiting him. Initially, his instinct was to strike the 'stupid woman' in her 'smug puss' and wake her up to the reality of the situation, but Windsor decided to be patient awhile in case his protégé had good reason to celebrate.

"I won't ask how you are, Robert. I know how you must feel", the smiling woman remarked, as the door closed behind her guest. Windsor stared blankly in response, although he noted his host's use of his first name.

"Anyway", she continued, "do sit down and have a drink". Launching herself into the double wraparound armchair and inviting her guest to join her with a wave of her left hand, she announced that she thought she might have something that would cheer him up. Hitting 'view' with the same hand in a theatrical gesture and grasping her glass of brandy in the other, Simpson smiled as Windsor sat down beside her to watch the show.

MCKENZIE WAS WORRIED. EARLIER on, hiding behind a filing screen, she had observed Simpson interfere with the mobility restriction grid. This was the electronic system whereby the individual access of every single person on the kolony was controlled and monitored. It was this system that would alert Security immediately if a prisoner was entering a restricted area (indeed McKenzie's first task on meeting Kane was always to neutralise the area in which she was about to meet him) or if a member of Kolony staff authorised to be in one area had actually entered another. If a member of the kitchen staff left the Kitchen Area, a functionary on library staff wandered into the Arrivals Area or a mechanic in the Despatch Port approached the Security Unit, the system would simultaneously alert security and the captain of the tyron guard.

When Simpson was finished, she left the area as surreptitiously as she had arrived. However, no sooner had she gone then McKenzie was in her place. Calling up 'last keyed direction' she discovered that the coordinates of Kontroller Windsor's confinement had been altered to allow him access to Simpson's suite.

Mm, McKenzie thought, the dark lady is feeling passionate tonight. But the young officer's awareness of the true nature of the Security Officer soon overcame any suspicions of a romantic nature. Simpson was up to no-good and McKenzie had better find out as quickly as possible what her plan was.

For Nevin, as for so many others in the kolony, this had been a significant moment in time. Having settled into a comfortable life of retirement on the kolony with his companion, on the other side of the mirror from his former life as an urban architect during the day and a planner of subversion and "director of information terrorism", as the court had termed him, at night, the last role he had expected to be playing at this stage in life was that of commander of a prisoner body of hundreds withstanding a tyron siege and assault. Once cast in that role, however, Nevin had been racked by the worry that the conclusion to it all would be disastrous and ignominious. It was one thing plotting and planning against the Administration on the streets and in the coffee rooms and bars that he once called home. Holding a mechanical plant in a controlled area against an assault by the most ruthless fighting force in the galaxy was another. Doing so at the head of large body of starving prisoners was raising the bar even higher. That the prisoners' resistance had been successful and an acceptable compromise solution obtained was an outcome Nevin was proud – and relieved – to have achieved. It could all have been so different but now this accomplishment would mean better conditions for the inmates of the kolony and a better life for all. Nevin was happy that, after all the years, he had passed the test when it counted and that everybody's future would be the better for it. The sports event would be a day of celebration, low-key but unambiguous in launching a new era for the prisoners of Korb-1.

Windsor didn't touch the glass of olive brandy in front of him. Equally, he seemed oblivious to the alluring lady beside him on the couch. Still in a daze, he sat on the edge of his seat, staring in stunned disbelief at the chaos on the screen. Almost immediately, his eyes became clouded with hatred on observing the 'prison rabble', as he regarded them, running riot in the prison. Even now, in the cold aftermath, the thought that a catastrophe of such magnitude, that he had so accurately and consistently predicted and attempted to prevent, was allowed to occur drove him to absolute rage. The efforts of the one who had chosen to ignore his well-informed warnings – the so called 'Master' – to actually blame *him* for causing the disaster was contemptuous in the extreme and an affront to his intelligence. The craven agreement of his fellow kontrollers to this perversion of the facts added unforgivable insult to serious injury. Because his advice had been ignored, subversives had been shamefully allowed to take control of the prison and inflict casualties on the finest combat body in the history of the world, whose hands had been tied behind their backs to prevent them from properly carrying out their duties and annihilating the insurgents.

Scene after scene on the viewer depicting the successful efforts of the prisoners to thwart the tyrons' attempts at restoring order drove Windsor's blood pressure through the ceiling. The failure of the tyrons to breech the defences established by the prisoners he regretfully regarded as inevitable, given the lack of support for the security forces evident at every level of the Administration. It was he and he only, Windsor thought, who had given the tyrons the backing and support necessary to do the job. But his hands had been tied by the cowardly incompetent in charge of the kolony.

Next to the angry ex-Kontroller, Simpson smiled a knowing smile of satisfaction as she watched her mentor's face grow darker and darker, like a volcano in which stirred immense power and violence. She was sure he would be ready to erupt soon.

VIEWS, TAKES AND TRACKS flashed on and off the screen at Assistant Security Officer McKenzie's work station in the Security Area. From the moment she realised that Simpson was up to something, McKenzie had made every effort to infiltrate her superior's personal security in order to establish the reason for her meeting with Windsor. Eventually, through a sidelink into Simpson's circuit, McKenzie got a view of what she had wanted to see. Activating the pinhole in the wall of Simpson's apartment, long deactivated by the dark lady, McKenzie soon realised what the tryst was all about. The feline shape of the scheming securocrat was clear, reclining comfortably and hugging her glass of brandy. Beside her, sitting still with eyes glued to the screen, was the 'imprisoned' Windsor.

McKenzie saw Windsor suddenly jump to his feet, gesticulating with a clenched right hand and pointing at the viewer with his left index finger.

McKenzie switched the lipreader on immediately, just in time to interpret the kontroller's outburst.

"My God! How could this rabble be allowed to go unpunished after this! Has anyone else seen this?"

"Yes", Simpson replied, calmly. "The Master".

"I knew it! The bastard! I knew it! What's he going to do about it? Nothing! Oh, yes!" he roared, looking for confirmation of his suspicions from his companion. A lazy nod of the head was enough to confirm. "Yes, I knew it, I knew it. The coward!" he seethed, emphasising the final word with clenched teeth.

McKenzie didn't need to see the viewer to realise what had animated the outlaw kontroller to such an extent. It was clear that Simpson had decided to make what could only be described as a serious and irresponsible intervention in an extremely volatile situation. Her action in revealing details of the riot footage at this stage, particularly to one as unstable as Windsor, was unquestionably calculated to move matters in a highly dangerous direction. If Windsor decided to bring the recording to the attention of the tyrons, nobody could predict what the outcome would be.

McKenzie witnessed her superior rising to place a hand on the shoulder of the frenzied kontroller. Fixing her eyes intimately on the hysterical man, his face red with anger, she announced assuredly: "Master, you know what you have to do!"

A shiver ran down McKenzie's spine as Windsor appeared to calm and reflect on what his companion had said. She watched with dread as he then took the viewer in his hand and left the room.

53 RETRIBUTION DAY

*K*ANE, ANSWER ME! PLEASE! *Warn everybody to stay in their cells! There could be something big about to happen! Be extremely careful!*

The emergency message flashed vainly on the prisoner's screen, as McKenzie frantically attempted to alert her companion to the backlash that Windsor was about to unleash. But there was no reply from the prisoner and McKenzie's alert went unheeded. Oblivious to the warning, Kane had just walked out the door and was heading confidently down the corridor towards the L+S.

Chest out, chin straight, Kane's thoughts concentrated on his future and that of his fellow inmates. Apparently Nevin was content that a 'fair' resolution had been achieved on the prisoners' concerns about the running of the regime and was happy that a 'new dispensation' was about to unfold. That was ok by Kane in the short term but such an outcome would be a far cry from Kane's own objective. Escape from Korb-1 was Kane's goal from day one and that hadn't changed. There might be those amongst the prisoners – maybe even a majority – who would be happy to spend the rest of their days in a reformed Korb-1, but they certainly didn't include him. And although Kane would have liked to have led a mass breakout from the kolony or have managed to carry out Dayton's master plan and set up a Prisoners' Republic, he realised that a small group of dedicated and focused individuals would probably have a better chance of breaching the defences of the kolony and breaking away than a marauding multitude would have.

Back in Kane's cell, another message flashed on the screen.

Whatever you do, don't leave your cell! Kane – answer me! You mustn't leave your cell!

At this stage, the prisoner was only a hundred metres from the L+S. Approaching the area, Kane could hear what he would normally expect to hear – balls hitting walls in the squash courts near the entrance, groups talking excitedly, the echoing cheer following a score. Unusually, however, the space directly outside the glass-walled sports and leisure area had a large contingent of onlookers reclining against the perimeter wall in anticipation of the entertainment to come. Above, the purple sky of Korb-1 watched ominously.

In Kane's cell, another message flashed on the communication player screen.

Kane, wherever you are, be careful! Windsor has a video take and is liable to use it to save his skin. I hope you're reading this. I'm afraid things are going to get out of control. Please reply!

But Kane was far from his cell screen at this stage. Standing just inside the L+S, he was talking to Dayton.

"Well, Andy, ready to win the high jump?" he asked playfully.

"No, I'm really warming up for the wrestling challenge!" Dayton responded, the usual smile breaking on to his lips.

"Oh, I see," replied Kane naughtily, "are you going to challenge Kenning to a tussle?"

"Ha, maybe I'll challenge *you*!" Dayton answered, suddenly throwing an arm around his companion's neck and attempting to pull him to the ground.

McKenzie was attempting to remain calm as she observed Simpson interfering with the mobility restriction grid again. The conspirator was obviously not going to remain idle in whatever was about to unfold, but the game the dark lady was playing was a high-risk one. She had passed a highly sensitive security item into the possession of a dangerous and unstable madman. What she expected him to do with it was now the crucial question. Was it her expectation that the mad kontroller would somehow challenge the Master with his new evidence? That was unlikely. Even if he did manage to escape from his restriction area, the Master would have him in a cell in a matter of seconds. If he approached the other kontrollers, they would be vying with one another to sell him out to the Master in double-quick time. The more McKenzie weighed up Windsor's options, the clearer Simpson's game plan became. There was only constituency in which Windsor's security footage would meet with keen interest and that was the tyrons themselves. McKenzie shuddered at the thought.

Watching keenly while her superior officer worked on the mobility restriction grid, the worried woman could see the screen reflecting in the dark lady's green eyes as she calmly keyed in her instructions. What was she doing? Was she returning Windsor's restriction to its original setting? Or was she extending his mobility even further? And what would the repercussions of her intervention be for everybody in the kolony? McKenzie could only wonder and wait patiently for the conspirator to conclude her task.

In the L+S, the Sports Day had well and truly begun. The atmosphere was cheerful as two teams from 5-3 and 27-2 engaged in a rip-roaring game of hurling-ball. A tight encounter was developing as both sides, including, as they did, former professionals, squeezed valuable scores from the tightest of angles and the closest of tackles. The crowd was animated as score matched score and tackle answered tackle. The lively crowd was getting behind the teams and they, in turn, were responding by heightening the contest for every ball.

"My dessert tomorrow says 5-3 will do it!" Dayton challenged Kane.

"Done! Mine is on 27-2!" Kane responded immediately.

No sooner had the prisoner spoken than the full forward on 27-2 shimmied and danced his way through the opposition defence to score a goal and give Kane's team a three point advantage with only ten minutes left. As the crowd reacted with enthusiasm, Dayton gave Kane a pseudo-dirty look. Kane smiled a wide smile of satisfaction.

There were strong challenges as the game entered the last few minutes and the 5-3 team tried repeatedly to get back into the game. Their efforts were in vain, however, as attack after attack met a stonewall defence which soaked up the pressure every time before clearing the ball up to their forwards and putting their opponents under pressure again. Kane licked his lips provocatively as Dayton looked on in feigned annoyance at his competitor's good luck. As the final hooter sounded, Kane thanked his disappointed friend.

"Fair play, Andy, my old friend. Mighty generous of you!"

"Double or quits on the next game?" Dayton suggested, attempting to turn his luck.

"Why not?" Kane replied, "Another dessert never did any harm!"

"Done!" Dayton confirmed.

As soon as Security Officer Simpson had departed and silence had returned to the security area, McKenzie made straight for the mobility restriction control. The heat from her predecessor's body that still warmed the seat when the younger woman sat down made McKenzie uncomfortable. The dark lady's seat exuded vibes of duplicity and merciless calculation that McKenzie could feel invading her very bones, but this was a feeling the younger woman must quickly overcome if she was to focus on the task in hand. McKenzie was well aware that what she was about to discover could have seismic ramifications for the prisoners in the kolony – Kevin Kane included. Carrying that heavy thought in the back of her mind, McKenzie's fingers hit the keyboard at lightning speed. Almost immediately, the young woman had reached her predecessor's last keyboard request. The light from the screen reflected in McKenzie's eyes now as she hesitated slightly before pressing the recall button. If the eventuality she feared most was about to take place, the repercussions could be catastrophic. Bracing herself, McKenzie hit 'last request recall'. Immediately 'REVISED MOBILITY RESTRICTION – KONTROLLER WINDSOR' flashed on screen. McKenzie's heart skipped a beat. Hesitating again, she stared at the message on the screen, almost seeing through it the disaster that those words could ultimately mean. Eventually, prepared for the worst, she hit the button again. Like a warning beacon, the revised mobility restriction map for Windsor flashed in red and green on the screen. The movement restriction had been adjusted to afford access to *tyron security quarters*. McKenzie sank back into the seat in stunned silence as she realised her worst fears were about to come true.

For Windsor, this was Retribution Day. Today the just man who had been wronged and vilified by the corrupt and incompetent would have his revenge. Today those who had thought to hide their iniquity behind the smokescreen of authority would be dragged out under the glare of their peers and made to pay a heavy price for their transgressions. Today a shameful episode in the history of the Administration would be brought to an end. Windsor began to swagger as he made his way unhindered through the security area and straight for the headquarters of the tyron guard. So often in the past had he been thwarted by lesser beings and left to take responsibility for their failings. So often had he been outmanoeuvred by the cunning and the guileful and left to carry the can for their crimes of inadequacy. So often had he to pay a high price for his high standards while those for whom the survival of their own career was paramount walked away unscathed. Today would see an end to all of that. Today was Retribution Day.

Strutting along towards the tyron camp, Windsor gathered confidence with every stride. Dressed in his best military fatigues and carrying his helmet under his arm, he was ready for the most important battle of his life – the battle for the support and confidence of his force. Like him, the tyrons were soldiers – straightforward, upfront men and women who feared no enemy and would never flinch from performing their duty. Like him, they knew that high standards always carried the day and, like him, they could be relied upon to stand by those high standards when others would abandon them for personal gain. Unlike those who, through corruption and sleaze, had been given the responsibility of high office, the tyrons were honest and direct. When faced by the enemy, they knew only one way – to attack, to fight and to win. Armed with superior weapons and higher moral fibre, the tyrons had always been victorious. Seeking reassurance, Windsor glanced at the viewer in his left hand. Appropriately armed for the encounter, he was under no doubt that this was a battle he *would* win.

The various competitions of the Korb-1 Sports Day were coming to a conclusion and spirits were high following an enjoyable day. The Acrobat was going through her paces to the delight of the crowd in the main arena in a final display to finish off proceedings. Landing on her feet after a triple somersault only to launch into a single-handed cartwheel, she had the crowd open-mouthed in amazement as she completed her performance. Kane and Dayton were among the impressed.

"Long time since I saw *you* doing that, Andy!" Kane quipped.

"Couldn't be bothered," Dayton replied. "It's mental gymnastics I do nowadays!"

Throwing a glance in the direction of the Acrobat, Kane continued: "I'd be worried that when she goes up there, she might forget to come back down!"

"A bit like the Master," Nevin joined in, as he joined the two, "he's still up in those purple clouds above our heads, pondering the miraculous wonder of it all!"

"I think he produces the gas himself", remarked Kane. "No wonder he feels at home up there!"

As Kane spoke those words, his lips moved on the lipreader on the screen in front of McKenzie and the software uttered his jest by proxy. McKenzie didn't even smile at the humorous comments. Instead, grim-faced, she turned her glance to another view on the screen. In that scene, there was no humour, no sport, no play. Instead she observed a small man with a deadly serious expression speaking animatedly to a large group of tyrons. While Kane and his comrades relaxed and joked, Windsor was playing his final deadly hand. Wondering when and how she could possibly intervene, McKenzie played an agonising waiting game as she awaited a decisive move from the tyron camp.

When the moment came, it appeared initially to be almost innocuous. Kane and Dayton were following the last of the group out of the L+S when they suddenly sensed a feeling of unease amongst those in front of them. The two were not in a position to see what was causing the problem ahead but the sudden silence of the crowd was enough to convince them that something was wrong. The crowd at the back waited nervously to discover the cause of the tension when suddenly they heard the sound of searers and the cries and shouts of those apparently at the receiving end of the blasts.

Drawing frightening conclusions from the activity ahead, the crowd immediately fragmented and prisoners ran in every direction. In the middle of the pandemonium that reigned in the large corridor, Kane saw an apparently seriously wounded prisoner being helped along by two others, one of whom himself carried a wound. Then Nevin, a look of horror on his face, appeared, running down through the prisoners, repeatedly calling out one clear order:

"Head for the Dining Hall. We're under attack. Head for the Dining Hall!"

Nevin was in shock – and it showed. All of a sudden, the cosy accommodation he had been so carefully constructing with the Master was being ripped apart. Who was responsible? Had the bald bastard been planning this all along? Or was there another, more sinister, hand at work? At the moment, it didn't really matter. The prisoners were under assault again and they had better protect themselves fast.

It hadn't taken Kane and Dayton long to realise that they'd better get moving too. Realising the gravity of the situation, the two men headed at speed towards the Dining Hall. As he ran, Kane tried to figure it all out. Why was there an outbreak of hostilities so soon? Was there not a deal?

Who was reneging? And why? A searer scorching the wall beside Kane's head woke him out of his contemplation and focused his mind on what was important now – getting to a safe place. Casting a quick glance at Dayton, he quickened his step towards the Dining Hall.

Frozen in horror, McKenzie watched a terrifying new chapter in the story of Korb-1 commence before her eyes.

54 FINAL STAND

The Dining Area was filling rapidly with prisoners escaping from the area of the L+S. In an atmosphere of chaos tinged with fear and tempered with the courage of those left with no choice but to take a stand, the prisoners assembled. The word quickly spread that the tyrons had attacked the prisoners leaving the L+S. Nobody knew how or why they had been incited so quickly into an assault but, at this stage, it didn't really matter. The important thing now was survival. Most of those present reluctantly accepted that if the security force in the kolony had taken to butchering prisoners in the corridors, there was no other option now but to make a stand as best they could and hope to survive the onslaught.

In a matter of minutes, the Dining Hall was almost full and when Nevin arrived a solemn silence descended on the assembled throng. The prisoners' leader was hoisted up onto the shoulders of some of the tallest prisoners in the Hall so that he was visible to all. Without ceremony, he began to address the prisoners.

"Free People of Korb", he began in a surprisingly clear and authoritative voice. "Fate has brought us all together in a prison kolony on a barren rock in space. For most of us, a simple attachment to the truth and a belief that the people's right to know was more important than any administration's right to conceal was sufficient to rip us away from our friends and families and cast us away on the Rock of Korb. We could have sat in our cells and worked in our chambers and accepted our lot. But Fate is answerable to no-one and Fate makes apologies to none. And Fate does not judge those on whom its hand dispassionately falls. Fate will deal evenly with all, and it is only those who lie down without a fight who will be ignored in the final movement of that hand."

The assembled prisoners listened intently to their leader's address. Most of them were surprised at the manner in which his dignified oration appeared to be so relevant to their plight this fateful day. Eyes firmly fixed on the man they hoped would help them make sense of it all, they felt strangely uplifted by his analysis of their struggle and his clear message that, despite all they had gone through and the imminent threat of another murderous assault, their fate was now in their own bare hands. His reassuring message assuaged much of the naked fear that had been palpable amongst the prisoners from the time the first shots were fired.

Nevin continued: "We have planned for this day for some time. That it is happening in the heightened atmosphere created by the murderous activities of our jailors is unplanned but hardly surprising. It is the nature of the beast to conceal and deny the truth. Let us now ensure that truth will win the battle this time around and that those who attempt to stop the gaps in the dam with their grubby claws will be washed away forever in a torrent of justice!"

A sudden salvo of searers heard from the direction of the L+S caused most of those present to focus their attention in that direction and momentarily stopped the leader's address. Gathering his composure,

Nevin went on: "It is now time for the well of truth to be tapped, for the spring to be sourced, for the torrent to flow. Fate may have dealt us poor hands in the past, but Fate holds no grudges, nor should we. If we cast ourselves into the path of Fate once more, we will given as fair a cast of the dice as anyone else. Our best chance now is to divide into combat groups, based on four KC teams. This must be done speedily. Those in charge of the groups will be told what their objectives are and, as soon as they have assembled their forces, they must move with speed to achieve those objectives. When all objectives have been realised, the teams will assemble at the entrance to the Korb Departure Area for the final push for freedom. You all know what is expected of you now. You all know what you have to do. Carry out your responsibilities courageously and Fate will smile on us today!"

Surveying the large throng in front of him, Nevin took a deep breath. Swelling his chest with pride and raising his left arm in a clenched fist salute, he exhorted his troops one more time: "Courage, Free People of Korb. Today freedom calls!"

At that, the prisoners, to a man and a woman, cheered aloud and, clenching their fists, moved en masse to the lower gate of the Dining Hall, leaving their fears and their past behind.

Despite Nevin's seemingly clear instructions, Kane found himself unable to distinguish between the prisoners' armies and, rather than waste time, fell in with a large group of prisoners who had come together under the command of Angela Karnassis, a tall dark woman from Korb 31-2, and marched out of the Dining Hall with that group. Dayton and Gibney took their place beside their comrade and moved off with the company to confront whatever Nevin's friend, Fate, had in store.

Looking around him at the mostly young men and women in the ranks, Kane wondered what chance of success their premature revolt really had. Marching along amongst them, he sensed a strange kind of tension in their ranks. It was as if this was an adventure in which they *had* to engage, an event that in some strange way they felt would reward their participation by bringing about some dramatic change in their lives. Kane felt this exciting idealism light up the atmosphere all around him. Initially, he found the buzz of optimism stimulating but, as the group turned down the corridor on their great adventure, the prisoner couldn't resist the thought that the expectations of idealism more often than not terminated in the cold embrace of failure. Kane experienced a certain sense of shame at the arrival of such a negative thought in his mind at a time of such unbridled bravery and hope. His shame was exacerbated by the events that were to follow. Moving at speed, the company soon found themselves at the eastern gate of the MKC. As they were about to enter, however, a force of seven tyrons arrived and downed eleven members of the raiding party. Another five casualties followed. The reaction of the prisoners was swift. Rather than retreat, as one might have expected an unarmed force to do in the face of armed and trained soldiers, the prisoners almost in unison threw themselves on the tyrons. Smothering the soldiers' fire with their own bodies, they silenced seven of the regime's best soldiers in almost an instant — though at a high personal cost. The hostilities ending as suddenly as they had begun, a moment of shocked silence followed. This had been a defining moment. At last, the prisoners had cast away their fears and grasped a stake in their future with both hands. As if realising the importance of seizing the initiative and denying those involved the opportunity to ponder too deeply on the ghastly events to which they had been a party, Karnassis immediately set about handing out tasks to as many prisoners as possible. One of those was to organise a casualty survey. While those instructed to tend to the wounded carried out their duties, Karnassis ordered the tyrons stripped of all weapons and equipment. Calling Pinter and Ap Gwilliam, both of whom had paramedical experience, to one side, she appointed them casualty officers. Their role would be to carry out casualty surveys after every clash and every hour in-between and arrange rudimentary aid. They were to appropriate first-aid materials at every given opportunity and were to be responsible for appropriately disposing of the bodies of prisoners killed in action. The appointments made, the commander turned her attention to Kane and Dayton, asking them to monitor arms and ammunition supplies taken from the tyrons and to get them into the hands of those trained in the use of arms. Both men accepted their responsibilities, though neither displayed any great enthusiasm. Kane would have preferred to have been able to concentrate on his own direct role in combating the tyrons but was impressed with the new commander's organisational approach.

Karnassis then ordered the company to enter the MKC, bringing all casualties, fatalities and arms with them. Once inside, the tyrons were placed in one corner while the bodies of the dead prisoners were placed respectfully in another. Kane and Dayton then moved amongst the prisoners, inviting those with experience of weapons to make themselves known. A variety of responses were received, one of the first of which was "I was a crack shot in the amusement arcade in NC City 7!" Kane gave the young woman a zennor. Soon the weapons were in the hands of those skilled in their use, Kane and Dayton deciding they themselves lacked sufficient experience to hold on to any yet. Karnassis immediately ordered all armed members of what she now termed the "Free Korb Army" to split up and cover the entrances.

After the initial horror, the success of their first skirmish was beginning to create a belief amongst the prisoners in their ability to meet the challenge that lay ahead, whatever form that might take. The initial buzz of enthusiasm was now being rooted in the reality of a successful encounter with the tyrons. The fact that the tyrons were hopelessly outnumbered was counterbalanced in the minds of the prisoners with the fact that the regime's soldiers had been the ones with the weapons. Even Kane began to believe that this 'army' might march a little longer then he had first expected. As the speed of their success against the tyrons and their acquisition of arms began to sink in, a flush of excitement swept amongst the members of the prisoners' army and some hurled shouts of defiance in the air as they took up their positions in the Chamber.

A remarkably calm Karnassis told the company, with the exception of the armed guards, to reform marching ranks, an order responded to immediately. She then outlined what the objective of the group in the MKC was.

"Our role here is to disable the main Korb Flush Channels so that the arrival of the next automatic flow in each Chamber will cause that Chamber to explode. It is hoped that this action will attract tyron forces away from the areas we need to penetrate. While members of the team carry out this operation, the rest will position themselves around the entrances to the MKC to prevent tyron forces entering."

The group listened eagerly to their commander's instructions and, as she bawled out with functional efficiency the names of those selected to take part in the action, all of those chosen moved with enthusiasm to carry out their tasks. The others were equally enthusiastic as she directed them to their positions around the entrances, behind the armed members of the team, Kane and Dayton amongst them.

Karnassis stood in the middle of the Chamber on top of a tool transporter as her troops worked quickly to sabotage the Flush Channels. With one eye on the korb klock hologram above one the doors and the other on the work being feverishly carried out at her command, the tall slim woman nervously brushed her long black hair over her ears. Impatiently, she burst out a command: "Faster, we've got to move faster. The longer we hang around here, the greater the danger we'll be interrupted. Faster!"

Those involved in the difficult and dangerous work of disabling the Flush Channels were covered in sweat as they stretched inside the operation panels to short the operating currents of the machines. The team released a joint sigh of relief as the last one finished and Karnassis jumped down to gather her force together. Just as her feet hit the floor, however, a force of tyrons appeared at the western gate and immediately opened fire. Prisoners dived for cover in every direction as the tyrons fired at will. The prisoners at the gate returned fire instantly and the tyrons, not expecting their prey to be armed and capable of defending themselves, made good targets. The armed prisoners at the other gates reacted fast, swinging around to join the response to the tyron attack, while the rest of the prisoners found whatever cover they could.

Three tyrons hit the ground dead, joining three prisoners who had also taken fatal hits. The weapon of one of the fallen tyrons slid across the floor as she fell, stopping beside Kane, who had taken cover behind a Tool Supply Box just inside the gate. Kane glanced at the weapon, unable to believe his luck in obtaining a passport to join the fray, and instantly popped out to grab it. Throwing himself back behind the Tool Box with the weapon, Kane studied it closely, accustoming himself to its weight and dimensions. Then, holding it in his welcoming arms, he got ready to pounce. Two tyrons, who had breached the defences where the three prisoners had fallen, raced past Kane. Without hesitation, the prisoner sprung out to open fire on the nearest tyron, felling him easily with a shot to the back of the knee. As he fell, the tyron turned to respond but Kane finished him with a shot to the throat. The second tyron turned to respond but another volley from Kane took him out of the action.

At the gate, two tyrons who had remained outside continued to direct fire into the Chamber. Kane observed one of them closely and then, waiting patiently for his man to overextend himself, despatched him with a single shot under the chin. The sole tyron survivor of the attack began to lose confidence at this stage, firing only intermittently as if waiting for reinforcements or the opportunity to escape. When he did make his move, the funfair lady from NC City 7 was ready and the tyron's move was his last. Kane looked at the crack shot woman, raising an eyebrow and bowing his head slightly in a gesture of appreciation. She acknowledged his compliment with a wide smile.

When the encounter was over, the prisoners stood up, the smell of battle strong in their nostrils, to count the cost. Five more were dead and another slightly wounded. The cost to the regime was heavier – another seven tyrons downed and a total of fourteen searers now in the hands of Karnassis' rebels. The wounded prisoners being treated and the bodies of their fallen comrades laid out in the corner, Karnassis called on the party to regroup and march on to the next phase of their mission – a rendezvous at the junction of the blue and yellow corridors. With the fire of battle burning in their veins, the party moved out of the MKC, leaving a scene of destruction in their wake.

55 FREEDOM MARCH

IF HOPES WERE HIGH as Karnassis' company left the Dining Hall with Nevin's inspiring words ringing in their ears, the feelings of the group were now somewhat different. Idealistic enthusiasm was the driving force then but now the party had seen combat twice and actually seen off the tyrons on both occasions. Despite losing seventeen of their number, this band of warriors now considered themselves a formidable fighting force. The myth of tyron invincibility had been blown to shreds and it was now a question of continuing on as planned until victory was secured. Marching along with the party, those armed with captured weapons, rather than being fearful of approaching tyrons, were almost eager to spot some so that they could up their tyron hit count.

Even Kane himself was affected by the general rush of adrenalin that had seized the group. Unlike the tyrons, for whom the battle was one of professional duty against illegality and anarchy, the prisoners were fighting for their very survival. Every skirmish that resulted in victory brought them that little bit closer to their eventual liberation. Any defeat in such an encounter set them back, possibly irreversibly, in their struggle to be free. Two victories on and now at least with some arms with which to defend themselves, the prisoners had greatly improved their position. Even Kane was beginning to believe that perhaps at long last the prisoners' day had come.

After about five minutes, the victorious prisoners' progress was halted unexpectedly by Gibney, who reminded Karnassis that, in the chaos of surviving the tyron assault, the unit had forgotten to destroy the communications equipment in the MKC. Gibney offered to double back, take out the equipment, and then catch up with the unit. After a moment's reflection, Karnassis nodded o.k., then added "Dayton, you go too – but both of you take care!" Some moments after the other two had vanished around the corner, Kane chipped up: "I'll go as well. Someone needs to watch their back!" Reluctantly, Karnassis agreed and Kane went after the other two, zennor in hand.

Kane took his time moving along the corridor after his comrades, watching for tyrons in every direction as he went. The prisoner experienced an eerie sensation as he patrolled the deserted corridors with a tyron weapon in his hand and wondered would he wake up soon, as he had so many times before from his escape fantasies. It was a short journey back to the MKC, though, and soon Kane found himself outside the main gate. Approaching the gate, Kane was stopped in his tracks, however, when he saw the spread-eagled body of Dayton lying face down on the ground. "Andy!" Kane uttered, almost inaudibly, but rather than running immediately towards his fallen colleague, Kane slowed down and moved cautiously towards the entrance.

Approaching the gate, Kane could hear a voice. It was Gibney's: "….almost a hundred. 14 tyrons down. Weapons in the hands of the insurgents. Next destination: junction of Blue and Yellow. Leader is

Karnassis. I'll wait for instructions before rejoining rebel force. Over!" A cold feeling came over Kane. It was the cold of the grave, the cold of betrayal. But it was soon replaced by another cold sensation. That was the cold of revenge, the steely determination that at long last a major debt would be paid. For Kane, it was an opportunity for vengeance that he had never expected to obtain, a chance to exorcise a ghost forever. Ever since the day in the tunnel that McKenzie had helped Kane recognise for once and for all the Face that had tormented him for so long and revealed to him the role played by that individual in the murder of Thorsen, it was all the prisoner could do to restrain himself from lunging at the traitor and tearing his throat out at the first opportunity. But Kane had decided to bide his time and wait until the traitor's time had come. That time was now.

As Kane prepared to move into the Chamber and confront the monstrous ghosts that resided in the person of Clarence Gibney, he saw that Dayton's body was being dragged away. Moving cautiously to the door, Kane observed as Gibney pulled the young man towards a korb chute. Opening the door and using all his strength, the NC agent lifted the young man and attempted to force his apparently lifeless body into the chute. The cold patience of the vengeful being gradually replaced by the anger of the betrayed, Kane prepared to pounce. Suddenly, however, Gibney's load came to life and a disorientated Dayton, awaking to find himself about to be despatched by a former comrade, struggled to get free. Taken aback, Gibney did his utmost to force the younger man into the chute. With his victim still at less than his full strength, Gibney appeared to be winning the death struggle when suddenly he heard a voice in his ear:

"Want a hand there, Gibney?"

Gibney froze, the voice of a man he had betrayed one time too many being the last sound he had expected to hear.

Turning slightly, but not looking Kane in the eye, he replied: "It's not what you think, Kane". His voice was weak, hesitant, as if he didn't really expect Kane to believe him.

"Oh, really!" Kane retorted, with a grin. "What is it then?"

Before Gibney could reply, Dayton gave his captor a knee in the face and dropped to the ground, free from the deadly clutches of his former friend.

"Over here, Andy!" Kane called to Dayton, and the young man was soon on his hands and knees, taking deep breaths beside Kane. Kane kept his zennor trained on Gibney.

"No, Kane, really – it's not what you think!"

"Save your breath, scumbag. I know what it is. I know you're the NC agent who shopped Sheena Strauss and me. I also know that you're the one who, after realising that the novo, Nathan Winslow, had recognised you and told Andrea Thorsen who you were, engineered Andrea's murder and probably that of the novo, who hasn't been seen since. I remember your pathetic little injury in the chamber that day and how you left so suddenly for the Treatment Unit. I just wish I'd recognised you then – Andrea would still be alive if I had!"

"Kane, I had nothing to do with any of that. I swear. You're all wrong! I …"

"Shut the fuck up!" Kane exploded angrily, " I know it all – the whole story! I've known it for some time. I've just been waiting for the chance to sear you – and now I catch you trying to despatch Andy!"

Dayton, who had been listening in shock to Kane's account of what had occurred, got to his feet, and took the opportunity to utter a dazed: "You bastard, Gibney!"

Gibney had the appearance of a cornered rat and his eyes betrayed the contempt in which he held his former 'comrades'. Kane was well aware the trapped traitor was weighing up his chances of disarming him in a sudden lunge. Gibney made his move. Throwing himself head first at Kane, he stretched out his arms to grab Kane's zennor as he landed. Expecting a sudden effort by the snared beast to escape his fate, Kane merely stepped back and emptied a searer blast into the NC agent's skull. Gibney landed at Kane's feet, still smouldering.

Dayton breathed an audible sigh of relief when his would-be murderer hit the ground, as if a vile monster had been slain. Kane was silent, the faces and voices of those whose lives had been destroyed by the creature he had once considered a companion passing through his mind as if in some final act of recognition and closure.

"Time to get back to the others, Andy!" Kane announced "Are you o.k.?"

"Yeah, I'm fine. But there's one more thing we have to do!"

As both men left the MKC to rejoin their comrades, the red light flashed on the side of the liquidiser tunnel in the Chamber behind them and the deadly ghost of Clarence Gibney left Korb-1 forever.

KARNASSIS WAS VISIBLY SHOCKED when Kane and Dayton rejoined the unit and told her what had happened in the MKC. That the enemy could get so close was a frightening thought that raised issues about who could really be trusted and when were the prisoners really safe. But Karnassis was as aware as anyone else that, from the beginning of time, anybody challenging the status quo must always be wary of the enemy within their own ranks. It was always a question of limiting the damage and getting them before they get you. After an initial shudder of horror, the unit leader congratulated the two on eliminating "the horrid creature" and hoped they would be ok. Then, in view of Gibney's actions in alerting the Administration to the prisoners' plans, she announced a change of course. Instead of heading straight for the junction of Blue and Yellow, the party would divert towards the Treatment Unit to see if the group sent there needed assistance. The combined bands could then proceed to the junction. The prisoners nodded their agreement and the group was on the march again.

The corridors were eerily quiet as the party made steady progress towards their next objective. Along the way, they looked anxiously in every direction for a sign of their comrades but none could be seen, the area seemingly deserted. Eventually, the party reached the Treatment Unit, having met no resistance whatsoever along the way. Karnassis, calm but focused, waited outside the TU for a while, occasionally casting a concerned glance in the direction from which the other party was expected to approach. As the korb seconds passed like an eternity, the prisoners nervously waited for the next move. Some looked at one another, perhaps seeking assurance. Others stared ahead without moving, their anxious gaze betraying the tension that was building up inside them. Then, with no sign of activity in any direction, Karnassis instructed her party to enter the TU, the majority of the armed members to lead while the remaining armed prisoners were to fall back to protect the rear.

The prisoners were extremely cautious on entering what had essentially been an off-limits area to prisoners. The unmistakeable antiseptic odour of a hospital unit faced them as they went in but there was no sign of doctors, patients or tyrons. There was no sign of any struggle either and it appeared that the other prisoner band hadn't yet reached the area. Karnassis decided not to waste time. Surveying the area, she instructed her team to create an obstruction at the junction outside by pulling furniture from the Treatment Unit and stacking it. This, she hoped, would delay any tyron re-enforcements that might attempt to catch up with the prisoners.

The team was soon at work, and anything that was mobile was carried or pushed out of the area and unceremoniously dumped outside.

Most of the furniture and fittings appeared to be either custom fitted or withdrawn into the wall but the team found enough to create a formidable barricade to delay the tyrons. Karnassis then instructed her troops to form up and prepare to march on. As they did, however, the sound of searer fire erupted to their right. Looking down the corridor, the prisoners saw what appeared to be the remnants of the other prisoner party retreating in their direction in panic, pursued by a party of tyrons.

"Take cover!" Karnassis roared. "Armed people to the front! Lie low behind the barricades until the tyrons are clearly in your sights. Aim carefully at targets and, when I give the word, take them out!"

Kane positioned himself flat on the floor, with a clear view through a gap between the heaped furniture. The fleeing prisoners were getting closer but were blocking a good aim at the pursuing tyrons. Karnassis studied the situation. Then, getting down on one knee, ordered the prisoners to wait until their fellow prisoners had jumped the barricades before opening fire. The defending prisoners looked on in anger as the tyrons picked off the retreating prisoners with ease. When the first of the fugitives clambered over the barricade, they were amazed to see their fellow prisoners lying in wait. Karnassis signalled to the escaping prisoners not to reveal their position and to continue on to the TU.

On more than one occasion, Kane winched with pain as prisoners clearing the barricade with speed landed right on top of him. With more and more running prisoners jumping wildly over the barricade, Kane and his fellow defenders sensed the itch in their fingers at the prospect of repaying the tyrons for their murderous pursuit of unarmed prisoners. Waiting impatiently for the last of the prisoners to clear the barricade, Kane recognised two of those fleeing for their lives – Pedersen and Nielsen. Blood streaming from a wound on his left shoulder, Pedersen's face revealed a smile of recognition as he cleared the barrier to see the welcome face of Kane and his colleagues ready to wreak vengeance on his brutal pursuers. Nielsen seemed unscathed but equally elated to see her comrades lying in wait for her tormentors. When the last prisoner had cleared the blockade, Karnassis gave the word: "Now!"

A hail of carefully aimed zennor fire sailed into the ranks of the bloodthirsty pursuing pack, stopping them in their tracks. One in particular who had almost reached the barricade in his eagerness to spill more prisoner blood received a blast straight to the throat from Kane, sending him flying a good ten korb feet, never to move again. Kane aimed again and picked off another tyron almost immediately.

The tyrons, taken totally by surprise by the intense fire directed towards them, were in disarray. Now open targets themselves in the corridor, they jumped to the ground to make the armed prisoners' task more difficult. But the insurgents had had time to aim well and, one by one, the prone tyrons shook as searer fire rocked into them. One defender, however, who in his enthusiasm had risen up to provide the tyrons with too easy a target, fell dead as a prone tyron seized his opportunity to strike back.

At the conclusion of the battle, Kane felt the thrill of victory run through every fibre in his body. At last, it was clear that the tyrons were far from invincible. At last, it was clear that the prisoners, if disciplined and focused, could take their fate into their own hands. At last, it was clear that apparent defeat could be turned into decisive victory. Spontaneously, the enlarged prisoner party stood and, the armed ones brandishing their weapons, emitted a defiant roar heard in many parts and in many times in the history of humankind – the roar of the oppressed as they clamber to their feet to demand their freedom.

Karnassis, standing on top of the barricade, congratulated the party on another stunning victory, then ordered them to organise: "Take care of the wounded – and the dead! Gather and distribute the weapons! Armed prisoners, guard all approaches!" Another seven tyrons had bitten the dust, though over thirty fleeing prisoners had been killed and one defender. Another seven complete set of weapons had been captured, however. The prisoners' band was rapidly becoming a well-armed experienced fighting force.

It was an ecstatic company of prisoners that moved on to its next objective. Armed and victorious, the party were following a path to what had previously appeared impossible – victory and freedom. The lonely cells and sweaty korb chambers of the forgotten rock in space would soon be a thing of the past, the prisoners now believed, and no matter what awaited them ahead there would be no going back. Freedom, once tasted, was a sweeter drink than any kind of oppression, be it benign, liberal or otherwise. Eyes peeled, none of the prisoners spoke as they marched to that meeting with Fate that Nevin had so passionately promised them.

McKenzie stared intently at the multi-image grid in front of her. Her full red lips were pursed with tension, her eyes focused on the scenes before her. She had been shocked at the speed at which the situation in the kolony had deteriorated. It was less than eight hours now since Windsor had played his hand and plunged the entire kolony into chaos and the ensuing mayhem had astounded even the most experienced in the Korb-1 administration. The Master was in a state of shock and his kommanders were being ignored by the tyrons who were bent on revenge for the deaths of their comrades. The tyrons were now acting as an autonomous army, patrolling the kolony in bands of seven – their usual formation – and seeking bloody vengeance on whatever prisoners they came across. The Master had called a meeting of his Korb Kouncil in an attempt to regain control of the situation but Windsor was reported to be moving around the kolony, capitalising on the disorder he had created and turning the rage of the tyrons to his own advantage. The entire situation now hinged on whether the Master could call the tyrons to heel or not. If he could, then some kind of normality could be restored. If he failed, the chaos and mayhem would continue and the kolony would face total disaster.

Scanning all available visual takes to gain an overview of the situation, McKenzie's aim was twofold. She had been instructed by Simpson to obtain hard information on the situation on the ground and construct a comprehensive security picture. But many of the security cameras were immobilised and McKenzie could access less than half of the kolony area. What she did see, though, were scenes of carnage and vicious fighting – much of it hand to hand – all over the kolony and in many cases – much to McKenzie's surprise – it was the tyrons who appeared to be coming off worse.

But McKenzie had another goal. She wanted to find Kane. The prisoner tracking system had been disabled when a band of prisoners attacked and destroyed one of the main security relay posts near the junction between the Green and Red corridors. Now, only visual scanning could establish if Kane was still alive. McKenzie loaded Kane's personal file into the visual scanner and hit *scan* on her control panel. Immediately, Kane's security image came on screen. The prisoner's facial image flashed first, showing (and dating) the latest security update. A body profile followed and then the system displayed a full multi-dimensional image of Kane, showing the prisoner from every conceivable angle. McKenzie hit *capture* and *find* in quick succession and then went about running all security views simultaneously. Steeling herself in preparation for a sight she might wish she had never seen, McKenzie examined every available image in an attempt to locate her separated comrade. The more the situation descended into all-out war, the more real became the likelihood of Kane ending up as just another casualty. Casting her eye over innumerable images, McKenzie scoured the scene for a glimpse of Kane. With the ring finger on her right hand, she passed over the sensor to produce yet another collection of images, some overlapping, some crystal clear, some obscure, all code-numbered. Touching a spot on the grid immediately enlarged the image at that spot on the viewing screen. Touching it again enlarged it once more and the process could be repeated *ad infinitum*. With increasing speed, McKenzie examined hundreds of images from all over the kolony, scrutinising a multitude of faces in the process.

As McKenzie strained her eyes to obtain a sighting of Kane, the system worked effectively and speedily away, scanning every single available view, every image, every frame and every angle. Suddenly an image froze on screen and a red square flashed over a face. Fixing on the image, McKenzie tensed on seeing a familiar visage. Focussing in on the view, she identified Kane, searer in hand, exchanging fire with a group of tyrons. Hitting *location*, McKenzie received confirmation of the site of the battle – the Triangular Junction between the Red Quarter and the Green Zone. McKenzie examined Kane's face closely as she read the intensity of the encounter on his features, knotted in fury as he fired off blast after blast at the enemy.

56 WINDSOR'S WAR

DESPITE THE HEAVY CASUALTIES inflicted on the fleeing prisoners who had joined up with Karnassis' company, the mood amongst the combat group was one of confidence as they moved on. Kane was particularly happy to see Pedersen escape from the clutches of the tyrons. His presence would certainly add to the cutting edge of Karnassis' company. There was no doubt either that Pedersen was delighted to see his colleagues rather than the Supreme Being around the corner from the Treatment Unit! He told his rescuers that his group, led by Mernagh of KC 7-1, had made good progress until they met with a large band of tyrons. The tyrons were accompanied by Kontroller Windsor and, on spotting the prisoners, immediately unleashed a massive hail of firepower that decimated the prisoner band. When the prisoners retreated, they were pursued by a group of tyrons and a massacre ensued, during which most of the fleeing prisoners were killed (Mernagh included). Then, thanks to Kane and his colleagues, the pursuing tyrons had been stopped in their tracks and the surviving prisoners rescued.

When Kane and Pedersen discussed the fate of Mernagh's band, their immediate thought was to follow a course that would ensure they avoided the large tyron force that had massacred their colleagues. Momentarily, however, it had occurred to the trio that a pre-emptive strike against the tyron force could in fact catch them off-guard and enable the prisoners to take a famous scalp if Windsor fell into their hands. McKenzie had briefed her companion on the demented kontroller's role in the kolony and Kane would have loved a shot at him, but wisely he and Pedersen let the thought pass and decided to follow their agreed course. Windsor would have to wait.

So far, all tyron attempts to halt Karnassis' group's progress had been effectively overcome. Most of the rebels in the company regarded this as proof that their uprising was already successful and that the Administration was collapsing. Kane saw the lack of resistance differently. The tyrons were a formidable force. They had proven themselves all over the planet and anywhere in the galaxy they had been asked to serve. They were not the type to run away. Granted, in all the skirmishes so far, the prisoners had shown their oppressors to be far from invincible, but Kane felt that surprise had played a large part in events up to now and that the real battle had still to be fought. The likelihood was, he feared, that the Administration had decided to confront the rebellion head on in circumstances chosen by, and controlled by, it. Kane was convinced that the ultimate battle for freedom would be a more difficult one than the various encounters up to now would suggest. But the prisoner kept these thoughts to himself, as he moved, searer at the ready, towards the rendezvous with the other insurgent groups.

Suddenly, Kane noticed two tyrons at the intersection ahead. Karnassis immediately ordered the company to take cover positions along the corridor and, as they did, searer fire began to blast in every direction. Kane, crouching at the angle of the floor and the wall to the right of the corridor, decided not to fire. All round him, prisoners with weapons were letting fly in the direction of the intersection but Kane noticed that the tyrons were much more economical with their firepower. Every few seconds, on an alternate basis, a tyron would pop head and shoulders around the corner, take aim and fire at a chosen target. Almost inevitably, the target would fall.

The company was in trouble. With little or no cover, the force would be easily held back and gradually decimated. Unless the tyrons were disabled, the uprising would soon be over for Karnassis' troop. Kane observed the tyrons' approach. He noticed that a tyron appeared every five seconds and fired. Then another tyron appeared from around the other corner and fired. Kane also noticed that the tyrons appeared alternately in a high or low position. The prisoner counted the time sequence and decided to act. Taking aim at a high position on the left, Kane waited until the targeted tyron appeared and fired a blast. Whaff! The tyron flew back with the force of the blast and landed six feet away. The other tyron did not show his face again for some seconds after the first was struck but soon re-appeared to aim at the crouched prisoners. Kane noted with relief that a third tyron did not appear to replace the fallen one on the left hand side. With determination, he decided to sequence the other one next. As fire from the rebel force sprayed in every direction, Kane again took aim at a high position on the right hand side. Within seconds, the second tyron had fallen. An apprehensive lull followed the second shooting as the prisoners waited for a reaction from the other side. After a while, it appeared that the two tyrons had not been part of a tyron seven-squad, as these groups were called. The way was clear to advance once more.

The tyrons stand had not been without some success, however. The corridor was strewn with the bodies of fallen prisoners, most of them fatalities. Eight prisoners lay dead and another four had serious burn wounds. Survivors tended the injured and placed the dead to one side as the armed prisoners kept watch for another tyron appearance. The prisoners had been badly hit by this attack. On top of the casualties, their confidence had been dented by the fact that two tyrons could inflict so much damage on a reasonably large force and severely hinder their attempt to progress towards their objective. Karnassis approached Kane.

"Well done, Kane", she said smiling, "Looks like you know how to handle those things". Both of them looked at the searer in Kane's arms with clear affection.

"Luck is important in all of this", was Kane's modest response.

Karnassis sat down beside her comrade, emitting a weary sigh as she did.

"It's going to get harder from now on in", she announced, the tone of her voice becoming serious. "They're not going to allow us to stroll out of here."

Kane nodded. "No doubt about that", the look on his face indicating reluctant agreement.

Silence between the two followed as they both surveyed the destruction before their eyes.

"There'll be a lot more of this", Kane added in a grave tone.

"I know", Karnassis concurred, "but we've got to keep going, got to keep hoping there'll be a way out."

"We've no other choice, Karnassis", Kane agreed. "They've left us none. Who knows? We may succeed – we've haven't been doing too badly so far!"

Smiling in agreement, Karnassis arose. "It's time to move on", she announced.

"Scout team ahead!" the tired woman ordered as the force prepared to move. With that, a team of four armed scouts went forward with caution to ensure the way ahead was clear. Throwing themselves across the floor at the junction further on before positioning themselves and aiming their weapons ahead, the scouts appraised the situation and then signalled for the force to follow. When the band had all turned the corner, lead by the other armed prisoners, the scouts waited until all had passed before rising and adopting the role of rear guard.

Marching along, Kane wondered aloud where the other five members of the tyron seven were.

"Maybe they were killed in another skirmish?" Dayton suggested, "or maybe they just retreated."

"I dunno." Kane worried. "Tyrons don't run away!"

A contemplative silence reigned between the two men as they considered what the answer to Kane's uncomfortable question might be. They didn't have to wonder long.

Whish! Without warning, the burning odour of searer rounds filled the air as prisoners fell in every direction. Diving for non-existent cover, the prisoners spread all over the floor like rodents when the light goes on. His weapon at the ready, Kane looked desperately for a sign of the attacking tyrons but, with the large number of prisoners that were falling in every direction, couldn't get a glimpse of a potential target. Prisoners roared in pain as searer shots made their mark, and Kane realised the situation was on the verge of becoming a disaster. Cowering against the base of the wall, the prisoner suddenly realised that the fire was coming not from either end of the long corridor – but from above! The tyrons had emerged from chutes above the heads of the prisoners and were picking them off with ease. Immediately Kane targeted a trigger-happy tyron only a few feet away and brought him down.

"They're above! They're above!" Kane roared at the top of his voice. His fellow prisoners heard his warning over the din and looked up to see the tyrons enjoying what amounted to a turkey shoot.

"Aim up!" Kane roared again, and his call was echoed amongst the prisoners as everyone with a weapon directed fire at the chutes above. In a savage fire fight, prisoners took many hits but eventually the red-helmeted attackers came down one by one to join the prisoner dead on the floor.

When the post-battle silence began to reign, the prisoners, although delighted to have survived, were badly shaken. The usual procedure of tending the wounded, assembling the dead and disarming the tyrons began almost automatically and, in shocked silence, the prisoners gathered themselves together again as a fighting force, better armed but badly depleted. No sooner had the prisoners prepared themselves to continue, however, then another unwelcome sight greeted them further down the tunnel. Yet another band of tyrons had entered the corridor area and had begun to open fire. Instinctively Kane and his comrades fired back, anger and frustration driving them into yet another confrontation with their relentless foe.

Prisoners were already hitting the floor as the tyrons made their first salvo count. Then the return fire took out two tyrons and the battle exploded. It was at this stage that McKenzie located her companion on the visual tracker. She could see the veins standing out on Kane's neck as he strained to return fire towards the tyrons without exposing himself to the lethal shower raining down on the prisoners from the end of the corridor. McKenzie could sense the heat of battle, even from her remote location, as she watched the prisoners hold their ground against the tyrons. She watched as Kane, having swung out from around the corner at medium height level, fired a single blast at a tyron in a kneeling position to the side of the corridor ahead. As he swung back around, Kane saw the tyron fall. His back pressed up against the wall, the prisoner took a deep breath. Every battle so far had claimed casualties. This one was no exception. Lying in front of him in the corridor lay at least ten prisoners who were now free of Korb-1 and joining their ancestors in the spirit world. For them, the battle for liberation was over. Three tyrons were laid low as well – victims also, Kane felt, of a system that was so corrupt that it had convinced itself that its every deed was not only justified but necessary and that those who questioned it were terrorists with no rights.

Observing the bodies of the tyrons, Kane felt it ironic that those who had made information the be-all and end-all of existence, the sophisticated currency of power, should have to resort to the oldest and crudest form of control known to the species – brute force. How thin was the mask of respectability worn by the Regime! How easy it was for them to revert to their real intent – utter and total control by whatever means necessary. In a strange way, Kane felt that the Master in his smug position of authority had really deluded *himself* into believing that violence would never be required as a tool of control on the kolony. For the Master, the regular and 'generous' helping of information regarding the impossibility of escape and the unrealistic nature of holding any hope of an alternative to a 'productive' life of labour on the kolony were to be sufficient to smother any urge to test the parameters. The Master's approach had succeeded to a certain extent, though whether the bird of freedom could be netted down and prevented from flying forever was arguable. Certainly Kane had never any intention of making Korb-1 his home for the rest of his natural life and no amount of preaching by the Master was ever going to change that. But maybe the Master knew what he was doing after all. If the majority of the prisoners could be demotivated and deprived of any real expectation of freedom, then the number of 'dedicated terrorists', as his security chiefs would describe them, would be limited. In that case, the securocrats could ignore the majority of the prisoners and focus all their energy on monitoring the malcontents who would never relax until they had either escaped or died in the attempt.

Kane was obviously one of them. Since his arrival on the kolony, every sinew of the prisoner's being had been focused on ultimately gaining the upper hand on his captors and regaining control over his existence. His sensual encounters with Thorsen almost always ended with a discussion on how to get free, how to fly away and leave the ugly nightmare that was Korb-1 behind. The Master's nauseating speeches served only to convince this prisoner that attempt at escape, whether successful or not, was an *imperative* for anyone hoping to retain his dignity and his sanity. At the end of the day – another irony – it appeared that it was the Master's security zealot, Windsor, who had imperilled his boss's carefully engineered strategy. It was Windsor who had goaded the prisoners to the point of insurrection, leaving them no option but to rise up. This was Windsor's rebellion, Windsor's war – not Nevin's or Kane's. If it were successful, it would be Windsor's damning legacy to the Korb-1 Experiment.

57 WHOSE TURN TO DIE?

Looking at the casualties of *Windsor's War* strewn around in front of him, Kane wondered when it would be his turn to die. Despite his regular tussles with the regime, the prisoner had never sensed his own mortality so keenly before. Any day – any moment – could be his last in the chaos that the Master used proudly proclaim 'an orderly society'. Kane realised that that moment could be waiting for him literally around the corner right now. All of a sudden, a strange feeling come over the prisoner. If this was to be his final moment, why not meet it head on? Why not look Fate right in the eye and ask it the question most people didn't dare to ask? Why not find out himself if this really was his time to go? In an impulsive split second, Kane launched himself out into the corridor, and rolled down towards the bodies of two of the dead tyrons. As he did, another prisoner fell dead behind him. Lying down behind the tyrons, Kane had a sense that the battle was actually taking place around him but not really involving him.

Stretched out flat on the floor, Kane observed the course of events as they unfolded. More prisoners fell as the tyrons doggedly held up the advancing column. So far, it was probably lucky hits that were downing tyrons and the advantage was still with the regime's hardened soldiers. As long as they held firm, prisoners would die and no progress would be made. Looking over the bodies of the slain, Kane could see that four tyrons were all that stood between the prisoners and their objective of rejoining the main party. Maybe now was the time to push Citizen Fate to answer his question for once and for all. The two fallen tyrons had stun-grenades in their belts. Stretching towards them, Kane removed three grenades, then, pausing for one deep breath, primed all three and hurled them over the fallen bodies towards the tyrons at the end of the corridor.

Exploding simultaneously, the grenades surprised the tyrons who had no expectation that anything other than searer fire would be trained on them and, indeed, so far in the conflict the prisoners had not tested any other element of their newfound tool-kit. In a state of confusion, the tyrons stumbled around in the corridor, one of them firing wildly as he bounced against the wall, killing a prisoner with a chance hit. Recognising that the initiative was now theirs, the prisoners made no mistakes. Everyone with a searer blasted the tyrons and soon the bloody battle was at an end.

McKenzie regarded the action with a mixture of horror and pride. Her knowledge of the military prowess of the tyrons made her pity anyone who had to stand against them, particularly untrained and semi-armed prisoners. But the manner in which the prisoners had bravely stood their ground and overcome great odds elated her. Perhaps the dream was about to come true? Perhaps it really *could* be done? McKenzie observed her companion with admiration.

In the aftermath of the encounter, Kane was surrounded by prisoners congratulating him on his heroism. Karnassis was amongst them.

"You're beginning to like this, aren't you?" she asked the hero of the hour, a confident smile on her face.

"I'll only like it when it's all over!" Kane replied, serious but trying hard not to appear sombre.

"Let's hope that won't be much longer!" Karnassis added.

Kane thought for a minute, then made a suggestion.

"I've been thinking, Angela. We seem to be always meeting these robots around the corner, just when we think we're in the clear. Wouldn't it be useful to know where they are and either avoid them or get them before they get us?"

"Of course it would, Kevin, but how would we do that?"

"I've an idea", was Kane's promising response.

Listening intently to her comrade's plan, Karnassis was more than surprised to hear that Kane had "some knowledge" of the layout of the kolony and would be able to scout ahead of the troop to establish the strength and location of the tyron forces.

"Where did you get this information, Kane?" Karnassis enquired eagerly.

"Well, Nevin wanted us to find out what we could – and I met with some success!"

Kane observed the troop leader looking in her mind's eye at the potential of the kind of operation Kane was offering to pull off. Then a smile broke on to her face and she nodded to her company's hero: "Go for it!"

Not wasting any time, Kane chose Dayton, Nielsen and Pedersen to accompany him on his reconnaissance. With these three, the prisoner was sure he had a team he could rely on. Kane agreed the approach with the other three. He would lead the team, while Pedersen would protect the rear. Silence was an absolute necessity. Disappearing into a hatch in the ceiling above their colleagues, the mission began.

Kane brought his unit in the direction of the Triple B Junction, where it was hoped his party would liase with the other prisoner bands. The overhead passage was surprisingly spacious and the four were able to make significant progress in a short time. After a while, the team stopped, following a signal from Kane, who pointed below and then proceeded to lift the grid in the passage floor. The other three tensed as Kane looked down into the corridor below. Closing the grid again, Kane used his hands to report to the others. Seven fingers signalled a tyron team of seven, while a slow movement of his hand gave the direction in which the tyrons were moving. Kane then indicated that the team should wait until the tyrons had passed below, then open the grid, drop down and take them from the rear, with Nielsen remaining at the hatch ready to open fire from above. Kane was to take the last two, Pedersen the second two, Dayton the first duo and Nielsen was to take out the leading tyron. Holding up his hand one more time, Kane signalled a count of five before the hit. All four took deep breaths and got ready. Then, as Kane signalled five, he burst the grill open and dropped down behind the tyrons, opening fire almost instantly. Pedersen and Dayton followed immediately, firing as they fell. Six of the tyrons were hit and went down. The leader, however, responded with speed and trained his weapon on Dayton, who had slipped after delivering his fatal message to his two target tyrons. But, as the tyron hit the trigger, Dayton managed to throw himself out of the line of fire and the shot hit the ground. With the tyron focussing his weapon on Dayton once more, it looked bad for Kane's close friend, but a sizzling shot from Nielsen downed the tyron and he joined his colleagues in the tyron afterworld.

On his back, Dayton looked up and smiled at Nielsen, who beamed a wide smile in response. Meanwhile, Kane and Pedersen looked up and down the corridor to see if the commotion had attracted any unwelcome attention. Nobody appeared. Within a minute, the tyrons' weapons had been collected and the team was back in the passage way, quietly congratulating one another on a successful operation. At Kane's signal, they moved on.

McKenzie was sitting on the edge of her seat watching a victorious band of prisoners marching along the Green Corridor towards the Purple Assembly Point. PAP was the nearest open area close to the Administrative Centre and only two corridors away from the Suite of the Master himself. Looking at the other views available, the Security Officer saw prisoners who had survived clashes with the tyrons appear from every direction and converge on the PAP. McKenzie wondered what this would mean. There was no way the security forces would allow anyone to advance beyond that point. To do so would be to allow control over the entire kolony to pass into the hands of the insurgents. No matter who was in control of the tyrons, they weren't going to allow that to happen.

McKenzie was wakened from her reverie by the shrill voice of Security Officer Simpson in her ear: "Update – what's the position?"

McKenzie hesitated, wondering what to say. Giving a truthful account would imperil the prisoners and seal their fate. Giving a totally misleading account would assist the prisoners but, in the event of their failure, expose McKenzie to the regime as a fifth column – the enemy within.

Simpson repeated her question, her voice more shrill: "I repeat: Security Position Global?"

McKenzie decided to compromise: "Position Global Compromised! Partial Convergence of Subjects in Area Central. Numbers under 400."

"Report Any Significant Change Immediately! Clear?" Simpson ordered sharply.

"Clear!" McKenzie responded, attempting to mask her betrayal of the regime with a vocal expression of enthusiasm.

When the echo of the Security Officer's harsh voice had left her head, McKenzie wondered what the reaction of the Security Forces would be now. The mutiny by the tyrons had taken the kontrollers as much by surprise as the prisoners' resultant revolt. It still wasn't clear to McKenzie who was calling the shots but she was convinced that Windsor was playing his final hand in the end-game. The Master hadn't been seen since the kolony exploded but was understood to be attempting to wrest back control of the situation. Was he considering his position? Would he end up losing no matter which side won? From what she knew of the man, McKenzie believed the Master wouldn't give up without a fight or a crafty trick or two. He loved his pretty little kolony too much to simply hand it over to either the prisoners or the mutineers. He was probably presently engaged in assuring himself of the support of the main group of kontrollers and desperately trying to make contact with loyal elements amongst the tyrons.

The more she thought about the situation, the more McKenzie was convinced that the prisoners now had a real chance of success – certainly the best they ever would. The regime was divided and crumbling. The tyrons were on the rampage, apparently following no central instructions, and the prisoners had proven the tyrons' reputation of invincibility to be less than totally deserved. Added to that was the fact that whatever branch of the kolony regime they were up against would not have the support of the other. In fact, victory for the prisoners over one side of the Administration would delight the other and set them up to blame their rivals for whatever went wrong.

More importantly for McKenzie, however, was not what the regime would do, but what would she do? If she was to make an intervention in favour of the prisoners it would have to be decisive. If not, then her cover would be blown and she herself would become just another casualty of a failed insurrection. If the insurrection appeared to be about to fail, no matter what the Assistant Security Officer did, then should she just bit her lip and not react at all and hope to get another chance another day? Realistically this was probably going to be the last opportunity for a long time. It could even be the last one ever. Deep in reflection, McKenzie viewed the latest incoming images from around the kolony. All the while, one thought was developing clearly in her mind – whatever she did, her conscience would not allow her to walk away. It was a question of finding the right way to make a telling intervention.

IN THE PASSAGE ABOVE the corridor, Kane and his colleagues paused once more. This time the reason was the presence below of a large force of tyrons, almost fifty in number. Kane signalled to his colleagues to halt and be particularly quiet while the enemy passed below. It would be suicide to attack such a large force and there was no other option but to let them pass. The presence of such a large force in close proximity to the prisoners posed an extremely serious threat. If they came across Karnassis group, the result could be devastating. Kane knew he must get back to the main group quickly and warn them. But first they would have to wait until the tyrons had moved on. The four sat in the passage, anxiously listening as the tyrons passed below, like prehistoric humans hiding in a cave from a ferocious predatory beast. The noise below fading into the distance, Kane decided to take a look through the nearest grid to see if the coast was now clear. As he did, the others waited eagerly for his report. Almost immediately, Kane closed the grid and looked towards his colleagues with a look of amazement in his eyes. The three, realising that something important was going down, eagerly awaited an explanation.

Kane signalled them to wait and then looked down again. Then, closing the grid once more, Kane whispered the news to his colleagues.

"It's Windsor, with two others. Right below us. I'm sure it's him. I recognise the bastard from the time of my arrest. I'll never forget him!"

The team pondered their options. Their first reaction was that they had got too close to the tyrons and should back off as soon as possible in order to warn the others. But soon another idea occurred to the four and the smiles they exchanged signalled the daring thought they now shared.

58 THUS BLOW THE WINDS OF WAR

THE FOUR PRISONERS OBSERVED the animated kontroller in the corridor below as he gestured to his accomplices. By their uniforms, Kane concluded the other two must be tyron officers, taking their instructions from their newfound hero. The officers listened intently as Windsor apparently dished out commands and they both nodded in unison at various stages to signal their agreement.

Kane and his friends looked at one another again. "It's now or never!" Kane announced in a whisper. If they move off, we'll hardly get this chance again. If we swoop now, we can grab Windsor and bring him back to the company!"

Accepting his comrades' silence as agreement, Kane gave the instructions. "We'll move on the count of ten", he announced. "You take the one on the right", he told Nielsen. "The one on the left is yours, Andy. You two will drop first and fire immediately. Tom and I will follow and grab

Windsor. After you down the officers, help us get Windsor under control, take the officers' weapons and then join us in the tunnel! Are we ready?"

The committed expressions on the faces of Kane's colleagues said it all and the prisoner didn't need to ask again. At the count of ten, the four were in the corridor and had the tyron officers down before Windsor knew what was happening. The look of horror on the kontroller's face as he realised what was taking place gave a particular sense of satisfaction to both Kane and Pedersen, who had seen the scarred face in a wholly different environment not too long ago. Then it was the arrogant face of domination and power. Now it was the face of one who was suddenly aware that the roles were about to be reversed. The hunter was becoming the prey and he didn't like it. Kane made sure to look Windsor in the eye for that brief decisive moment. Nielsen and Dayton were splendid. Landing on their feet together and opening fire simultaneously, their intervention was clinical. In a matter of seconds, the man who controlled the entire tyron force was on his own and facing those who would hold him to account for his actions. As soon as Nielsen and Dayton had closed the grill behind them, a stun shot rendered Windsor immobile and an ecstatic quartet made their way back towards their comrades with their unexpected booty.

MCKENZIE COULDN'T BELIEVE HER eyes when she saw the incident unfolding on her security screen. The arrival of Kane and his colleagues out of the blue to snatch Windsor was an action of such daring that it left the assistant security officer almost speechless. Time and again, she played the visual to take in the audacity of it all. Her admiration for Kane's achievement was mixed with a sense of pride that it was the knowledge of the kolony layout that she had given the prisoner that had made it all possible. But the sheer clinical nature of the operation amazed McKenzie. These prisoners were obviously no pushovers. In one brief action, they had taken the initiative and taken out one of the main players in the game. This would be a serious setback for the hawks in the security camp and a major boost for the Master and his establishment. It was also a significant triumph for the prisoners but the extent to which this turn of events would actually change the course of the game depended on the use they would make of their new asset. Still awestruck, McKenzie wondered what *she* should do next. The later the regime found out about Windsor's capture, the better. The prisoners would have more time to decide on how best to capitalise on their good fortune and the hawks less of an opportunity to prepare a response. McKenzie decided to sit on her remarkable discovery until word came in that Windsor was actually missing. Then she would probably do a scan to see if there was any sign of the maniac. In the meantime, she would enjoy with pride her comrade's monumental achievement.

When Kane's fellow insurgents saw him and his accomplices drop down into the corridor to rejoin them, they were relieved that their comrades had returned safely and impressed by their daring. When they dragged a fifth party down after them, the prisoners stopped to stare. When the extra man turned out to be Kontroller Windsor himself, the personification of all that was oppressive for the prisoners in the kolony, a wild spontaneous deafening cheer went up.

"Jeez, Kane, How did you manage *that?*" Karnassis asked in amazement.

"A present from the gods! Looks like Fate might be taking a shine to us after all!" Kane responded with a broad smile.

"What are we going to do with him?" the commander asked.

"Oh, we've lots of options", Kane responded. "We can try him and execute him. We can interrogate him to find out where we should concentrate our forces in order to escape. We can even take him with us, if we succeed – just for fun!"

"I like it, Kane. You're impressive!" the woman responded, displaying a warm smile.

SIMPSON WAS ENJOYING THE chaos in the kolony to the full – the Master locked away in his quarters attempting to regain control of his precious creation, the prisoners running riot throughout the facility, the tyrons wreaking bloody vengeance for their murdered colleagues and Kommander Windsor taking his rightful place as *de facto* Master of the entire kolony – Destiny was taking a hand in events at last, she believed. The Master's determination to contain the mayhem to the prison area and not to allow it to spill out into the other areas of the kolony, nor indeed to allow word of it to get back to NC authorities, played straight into Windsor's hands. The longer he had to create chaos, the harder it would be for the Master to contain it, and the more likely it was that 'the old fool', as both Windsor and Simpson referred to him, would lose total control of events. With Windsor in control, Simpson would once again be in a position of influence – in reality, the 'real Master', reading every situation astutely and providing Windsor with a vital insight that his more military approach would lack. In essence, she would be the first lady of Korb-1, the leader in everything but name.

All of the prisoner bands were eager to be present when Windsor awoke to find himself in the hands of the prisoners he despised so much. They were granted their wish soon when Karnassis ordered that the still lifeless form of the kontroller be tied to a pipe on a raised area so that everyone would get a good view as the bully awoke and took in the reality of his new situation. There was general silence in the Chamber as Windsor started to rouse himself from his zennor-induced slumber. First, to the amusement of the assembled prisoners, he emitted a few low grunts, followed by a number of louder snorts. Then as the powerful leader of the rampant tyrons focused on the scene before him, the obvious realisation set in that, rather than being at the head of a formidable force of tyron soldiers, the man who regarded himself as a natural leader of men and women was in fact a captive in the hands of the very people whose lives he had vowed to make miserable – the vile gang of subversives that the Master had failed so miserably to control. Many in the crowd laughed as Windsor attempted to weigh up his newfound situation while at the same time retaining his military bearing and dignity. When the subject had regained his composure, Karnassis spoke.

"Welcome to our merry little band, Citizen Windsor!" she announced, deliberately using the egalitarian term of address adopted centuries before by those who would reject titles of domination and distinction.

"I am Kontroller Windsor!" the bound brute barked in response.

"Not so, Citizen. There are no kontrollers here, no Masters either – just citizens. Citizens of a free society called Korb. You are welcome to join us in our society if you are capable of purging yourself of hatred, domination and control", was Karnassis' dignified reply.

The prisoners were impressed by their leader's ability to gain the upper hand in the initial verbal encounter with a man used only to barking out orders to the compliant.

"There are no citizens here – you are prisoners, dangerous subversive prisoners!" Windsor roared again.

Observing the once arrogant hunter now snared in a trap of his own making, Kane felt little respect for Windsor. *Windsor's World* was a small one, inhabited by nasty monsters that the wild kontroller knew it was his duty to destroy. He was, and would always be, blind to that middle universe where most people dwelt, where life was rarely black and white and people attempted to live their lives, take the hard decisions when they had to, and be as happy as they could in their circumstances. To Windsor, such a life was a cowardly choice, involving, as it did, the avoidance of confrontation. Confrontation was the essence of *his* existence and he had spent his life looking for demons to confront. Most of the prisoners listening to the diatribe now had themselves attempted to live the easy life once upon a time, but brutes like Windsor had ultimately left them little choice but to take action and, when they did, there was no going back.

SIMPSON WAS BECOMING A little uneasy. Something was bothering her but she couldn't really make out what it was. Something was wrong. Then, suddenly, a message arrived. It was McKenzie. A tyron report had been received that Kontroller Windsor was missing. Two tyron officers in whose company he had last been seen had been found seared – there was no sign of Windsor. The dark lady jumped to her feet, the serious expression on her face betraying her worst fears. If Windsor was gone ……..

Rushing in to the Security Centre, Simpson demanded that McKenzie locate the last visual of the kontroller immediately. McKenzie replied that she had just completed the search and had concluded that Windsor had been captured by the prisoners. In evidence, she ran a carefully edited version of her original take, with the faces of the prisoners excluded from every scene.

Simpson was horrified. "Captured?" she asked incredulously. "Captured? He can't be captured – he's the most powerful man in the kolony! He can't be captured! He can't be! My God!"

With Simpson staring deep into an uncertain future without Windsor, McKenzie put on a suitably grave face in order to conceal her real feelings. Enjoying the sight of the manipulative mistress in a state of panic, she smiled an invisible smile. McKenzie wasn't blind to the real reason for her senior accomplice's distress. Anyone who knew the dark lady knew that her only real concern in the world was her own carefully calculated agenda. Simpson's main player had been removed from the board and now she realised that she herself could soon be out of the game.

Putting her left hand to her forehead, Simpson asked herself aloud what she should do. Then, almost automatically, she touched her communicator and sought to contact the missing kontroller. "Kontroller Windsor! Kontroller Windsor! Please respond!" Waiting a while, she repeated: "Kontroller Windsor! Please respond!" But there was no response from Windsor.

IN A KORB SUPERVISION Chamber in the Blue Corridor, Kontroller Windsor was not in a position to respond to the message crackling on his communicator. Struggling to free his hands to communicate with Simpson, he saw Dayton approach and attempt to grab the communicator. Windsor, furious at the audacity of the prisoner, continued to wriggle and twist in order to free his hands. As Dayton struggled to get control of the communication device, Windsor at last managed to get a hand free. Wasting no time, the kontroller, noticing the young man's zennor hanging idly on his shoulder, grabbed the weapon and immediately released a number of rounds. Dayton jumped back in a response of self-protection only to see two prisoners who had got too close to the raging captive fall to the ground. The bulk of the prisoners who had crammed around to view their captive retreated and sought cover as Windsor fired indiscriminately into their ranks, and another prisoner fell dead. Panic filled the air as Windsor continued to fire, then suddenly a final shot ended the crisis as Windsor fell limp, the zennor falling out of his hand. With Dayton seizing the weapon lest Windsor use it again, all eyes turned to look at Pedersen, a serious look on his face and his zennor still focused on Windsor.

Immediately, Kane and Karnassis ran towards Windsor, Karnassis announcing, after failing to locate a pulse, that the kontroller was dead.

The suddenness of the incident took everyone by surprise. Windsor had been the prisoners' prize catch in the whole campaign, having fallen unexpectedly into their hands. He was to be their vital card, their hostage, their door-opener, their ticket out. Now he was dead, a useless piece of space detritus, a former player in the game, a dead card. The prisoners looked at one another, wondering how to deal with this latest unexpected turn in events. Kane broke the silence: "Well done, Tom! You saved many lives! Well done!"

Pedersen, himself still taken aback by the incident, nodded slowly in response.

"Thus blow the winds of war!" Karnassis proclaimed, attempting to give a meaning to what had taken place. Then she continued in an upbeat tone: "Put a rope on him and we'll drag him along in case we need him. He might come in useful yet!"

59 FREE KORB

THE EXCITEMENT WAS RUNNING through the air like electricity through water. Nevin and his team of leaders stood on the plinth of a larger than life statue entitled 'Korb Kooperation', an ugly piece of work showing the various participants (willing and otherwise) in the korb project, all carrying out their roles in perfect harmony. Nevin considered it an appropriate backdrop for the events that were now taking place and the irony of it all wasn't lost on the multitude of prisoners now gathering for their final rendezvous with Fate. The triumphant companies of prisoners marched proudly into the hall, some badly battered and depleted, others in relatively good shape and obviously boosted by their unexpected successes against their oppressors. Many showed all the signs of having been through the mill. Battered and bruised, they hobbled, limped and staggered in to join their fellow combatants. Every new group was greeted by those gathered inside with a resounding cheer of welcome and congratulations. The welcome was not only for the individuals involved, but also for what they represented. Every prisoner that made his or her way into the Purple Junction Area was one who had stood up to the terror of the tyrons and survived. Battered and shaken as they were, these men and women were living proof that the regime and its army were not invincible. As powerful as it might be, the regime could in fact be defeated. The motley bunch of victorious prisoners marching into the junction outside the Despatch Port were literally living proof that from now on the old presumption of the inevitability of victory for the powerful was dead.

And what a mix they were! The blood- and sweat-soaked survivors represented all sections of the prisoner population. Regardless of background or political persuasion, all of the prisoners had united against the attack by the tyrons and a new alliance had been formed including those who had up to then had much to complain about but little to motivate them into rebellion. Now, rebels all, complete with experience of battle, they came together to face the last and most crucial step in their march towards freedom.

Kane's company was one of the first to arrive and the prisoner's eyes focused sharply on those he found before him as he attempted to establish which of his colleagues had survived the fighting – and who had not. With the group making its way into the Area, friends and comrades were recognised and spirited greetings exchanged. Kane was struck by the appearance of those in the hall before him. Many were injured or maimed and almost all the faces he saw before him betrayed the effects of a great struggle, both physical and mental, to survive. The welcome they gave their comrades on arrival was also an applause of assurance to themselves that, so far, they had survived and so had others, others who would share the rest of the journey over even rougher terrain.

Kane himself felt this feeling of support – of solidarity – as he in turn watched more bands of prisoners rejoin their comrades. Some of the companies were reduced to a pathetic handful of battle-scarred individuals while others appeared to have fared better and managed to get through with minimum casualties. Kane carefully studied the different faces as they came in and saw the same signs of battle-weariness and stress on them all. It was clear, though, that the mood of the prisoners had been transformed since their first assembly only two days before from one of nervous foreboding to one of confident celebration. Battles had been won, lives had been changed, hope had lived to fight another day. Kane joined in the tumultuous applause, as his comrades returned from their various brushes with the forces of death, and cheered loudly when he noticed friends arriving through the gate. O'Hara, Gilmore, Reilly and others joined the throng and returned Kane's warm salute in the sea of hands.

The natural exhilaration that most prisoners experienced on rejoining their comrades was pushed to levels of hysteria when Karnassis' band arrived carrying the limp body of Kontroller Windsor on a stretcher. That the prisoners had not only fought the tyrons and scattered them in their path but had done to death one of the regimes most belligerent leaders was a cause of amazement amongst the prisoners and a source of inspiration to many. That the body of the one who had led the campaign to turn the difficult life of the prisoners of Korb-1 to one of slavery and oppression was now on display amongst his former victims as a trophy of war gave reality to the prisoners' belief that they could now snap the chains that had for so long shackled their lives and tied down their very imagination. That the prisoners of Korb-1 now believed they could be free was the proof that the first of these shackles had been broken.

Gradually, the tumult died down to a buzz of conversation all over the hall as the survivors swapped tales of exchanging searer fire with the devil and wrestling with death. Kane, Dayton, Pedersen and Nielsen sat down together, proud to have got this far and conscious of the dangerous path that lay ahead. Their tunics stained with the soil of battle, they were older and wiser now than the group that had so often sat together in the Dining Hall to exchange fantasies of escape from Korb-1. Now, perhaps, those fanciful dreams were about to be realised. The new lives, the organic vegetable store, the dancing school, the journalist job with the local newsite – maybe they could all come true. Maybe it was all possible now.

Word went around the hall that Nevin was about to speak and a hush descended. Kane observed Nevin closely. The veteran had the appearance of someone who had taken a big gamble and was just beginning to believe it might actually pay off. Kenning stood by his side, offering a quiet reassuring glance as the leader prepared to address his forces.

"Fellow citizens of Free Korb", Nevin began, "welcome to the gateway to freedom!"

A loud cheer of acclaim around the hall greeted Nevin's opening words. The confirmation that their heroic struggle against the tyrons had delivered them to the very threshold of liberation was balm to their ears. The years of imprisonment, the denial of life on Earth and of all the human relationships that had been left behind, the removal of hope and the bloody battles of the last few days would not have been in vain if they ultimately led the prisoners of Korb-1 to their freedom. That that freedom was now only a few steps away put all the years of suffering and oppression in context, and that context was one of final vindication and liberation. And ultimate liberation was the theme taken up by the prisoners' leader.

"We have seen the dark days of imprisonment and despair but now we have taken our destiny into our own hands. Those who told us we had no chance of escape, no chance of liberation, no chance of regaining control over our own destiny have been given a fitting response. Their tyrons have experienced defeat for the first time – at our hands. Their so-called kontrollers have seen themselves outwitted by those whose motivation far exceeds their own. And, let us not forget, the one whose arrogance told us all we had no chance of freedom now faces eternity in Korb-1 while we make our way along the road to freedom."

More applause followed as Nevin told the assembled prisoners that their future was now in their own hands. He warned them not to become complacent, however – that the regime would still do everything in its power to prevent their escape.

"Our next stop is the Despatch Port Departure Area. We do not seek confrontation with the enemy but if Fate decides we must face down the tyrons for once and for all, that we will do. If we do that, nothing will stand between us and total control of the kolony. But every one of you must fight – and fight as never before. From here on in, you are fighting not only for those who have died along the way, not only for yourselves, and not only for the truth – but for a new generation, for the children you never had, for a new world where there are no tyrons, no kontrollers and no masters. Let us go there – now!"

The assembled crowd burst into spontaneous celebration as their leader finished. Then, gradually, a strange quiet descended as they prepared themselves for what could be their final battle.

DAYTON SPOKE TO KANE. "It looks like we're almost there!" he said optimistically.

Kane smiled. "Don't be so sure, Andy. There's a long way to go yet. The regime may seem to be in disarray but they have a lot of resources at their disposal that haven't even come into play yet."

Dayton thought for a minute, considering Kane's negative reply.

"Surely there can be no going back now?" he asked his friend, his eyes looking into a distant future. "The only way has to be out."

"You've only won when the game's over," Kane replied, pausing momentarily before announcing cautiously: "and the game isn't over yet!"

The two men's thoughts were abruptly interrupted when two prisoners suddenly came rushing in from the Green Sector Gate. They were dirty and dishevelled and showed all the signs of having recently been in battle. Rushing up to Nevin, they announced in urgent tones: "Tyrons. A large troop. Only minutes away!"

Immediately an atmosphere of emergency bordering on panic swept through the assembled prisoners. Dayton looked at Kane as if realising that his friend may not have been unjustified in questioning his enthusiasm. Without saying anymore, both men clasped hands in a reassuring gesture, then parted to take up their respective positions.

The area was now a mass of moving bodies urgently attempting to link up with their groups and move on to their objectives before their mortal enemies arrived in force. Enthusiasm and reluctance, fear and courage, hope and despair all joined together to create a force that the oppressor would now have to reckon with.

The prisoners left the Purple Junction speedily but without losing their shape as a fighting force. Whether they feared the arrival of a large band of tyrons or not, they were determined not to allow the threat of yet another, though more serious, confrontation upset their composure and organisation. Band after band marched out and up the wide passage towards the Despatch Port, their speed and formation belying the impact of two days fighting and little sleep on their strained bodies and stressed minds and giving an impression of courage and determination that was in itself a motivator for those whose spirits were flagging.

Their step gaining confidence with every metre they progressed, the prisoners soon found themselves at the gate of the Despatch Port. Massing together again, Nevin realised his team had a problem. The gate was a secure structure, built as part of the surrounding wall and only capable of being opened by palm security code. How on Korb were the prisoners to get through this? "Let's ram it!" one enthusiastic prisoner roared, and his sincere but unrealistic suggestion was taken up by other prisoners and soon echoed throughout the area.

Nevin and his lieutenants looked at one another, hoping an inspirational thought would emerge to resolve the situation but nobody seemed to have a useful idea. Dayton's "can we shoot it open?" was met with a sad and silent nod of negativity. Then Kane and Karnassis spoke to one another before calling the team who were carrying Windsor to the front.

"Let's not forget our illustrious guest!" Karnassis suggested, while Kane smiled a broad smile.

"Yes!" added Pedersen enthusiastically, "I knew he would be willing to give us a hand!"

Grasping the meaning of his colleagues' sarcastic announcements, Nevin's eyes lit up. "Bring the good man forward!" he ordered. Streever and Pedersen carried the former kontroller and tyron war hero to the front. Bringing their trophy towards the gateway and propping him against the wall, they placed the palm of the dead man's right hand on the palm-print sensor. Immediately, the gate opened and a mechanical voice announced "Enter, Kontroller Windsor!" To a loud cheer, the band marched through and headed for the Despatch Port.

60 BATTLE FURY

THE SENSE AMONGST THE prisoners of being pursued as prey diminished somewhat with the successful entry of the insurgent army into the Despatch Port. The fact that the limp figure of the scourge of the inmates for so long, Kontroller Windsor, could be used to gain access to this previously inapproachable sector of their confined little world enhanced the new-found feeling of confidence that inspired the otherwise weary and starving prisoners. Now they really could believe that, in the new order of things on Korb-1, anything was possible.

As they had done from the beginning of the campaign, Kane and Dayton marched with Karnassis' band. Many who had begun that march with enthusiasm and hope were no longer with their comrades, having fallen along the way, and Kane found himself thinking of those who had not made it this far. What factors, he wondered, determined who would die and who would live to fight another day, what decided who would fail and who would succeed? Before this day was over, Kane knew well, more lives would have been ended. Looking around at those who were marching with him along a wide passageway, he wondered how many would see tomorrow, not to mention the freedom they had all so ferociously fought to attain. He wondered would he himself survive another day.

CRRRRRGGH! A loud explosion from the direction of the rear brought Kane's mind back to the immediate. Most of the prisoners turned to look back towards the source of the deafening blast, others – including Kane – deliberately fixed their gaze ahead and marched with determination towards their destination. This was not a time to reconsider, not a time to look back. CRRRRRGGH! A second deafening explosion reverberated up through the passageway. The prisoners seemed to quicken their step on hearing the second blast and the atmosphere darkened as a threatening cloud from the direction of the explosions moved up over the throng. As the cloud – a light green colour – floated over the rear guard of the marching prisoners, a number of them fainted, hitting the ground hard – whatever weapons they had skidding along the floor to be picked up by fleeing comrades. Some of the prisoners stopped in their tracks momentarily, as if attempting to work out what exactly was happening.

"Gas!" shouted a bearded man with nervous eyes darting around in his head.

"Nerve gas! They're going to gas us!" added a slender woman with short black hair.

As the realisation grew that the regime was resorting to poisonous gas to stop the prisoners, there was a stampede from the back of the column up through the lines of those ahead. "Gas! Gas!" many shouted, as they attempted to flee the danger. Like a landslide on a rocky mountain, the ripples of fleeing prisoners moving through the ranks of their fellows soon became an avalanche. Leaders amongst the prisoners tried to stop the headlong rush by calling for calm and discipline but, at this stage, their calls were falling on the ears of those who believed their hard-fought campaign for freedom was about to end in a sudden convulsive death at the hands of their enemies. Eventually, the only option for everybody, leaders and led alike, was to join the torrent of fleeing forms in a macabre marathon. Kane reluctantly joined in and soon found himself part of an uncontrollable mob hurtling along the passageway with no clear view of where they were going. A prisoner carrying a weapon made out of a piece of piping from a korb station lost his footing and was trampled by the crowd. Kane stopped to extricate him and drag him over to the side. The man appeared to be already dead. Rejoining the running herd once more, Kane was horrified that, after all they had gone through, the prisoners' army was suddenly being reduced to what they had tried so hard to avoid becoming – a fleeing rabble.

The atmosphere in the passageway was stifling, the heat and lack of oxygen almost unbearable. A sense of claustrophobia and paranoia set in amongst the prisoners, who were now a leaderless horde, running in panic, their destination irrelevant. After about 300 metres of blank passageway, the path began to turn to the right and slope down, widening out into a chamber. At the bend in the passageway, the multitude unhesitatingly rushed on. On entering the exit chamber, however, they came to a sudden halt. For there, lined up before them, the fleeing prisoners saw a massive phalanx of tyrons, perhaps five hundred in all, armed and fully battle clad, helmet visors with gas protectors included. As each new wave of prisoners arrived down from the corridor, they stopped and stared at the nemesis that faced them, the less tall at the back sensing the threat and only imagining what lay ahead. The lines of tyrons seemed to the prisoners to be an impregnable wall – inapproachable, unassailable and impassable. An eerie silence descended as the stampede ground to a halt, the faces of the massed prisoners betraying an anxiety that had so quickly replaced their soaring confidence. The citizens of Free Korb now faced their most perilous challenge yet.

The tyrons stood motionless before the prisoners, who looked aghast at the force confronting them and attempted to assess their predicament.

None of the faces behind the myriad of darkened visors was visible to the prisoners, adding to the threat felt by the poorly armed and disorientated prisoners. Every moment felt like an hour as even the bravest in the prisoners' army realised the initiative was no longer theirs and that they were now facing the enemy in a situation not of their choosing. The tyrons remained still, their commander aware that every moment that passed would weaken the resolve of those who could now only gasp in awe at the strength that opposed them. Nevin, having just arrived, pushed his way to the front and, casting a cold eye on the tyron force ahead, immediately realised the gravity of the new situation. His flushed features soon turned sallow.

Eventually, all the prisoners were assembled on the slanting corridor in full view of the massive tyron force. Total silence reigned on all sides, as the prisoner's expressions barely concealed the fear and panic that raced through their veins. The tyrons darkened visors revealed nothing, but suggested that the rebels' account was about to be reckoned and paid in full.

After what seemed like an eternity to the trapped prisoners, a gap opened up in the tyrons front line and a figure emerged. It was the Master. Resplendent in his purple robes, he calmly viewed the host of prisoners crammed into the space in front of him. Then, pushing back his cloak in theatrical fashion, he began to speak.

"Prisoners of Korb-1, I am aghast that my efforts to reach an accommodation with you, despite your criminal activities in the past, have been thrown back in my face. I realise that others may have made serious errors and brought us all to the edge of oblivion. But I, at all times, have striven to create an atmosphere of harmony and cooperation amongst us that would be to the mutual advantage of all. I beseech you, for the last time, to finally come to your senses and accept the lawful authority that has the onerous responsibility of running this kolony for the benefit of all."

There was a long moment of silence and then a bearded man with a deep voice responded: "Never! Never! We want freedom now!" As soon as these words of defiance were uttered, they were taken up by those around the bearded man and were soon echoed around the chamber. Before long, the entire body of prisoners was chanting fearlessly: "Freedom now! Freedom now! Freedom now!"

As the prisoners' response rained down on the Master, a movement on their right hand side began to attract the attention of the prisoners. Nevin, looking tired and worn-out, had moved to mount a stanchion at the sidewall. Quiet returned as he began to speak.

"Prisoners of Korb", he roared, "That red line lies between us and freedom. We must consider carefully what our hearts and minds tell us now! It may be ......"

Suddenly, the attention of all assembled moved from Nevin and focused on an object that had been hurled from amongst the prisoners and had landed a few feet away from the tyrons. For a frozen millisecond, those focussing on the object attempted to identify it. Kane soon realised what it was. A scatter bomb! Almost simultaneously, two tyrons ran forward and kicked the object back towards the prisoners. In an instant, it detonated, blasting prisoners in every direction. At the same time, a zennor shot cracked into Nevin's head and the veteran leader fell to the ground. Mayhem ensued as firing broke out in every direction. Almost simultaneously, a communal roar of anger swept up from the prisoners' ranks towards their oppressors, and the insurgents, an army once again, surged forward like a mighty wave. Ignoring the overwhelming advantage carried by the forces lined up against them, the prisoners ran like wild beasts at their tormentors.

As The Master vanished behind the ranks of the tyrons, the tyron kommander responded without delay. Whispering into his mouthpiece, he gave the order to "fire at will – zennor cannon!" Instantly, a volley of fire crashed across the body of prisoners moving forward. In a cacophony of screams and roars, an entire line of prisoners fell. Without hesitating, the prisoners behind continued on, uttering what seemed above the din to be a primitive and unrecognisable war cry as they went. Another zennor blast decimated their ranks. Still, the prisoners advanced.

Dayton, four or five lines back, stopped, assessed the situation and roared: "Those with arms, lie down and take aim. Make every shot count!" Many of those within earshot reacted immediately, and soon the sight of falling tyrons welcomed the advancing prisoners.

The scene soon became one of total carnage, tyrons firing at will and making every shot count, armed prisoners returning fire with equal success, and unarmed prisoners rushing headlong at the enemy lines in the knowledge that to do anything else now would be to die dishonourably. Kane observed his colleague Dayton, assisted by Nielsen, marshalling more and more of the prisoners and organising them into an effective fighting force once more. Under their direction, those prisoners with arms utilised them to maximum effect, raining fire on the enemy with great success. Kane installed himself behind the piled-up bodies of fallen prisoners and downed a tyron with every shot. The prisoner sensed that the situation was beginning to change. The insurgents had suddenly succeeded in making a battle out of what had at first looked like being a total massacre. All across the battle zone, leadership was emerging from unexpected sources. As Dayton led the surrounding fighters with phenomenal success, directing fire and maintaining discipline, others – Streever, Schnellinger, Kieft, Iribar, O'Hara – organised the prisoners in their vicinity and together created an army once more. The number of killed and wounded was high, however, and once the casualty plateau was reached the prisoners advance slowed down and eventually ground to a halt. Both sides were now dug in behind the fallen, trading fire in a savage battle of attrition.

The surviving prisoners sensed that perhaps their journey might not have to end here after all. Perhaps Fate had not yet dealt its final hand. Perhaps, despite the loss of their leader, the rebel forces would see the victory he had motivated them so much to achieve. The prisoners began to believe in themselves once more.

Suddenly – disaster! Dayton, down on one knee directing his forces, took a blast on the side of the head and, uttering a short muffled sound, fell on the spot. Observing her partner falling, Nielsen froze in horror, only to receive a shot in the face and join him on the ground. Soon Karnassis and other leaders were also downed. Kane was aghast. Running over to his colleague, despite the tyron fire, he lifted up his friend's head and called to him: "Andy! Andy! Don't go now! We're going to make it! Don't go now!" Kane thought he saw a slight smile on his friend's lips in response to his call, but then – nothing more. Despite the chaos of battle surrounding him, Kane felt his mind being pulled back to the first time he had met Andrew Dayton. Taking an immediate liking to the good-humoured young man, who was wakening up in a strange new world, Kane had done his best to make the young novo feel, if not at home, at least welcome amongst his fellow prisoners. Soon they were close friends, kindred spirits in an alien world. Now he was gone.

Zzzsh! Kane fell to the floor in pain, his shoulder hit by a tyron searer blast. His immediate reaction was to roll over and away from the scene. Hitting the base of the right wall, he found himself lying beside the fallen Nevin. Kane looked at his stricken leader. Apart from the scorch mark on the side of his face, the prisoners' chief seemed to be merely resting for the next battle. But Nevin's battles were over now. He was in peace, his contribution made, his war over.

More fire shook the area around Kane. Huddling low against the wall, he observed the course of the battle. Bodies lay scattered in every direction, yet fire still rained all around. The red-clad bodies of the fallen tyrons made an encouraging spectacle for the prisoners but the sight of their own fallen comrades brought home the seriousness of their plight.

Gradually Kane noticed the tyrons had stopped firing. Then the prisoners' fire began to die down in response. Kane watched closely, wondering what the next step was going to be. Would there be a truce? Would there be negotiations? Was there going to be a way-out, after all? Silence descended on the vast chamber as everybody waited for the next step to become clear.

Kane observed the now decimated prisoner force. Tired, weary and anxious faces, unwilling veterans of an unexpected war, watched eagerly for an indication of what was in store. They hadn't long to wait. Suddenly, a voice shouted in panic: "Gas!" The warning was repeated with varying degrees of alarm around the Chamber. "Gas! Gas!" The short simple monosyllabic word that had caused so much terror earlier had the same disastrous effect once more. Almost immediately, the surviving prisoners, most of them bearing arms now, recommenced firing and a ferocious fire fight blasted the tyron front line. Kane tried to get to his feet to gather a zennor from a fallen comrade, but couldn't make it and stumbled to the ground. As the gas was siphoned into the Chamber, the lights went out, adding to the chaotic atmosphere. In the darkness, with the smell of scorched flesh in his nostrils, Kane could sense people running in every direction, the zennor blasts creating a dance macabre effect as the faces of the panicking prisoners flashed before him. In one surreal glimpse, Kane saw Pedersen downed by a zennor blast. Stunned into inaction, the prisoner's heart fell as he realised that yet another valuable member of the prisoner cadre was now gone. Suddenly, Kane felt a hand on his shoulder. Presuming it to be that of an enemy, he grabbed the assailant by the wrist and pulled them to the ground. "It's me, Kevin!" a familiar voice spoke, in reassurance. "Come on! We've got to get out of here!"

61 FREEDOM RUN

KANE AND MCKENZIE SCRAMBLED in behind the panel that McKenzie had opened in the wall and fell exhausted on the ground as it closed behind them. Trying to catch their breath and attempting to compose themselves, they looked at one another in disbelief at what had just occurred. Merciless slaughter had taken place before their very eyes. Nevin and his army had marched into a trap and paid for their desire to be free with their lives. Fate had finally made its call for the prisoners of Korb-1. Escape from the kolony had turned into what the Master had always claimed it would be – escape to oblivion.

Still in shock, Kane and McKenzie looked at one another as if to ask *'what now?'* Was a similar fate in store for them at the next stage of this dangerous journey? Neither spoke. Words would be superfluous to describe what was transpiring on the other side of the panel. Instinctively, the pair embraced, holding on tight to each other. Kane felt an energy in McKenzie's body that reinvigorated him in some strange way. It was as if she was some kind of motivational source, lifting him when he fell and driving him on when, as now, he seemed to be on the verge of defeat. For a time, their embrace gave both of them something simple that had been denied them for so long – a sense of being alone together – the only ones in a dark abandoned universe, relying on one another for heat and light, and kindness. Releasing their embrace, the two stood up slowly, realising it was time to let go. Then, following a knowing glance, they set off down the narrow tunnel together.

The service tunnel through which the fleeing duo moved to leave the bloody chaos behind curved gradually to the right and was lit by a long continuous stringer light running along the ceiling. The fugitives travelled quickly down the long tunnel, listening at every moment along the way for an indication that they were being pursued. They moved at a fast jogging pace, intent on putting as much distance as possible between themselves and the mayhem they had left behind. Side by side, they moved along the tunnel, not knowing what to expect as they followed the curvature of the shaft with its limited view of what lay ahead. After they had progressed about 300 metres, the pair slowed down and began to look at the walls of the tunnel on each side. In a few moments, McKenzie announced with a note of achievement: "Got it!" Then, as her hand touched the pressure point on the wall, the hatch opened and the pair found themselves looking into another tunnel, identical to the one through which they had just travelled. Exchanging a glance, the runaways entered and looked back as the hatch closed behind them.

Kane sensed something symbolic in the closure of the hatch behind the pair. He regarded it as a door that was closing on the unhappiest period in his life and allowing him to move on to a newer, happier phase – whatever that might entail. A strange unexpected feeling overcame him and he recalled his first day on Korb-1. He remembered waking in the confinement tray, stunned at his new surroundings, still hurt at the trauma of his arrest and mock trial. He remembered the Master's speech as the unfortunate prisoners attempted to grasp the reality of their new situation, and he remembered walking into his new prison cell for the first time. Now, Kane hoped, the hatch that had closed behind him would mark another important step on his journey into a new reality, the reality of freedom regained, whatever form that was going to take. McKenzie appeared to sense her companion's reaction to the progress they were making and, smiling, took his hand in hers, indicating her support with a tight squeeze.

The two moved at the same regular pace down the new tunnel. On reaching the end, they were presented with a choice to go right or left. Both hesitated only slightly to consult before, nodding agreement, they turned left. Soon, this tunnel would veer to the left and then, about halfway down, to the right. Just after that half-way point, the runners stopped once more, this time to survey the roof of the tunnel, just above their heads. Again, a pressure point was located and a hatch opened in the ceiling to one side of the light. Kane went up first, McKenzie followed. Once up, the pair found themselves in another tunnel, this time lit with a green stringer bulb. Two large pipes ran along the left wall. The pair continued along the green tunnel for what seemed to Kane to be a long time. The tunnel ran mostly straight but occasionally veered slightly to the left or right. Twice the escapees passed a junction but chose to continue on straight. On reaching the end of the green tunnel, the two came to a t-junction. Looking at one another teasingly, they both smiled and, looking above their heads, sought and found another pressure point. Another opening hatch brought them into a wider tunnel that seemed to stretch forever.

The fugitives had been travelling through the tunnel network for almost an hour when they came to a major junction. Kane instantly recognised the multitude of pathways from the Kolony Plan. This was the Star Junction. Only three more layers of tunnels to travel and the kolony perimeter would be reached. Kane felt a sense of excitement tingle along his spine at the thought of having got this far. No amount of wanting and yearning and imagining can prepare the fugitive for this moment. The journey from plotting and planning and hoping against hope to the penultimate step of freedom is a leap in time and reality that only those who have made it can understand. Kane now stood on that hallowed spot – the threshold of freedom. Anything beyond this was a new game. To get this far had been an achievement, but in the prisoner's mind the elation at finding himself so close to escape was tinged with the realisation that getting this far wasn't enough. To escape, the prisoner had to make it *all* the way. Kane's journey since the initial attack on the prisoners had been a success – even remembering the lay-out of the tunnels in the Kolony Plan had turned out to be an easy task – but sooner or later, he feared, the luck of the fugitive might run out. One chance meeting with a group of tyrons would be enough to render all that had been achieved so far to nought. One bad break, and the vision of freedom tantalisingly forming in the prisoner's mind could be clouded once more with the reality of incarceration or even death in the footsteps of Thorsen, Dayton, Nevin, Karnassis and all the others who had bravely attempted to grasp the freedom that was rightfully theirs.

Almost as if reading the heavy thoughts in her companion's mind, McKenzie stopped and pointed at a panel in the wall. With a nod of her head, she invited Kane inside while touching the pressure point to open the door. Once inside, McKenzie's expression became serious. Looking him straight in the eye, the woman in the red uniform, as Kane had known her for so long, spoke earnestly.

"Listen, Kevin, from here on out, it's going to become more difficult. If we meet resistance, we'll be obliterated. The system is in chaos and there's no way there'll be anybody tracking you electronically but sooner or later we'll run into someone. Here's what we've got to do. As far as I'm concerned, nobody is aware of my involvement with you. Windsor is dead. In the aftermath, he'll probably be blamed for everything that happened during the chaos. If we make it out easily, well and good, though I have my doubts. If we're stopped, you've got to use me as a hostage. I ….."

"What!" No way!" Kane interrupted, "you must be mad! We're going out of here – together!"

"Look", McKenzie returned, "be sensible. I'm an officer of the Administration. You're a prisoner. If we're stopped going out of here together, we're both finished. If, on the other hand, you use me as a shield to engineer your escape, there's a chance you'll manage to get out, and I'll be treated as the brave victim of an information terrorist who used me as a screen to make good his escape. I can get out myself then and we can meet together later."

"Look, this doesn't make sense. How are we going to meet again later? And anyway, how are we going to survive once we get out. Won't we be poisoned by the atmosphere?"

Kane hesitated, as if realising something that he hadn't considered before. Up to know, the plan had been to commandeer an Administration vessel and sail away into the sun. Now Nevin's intentions were as dead as the man himself and Kane had no other game plan. Getting to the perimeter was wonderful but if there was no safe way of leaving the kolony, all his achievements would have been in vain. The prisoner looked to McKenzie for guidance. The woman's response to Kane's concerns was hesitant. After thinking for a while, however, she appeared to have conscientiously decided what she had to say. "Kevin, once you get out of the kolony kompound, you'll know what to do. Believe me, you will. You've got to trust me now. Haven't we been through enough at this stage for you to do that?"

Kane reflected on his companion's words. It was true that she had never let the prisoner down. There was no question in his mind at all now that everything she had told him had been true, that her confidence in his ability to escape had been justified. Now, with Nevin, Dayton, and the others dead, he was the only one, thanks to her, with a chance of making it out alive. If she wanted to play it a certain way, why should he argue? Reluctantly, Kane agreed to McKenzie's plan.

"O.k.", McKenzie confirmed. "Now from here on in, we've got to play our new roles to perfection. If we're spotted running together, the game will be up. If we're seen talking, I'm implicated and we're both dead. We've got to behave like escapee and hostage. That's the only way. Understood?"

"Understood!" Kane repeated, reluctantly.

The two looked at one another, enjoying what could possibly be their last intimate moment, embraced for a long time, then turned to re-enter the main tunnel. Emerging from the hatch, Kane immediately pointed his zennor at McKenzie's head, took the Administration official by the upper arm and marched her along.

As they walked, Kane tried to keep a clear head. Events were happening so fast and furious now that it was difficult to get a focus on what could possibly happen next. As well as that, he was becoming conscious of the wound he had suffered in his shoulder, though, thankfully, it didn't seem to be too serious. Coupled with the wound was the nagging feeling in his gut that many of the questions that Kane had harboured in his mind since he first came into contact with McKenzie remained unanswered. Why was she helping him? What was her angle? Why couldn't she come with him? Kane decided that now was as good a time as any to try to establish what his benefactor's motivation really was. "Zeena, there's one thing I really would like to know …….", he ventured. "Ask!" was McKenzie's simple response.

From a distance, the two were an odd sight. A prisoner, dishevelled and battered, apparently leading a member of the administration staff, in pristine kolony uniform, as a hostage through the interconnecting tunnels in the bowels of Korb-1, the zennor trained on the young woman's head confirmation that her life was at risk. What the distant observer would not have seen, however, was the slight movement of their lips as the pair talked in detail about the most intimate details of their tragic lives. For the sad figures that made their way together along the tunnels of Korb-1, the ones they had left behind still lived in their painful memories. As the two moved along, the stories of Sheena Strauss, Andrea Thorsen and Ruyan Kendrick were told, their lives providing the prime motivation for the final acts being carried out in the personal dramas of Zeena McKenzie and Kevin Kane.

Through the tunnel system, which Kane thought was becoming more complex than before, the pair progressed, McKenzie a half step in front of her 'escort'. The prisoner now believed that he understood his companion at long last. She indeed *was* a kindred spirit, one of the few who had seen the face of the monster and understood its true nature. She was one who would never – could never – walk away but would instead wreak vengeance on the system that had deprived her of that which she held most dear. Both of them, he believed, were on the same journey – the same quest. He hoped they would complete that quest together.

Both of the tunnel travellers had their eyes peeled, as they made their way steadily towards their goal. McKenzie had determined that the Eastern Gate was the only alternative place at which the perimeter could be breached. Kane presumed that this was one of the main gates out of the kolony and that perhaps an *omni* (omniphibious vehicle) could be seized there. His expectation all along had been that the Despatch Port would be where the final action would take place. Either a large party of prisoners would battle their way on to a vessel and depart or a small group of prisoners would secret themselves on a ship and make good their escape. An exit through the Eastern Gate was an unexpected and previously unconsidered departure from the script for him.

Kane was tossing his concerns around in his mind, wondering when things would go wrong, when suddenly *pzzzzzzzzzz*! A searer shot ripped into the wall behind his left shoulder. Startled, Kane threw himself and McKenzie on the ground and returned fire. The tops of two red tyron helmets were all Kane could see around the bend in the tunnel. Kane waited silently, then signalled to McKenzie to run away. An anxious look on her face, McKenzie moved her head in disapproval.

"No, tell them you have a hostage!" she insisted.

"That comes later", Kane declared confidently. "Make sure they hear all *four* feet!" he added.

Getting the message, McKenzie moved noisily down the tunnel. Almost immediately, the two tyrons lurched out into view, ready to chase their prey. Already aiming, Kane despatched them with a precision he found exhilarating. Sparing a moment to enjoy what he felt was a small measure of revenge for Dayton, he waited for his 'hostage' to rejoin him and the two moved at a quicker pace than before towards the next junction.

"They probably came across us by accident, but they more than likely alerted the entire kolony to our presence here", McKenzie opined solemnly as the two moved along. "At least we're nearly there", she added, with a note of optimism, "and if we don't meet any more resistance, we might make it. My guess is that most of the kolony security forces will be in the Security Area, mopping up after the battle. Getting through the Gate shouldn't be too difficult."

Kane liked the sound of his companion's confidence. Somehow, though, he didn't entirely share it. If the kolony authorities were of the same view as McKenzie that escaping through the Eastern Gate was that easy, surely they would make sure nobody tried it. It all seemed too easy to be true!

62 ASCENT TO THE FUTURE

KANE AND MCKENZIE WERE a strange and somewhat lonely sight as they travelled through the maze of tunnels that comprised the heart of Korb-1. A network of passages constructed to ensure the efficient and secure running of this "innovative and radical project", as the Master sold it to the Administration so long ago, was now the channel through which the prisoner would find his way to freedom. "These tunnels were built to ensure that the supply of korb would never be disrupted. It's ironic that they might yet lead you out of here!" McKenzie quipped. "Us!" Kane corrected. "We're going out together!" McKenzie didn't reply and Kane fell quiet again, reflecting on the truth of his companion's words. He had always maintained that if the production of korb had deprived him of his liberty, he would use the production of korb to regain it. That that moment was now so close was a sobering thought for the prisoner. While the Master and his kontrol structure concentrated on quelling the biggest threat to the kolony since its establishment, the structure of Korb-1 itself was being used under his very nose to convey one of its most forceful opponents to freedom – with a trained member of the Korb-1 security staff as his guide! Kane smiled at the thought.

"This is the last tunnel before the Gate", McKenzie announced as the pair emerged from a hatch and stepped into a wider tunnel than those travelled so far. But the pair were not out of the woods yet. Almost immediately, Kane spotted a tyron getting into a firing position at the wall of the tunnel opening out in front of him. Without hesitation, Kane sent a searer shot that blasted the tyron just as he was about to fire. The tyron's riposte ripped into the ceiling of the tunnel as he fell. A second tyron appeared behind the first one and fired in Kane's direction. As he did, Kane slipped and luckily the shot roared against the hatch that was still open behind him. A quick return from Kane saw the tyron hit the ground, his red helmet making a cracking sound as he fell. With McKenzie lying prostrate behind him, Kane waited awhile, adopting a firing position beside the hatch, but no other tyrons appeared. After an anxious wait, the two decided to continue their journey.

"It looks like we're not going to stroll out of here!" Kane observed, dryly.

"Don't worry, we're nearly there", McKenzie reassured. "Just don't forget our plan for when things get hot!" Kane's glance suggested a less than total agreement to co-operate.

The Eastern Gate Area was illuminated with purple lights. An appropriate colour, Kane felt, for his departure from Korb-1. The purple sluggish threatening sky of Korb had always been like a heavy immovable lid above the prisoner's head, perpetually weighing on his mind and reminding him of his place in the kolony. Kane thought of this, and of other unfinished issues that floated around in his head now that escape from Korb-1 appeared to be becoming a possibility. His main thoughts were of those he had left behind and would never see again – Thorsen, Dayton, Nielsen, Karnassis, Nevin – and he wondered how wise it would be to leave without McKenzie. After he left the kolony, Kane would just keep running. Where to, he didn't even know. How could he and the woman who had done so much to help him escape ever hope to meet again?

"Maybe we can get out together?" Kane said suddenly, breaking the silence as the two made their way towards the final junction. He wanted to say more, to plead with her to come with him but he knew that, if she stayed, she had a chance of surviving, of escaping detection and maybe of helping someone else, if not meeting him again.

"You know it's the best way, Kevin", McKenzie replied. If we can waltz out of here together, we'll do it. If not, follow the plan and …" – she hesitated, looking sideways at Kane as she spoke – "I promise we'll meet again."

Kane detected a significance in the way his companion stressed the word *promise*. There was something positive in the manner in which she seemed to foresee events unfolding. There was no way, in his view, that the two would sail out of the kolony in an *omni*, eating korb kaviar and drinking arctic ice juice but if McKenzie was confident they would meet again, that had to be reassuring for him. Kane promised himself that, whatever happened, if he survived, he would discover some way to find the woman who had made him a free man again.

Zzzzzztztz! Suddenly, a searer shot ripped into the wall beside Kane, as the pair approached the junction. Both dived to the floor, a second and a third shot lashing off the wall. Kane returned fire blindly as more shots retorted. Sparks and flashes flew as Kane desperately attempted to retreat. Both he and McKenzie struggled to get back up the tunnel, neither of them noticing the hatch above their heads opening slowly. More shots came as the two inched their way back. Then, with Kane's attention directed at the corners of the junction, a tyron suddenly emerged from the hatch, wrapping his legs around the prisoner's neck. Kane was caught unaware and struggled to break free. The tyron held on to the hatch opening and, swinging above the prisoner's head, attempted to strangle him with his legs. McKenzie looked on at the death struggle, aware that another few seconds would allow the other tyrons to close in on Kane and bring the contest to a close. In a millisecond, she approached the struggling pair, grabbed the tyron's searer from his belt, and fired a shot at him. The glancing shot was enough and the tyron fell unconscious on top of Kane. The prisoner threw off the fallen tyron and immediately trained fire towards the junction where other tyrons were beginning to emerge. Under this fire, the tyrons reluctantly retreated around the corner.

As Kane steadied himself behind the groaning tyron, aiming his fire at the corners of the junction, McKenzie whispered in his ear: "Kevin, it's time." Kane hesitated to absorb the meaning of his friend's brief remark, but he really understood the import of her words.

"Let me go, you bastard!" McKenzie suddenly shouted. "Let me go!" she roared and followed that with an impressive screech. At that, firing stopped and a threatening silence ensued. Kane cast a knowing glance at McKenzie, recognising that the moment of truth had indeed arrived. The tyrons were silent, obviously trying to make sense of what they had just heard. It was likely they were contacting their superiors for instructions on how to proceed. If they didn't buy the story, Kane was a dead man. If they did, Kane had to figure out how to use his 'hostage' to get himself near enough to the Gate to make a run for it.

"This is Kommander Denning! Identify yourself!" a voice suddenly called out.

"Kane. Prisoner 313. I have two of your people here – and I want out!" Kane replied with authority.

There was silence for another few moments as the tyrons digested what they had heard. Then the same voice announced:

"Don't be stupid! Everybody knows there's no way out of here. Even if we wanted to, we couldn't let you go. There's nowhere to go *to*!" Then silence again.

Kane decided not to say anything, knowing the less he said the better. His strategy would be to let the tyrons do the talking, ignore what they were saying, and try to work out how to get out. He knew the longer he delayed, the more forces the tyrons would move in, leaving him hopelessly surrounded.

"313, who is with you?" the voice returned.

"Tell them who you are!" Kane demanded of McKenzie, harshly.

"Security Officer McKenzie!" she responded. Then added hysterically: "He's got a tyron too! Please don't let him kill us!" followed by another pained screech.

Silence again. Kane knew that every second that passed was another nail in his coffin. He looked at McKenzie. She responded with a loud grunt, as if she had been thumped, then nodded towards the wall beside Kane. A vent, obviously hit in the crossfire was hanging open. Kane looked at McKenzie again, eager to understand her message clearly. McKenzie again nodded at the vent, this time with an earnest look in her eyes.

"We want visual confirmation on this. Show us who you've got", demanded the surly voice of the tyron kommander.

Kane looked at McKenzie again. She nodded. Then Kane arose, holding McKenzie in front of him. McKenzie feigned terror as Kane announced he would kill his hostages unless the tyrons withdrew within two minutes. As the tyrons considered Kane's demand, the prisoner grabbed the tyron by the shoulders, placed his own feet in the narrow vent, and then allowed himself to slide in. Kane held on to his hostage, who was now hanging inside the vent from the waist up, his lower body and legs outside in the tunnel. Swinging inside the vent, Kane struggled to get his bearings. If he let the tyron go, he would slide down the vent. If he held onto the tyron, he would be soon be seared by the reception committee he could hear rapidly approaching outside. Kane frantically wondered what to do. Suddenly and unexpectedly, however, the tyron's eyes opened and the trained soldier began to realise where he was. With both hands, he grabbed Kane by the throat. Taken by surprise, Kane struggled to free himself while still holding on to the tyron. The prisoner's face was turning blue as the tyron's second effort at strangling him appeared to be about to achieve more success than the first. In the excitement, he could hear the sound of activity in the tunnel outside and McKenzie's voice screaming "I'm free! I'm free! He's gone!"

Kane realised this could be it. Hanging in the air, face to face with the tyron in the semi-darkness, he could see the cold hatred in the other man's eyes. Only the prisoner's ignominious delivery to the tyrons gathering outside or death at his hands would satisfy this fighting automaton now. Kane felt himself being pulled up by tyron, who was just about able to use his supple body to manoeuvre the prisoner back towards the hatch. Kane's now had only one way to escape – loosen his assailant's grip immediately and slide down to whatever fate awaited below. If he didn't, he would be pulled out by the tyrons and his fate would be sealed there and then. In one final effort, Kane grappled with his attacker, trying desperately to release his grip. Then an idea occurred to Kane – one last hope. Reaching towards the tyron's left cuff, Kane felt his way towards the tyron's armour activator. Feeling his consciousness slipping away, Kane pressed the activator pad. Immediately the tyron's suit began to harden and lose the flexibility that had allowed the soldier to grapple so successfully with the prisoner in the narrow hatch. Surprised by the unexpected development and deprived of his agility, the tyron lost the initiative. Four solid blows to the face delivered by both hands dazed the tyron, and he let go his grip on Kane. With the tyron, in his hardened suit, stuck in the opening of the chute, the prisoner, still gasping for breath, hurtled down towards the unknown.

In the ensuing seconds, Kane's heart stopped as he prepared to accept whatever fate lay in store for him. Would this be the end? Would he be killed in the fall or, worse, would he just break his legs, leaving him easy prey for the pursuing tyrons. Before he could tease out all the terrible possibilities that might await him, the prisoner suddenly found himself bouncing onto a metal passageway that seemed to curve into the distance in both directions. Realising he was still very much in the game, Kane took only a second to refocus, pick up the zennor gun that had fallen before him and look around for options. A short distance away, he noticed a stream of light shining down through what appeared to be a shaft. The glow was shifting but strong, to such an extent that it seemed to be throwing a beam along the passageway for some distance in each direction. Kane didn't hesitate. Looking around once more, he headed straight for the source of the radiance.

Arriving at the bottom of the shaft, Kane looked up to see a duct wide enough for a human to travel in, with a climbing rail up one side. At the top, he saw a powerful fluctuating light. The prisoner decided it was time to make a move before all the tyrons forces on the kolony descended on him, and the duct seemed to be the only option presenting itself. Prisoner 313 launched himself up the climbing rail, the zennor gun over his shoulder. Every step he took up the rail seemed to Kane to be an eternity. His boots weighed heavier and heavier with every rung he climbed and his arms seemed to become weaker and weaker as he attempted to hold on to the rail. Halfway up, he experienced a feeling of lightness in the head and wondered was he going to lose consciousness and fall to his death or recapture – and he didn't see much of a difference between those two options now. Stopping momentarily, the prisoner cleared his head and, refocused, applied himself once more to the task of reaching the top.

Nearing the top of the shaft, Kane realised he was approaching a giant fan, which moved slowly but steadily in an anti-clockwise motion before him. Now at the top, the challenge presenting itself to the prisoner was how to get through the large mechanism. Any attempt to push through would almost certainly result in mutilation or death. But what other choice did he have? Kane stared at the object as it turned incessantly. How could he get it to stop long enough to force himself through? Then, grabbing the zennor from his shoulder with his left hand while holding on to the rail with his right, Kane compared the length of the weapon to the space between the blades of the fan as it turned. Sensing he might have a key with which to unlock the door, Kane prepared himself to wedge the weapon in the fan. Aware that misjudging the movement or strength of the fan would almost certainly result in the weapon hurtling down to the bottom of the shaft, he took three deep breaths to compose himself. Then, with one mighty effort, the prisoner wedged the zennor in between one of the fan blades and the rim of the opening and the giant machine came to a sudden halt. Without hesitation, Kane raised himself up between the blades and, despite knocking out the wedged weapon with his feet as he cleared the gap, emerged on the other side.

63 A LAKE BESIDE A SMALL WOOD

THE FIRST THING KANE noticed after he had struggled through the giant fan was the texture of the ground beneath his feet. It felt and appeared just like grass. Almost simultaneously, his senses became aware of something else. The air was much cleaner, purer than that with which he had been filling his lungs for the past three years. Flexing his body, particularly his injured shoulder, in an attempt to recover from the gruelling treatment of the last few days and, more immediately, the death tussle with the tyron only minutes before, Kane noticed other things too. In almost every direction, the grass stretched for as far as the eye could see. In one direction, however, it vanished into a small wooded area. The prisoner's first reaction was anger – anger that his jailors had been capable of so convincingly replicating an earth environment for themselves while leaving the prisoners to languish in the oppressive, claustrophobic atmosphere of the prison. Would it have harmed anyone, he wondered, to have shared this oasis with the prisoners even one day a week? But Kane's anger was almost immediately surpassed by an even stronger emotion – the desire to escape. Looking around for a sign of tyron activity and seeing none, he wondered what was the best way to go. Adjudging the wooded area to provide the only decent cover available and therefore the possibility of avoiding immediate recapture by the tyrons, Kane took off in that direction as fast as his weary feet could carry him.

It took Kane about five minutes to make it to the wood after an all-out sprint. Then, in the relative safety of the trees, he rested to regain his breath and consider his next move. He knew his immediate aim had to be to finally shake off his pursuers. Once they had lost the scent, he would have time to think and plan ahead. But what options would he have? To escape from the kolony, he would need a craft of some kind. He would either have to commandeer one or conceal himself in one. But where was he going to locate a craft at this stage? At present, he seemed to be in an earth replication recreation area, probably reserved for kolony staff. He was unlikely to find a craft here. Kane decided to park these considerations until he had achieved some kind of relative security from the pursuing tyrons. Putting distance between himself and the chasing pack was not necessarily the solution, in that he would eventually reach the perimeter – and what was he to do then? Maybe staying one step ahead of his pursuers, while all the time getting closer to a way out, was the best way to proceed. Kane took a deep breath and headed further into the wood.

Moving through the trees, Kane was almost overcome by the strong natural scent of the growth that surrounded him. Even the twigs that cracked under foot as he ran along were like crackers going off in his mind to remind him of a world so far away. *The bastards!, he thought, the bastards! They could arrange all this for themselves, yet leave us in a world of plastic and aluminium. They wouldn't even share a taste of synthetic Earth with us! The swine!*

On the prisoner ran, confused but exhilarated at still being free. Occasionally he would catch a glimpse of the artificial sun shining through the upper branches of the trees and immediately another memory would be revived, breathing life into a myriad of connected remembrances once more. Out of breath, Kane stopped again. Placing his forehead against a tree, the exhausted man noticed a heart carved in the bark with an arrow dividing the initials LK and KD. Disgusted, Kane stared at the fake pledge of love, his heart filled with revulsion for those who would pull so many young people from their real world of love only to create a false one for themselves. *How sick! How repulsive!*, he thought. The prisoner listened for any sound of his pursuers but nothing could be heard except the sound of fake bird song. Kane decided to move further away.

Approaching the edge of the wood, the prisoner noticed what appeared to be a lake nestled nearby. It was a small lake, not unlike the one he and Strauss had swum in so many years ago. Kane paused again, wondering which way to go. Then, deciding to hold on to the cover of the trees, made his way across the wood to see what his options might be in another direction. The artificially fresh air filled his lungs and the sights, sounds and smells filled his mind with distant memories as he moved amongst the trees. Reaching the other side of the woodland, Kane stopped immediately. About a hundred yards away, he saw a number of *ptvs* parked together. Focussing as carefully as possible, the prisoner noticed what appeared to be a hatch door fitted into a small hummock in the grass. Kane wondered what to do. If he left the shelter of the wood, he could be spotted. But, at the same time, he knew he wasn't going to be able to stay in the wood forever. On the other hand, he could be walking straight back into the hands of the tyrons. Observing the scene while in his mind he attempted to make the best call, Kane decided that *ptvs* could only be in use to facilitate kolony personnel in moving from one area of the kolony to another. If he stowed away in one of them, the chances were, although remote, that he would manage to get to another area of the kolony where he would not be suspected of hiding, and then make contact with McKenzie or succeed in spiriting himself into an Earth-bound transporter. Kane decided to take his chances in one of the *ptvs*.

After waiting a little while to get his energy up, Kane was ready to move. Having looked in every direction to make sure he was not being observed, he scurried like a fox on the run towards the vehicles. Having reached his destination, the prisoner cast a speedy glance over the vehicles to see which one would give him most cover. One, a green one, had a number of sacks in the back and Kane decided to conceal himself amongst them. Luckily the back hatch was unlocked and soon the prisoner was hidden from view and ready for the next phase in the extraordinary adventure that Fate had decided should be his.

Lying in the back of the *ptv*, Kane waited patiently for the next event in what had easily been the most eventful day of his life. Although exhausted, he knew that to fall asleep could be disastrous in that he would either be discovered and easily overpowered or miss an opportunity to locate himself in a more suitable hideout. In his mind, the prisoner went through the dreadful happenings of the last few days. Dayton and Nevin and many others were now dead. Windsor and over a hundred tyrons killed. Gibney exposed as a spy and executed. Large areas of the kolony destroyed. The Master's great project in total chaos. McKenzie gone and maybe even arrested, and he himself concealed in a *ptv* in a synthetic earthworld, awaiting another slim chance to get on board a korb-karrier and make good his escape. The prisoner wondered would his sanity hold out.

As it happened, he didn't get too much more time to think. Before long, he heard a muffled noise and then what appeared to be two voices in conversation, although Kane couldn't make out what they were saying. Listening intently, the fugitive supposed they had emerged from the hatch in the grass and were probably about to enter at least one of the vehicles. Suddenly, the door of the green *ptv* opened. Kane tensed, realising his cover could be blown at any minute. The two were now apparently right outside the vehicle. Kane could clearly hear the conversation between them.

"Yeah, it's crazy down there! I'm told there are hundreds dead, including Windsor, and there may be some prisoners on the loose. It's scary!" a male voice spoke.

"The tyrons are on the rampage. They want blood. I hope somebody can control them", a female voice returned.

"Better lock your door tonight. You don't want the tyrons to break in and think you're a prisoner!"

"Damn sure," came the reply, followed by a "See yah, Mike!"

"Good luck, Tina! Take care!" ended the conversation and the door of the *ptv* closed.

His heart pounding, Kane didn't move a muscle. Hearing the *ptv* starting instantly, he steadied himself for another journey and listened to the smooth, almost comforting, sound of the engine as the vehicle glided along. Everything he had heard the two say he knew himself to be true, but they hadn't revealed anything new or useful for him. It appeared from the last exchange that at last one of the pair could be finishing work and heading off to some kind of staff accommodation. If this was the case, Kane was confident he might manage to secret himself somewhere for a while and give himself time. After about ten minutes, the vehicle slowly came to a stop and the driver lowered the window, exchanging a brief comment with someone outside.

"Good luck, Tina! Safe home! Let's hope things will be under control when you come back in the morning!" a male voice spoke.

"Hope so, Howard! Take care you!" the driver returned.

"Will do! Bye!"

"Bye!"

With that simple exchange of pleasantries, the vehicle began to move again and the window closed.

Kane was now convinced that his unwitting chauffeuse was going back to her accommodation for the night and that, with some luck, he might manage to find somewhere relatively safe to hide. Gaining confidence, he stretched his head up slightly to gain a view through the rear side window of the *ptv* at the area he was passing through. The vehicle seemed to be out on a road now and moving slowly. It was still travelling through the synthetic earth environment. The prisoner was dazzled as what appeared to be an evening 'sun' drenched the land. The large meadowland that Kane and his unsuspecting driver had travelled through was visible now through a wooden rustic fence. Kane stared out at the scene longingly, thinking of his experience in the real world of the past, feeling the pain of separation with so many treasured moments. The dull sense of pain and anger that only the cruelly oppressed can understand filled every tissue of his body, fuelled by the realisation that he was never going to retrieve that which he could now only think of as his 'former life', two words that encapsulated every feeling, emotion and experience he had ever possessed, even fleetingly, but which were uniquely his.

Staring through the window, Kane regarded the 'countryside', as the vehicle travelled slowly along the length of the white country fence. Wouldn't it be nice, he wondered, if even this phoney version of real life could be *his* world for a while? Wouldn't it be *something*? Suddenly, Kane blinked in wonder. The *ptv* was passing a sign on the fence. It was a yellow rustic sign that read "Chestnut Farm – No Entry" Something stung Kane deep inside. Straining to keep his eye on what appeared to be a strangely familiar sight, he wondered how such accuracy could be achieved in simulating an earth environment so many light years away from the home planet. But Kane had no time to consider that question.

His mind had already moved on to a more pressing one – what was next along the road?

A cold sensation came over the prisoner when the view through the fence unfolded. It was as if he had died and come back and died again. Down a gravel avenue, just about big enough to hold a *ptv*, Kane's frozen eye observed a lake beside a small wood. As the view passed into the distance, a tear reluctantly emerged and passed slowly down the prisoner's cheek. Too devastated to think, too distraught to cry out in anger, Kane lay back under the weight of the realisation that was grasping him in a cold embrace. Not even the traffic reports from NCC 48 on the car radio that confirmed his cruel suspicion could move Kevin Kane to react.

The horrible truth had hit the prisoner's consciousness at last. The key that had locked him and all the others into their kolony prison for all those years had not been an impossible distance and the poisonous atmosphere on a rock in space. It had been the extinction of hope. Convinced that they could never escape and that everyone and everything they had held dear was gone forever, the bravest and strongest men and women had despaired and given up the fight, becoming mere cogs in a korb production plant a few kilometres outside NC City 48.

How cruel! Kane thought. *How clinically merciless and effective! The extinction of hope! What a pitiless sentence for any prisoner to endure. What a deception! What a crime! All the lives, all the hopes, all the expectations – dumped at a gate marked 'Chestnut Farm' and left to decay into the dust of eternity on an old country road.*

Almost like a wave of nausea, Andrea Thorsen's last gasping words came surging up through the prisoner's consciousness – "it isn't there.... doesn't ..... exist!" Was it this his soul-companion had been trying so hard to tell him? Was it this cruel secret that had actually cost the beautiful young woman her life? Kane felt a dagger of anger pierce his breast at the thought that Thorsen's dying words had revealed the horrifying truth behind the Master's cruel experiment – and that he had failed to realise their significance. Was there now yet another layer of guilt to be laid on the conscience of Prisoner 313?

Still, despite the hurt and pain that gnawed on the core of his bones like an insatiable rat, Kane was aware that, for him, the realisation of the truth was the beginning of his revival. In spite of the Master and his cruel deception, he now had the key with which to open *his* prison gate. Where that open gate would lead to was something he couldn't know but, as the Chestnut Farm faded into the distance, one thing was certain: the prisoner was a prisoner no more.

Made in the USA
Charleston, SC
13 November 2014